CW00408859

GUARDIAN ANGEL

Brian John

Greencroft Books

2007

First Impression 2007

Copyright © Brian S John

Published by Greencroft Books
Trefelin, Cilgwyn, Newport, Pembrokeshire SA42 0QN
Tel 01239-820470. Fax 01239-821245
Email: greencroft4@mac.com
Web: www.books-wales.co.uk

*All characters in this story other than those clearly in the public domain
are fictitious and any resemblance to real persons, living or dead,
is purely coincidental*

All rights reserved. No part of this publication may be reproduced,
stored in a retrieval system, or transmitted, in any form or by any
means, without the prior permission in writing of the publisher,
nor be otherwise circulated in any form of binding or
cover other than that in which it is published and without
a similar condition including this condition being imposed
on the subsequent purchaser.

ISBN 978-0-905559-86-5

Typeset by the author in Palatino 10 pt and designed on
Apple iMac G5 computer using Pages 2.0.2

*Printed and bound in Great Britain by
Biddles Ltd, King's Lynn, Norfolk PE30 4LS*

Contents

For
all who love the mountain

DRAMATIS PERSONAE

The Group of Twenty-five

Betsi and Ioan Rhys, Daisy and George Havard, Bessie Walter, Will Owen, Brendan and Mary O'Connell, Rose and Henry Evans, Wilmot and Delilah Gwynne, Patty and Jake Nicholas, Skiff and Maria Abraham, Shemi and Sian Jenkins, Abel and Susan Rhys, Myfanwy Owen, Blodwen Bebb, Gerallt Owen, Gomer and Gwenno Jenkins

The men who loved Martha

David Morgan, b 1777. Married Martha 1796. Murdered by enemies 1805.
Moses Lloyd of Cwmgloyn, b 1773. Killed by Martha in self-defence 1797.
Ceredig ap Tomos of New Moat, b 1769. Betrothed to Martha 1822.
    Committed suicide after cancelled wedding.
Iestyn Price, b 1771, army officer (presumed dead) 1807, actually died 1822.
Joseph Harries of Werndew, b 1761, wizard, herbalist, doctor, and sleuth.
    Died after accident 1826. Martha's friend and mentor.
Owain Laugharne, b 1780, squire of Llannerch 1802. Missing for 15 years.
    Betrothed to Martha but never married. Died 1825.
Amos Jones (Jones Minor Prophet) b 1785, itinerant preacher. The last love
    of Martha's life. Murdered 1855.

The Morgan Family in 1855

Martha, b 12 May 1778 at Brawdy. Married to David 21 August 1796. Date
    of death recorded as 27 February 1855, aged 76.
Nansi, aged widow of Martha's brother Morys.
Elen, Martha's sister, b 1773. Illegitimate son Brynach b 1807. Emigrated to
    USA, m Tom Bradshaw 1810. Two other children.
Catrin, Martha's sister b 1776, m James Bowen 1800. Sons John and Mark.
Betsi, daughter b 1798,m Ioan Rhys 1818. Sons Benjamin, Joshua, Abel,
    and Owain.
Daisy, daughter b 1801. Went to London 1821 and returned 1844. M George

Havard 1846. Illegitimate children Amy, John, William. Brynach, adopted son b 1807. Wife Anne d 1837. Daughter Rose, son David. Inherited Llanychaer estate from George Price in 1832.

Other Key Characters

Skiff Abraham, b 1782. M Maria 1812, children, Rhiannon, Josie, and Annie. One-time petty criminal, now a wealthy merchant .

Henry Evans, b 1826, m Rose Morgan 1849. Son Levi, b 1852.

Lady Charlotte Guest, b 1812, wife of Josiah John Guest. Philanthropist, translator of the Mabinogion, and on her husband's death head of the Dowlais Iron Works.

Wilmot Gwynne, b 1895, from Swansea, squire of Llanychaer and Plas Ingli 1845. M Delilah 1820. Children Samson, Joshua, Maria.

Jonas Harry, b 1890, from Plas Glas, Mumbles. Industrialist and financier.

George Havard Medical, b 1790, doctor from 1822. M Daisy 1846.

Merlin Ifans, b 1845, orphan from Cardigan. Destined to take over from Shemi as wizard.

Shemi Jenkins of Werndew, wizard, b 1782. Servant at the Plas from 1797. M 1810 to Sian. Left to be a wizard 1836.

Sir Mervyn Lloyd, Lord Marcher 1845 - 1876. Lived in Cardiganshire (Bronwydd estate) by preference.

Patty Nicholas, ex-prostitute and close friend of Martha, b 1776. M Jake 1807. Children Mary, Jack, Hubert, Amy.

Brendan O'Connell, b 1801. Wife Mary and 6 children. Fled from the Potato Famine 1848. Settled at Garfeth.

Donal O'Connell, b 1815, from County Cork in Ireland. Related to Brendan. Special investigator.

Will Owen, b 1780, head man at the Plas from 1836. Children, Gerallt, Myfanwy, Bronwen.

Silas Reynolds, b 1828, from Gowerton, one of Harry's henchmen.

Bessie Walter, b 1776. Servant at the Plas 1795-1855. Martha's oldest friend.

Iago Woodward, b 1826, from Swansea, one of Harry's henchmen.

John Wylde, b 1818. Emperor of China, and his lady Mags Williams. Head criminal of the gangs inhabiting Pont-storehouse, Merthyr Tydfil.

Pickersniff, Jebson and the Woman in Black

"Pickersniff and Jebson?" I asked. "Never heard of them. They sound like a pair of Dickensian attorneys -- correct?"

"Not far off. They were London publishers at the time of Queen Victoria. They published penny dreadfuls and truly terrible Gothic melodramas -- but also some obscure works by Mrs Gaskell and others including Charlotte Bronte, under one of her pseudonyms."

"Indeed? That's very good to know -- but I don't see why this should be of particular interest to me down here in West Wales."

The young lady, who had already introduced herself over the phone as Carol Wise from Hyde Park Publishers, picked up from my voice that my brow was furrowed. She laughed. "If you have a moment to spare," she said, "I'll explain." And she did.

She said that her publishing house, one of the biggest and most successful in the world, was involved in that mysterious process called rationalization, and was disposing of various premises in London. One such office, originally belonging to Pickersniff and Jebson Ltd of Gabriel Lane, SW1, had been taken over in 1859 in order to save that company from bankruptcy and to acquire the publishing rights to three authors who later became best-sellers. For almost 150 years the old office had been used by proof-readers and as a repository for company records, unpublished manuscripts and so forth -- but now the decision had been made that the site was too valuable to remain effectively unused in central London. It was on the market, valued at £6 million, and the publishing records were all being moved out to new offices in Basingstoke. Carol, who was a junior editor with one of the Hyde Park imprints, had been seconded from her duties for six months and told to decide what should be kept and what should be thrown away. On going through the old papers she had come across some 1858 correspondence between Samuel Pickersniff and James Jebson in which mention was made several times of an unpublished memoir called *The Ghost of Inglestone* by an unknown writer called Mrs Susanna Ravenhill.

Carol said that there were mentions of Wales in the letters.

"I thought of you," she explained, "since this correspondence is about a memoir, not a novel. Many writers at that time used pseudonyms. I love the published diaries of your famous Mistress Martha Morgan, and I just thought.........."

I stopped her in her tracks. "But Carol," I said reprovingly, "Martha died in 1855. She wrote diaries all her life, but I have never had any indication that she wrote memoirs or novels. She was a competent wordsmith, but seems to have had absolutely no pretensions as an author."

"But what about her sisters, or her daughters or grand-daughters? Couldn't one of them have had a story to tell, either on their own account, or maybe relating to Martha herself? There may have been episodes in her life that haven't as yet been recorded, and which moved somebody to put pen to paper after her death. Are you OK with that?"

"Yes, that's possible," I conceded. "Any one of Martha's female descendants might have had a story to tell, and the inclination to do it. But this is still a very long shot. Have we nothing more to go on?"

"Not much, I admit. There's no book with the right title on Pickersniff and Jebson's list of published works, and no author with the right name either in their catalogue or in their ledgers. Unfortunately there's no sign of a manuscript.........."

"So what's the date on the correspondence?" I asked.

Carol shuffled through her papers for a moment, and then said: "All in the month of June 1858."

"That's too late to have had anything to do with Mistress Martha personally, unless she left something behind her relating to one of the "mystery periods" in her life. There were certainly some gaps in her diaries, the longest of which lasted for ten years. I suppose something from one or more of those intervals might have come to light after her death, and might then have been brought forward by one of her family with a view to publication. But Mrs Susanna Ravenhill? I've never come across anybody with that name in all my researches of the gentry families of North Pembrokeshire. Ravenhill has to be an English name, but it has a nice ring about it as a pseudonym."

Even as I spoke, I was tuning in to the fact that both the name of the "memoir" and the name of the author indicated a connection with Carningli. I assumed, without knowing, that there could be various places called Inglestone in England or Scotland. On the other hand "carn" in Welsh means a stony or rocky summit, so "Inglestone" could also be a frivolous play on the Welsh name of the mountain so beloved of Martha and her family, with "ingli" turned into "ingle". "Ravenhill" could also be a fanciful name for the mountain, since it was and is a hill inhabited and indeed protected by ravens. Martha -- and probably her daughters too -- saw these great black birds as the guardian angels of a special, sacred place.

I pulled myself up short, and realized, not for the first time in my life, that my mind was racing ahead in a manner that was quite unjustified by the quality of the information on the table. I laughed. "Hold on a moment, Carol," I said. "We're getting somewhat ahead of ourselves here. With all due respect, why should you be interested in this missing memoir? What's so special about the title or the writer?"

"Nothing, but I have an intuition. We women have intuitions......... "

"Yes, yes, I had noticed."

"....... and sometimes they are well founded. Some of the letters say the tale is set in Wales."

"But Carol, Wales is a big place -- the story could be set anywhere."

"So it could. But there are mentions of Carningli and Newport in the correspondence about the book!"

"Well, that is more interesting, I suppose. But they're both romantic and picturesque places -- and atmospheric too. I wouldn't be surprised if some budding author used them as settings for a ghost story."

I was still sceptical, and said so. But the young lady in the dusty London office was not in the least bit discouraged. She said that she had thus far currently only found James Jebson's folder of "correspondence received", but promised to search for other information. I encouraged her to delve deeper, since it would have been churlish to dampen her enthusiasm.

Two weeks passed. It was mid June, a time of mellow days and short nights. One day, shortly after I returned from a bracing walk on the mountain, Carol rang back, and there was excitement in her voice. She said that she had found Samuel Pickersniff's folder as well, and was now able to recreate the sequence of letters passing between the two men. "This begins to look exciting!" she enthused. "Much more interesting than packing piles of dusty old first editions into cardboard boxes and working out what else should go into the skip at the back entrance."

"So what is it that makes you so excited?"

"I think you should read these letters for yourself. There are a few pages relating to Mrs Susanna Ravenhill and her strange memoir -- OK if I pop copies into an envelope and send them through to you?"

"Are you sure you are allowed to do that?"

"Good God, yes! Not a problem! I've got absolute discretion in getting this place sorted. If you aren't interested the letters will go into the skip or the shredder anyway. Please look at them. You'll be intrigued!"

So it was that three days later a package arrived from Carol, with a brief covering note and photocopies of some touching correspondence between Samuel Pickersniff and James Jebson. These are some of the crucial extracts:

Bow Street
Friday the 4th day of June in the year of our Lord 1858
My dear Pickersniff
I trust that this finds you in better health than you displayed at the time of our recent conference. No doubt your good lady has kept you under appropriate restraint and has resisted all your pleadings to sally forth and put the world to rights. A deep chill upon the chest is not a trifling matter, and if I may make so bold I heartily recommend five spoons a day of Dr Abraham's Patent Lemon and Balsam Medicament which I found to be wonderfully efficacious on the occasion of my last unfortunate indisposition.

My dear fellow, I hesitate to inform you, when you have quite enough upon your chest as it is, that the wolves are still at the door, not simply howling but seeking to batter it down. I have had yet another note from that wretched fellow Gobbings who is supposed to be printing our ill-fated "Mystery of the Flaming Galleon", complaining that he will not print part fifteen of the story until we have paid for the printing of part six. I was sure that we had paid him up to and including part eight, but perhaps I am mistaken in that, since the ledger is, I think, at home with you and under your bed. Perhaps, if it is not too much of an exertion, you will be good enough to reach down and fetch it forth, and to let me know the extent of our indebtedness in this matter. Gobbings requires at least £100 from us, but there is less than £23 in the cash box in the office.

Then that rough fellow from South Wales who sold us 10 cwt of coal in January came and demanded his money, and I had to explain to him that the fearsome winter weather which followed in February had not only caught us unawares and had necessitated a continuous use of our fireplaces in Gabriel Lane, but had also had a dismal effect upon the profitability of our enterprise since it had been all but impossible for us to receive deliveries from our printers or to pack off books and journals to the far-flung corners of the land. "Your problem, not mine, Master Jebson," said he. "It always snows in February, and I like nothing better than a fireplace going like a blast-furnace around the clock. If I do not get my money next week, I fear that I shall have to pay you a little visit with two of my sturdy friends for company. They are as soft as kittens, but they are not at all lovable when they meet gentlemen who upset me. Do you take my meaning, sir?" I threw him out, of course. But he will be back, with his friends, and I suppose I shall have to conjure a few shillings or pounds from somewhere if I am to avoid unpleasantness.

There have been others seeking pecuniary satisfaction as well, my dear fellow, but this is not the time to upset you with the sordid trivia of commerce. It is June, after all, and truly all is well with the world! This very day I counted no less than six blackbirds in full voice on my walk from my house to the office. Was that not a splendid thing?

I fear that I have failed in my attempts to encourage that fellow Dickens to join our happy band of authors, and my communications (which I thought remarkably diplomatic) to Master Collins and Master Thackeray have sadly elicited no response. They are no doubt too busy writing like men possessed, and lining the pockets of others. Mrs Gaskell promises that we will have something new from her, in due course, but I think it a racing certainty that she has not even started work yet and that she is in any case fully occupied on her latest popular fiction. Rumour has it that it will be serialized by Mr Dickens in "Household Words".

We must remain optimistic, even in the face of straightened circumstances. My dear fellow, it is too early yet to be sure about matters, but I fancy that I might have found the author who will transform our fortunes! I must relate for you a singular occurrence. This very morning, within five minutes of my turning up at the office, an elderly lady came in off the street and asked young Martin in my hearing if she might meet "the proprietor" on a matter of some urgency. Indeed she might, said I directly, and so in she came. She was dressed in full mourning clothes, and had her veil over her face for the duration of our interview, but I would guess from her voice that she might be more than sixty years of age. A good clear voice she has, with a touch of a Welsh lilt. Medium height, and a good upright posture. Every inch a lady, I would say. She would not give her name, but said she was acting for a friend. She said she was charged with finding a publisher for a memoir entitled "The Ghost of Inglestone" and would be keen -- on behalf of this friend -- to find out how much I might offer for the serial and book rights.

I said that that would depend upon the quality of the authorship, and offered to read it and come to a view as to what its value might be. She nodded, and I asked her if I might have a glance at said work. She said it was presently locked away, but that she would bring it in for inspection some time next week. "Perfectly acceptable, Madam," said I. "It is our pleasure, as old-established publishers of high-class literature, to serve both new and established authors to the best of our ability, and to ensure the highest possible remuneration and the greatest possible readership for worthy works."

She gave a little curtsey, and I think she smiled beneath her veil. I invited her to join me for a cup of tea, and to say a little about this memoir of hers -- for I think this "friend" is nothing but a little artifice or conceit -- and she was remarkably forthcoming. We talked of this and that for near two hours, in a perfectly easy fashion. During our conversation, she summarized her narrative for me. Absolutely extraordinary! I must say, my dear Pickersniff, that we might have a very big thing here, if we can just get our hands on it!

The lady courier says that the story ranges right across Europe, and that in order to protect anonymity Mrs Ravenhill has changed the names of people and places. But she admitted to me, on being politely pressed on the matter of authenticity, that several places in Wales feature large in the tale -- with names that are carefully disguised. One, so I gather, is a town called Newport and the other is a mountain that goes by the name of Karren Iggly or some such thing. The tale is truly remarkable, and if it is as fluent and fascinating as the abbreviated verbal narrative given to me by The Woman in Black, it will surely weave a charming web around her readers and leave them trapped and entranced. "But you say this is a memoir, Madam?" said I. "It is a truly fantastical one, in the tradition of the great Gothick tales of years gone by, but with a modern slant to it. Be honest with me if you please -- this is a product of a vivid imagination, is it not?"

"Sir, you do my friend and myself a grave disservice," she replied. "I give you my word that when you read this narrative from first page to last, you will be reading a true narrative of real events, recalled and described faithfully by the author."

Then without another word, she rose to her feet, gave another curtsey, and indicated to young Martin with a nod of her head that she would take her leave. She would take no assistance in the hailing of a phaeton, so I kissed her hand, and down the stairs she went. I chanced to look out through the window as she went out into the street, and I saw that she met up with another mature lady, with whom she strode off towards Piccadilly, arm in arm.

I await developments. Get well again as soon as may be, my dear fellow. In truth it would be a fine thing to have you here again in the office, in case any more angry coalmen or exotic ladies in mourning dress come calling. There is too much blackness about for me to cope with all alone.

I send fond greetings to your good lady,
and remain your dear friend
Jebson

Russell Square
June the 7th 1858
My dear good friend,
Thank you indeed for your kind felicitations and for your encouragement for me to return to the rudest of health as soon as God may permit it. In his infinite wisdom He has decreed that Dr Abraham's Patent Lemon and Balsam Medicament should work miracles for other gentlemen but should do nothing whatsoever in the calming of my own troubled breast. I am therefore still confined to bed with a horrid cough and a fevered brow, and fear that it will be some days yet before I can return to work. In the meantime, I advise you to lay in cudgels and a few bottles of unpretentious wine so as to deal with irate coalmen and exotic tellers of tall tales.

In all seriousness, my dear fellow, things are not looking too good. I fished out the ledger from beneath my bed and discovered that we have thus far paid only for parts one to five of "Mystery of the Flaming Galleon", and that parts six to fourteen are still to be paid for. If Gobbings calls again, or sends round his attorney, for God's sake convince him that parts fifteen to twenty must be printed, if we are to prevent revolution and mayhem; that the eager reading public is more and more absorbed with the mystery as week succeeds week; and that when the full book is published there will be fortunes to be made by all three of us -- Gobbings, Pickersniff and Jebson. Tell him that the word among both critics and publishing gentlemen of discernment is that sales will be truly enormous! I fear that I do not believe a word of that myself, and I suppose that neither do you; but when the wolves are at the door some small exaggeration is required if one is to encourage them to go away. I confess to feeling somewhat depressed with regard to our prospects, my dear old friend. But one must battle on, must one not?

Now then, to this exotic lady and her fanciful memoir called "The Ghost of Inglestone". Is there anything further to report? Why should her book be any better than the dross which pours in, week after week, from aspiring novelists, and which washes across our office floor? It would indeed be a miracle if her memoir was to be the very thing to rescue us from penury. But there have been miracles before, as the Good Book assures us.

By the way, Newport I know about. A big sea-port, so I believe, with coal and iron coming and going, and dark and dismal streets where dastardly deeds are probably commonplace. A good place for a novel, if I am not mistaken. Next, this peak you call Karren Iggli. Is it a place of beetling crags, swirling mists and tumbling glaciers and snowfields, where sturdy mountaineers faint with terror and disappear without trace, and where fearsome demons or monsters lurk? Is the Abominable Snowman stamping about across the pages? If so, I suppose we are in with a chance of giving the modern reader what he or she wants.

Grateful thanks for the currant cake, which I shall consume when I am better. My beloved Ellen sends her kindest regards, as do I.

Your old friend

Pickersniff

Bow Street

The 14th day of June, year of our Lord 1858

My dear Pickersniff

I have more news for you, and I trust this finds you in your convalescent wicker chair in the garden rather than in your sick bed.

The coal-man and his two friends from Merthyr Tydfil came for their money, so I paid him £8 on account, and gave each of them a glass of red wine.

14

That seemed like a more sensible strategy than defending myself with a cudgel, as I hope you will agree.

While we were chatting amiably, who should come knocking on the door than my aspiring author! My clerk Martin let her in, and -- blow me down with a breeze -- when she was introduced to those thugs from South Wales she forgot all about her mourning, lifted her veil and started chatting to them nineteen to the dozen, in Welsh, just as if they were all lifelong friends! Perhaps they were, for she called them Twm and Ianto. I had no idea what it was all about, but very soon they were rolling about and hooting with laughter. It was very infectious, and I admit to having a giggle myself. The lady was kind enough to explain, after they had gone, that they were reminiscing about good old times.

With the return of sobriety, I noticed what a handsome woman Mrs Ravenhill is. (I shall call her that, although she still claims that she is someone else, and is acting as an agent for our mysterious author.) She has the most beautiful brown eyes, a straight nose and lips that are still full in spite of her age. Her high cheek-bones and a ruddy complexion suggest a liking for the fresh air and sunshine. Her brown hair has a touch of grey in it. She has her fair share of wrinkles, but I estimate that they are more to do with laughter than with sadness, and I declare that I cannot for the life of me decide whether she is a lady who has seen and done everything in her sixty years, or a lady who is remarkably well preserved at eighty. It matters not, my dear fellow; I judge that she has a good deal of life left in her yet, and that is an important consideration if she is to be our next big author. She seems to know London very well, and to have good connections. To tell the truth, I have more faith in this dear lady than I do in Mrs Gaskell.

Apologies, Samuel. I ramble on, and must get to the point. Mrs Ravenhill did not stay long. She left me a bundle, and took her leave, having promised to return in one week. So now I have the manuscript in my possession. On the first page these words are inscribed: **"The Ghost of Inglestone: Being the memoir of a phantom or lost soul whose destiny it is to wander the earth and to find redemption for a wicked life through the completion of good works, the prevention of evil and the saving of that which is sacred."** *A strange title, and somewhat pretentious, don't you think? We can probably advise her of the merits of something shorter.*

However and notwithstanding, it is an unusual pleasure to be given something complete, instead of receiving a few pages at a time, for our next weekly episode, from some aspiring author who probably has not the faintest idea how his story is going to end. I am truly tired of penny dreadfuls and turgid episodes of "Mystery of the Flaming Galleon", and long for a good tale, well told, fit to make us a fortune. As I have indicated, I know the outline of this dear lady's tale already. All I need now is good writing.

I will read the tale, and report to you again in some days. On the matter of tumbling glaciers and fearsome demons at the heart of the narrative, I am at present uncertain; but you may rest assured that I will look out for them.

> *I remain*
> *Your ever faithful friend*
> *Jebson*

Russell Square
16th day of June 1858
My Dear Jebson
I have received your narrative of laughing coalmen and the beautiful old lady -- I am truly glad to see that you are bearing up well in spite of the fact that we still face a financial disaster. I wish I could share your eternal optimism, my dear fellow.

As for me, optimism does not come easily just now, since my doctor has just told me the dismal news that this bother on my chest has turned into pneumonia. I wish that I was younger and stronger. So I fear that I am out of action for a good while yet -- a matter of great regret to me, in view of the hard times that are upon us and because a great weight is now pressed upon your shoulders alone.

I declare that your mysterious lady author has made a profound impression upon you! Beware, Master Jebson! An old bachelor like you should look to his laurels. You always did have a tendency to be swept away by a shapely figure, a flashing smile and a furtive glance. I see bunches of red roses coming on. However, I will not complain so long as you retain objectivity in all things, especially when it comes to publishing decisions; and I trust that when you read this lady's manuscript, you will see before you her words rather than her brown eyes............

> *Now Ellen tells me that I must sleep, and I always obey instructions*
> *Your dear friend*
> *Pickersniff*

The Woman in Black

Bow Street, on the 22nd day of June 1858
Dearest Pickersniff,
I received news of your deteriorated condition from our lad Martin, and also from your beloved Ellen when she called in at the office this very morning, and I write this with a heavy heart. I am mortified that no visitors are allowed to your sick room, for I was intent upon calling in to see you with a little box of things designed to bring you good cheer, and a manuscript for you to read. But you must remain brave, my good fellow, and hold to the belief that the great advances in medical science that mark our era will shortly enable you to cast off the shadow of that dismal disease and turn the corner into a bright new day and a full recovery. You have in Doctor Snugget a skillful and wise practitioner, and I have it on the soundest authority that there is no better man on this side of the Thames.

Now then, news to cheer you and to speed you to a full recovery. Mrs Susanna Ravenhill is the woman who holds our future in her hands! I have no doubt about it. She writes good English, and her tale is even more remarkable than I had perceived from that conversation of some weeks back. I know, my dear old friend, that your instinct has always been to find a genius of tender years who will write us a never-ending stream of episodes and a three-part novel each year for the next twenty years; but bright young things such as Miss Austen and the Bronte sisters tend not to reproduce, and to die young. Then I know that your instinct tends towards the Gothick. I fear that on that score I must disappoint you, since there appears not to be a trace of a dragon or a demon, or a glacier or a sturdy mountaineer, in the narrative which I have recently perused; neither is there an insane murderer on the loose, or a ravished heroine, or a vampire desperate for the blood of virgins. But never fear -- there are many compensatory virtues in this tale, and in any case it is my judgement that the taste for Gothick nonsense is now greatly reduced. Is that not shown already by the success of the tales of Mr Dickens, Mr Collins and others who write about poverty, injustice and strange and convoluted family histories? They may fill their books with caricatures, but they know how to spin their yarns and to weave pretty tales, and it is our misfortune that we have no such writer on our publication list.

But now all that is about to change, my dear fellow. I feel it in my creaky old bones............... Damnation! I was about to elaborate. But young Martin tells me that that fellow Gobbings is at the door again, with a countenance as black as thunder. I will get out the best bottle of red wine I can find, and try to placate him.

I will send this off to you with a view to bringing you a little comfort; and I will continue my hopeful narrative later.

Take care, my dear old friend, and hurry along to a full and speedy recovery. I need you to be well again. I recommend a slice of that moist currant cake, which is now mature enough to have reached perfection. Give my kindest regards to your beloved Ellen.

Your ever affectionate

Jebson

That is where the correspondence stopped. When I reached the last words of the gentle Jebson, I was just beginning to develop a real affection for him and his ailing friend, and to become more than a little involved in their struggle to keep their ancient publishing house afloat far out in a sea of troubles. I was irritated that I had no further news of Pickersniff's illness, or of Mrs Ravenhill's narrative, or of the further twists and turns in the fortunes of the Pickersniff and Jebson publishing enterprise. So I rang Carol on her mobile phone, to find that she was still packing up books and dusty piles of documents in the office in Gabriel Lane.

I thanked her for the copied bundle of letters, and confirmed that I had read them and become quite attached to these elderly gentlemen from another age. "Was that all the correspondence that passed between them?" I asked. "It's frustrating that it all stops, just as it's getting interesting......"

"That's all there is," said Carol. "When I read it myself, I was just as hacked off when I could find no more letters from either gentleman. Then I did some digging about, and discovered why. When James Jebson wrote his last letter, on the afternoon of 22nd June, poor Samuel Pickersniff was already dead. I found an Obituary in *The Times*. In his letters he clearly didn't want to admit how seriousness his illness really was. He must have gone downhill very fast towards the end, and he died around mid-day, with his devoted wife Ellen at his side."

"Oh, what a sad tale! That's really terrible.........."

"I know. I shed a tear when I discovered the truth too. I admit that like you I've grown very fond of this eccentric little publishing house and the colourful gentlemen who tried to pay their bills and keep up some sort of publication programme that would tickle the fancy of the reading public.

I think the two old fellows really loved one another, and from what I can see of the early days of their business they worked very well together and made a good living for almost fifty years. But by 1858 their debts were too large for them to survive."

"So bankruptcy followed, and the business fell apart?"

"After Pickersniff's death, Jebson seems to have become very dispirited," said Carol. "As an honourable man, he didn't want the company to become bankrupt, so he tried to sell out to another publisher. He did a deal with Hyde Park Publishers, which included a guarantee that all creditors would be paid in full. So Gobbings the printer, and the coalman from Wales, and everybody else, got the money that was owing to them. Hyde Park finished publishing the serialized *Mystery of the Flaming Galleon*, but it was rubbish. Sales figures were mediocre, and it never appeared in book form. Then Hyde Park Publishers itself fell upon hard times, and the bosses shut up the office in Gabriel Lane with a view to reopening it for the publication of illustrated magazines when matters improved."

"And matters never did improve?"

"Well, they did, and Hyde Park went on the become one of the greatest publishers in London. But the men in charge were very busy and ambitious. Some editors left and others came to take their places, and somehow or other the Gabriel Lane office was forgotten about. Rent was coming in from the other offices in the building, which was after all a pretty good capital asset. From the company's point of view, the situation was stable, and quite satisfactory."

Neither of us spoke for a moment; it felt to me as if we were both mourning for something special, something lost. Then Carol, who was a very pragmatic and efficient young lady, reminded me why it was that we had started talking in the first place. "Don't you wonder what happened to Mrs Ravenhill and her memoir?" she asked.

"Of course I do. Have you found anything else in your searches through cupboards and along shelves?"

"Not yet. There are boxes galore of unpublished manuscripts in the office. I've no idea whether *The Ghost of Inglestone* might be among them. It's quite possible that the strange Welsh lady came and collected her manuscript following Pickersniff's death, when she realized that her chosen publisher was about to cease trading. She might have called in and might indeed have had further chats with Mr Jebson -- but there's no trace of such meetings in his appointment books or papers for the months following the death of his old friend."

"Well, that might be a good sign," I concluded. "Maybe she went back to Wales, or died, or lost interest. Whatever the truth of the matter may be, the manuscript may still be there!"

"Now it's **you** who's bubbling with enthusiasm! So what happened to your scepticism?"

"Shall we say that it's still there, but in the background. I'm rather attracted by the sad tale of these two old gentlemen, and fancy a trip to London so that I can see for myself where their little drama was played out. May I call in and help you with your task of hunting for treasures and throwing away rubbish?"

So it was that a few days later I travelled up to London by train. I recall that it was a Wednesday, and that the countryside which raced by looked bright and fresh beneath a cloudless sky. I jumped down onto platform nine and three-quarters at Paddington and made my way via the Underground to Green Park and thence to the ancient office of Pickersniff and Jebson in Gabriel Lane. I was not at all convinced that anything interesting would come out of the trip, but with the garden all planted up I had nothing better to do, and I planned to combine the manuscript search with a visit to my son Tom, who needed help with the redecoration of his small apartment. I thought I should be away for four days.

As I travelled, I pondered. I was quite certain that the woman who called in at the office in 1858 was not Martha -- she was long since in her grave, and in any case she had long white hair and was above medium height. But might the mysterious woman have been her daughter Betsi? She would have been over 60 years old, and might fit the description. Or maybe the author was Martha's second daughter Daisy? She was three years younger than Betsi, but perhaps more wrinkled and battered by the excesses of her younger days. She had certainly been very beautiful when she was young. She had spent much of her wayward early life in London, consorting with noblemen and politicians. And in 1858 she had two of her illegitimate children (and possibly some grandchildren) living in London.

So she would have had a reason for visiting. She would also have been comfortable here, and she would certainly have known her way around.

So Daisy it was. She would of course not have used her own name -- given her somewhat interesting past in London. I felt very pleased with my powers of deduction, and further deduced that she might have been inspired to take up her pen and write a book following her mother's death, since she would have been in comfortable circumstances as George Havard's wife, with no children of her own at home, and time on her hands. And the pseudonym - Mrs Susanna Ravenhill - would have been a good one for Daisy to use, since as a child she had once been lost upon the mountain and had been found only after a frantic search extending into the hours of darkness. Daisy had stormed off to London as a girl, after a dispute with her mother. She had been effectively dead as far as Martha was concerned, and had later been "brought back to life" when she suddenly reappeared in 1844 after an absence of more than 20 years. Even the name Susanna was apposite, since it was a family name used in Brawdy, on Martha's side of the family. It all added up...... but to call her tome "a memoir"? I began to get excited, since I saw before me a book of scandals involving the Prince of Wales, assorted Prime Ministers, and several bishops, the like of which even the steamy side of London had never seen before. Had Daisy really revealed all in her manuscript? Could that be the explanation of the manuscript's convoluted sub-title? It all made perfect sense. I was looking for Daisy's confession before God and man -- her belated attempt, as a woman of mature years, to find redemption and to warn others who might be tempted into lives of hedonism and fornication.

But why would she want a scandalous memoir published? As an act of revenge, maybe against the fathers of her illegitimate children? As a desperate means of making money? But what would her gentle husband, Doctor George Havard, have made of Daisy's revelations? Perhaps he had died some time between 1855 and 1858, thus releasing Daisy from any obligations she might have had towards his family and towards the ideals of gentility and discretion? Questions, and more questions..........

When I arrived at the Gabriel Lane address at around 2 pm I looked up from the street at an imposing Regency building of four stories. The stone facade was clean, and the windows were in perfectly good repair.

The owners had looked after it well, I thought. Between a sandwich bar on one side and a small private art gallery on the other, I found a heavy wooden door which was of course locked. On the adjacent wall there was a long list of names and buzzer buttons. Most of the little name-plates belonged to assorted small businesses which clearly had no great need for visits from the public. I supposed that this situation had been very convenient in ensuring the survival of the offices of Pickersniff and Jebson. I pressed the button for "Hyde Park Publishers" and a voice came from somewhere. "Yes? Who is it?"

I recognized Carol's voice at once. I introduced myself, and she sounded pleased as she pressed a button to release the lock and let me in. I had to climb a winding stone staircase to the third floor, and found Carol waiting for me on a landing. She was a very pretty young lady with short blonde hair, and she wore jeans and a large Harlequins rugby shirt which she said were just the right clothes for sorting out a dusty office. She was not at all bookish, and proved to be a thoroughly vivacious and intelligent girl. We drank some coffee and then started to look around.

The office suite which had been the centre of the Pickersniff and Jebson publishing empire was just as Dickensian as I had imagined. Luckily, Carol had had the cleaners in before she started work, so most of the accumulated dust and cobwebs of a century and a half had been taken away. But there was still dust dancing in the sunbeams that shafted through the open window. There were three rooms, two of which were well lit by substantial sash windows. The biggest room, which had two windows looking down on Gabriel Lane, must have been the office used by Messrs Pickersniff and Jebson, for there were two very fine oak desks with leather tops, facing each other across the room. Behind these desks there were highly polished captain's chairs, their sheen now somewhat dulled by Father Time. There were finely crafted wooden shelves ranged along two of the walls, packed with leather-bound volumes of all shapes and sizes, and with bundles of papers tied up with red ribbons. In a corner there was a high desk with a sloping hinged lid which had been used, perhaps, by the young clerk Martin for copying and editing manuscripts and for writing letters. The back wall of this office had a fine stained glass screen allowing light to penetrate through to the larger back room, which had only a small window looking down on a dark courtyard. This room was filled with tables, shelves and heavy cupboards, all heavily laden with piles of papers, ledgers and tin boxes. There were no carpets anywhere, and here and there between the piles of boxes one could see ten-inch floorboards, finely polished and well worn. The final room, approached along a dingy passage, was small but brightly lit, and it was filled with what can only be described as junk. There were broken chairs, two hat-stands, a wash-stand with a cracked marble top and a tiled splashback from which two tiles were missing, assorted leather bags, a jumble of tin boxes, and yet more piles of leather-bound books, penny dreadfuls and manuscripts tied with red ribbon. Two or three of these piles literally reached up to the ceiling, and posed a threat to the safety of anybody who dared to disturb them. When I saw the sheer scale of the task facing Carol, my heart sank; and I realized that she had not even started on this room yet. I looked at her and raised my eyebrows, and she shrugged her shoulders and giggled.

"Yes, I know what you're thinking!" she said. "This is needle in haystack territory, if ever I saw it. I've no idea where to start, and I've not touched this room yet. I've been working my way through the front office, and I'll get to the back eventually. You can help me if you like, but I can't give you a clue as to where to begin, or what to look for. I reckon we should be looking for a hefty bundle of papers, maybe six inches think, and tied up with a ribbon. They seem to have liked tying things with red ribbon at Pickersniff and Jebson."

"Have you not been able to discern a system of some sort? Surely those old fellows must have had a method in their madness? For example, accounts and ledgers here, printers' correspondence up there, published volumes down there, and publications pending somewhere else?"

"That's what I assumed from the beginning," sighed Carol. "But I've been forced to give up on it. Now I think that their state of disorganization must have contributed to their downfall. We know already that Pickersniff kept the ledger of debtors' and creditors' accounts at home, under his bed. This wasn't the best-run office in London."

There was nothing for it but to go rooting through every pile of manuscripts in every room, in the hope of coming across something labelled *The Ghost of Inglestone*. So Carol and I searched, without success, for the rest of the afternoon, until it was time for her to go off home and for me to meet up with my son Tom. Next morning I turned up in Gabriel Street again, and the whole day passed in another prolonged, dusty and ultimately fruitless search. Both Carol and I began to feel that we were going nowhere, and that this expenditure of effort was just a waste of time. At 5 pm we went our separate ways, and I told Carol that I could only afford one more day in the city before picking up my paint-brush in my son's apartment.

As on the previous evening, I had to travel across London on the Underground, in the rush hour. That was not a happy experience, and although I had done it many times before, I still hated the cold anonymity of stuffy packed carriages, impassive faces, and hordes of human beings of all shapes, sizes and colours rushing, rushing, rushing............

I was feeling miserable anyway, because my nose was running like a tap, as it always does when exposed to clouds of dust and the strange micro-organisms that inhabit ancient piles of paper. But I was also irritated by the fruitlessness of the search in the Gabriel Street office, and because I could see my high hopes of progress crashing into the ground. I began to resent those eccentric old men and their chaotic publishing house, and somewhere beneath Oxford Circus I vowed that I would never again rise to the bait of discarded documents, missing memoirs and fantastical works of fiction. I would henceforth remain back home in Wales, where the air was fresh and clear, and where there was room to move beneath a wide sky on my heather-clad mountain.

The carriage, packed even more tightly with human flesh, rattled and rushed its way towards Baker Street and a change to the Circle Line. Blank faces, bored faces, tired faces; hardly any animated faces. Idly, I glanced at the front page of somebody's *Evening Standard* while he was reading the inside pages. I was jolted out of my state of jaded discomfort when I read these words, printed bold and brash in red ink: *TOWER RAVENS DISAPPEAR.* Beneath the headline were these words: *Ravenmaster Mystified -- will White Tower now crumble?* Suddenly I was fully alert, with my mind racing. Something was going on here, but I was not sure what it was. Ravens were the guardian angels of Carningli, and Martha Morgan, Mistress of Plas Ingli, had had a very special relationship

24

with them. Indeed, a raven had been instrumental in helping me to discover the final part of Martha's diary which I had published as *Flying with Angels*. Were the Tower ravens about to lead me to Mrs Ravenhill? I tried to read more, but the newsprint was too small for me to decipher. The carriage was turned inside out as some (including the man with the newspaper) poured out and others poured in at Regent Street. At Baker Street I had to get off and walk to the eastbound Circle Line platform, with my thoughts still whirling around inside my head. On we juddered and shuddered towards Aldgate, and as station succeeded station the crush was lessened. At last, at Moorgate, I managed to find a seat. On it was an abandoned copy of the *Evening Standard*. I grabbed it and read on.

According to the legend, the White Tower will fall and England will suffer from a spectacular disaster, should the resident ravens disappear. It's said that the monarchy will fall, and that the state itself will also collapse. Well, the ravens have gone, and nobody knows what has happened to them, or what will happen next. Our reporter Tom Willis has been to the Tower, and here is his report.

Tower of London, 3 pm -- Ravenmaster Ivan Stobbings noticed that the birds were missing around mid-day. He told me that there were six birds which were free to wander around across four territories, at Tower Green, Tower Steps, Coldharbour and Roman Wall. He first noticed that the two birds from Tower Green were nowhere to be seen. He called for them, and they didn't appear. Feeling apprehensive, he then searched the other territories and called each of the missing birds by name, with no result. Next he searched all of the buildings of the Tower, for more than an hour, and again found no trace of the birds.

"That's the first time this has ever happened to me in twelve years at the Tower," said Mr Stobbings. "The birds respond to my voice only. If anybody else tried to attract them or feed them, they would move away. And if anybody tried to grab them they would defend themselves. They are big birds, and an angry raven can go for your eyes. They are not to be tampered with."

Having lost the six birds from the stations around the Tower, the Ravenmaster then checked the nesting cages where two auxiliary young birds were kept. The cages were still locked, but the birds were gone. With eight ravens now missing from the Tower, this is the first time since 1946 that the ancient and iconic fortress has not had a single bird in residence. The police were called in at around 2 pm, and are now working on the theory that the bird-food might have been poisoned so that the ravens could be picked up in a drugged state. They have set about a systematic questioning of all the visitors who were at the Tower around 12 noon and who have not yet left the premises. But thousands of others are of course long gone, since the total number who buy tickets during the day is almost always over 5,000. I have questioned all the Yeoman Warders (Beefeaters) who were on duty, and none of them saw anything untoward.

One possibility which can be discounted is that the birds have flown away. They have the flight feathers of one wing regularly clipped, so that they can flap about but not actually fly for any distance.

The legend of the Tower ravens probably goes back to the Middle Ages. In the seventeenth century King Charles II wanted to move the birds out of the Tower, but thought better of it when he was told that should they leave, the monarchy and the kingdom would fall.

Will the Queen and her United Kingdom now collapse? We hope not. We are not quite so concerned about the fate of the Government. But the Tower authorities are taking no chances, and messages have gone out to zoos and aviaries across the UK where young ravens (some of them raised at the Tower) are kept, in the hope that there will be at least some birds back in residence by tomorrow.

It was now a quarter to six, and on checking the route map on the wall of the carriage I realized that my destination station, Aldgate, was only one stop away from Tower Hill. On impulse or intuition I continued to the stop used by many thousands of tourists each year who flock to Britain's top tourist destination. An idea connected with the name "Jebson" was beginning to take shape in my mind, but I had no idea what it would look like when fully formed. I rang through to my son Tom on my mobile to tell him that I would be late, and hurried to the main entrance of the Tower in a state of rising excitement. It was close to closing time, but I was confident that it would not be locked this evening, of all evenings, with a full-scale investigation under way. Having talked my way in on the pretext that I had information about the ravens, my next task was to find the Ravenmaster, Ivan Stobbings, and to have a word with him. However, the media scrum had arrived before me, and there were reporters, press photographers, police and TV crews everywhere. I realized then that this was a story of international interest, and that the evening news programmes across the globe would all be reporting on the loss of the ravens and speculating on terrorist plots and on the downfall of both the British monarchy and the government. I made my way along Water Lane and at last reached the oldest part of the Tower site. There was a security cordon around the great door of the White Tower, and the police would not let anybody pass through it. There was virtually no chance of me getting inside the imposing gleaming white structure, since I did not even have a press badge.

A dozen or so Beefeaters were milling around on the lawn, some of them talking to reporters holding microphones and others positioned carefully in front of TV cameras. One of the Beefeaters was in particular demand, and I deduced that he must be the Ravenmaster. I could get nowhere near him, so with my mad idea now fixed in my mind I decided to try my luck. "Ivan!" I shouted. "I think I know where the birds are!" That caught the attention of almost everybody in the melee, and suddenly there was silence. The police, who were doing their best to control proceedings, were uncertain where my voice had come from, and so a senior officer said in measured tones: "Would the gentleman who just shouted please come forward, if he thinks that he can give us useful information?" I swallowed hard and pushed through the throng to the plastic barrier which the police had erected around the door. "I think that I may be able to help," I said, "but I need to speak to the Ravenmaster first, and preferably away from the eyes of the world." The officer nodded and opened a section of the barrier so that I could pass through. As I walked forward I realized that now I was the centre of attention, and that made me very uncomfortable. Press cameras flashed and TV lenses were pointed towards me, and my instinct was to defend myself by holding my copy of the *Evening Standard* over my face. Before they would allow me into the White Tower the police frisked me, presumably on the basis that I looked like an Al Khaida suicide bomber, and then I was admitted. Ivan the Ravenmaster followed me, and I agreed that I would talk to him and the Police Inspector in private. We went into one of the cavernous rooms on the ground floor, and it struck me that I was about to become either a hero or a prize buffoon. I swallowed hard, and the Inspector picked up on my nervousness.

"Well, sir? Would you care to give us your name?"

"All in good time, Inspector. There is no time for formalities. The sun is still well up, and if we work fast I hope we might get the birds back here before nightfall. Ivan -- may I call you that?"

"Not a problem."

"Thanks. Ivan -- those eight birds. How long have they been here?"

"Well, some are old and others are young. Hardey is the oldest male, who came from Dorset in 1992. Cedric is another male, brought from Lincoln in 1995. Then there are two females who are their mates -- Munin and Hugine, who both came from North Uist in 1996. Odin and Thor are both males, from Hampshire. They came here in recently, in 2006, and we keep them as the auxiliary birds. They were locked inside their nest-boxes this morning, so God knows how they got out. The last two of the established birds are Sigmund, who came from Cumbria in 2001, and Rhiannon......"

"Did I hear that correctly? Rhiannon?"

"Yes. A pretty name. She came from Wales two years ago."

"Can I guess where she came from? Pembrokeshire, by any chance?"

"Quite correct, my friend! Now how did you know that? She's from a mountain near a little place called Newport. Came as a young bird, with a damaged wing, but she's done wonderfully well since she recovered."

"May I ask which is the dominant male?"

"Funny that you should ask that," said the Ravenmaster. "For the first time ever, we have a dominant female. Cedric was the dominant male until a few months ago, and then, without any warning of any sort, Rhiannon took over as the dominant bird in the group. She is always the first one out in the morning, and the first one in at night. She threatens me and challenges me all the time, but it's all show, and she is perfectly harmless if you know how to deal with her."

I laughed. "I quite understand. She hasn't changed a bit."

"Pardon me?"

"Never mind. I'll explain some other time." My mind was still racing, and suddenly it occurred to me what I had to do next. "Do you have a full London Telephone Directory?" I asked.

"Why yes, in the office, in the barracks."

"Will you take me there, please? We must hurry -- there's not a moment to spare."

We walked across to the Waterloo Block, trailed by the jostling media pack, and five minutes later the three of us were in the office. I opened up the Directory at the appropriate page, and thumbed down the list from Jabber to Jackson and from James to Jawecki. Onto the next column, and a dozen or so Jebsons, all but one of whom lived in the suburbs. My eyes focussed on this one: JEBSON A.C. 26 Bow Street, and then the number. "Aha!" I exclaimed, causing eyebrows to be raised. "I am on the trail, gentlemen. The mystery is almost solved. May I please use the phone?"

"By all means."

In a state of high anticipation I dialled the number. A small child answered the phone. "Sally speaking," she said.

"Hello Sally. Is your Mum or Dad available at the moment, so that I can have a word?"

"Dad isn't back from work yet, and Mum is in the shower."

"Oh dear." I thought for a moment, and then continued. "Sally, can you do me a favour?"

"I don't do favours for strange men."

I laughed. "Don't worry. Will you be kind enough to look out through your front window and tell me what you see?"

"Oh, all right. Hold on a minute." Off she went, and returned to the phone about a minute later. "Just people and cars."

"And have you got a garden at the back of the house?"

"Oh yes, it's very nice. I've got a Wendy house too."

"Have you? You lucky thing! Would you please look out through one of your back windows and tell me what you see?"

"Must I really? This is getting boring."

"It's really quite important. Please! Just this once."

"All right then. But then I have to go. I'm in the middle of a very hard computer game. Hold on a minute."

And off she went again. After a few seconds I heard a squeal of delight, followed by running footsteps as she returned to the phone. "Ooh!" she exclaimed. "On a big branch of the tree just outside the window of Dad's study, there are masses of big black birds, and they're just sitting there in a row."

"Thank you very much, Sally. You've been very clever and helpful. But can I ask how many big black birds there are?"

"Oh, I forgot to count. Hold on again!" Down went the phone

again, and I could hear the patter of her little feet on a wooden floor as she ran to the window once again. Back she came to the phone.

"I've been very good at counting since I was four. Now I can count up to 925, and perhaps even more if I try hard! Eight birds."

"As I thought! Excellent, Sally. You are a star! Now, you go back to your game. Just tell your Mum, when she gets out of the shower, that some Beefeaters will be calling to see her before too long. Have you got that?"

"Beefeaters? What a funny name! What are they?"

"Gentlemen in funny costumes, who like to eat beef for their supper. Thank you ever so much for your brilliant help. Bye bye."

"Cheery-bye."

I turned to the Police Inspector and the Ravenmaster. "All sorted, gentlemen," I said, no doubt with triumph in my voice. "If you take your portable cages, Ivan, and go as fast as you can to 26 Bow Street, you'll find eight ravens in the garden at the back of the property. If you talk to them nicely they'll probably be glad to flutter down off that tree and to get home, just in time for a snack before settling down for the night."

The Inspector and the Beefeater looked entirely mystified, but to their credit they sprang into action. They rushed out onto the green and off towards the tower in which Ivan stored his cages. The media followed them in a great phalanx, shouting questions but getting no answers, and with cameras flashing and whirring. Everybody forgot about me, and I took the opportunity to slip out of the office, closing the door behind me as I sidled away in the shadows. My work at the Tower was done, and ten minutes later I stood at the entrance of Tower Hill tube station as a convoy of unmarked vans and police cars with sirens blaring went rushing past. I could not resist grinning like a happy Dalmatian puppy as I descended towards the northbound Circle Line platform, and I did not particularly mind it when people gave me some very strange looks. Is it actually a crime to look happy on the London Underground? Who cares........

Later that evening, while my son was completing some office work, I decided to watch the Ten o'clock News on the BBC. The strange saga of the ravens lost and found was the lead story, with live reporting from the Tower and with recorded footage from earlier in the evening. There were interviews with the police inspector, the Ravenmaster, and the Prime Minister. The Queen was probably unavailable. How on earth, all the experts wondered, had the birds travelled from the Tower to Bow Street, and up into the branches of a tall tree, when they are unable to fly? There had been no sightings of them flying across the city. How had the two youngest birds got out of their cages, leaving them still locked after their departure? Then I found that I was a nameless hero, held up by the BBC Court Correspondent as the man who might well have saved both the Queen and the country. Luckily, there were no clear pictures of my face, but there was speculation as to who I was, where I had come from, and how it was that I had identified the location of the missing ravens. They had obviously decided that I was a psychic, and they even had an interview with a strange lady who explained dowsing and the paranormal sensing of crime locations. The next item on the News was about the economy, so I turned the telly off and picked up the phone.

First I rang my wife and told her briefly about the Tower of London episode. I said that I might have to stay in London for a few more days since I had not yet been able to give any help at all on the redecoration of Tom's apartment. In any case, I was hot on the trail of the missing manuscript. She was very understanding. Then I rang Carol on her mobile phone and told her the story too. She had heard the news about the ravens, but had not made any connection with me. To her credit she swore an oath of secrecy. I hoped that the raven story would die down within 24 hours, and decided to lie low over the weekend. So I told Carol that she might not see me again until the beginning of the next week. I stayed for the next day at the apartment in Aldgate while Tom was out at work, stripping wallpaper and sanding down door frames and other things that needed to be repainted. Intermittently I watched the ongoing coverage of the story on the BBC's News 24 channel, and was fascinated to discover that as the day went on the focus shifted from the missing ravens and the downfall of the state to the identity of the "shy Welsh hero" who had facilitated the recovery of the missing birds before the fall of darkness. There was endless speculation as to my identity, and the BBC reporter who had seen me when I shouted from the back of the crowd on the previous evening managed to give a reasonably accurate description of me and the clothes I was wearing.

When Tom came back from work, he carried with him a copy of

Friday's *Evening Standard*. "Take a look at this!" he chuckled. "Entertaining, don't you think?"

There was another banner headline, and my heart sank when I read it. This is what the front page article said:

TOWER RAVENS -- MYSTERY DEEPENS

Following the recovery of the Tower ravens, in which this newspaper played no little part, the hunt is on for the Welshman who identified the address in Bow Street where the birds were found.

The Tower of London has offered him a reward of £5,000 if he will come forward and identify himself, and this paper is pleased to match that sum. If he reads this article, and wants to reveal for the Standard the full story of how the ravens went missing, and how he found them, he simply needs to ring us on this number -- 0800 576442.

We also offer a reward of £2,000 to any other reader of this paper who can point us to the man who saved the nation. All we know about him at this stage is that he's probably in his sixties, of medium height and build and with a weather-beaten face and greying short hair. Yesterday he wore dark blue chinos and a green sweatshirt, and carried a red rucksack on his back. He had a copy of the Evening Standard in his hand. He has quite a strong Welsh accent, and according to the Tower Ravenmaster he might have some connection with Pembrokeshire. That's all we know for the present, but our investigations are continuing.

According to legend, the monarchy and the nation will fall if the Tower ravens should ever go missing. Yesterday they were absent from the Tower for around eight hours, but they were back in their cages by nightfall, and that was obviously enough to deflect the arrows of fate. At the time of going to press, the Queen is still in rude health, Buckingham Palace still stands, and the state seems to be working with something resembling efficiency.

On an inside double spread, there were features on the Tower ravens, on legends connected with the Tower, and on past connections between the Tower and Wales. There was a list of famous Welshmen who had been incarcerated in the Tower and even executed there, and a pompous and convoluted "Comment" column from the Editor in which he remarked upon the fact that so many previous Welsh visitors to the Tower had plotted the downfall of England and espoused the cause of Welsh independence, and concluded that this latest act of grace from a Welshman showed that Wales was now truly integrated as part of the UK.

"Oh my God!" I moaned. "Now they have turned this into a political gesture. Tom, do they always do this in London?"

"Don't take it seriously, Dad. This is all about circulation. This is a nice feel-good story. The Editor wants to keep it alive for a day or two, and he's trying to stir up a reaction on his letters page. Of course, he'll get a few letters from irate Welshmen. But by Monday the next big story will have taken its place. Now, shall I put the kettle on for a cup of tea?"

"But they are after me. I hope that neither you nor Carol is open to bribery. I wonder how many others there are who might betray me?"

"I shouldn't think there is anybody else, Dad. Nobody else knows you in London, and I suppose only a few of your friends at home in Wales know that you're here. They'll watch the news on the box and read the papers, I dare say, but there's no reason for them to make any connection between you and the Tower of London. Somebody might recognize you from the fleeting images of you that were shown on the news, but images are very ephemeral, and I wouldn't mind betting that they won't be shown again. Just take it easy, old man."

"Oh, all right. But what about these blood-thirsty investigative journalists that one hears about? They may all be heading for Pembroke-shire as we speak, determined to track me down."

Tom laughed. "The world has changed, Dad. There are a few such reporters who dig deep and travel. But take it from me that most reporters these days work from their desks, by phone and Email. It's far more efficient. I guarantee that by Monday this story will be dead."

On Sunday it was anything but dead, with big features in most of the popular Sunday papers. So I remained in hiding and made good progress with my painting and decorating. On Monday morning I thought heavy disguise was in order, so I dressed in the most casual clothes I could find in Tom's wardrobe. Luckily, he and I were almost the same size. A baseball cap on my head, dark shades over my eyes, and two days' worth of stubble on my chin completed my transformation. I emerged onto the street at 8 am, bought half a dozen daily papers on the nearest news-stand, and returned to the apartment to read them over breakfast. There was no mention of the Tower of London, or ravens, or Wales. I breathed a sigh of relief. So ended my five minutes of fame, which in retrospect I quite enjoyed, in spite of the fact that my name was never discovered.

Now I had various things to do. First, I rang Carol at the office in Gabriel Lane, and told her that I was busy, but would call in tomorrow, hopefully with something interesting to show her. Then I rang the Jebson household. "Hello," said a female voice. "Helen Jebson speaking."

"Good morning, Mrs Jebson. Please excuse this call out of the blue. You won't know me, but I'm ringing about this raven business."

"Oh no! Not again!" she exclaimed. "Who are you?"

I had to explain who I was, and had to hope that her natural suspicion would be ameliorated. She continued: "The last few days have been completely mad. The phone has hardly stopped, and we've had journalists and film crews here from all over the world. My daughter Sally has loved every minute of it, and thinks that she's now a film star. But normal life has been on hold, and I'll be glad when the story fades away. I've no more information to give you -- it's all been reported already."

"The story is now dead and buried, I assure you. I'm the one who spoke to Sally some days ago.........."

She was silent for a moment. "You know that reporters are hunting for you all over London?"

"And in Wales as well. That's why I've been lying low. There's a matter on which you might be able to help me, and I promise that it's got nothing to do with ravens."

"Well............" She sounded uncertain.

"Please! It has something to do with old Mr Jebson the publisher, who was, I assume, an ancestor of your husband?"

"No, he wasn't. He was a bachelor who lived in the upper part of the house, which he owned jointly with his married brother Morton. Morton had several children, and he would be my husband's ancestor -- maybe five generations back. Andrew has made a family tree, and he's mentioned "Old Uncle James" sometimes. He was greatly loved as a kind and eccentric old fellow; and there are mentions of him in various family papers. This house has been in the family since the eighteenth century."

"Dare I ask if any of Uncle James's things are still in the house?"

"They might be. There's a top-floor tenement -- more like an attic, really-- with lots of stuff in boxes and cupboards. And there's another cupboard in Andrew's study."

"Wonderful! This might be very important. Do you think that Andrew might allow me to look at some of the old man's things?"

"You'd better ask him yourself. I don't suppose he would object."

"I'm not in London for very long. May I call in today, when he comes home from work?"

There was a long silence, while Helen Jebson considered whether she should trust me. I did not want to force anything, and held my breath. "Very well," she said at last. "He normally comes home at about 5.30. I'll tell him that you rang. Call in at about 6 pm, if you will."

Now I had the rest of the day at my disposal. Tom was out at work, and so I spent the morning finishing off the painting of his kitchen. After lunch I took a brisk walk to the Tower, driven by an urge to see the ravens back on their home territory. I had to see Rhiannon in particular. I hoped that I would not meet Ivan the Ravenmaster, since I wanted to remain anonymous, and feared that he might recognize me. Having bought my entrance ticket I wandered about, marvelling at the sheer scale of the place and at the austere and ancient majesty of the White Tower in particular. On my previous visit, just a few days earlier, I had not had a chance to be a proper tourist. The buildings and precincts were heaving with visitors from every corner of the planet; visitor numbers for the day had probably doubled because of the publicity over the weekend. I looked for the ravens. There were two on a low wall close to the river, preening themselves and looking content in the warmth of the midsummer sun. I had no idea which of the four stations might be the one occupied by Rhiannon and her mate. So I explored rather aimlessly, guide book in hand, until I came once again to Tower Green, not knowing what to expect. Suddenly, there she was, just a few feet in front of me, stock still, and looking me straight in the eye, with her head slightly cocked. It was Rhiannon all right, the same bird which I had seen countless times before on my visits to Carningli. I dare say that all ravens are supposed to look the same, except that females are slightly smaller than the males. But I was surprised by her size, and impressed as ever with the beautiful silvery blue and green iridescence which gave colour to her otherwise pitch black plumage. I did not know what to do next, but then she hopped towards me. Instinctively I dropped to one knee and put out my hand. I thought that she might peck at it, but she rubbed against my fingers with her beak and head. If she had been a kitten, she would certainly have purred. For a few seconds, something passed between us.

"Be careful, sir! Ravens are dangerous birds, and that one in particular is very unpredictable."

The magic disappeared. The voice was that of Ivan the Ravenmaster, who was naturally more watchful than he might have been a week ago, and intent on protecting both his beloved birds and the inquisitive public. I got to my feet as he approached, and the raven hopped away to join her mate in pecking about in the weeds at the base of the high wall of the White Tower. Luckily Ivan did not penetrate my disguise, and I said nothing to him. I shrugged my shoulders and held my hands out wide, in the hope that he might mistake me for a Polish builder who spoke no English. It seemed to work, for he ticked me off very briefly with a smile on his face and then explained, in a very loud voice, the he had to go off to check the birds near the Roman Wall.

Shortly after six o'clock I knocked on the door of Number 26 Bow Street. The door was opened by Sally, who turned out to be a sweet child with blue eyes and a mop of golden curls on her head. "Are you the man from Wales?" she asked.

"Yes, I am," I replied. "It's very nice to meet you, Sally. Is your dad home from work yet?"

"Oh yes -- he was home early today. Come in, please."

So I spent a delightful evening with the Jebson family, talking about ravens (that could not be avoided), about my obsession with the diaries of Mistress Martha Morgan, and about the strange and tortuous trail which had led me to London and to their delightful home in search of something or other. Andrew and Helen invited me to join them for supper, and I gladly accepted. As we talked they became more and more intrigued themselves by the puzzle of *The Ghost of Inglestone* and the mysterious Mrs Susanna Ravenhill. Immediately after supper, while Sally enjoyed the special privilege of a short video before bed-time, we three adults set about the task of finding the lost manuscript; I was absolutely certain that the ravens had led me to it, and that it would be somewhere in the house. Andrew and Helen were more sceptical, but entered into the spirit of the hunt with gusto in any case.

It did not take us long. In Andrew's study there was one tall cupboard, beautifully made and with Regency styling. We opened it up, and found that there were six shelves inside, all heavily laden with bundles of papers. Some of them were tied with red ribbon. "Aha!" said I. "James Jebson liked red ribbon. He must have bought a giant roll of it once, maybe from a street vendor on Piccadilly." On one shelf were about twenty manuscripts of unpublished -- and probably unpublishable -- novels. One was called *The Virgin's Revenge*. Another was called *The Monster of Kilimanjaro*. A third had the enticing title *The Master Gunner and the Bluestocking*. And then, in a bundle somewhat smaller than the others, wrapped in brown paper and tied with crossing red ribbons and a flattened bow, there was a manuscript called **The Ghost of Inglestone.** There was also a label stuck on with glue, with these hand-written words: *Author: Mrs Susanna Ravenhill (pseudonym). NB subtitle removed by agreement. JJ.*

"Hooray! I've found it!" I shouted, as excited as a small child on Christmas morning. "I knew it would be here somewhere! And it was just outside this window that Sally saw the eight ravens perching on the branch, if I remember rightly. Best piece of guidance I've ever had."

With shaking fingers I untied the ribbon and removed the brown paper. I thumbed through some of the pages, and saw at once that the text was written in a hand which I did not recognize. It was not in the form of a diary, and neither was it written in Dimetian Welsh. It was a conventional first-person narrative, written in English. After reading just a few pages I became convinced that the tale was an extraordinary one, some of it set in Cardiff, Merthyr Tydfil and even Paris. But some of it was set in the landscape of Cilgwyn, Carningli and Newport, which was familiar to all the readers of the journals of Martha Morgan. But the names were all changed. Cilgwyn was called "Whitebank", Carningli was (of course) "Inglestone Mountain" and Newport was "Tidrath". Many personal names were falsified, but there were familiar ones too -- including Wilmot, Bessie, Will and other friends who had survived Martha, and younger members of the

Morgan family including grand-daughter Rose. Whoever the author was, I knew that there would be readers who would want to read the narrative. Fact or fiction? Was the writing really Daisy's, as I suspected? More to the point, was she "Mrs Ravenhill", or was she simply the medium for something written by somebody else?

I asked Andrew for his permission to take the manuscript away so that I could read it at my leisure and decide whether it should be published. "By all means," he said. "Although it was found on my premises I've no idea who really owns it -- maybe it's actually owned by the descendants of the writer, wherever they may be. But if the text does become a book, could I ask for twenty copies on publication? We're a large family, and many of us have heard tales of Old Uncle James."

"Done! You have a deal. When I get home, and have a chance to go through the text, I'll decide what to do, and give you a call."

I thanked them for their hospitality and cooperation, took my leave, and set off for Tom's apartment for my last night in London. I reached it without being mugged, and since Tom was out with some friends I could not resist settling down and getting stuck in. It was an incredible tale indeed, well written and easy to follow once I had got used to the precise and tidy handwriting. It was very different from Martha's hand-writing, which was strong, fluid and heavily slanted. At 2 am Tom came in, somewhat the worse for wear, and went to bed. At breakfast time I had almost finished the tale, and when Tom went off to work I had just two chapters to go. I finished reading by mid-morning, and knew immediately that *The Ghost of Inglestone* had to be published. Then I collapsed into bed and fell asleep. When I woke up it was late afternoon. I rang my wife to tell her the hot news, and promised to tell her everything else when I got home tomorrow. Then I rang Carol, who was still in the Gabriel Lane office.

She was thoroughly delighted. I told her that I wanted to edit the manuscript and publish it, probably for a limited readership, and wondered whether Hyde Park Publishers might have inherited the publishing rights to the manuscript. Carol said that she had already checked all her records, and confirmed that no contracts had ever been signed between Mrs Ravenhill (or her representative) and Pickersniff and Jebson. Therefore it was reasonable to assume that the manuscript had been rejected or abandoned through force of circumstances. There were no inherited rights, and the publisher had no claim to ownership. In any case, the manuscript had not been found in the office, but in a private home. She said that I probably had far more of a claim to ownership since I had already published Martha's diaries without any legal issues being raised, and since there was probably some sort of family link between those diaries and this new text. I confirmed that there was indeed a link.

"Take it away back to Wales," she said. "If you don't publish it nobody will -- there's not much taste for Victorian melodramas these days, and our current priorities are the publication of autobiographies of twenty-year-old football players who have their brains in their feet, failed politicians who think that their mediocre careers are of interest to the world, and others who are famous for being famous. By the time they've all had their six-figure advances, there's not much left for titles featuring Victorian ghosts. And even if I do pull it into our system and recommend it for publication, I've got to convince my editorial and marketing colleagues, and they have to convince the book trade. In the best possible scenario, the book wouldn't see the light of day for years."

"But what if it becomes a massive best-seller? And what if your MD finds out that the manuscript came from the Pickersniff and Jebson stable? Won't he put you on the carpet and wipe his feet on you?"

She laughed. "God, no. This wouldn't be the first or the last book to get away. If anybody asks me, I'll simply say that I didn't think the memoir would sell. Publishing is a very imperfect science indeed. We make misjudgments, and lose auctions, all the time............"

So next day I took the manuscript home with me on the train to Wales, and started work on it. I had to do much research in order to decipher some of the place names and the names of leading characters who are well known to history. As I read through it for the second time, this time in a state of greater wakefulness, I became more and more amazed by the extraordinary tale related. Fact or fantasy? Affectation or profound insight into the human condition? A fairy tale for adults? I leave the reader to judge. Here, with some long descriptive passages edited out, is the fantastical memoir of the mysterious Mrs Susanna Ravenhill, written down in the year 1857.

1. A Crime Against The Truth

Dying was, as I recall, a very easy thing, peaceful and painless. It was the sort of thing that everybody should experience. But what came afterwards was, in my case, very bothersome indeed. If I had been given some premonition of what would transpire, I should certainly not have bothered to die in the first place.

But I write in riddles, and I had better explain. When I opened my eyes and managed to focus them, with difficulty, on my surroundings, I found that I was in a room full of people. I recognized the place immediately as my own kitchen, and observed that I was lying on my back on the great oak table that had stood there, as sacred as an altar, for well nigh sixty years. How many corpses had been laid out upon it? How many surgical operations had been conducted upon its scrubbed and spotless surface? How many feasts had it supported, and how many breakfasts and dinners and suppers? How many times had it been anointed with wine, and ale, and even blood? How many legal documents had been signed upon it? How many hands had been shaken across it? How many midwinter ploughs had been stored beneath it? My mind was wandering about, befuddled with a dull sort of pain, as I drifted in and out of consciousness............

I felt cold, cold, as cold as death. My teeth chattered, and I was aware that I was shivering uncontrollably.

I looked around me for a few seconds, and saw that the table was surrounded by my nearest and dearest. They all had tears on their cheeks, and several of the women were sobbing, one of them uncontrollably and inconsolably. On one side stood Will Owen, my head man at Plas Ingli for many years, and his son Gerallt. On the other side I recognized the Irishman Brendan O'Connell and Henry Evans, the husband of my sweet grand-daughter Rose. There were two other men present -- Gomer Jenkins, once my servant and now the tenant farmer of Penrhiw, and my grandson Abel Rhys. They all wore heavy coats and scarves, and showed every appearance of having just come in from the cold. There were five or six women -- I was in no fit state to count. I recall that Blodwen Bebb, my tough milkmaid, who never cried, was wailing as if the end of the world had come, and that Will's daughter Myfanwy had her arms around her in some attempt to bring her comfort, even though she was sobbing herself. My beloved housekeeper Bessie stood motionless to my right, dabbing her eyes and blowing her nose on a kerchief. My dear daughters Betsi and Daisy were also there, locked in a silent embrace, rocking gently back and forth and no doubt seeking to hold their emotions under control. Somebody was moaning. The fire was sparkling and crackling. A sheepdog was howling outside the kitchen door. That much I recall, from the first moments of my new life.

"Good God. It's a miracle!" said somebody. "The Mistress is breathing and moving!"

Then I said: "I am very cold. Will you please stop weeping and move me nearer to the fire?"

The weeping and wailing stopped in an instant, and was replaced by an eerie silence as shock replaced grief. "*Diawch*, it's true!" said Will. "Blessed is his name," said Brendan, who was a good Catholic. "A miracle indeed," said Myfanwy. Then there was pandemonium, with laughter and more tears, and everybody talking at once. I was lifted off the table as if I was a small baby, and placed in the settle at the side of the everlasting fire in the *simnai fawr*, where Grandpa Isaac had seen out the last years of his life, half a lifetime ago. Shawls were wrapped around my shoulders; Myfanwy massaged my hands while Blodwen dealt with my feet; and Bessie poured some steaming hot milk and honey down my throat. The men looked on, lost for words and not knowing what to do next.

Time stood still. Those around me appeared to be part of a tableaux. Were they real people, or phantoms conjured up in death, for my comfort? Was I alive or dead? Recollections drifted into my mind, of a long, slow walk up onto the mountain as a rosy dusk turned to night, and then of a velvet sky glittering with diamonds, and of settling down on my back on the cool green grass near the summit, and of drifting off to sleep............

Then Abel said: "Grandmother, the whole world will be knocking on the door within the next half hour. News travels very fast in these parts, as we all know. Shall I invite people in, or tell them of the miracle and invite them to leave us in peace for the present?"

A Crime against the Truth

With those words, my dream-like state suddenly disappeared, and I experienced a most powerful and terrifying premonition. I had been led by many others between childhood and old age, but never anything as strongly as this. I could not understand it, but neither could I resist it. So my puzzlement on being alive was replaced in an instant by a strange (and as it happened, fateful) determination to embark upon a hazardous and utterly preposterous adventure. I knew with absolute certainty that I had to stay alive, but pretend to be dead. "No, Abel!" I said. "If people call, and know that my body has been found, and wish to pay their respects, I beg you not to disabuse them. Confirm that I am dead. Do not let anybody else into the house. Lock the kitchen door from the inside, if you please, and station yourself at the front door, as is appropriate in the circumstances. Blodwen and Myfanwy, will you please close the shutters on all of the windows?"

Nobody moved. They all stood with their eyes wide and their mouths agape. Not a word was uttered, but then Abel blurted out: "Grandmother, did you really say that? We cannot hide the truth of the matter from the neighbourhood. For a few hours, maybe, but after that, it will be impossible!"

"Please, Abel, I beg of you. I know that this is what we have to do..."

Suddenly Betsi found her tongue. "Mother, you are confused and unwell, and although we love you dearly we cannot possibly act on any instructions you may give so soon after your terrifying experience on the mountain. Please allow us to make a judgement as to what may be the best course of action. We have seen a miracle; we must let the world know!"

"Betsi, my experience on the mountain was not at all terrifying. It was beautiful, and as serene as may be. And I am perfectly in control of my senses, so please do not patronise me."

There was another silence, which probably lasted for no more than a few seconds but which felt like a lifetime. Time was short, and we all knew it. Time for one last throw of the dice. "My dear friends," I pleaded. "You know that I have special powers, which may lie dormant for years or decades and which may suddenly reappear. Through the use of these powers I have saved this house of angels, and this family, on many occasions in the past. Well, I will be truthful with you, and I beg of you to

42

believe me. Some minutes since I had a most powerful vision which I cannot resist -- I saw that I must live, but be dead to the world, and that I have been spared because there is one great thing that must be done before I truly go to my grave. I can only do it if the rest of the world, and my enemies in particular, think me dead. Do not ask me what that task may be -- I only know that it is my destiny to see it through. No doubt it will be revealed to me in due course. It may well be that the destinies of all of you, and your families for generations to come, are also dependent upon my acceptance of this high duty. Please, please -- I beg you, all of you, to help me........" I think that I was close to tears, and truly I did not have the strength to argue more. Only the ticking kitchen clock broke the silence.

I was saved, not for the first time, by my angels. To this day I still cannot explain the reactions of my nearest and dearest when confronted by what must have appeared to them as madness. First, my good friend and housekeeper Bessie stood before the fire and demonstrated both her loyalty and her willingness to take risks. "I will support Mistress Martha in this business, though a part of me feels that it is surely madness," she declared. "We have trusted her before, and we must do so again. We must share an oath that we will not betray her or let slip a single word that might lead others to the truth."

"I agree with Bessie," said Daisy, after a pause. "I venture to suggest that she knows Mother better than any of the family. If she sees something of deep importance behind what may appear to be a whim, or a moment of insanity, that is good enough for me. Anyway, this sounds like a considerable adventure for all of us. I admit to being quite excited! We will all have to lie through our teeth, over and again, to keep this secret, but if we lie in a good cause, God will surely forgive us. He has, I trust, already forgiven us for far worse sins."

Then Will stepped forward and broke his silence. "I will support you too, Mistress," he said, with his blue eyes glittering. "You have led us into many adventures over the years as it is, so we can all surely cope with another one. It will keep us all young. If we conspire with you we will not be breaking any of the laws of the land, I think. For you it will be a serious matter indeed, but for the rest of us it will be like a game of charades!"

Then there was a heavy knocking on the kitchen door, and we all froze with horror. Abel seized the moment and motioned for the others to surround me lest I should be seen from the door when it was opened. He opened the door very slightly, and I heard him say "Ah, Mr Harries! Kind of you to call."

I heard the voice of Billy Harries, one of the Newport carters. "I was passing by along the Cilgwyn Road a while back," he said, "and I saw a little group of men coming down off the mountain and heading for the Plas, carrying a short ladder with a burden upon it. Dammo, that looks like a bad business, I thought to meself. And straight after that fearsome earthquake which shook the mountain to its foundations. Would it be impertinent of me to ask, young fellow, whether there has been a sad accident up among the rocks, and to enquire further of you whether commiserations might be in order?"

"Excuse me if I do not invite you in," said Abel, "but there is a very sad scene in the kitchen just now, and it is best that I speak to you in the yard, if I may." With that, he sidled out through the door and closed it behind him. We all breathed a sigh of relief, and Bessie motioned to Myfanwy and Blodwen to start on the task of closing the shutters before any other unwelcome guests should turn up and start peeping through the windows. The house was thus plunged into darkness, although it was a bright and crisp winter morning, and candles had to be lit in every room.

I turned to Betsi. "Earthquake?" I whispered, with incredulity in my voice. "Billy mentioned an earthquake. There are never earthquakes in this area."

"There was a very great tremor last night, Mother," she replied. "Do you mean that you were unaware of it?"

"I promise you that I was unaware of any noise or shaking. I can only assume that when it happened I was dead to the world."

I was in no mood to pursue the matter. I sat by the fire, desperately seeking to get some warmth back into my body, as Bessie poured more hot sweet milk down my throat. After a few minutes, Abel came back inside, and locked the kitchen door behind him.

"It is done," he announced in a voice laden with doom, as if announcing the end of the world. "Billy Harries has the biggest mouth in town, and he will take that cart of his down Greystone Hill and past the church at the gallop. It's a Sunday morning, and people will be out and about in the church and the chapels. Within five minutes the whole town will know that Mistress Martha Morgan of Plas Ingli is dead."

For what seemed like an eternity, we all looked at him and absorbed the import of what he had said. Once again, the only sound came from the ticking clock. At last Rose asked him: "Do you mean that you have begun the process of misleading the community, as Grandmother requested?"

He nodded. "I had to make an instant decision, and for better or worse, that is what I said. I reported that Grandmother had been found upon the mountain summit early this morning, having died in the night possibly as a consequence of the earth tremor that rocked this house and rattled the mountain. I said that we were waiting for the doctor to conduct a post-mortem examination and to pronounce upon the cause of death, and that we were in such a state of shock that no visitors would be received for the time being. The first few of a thousand lies."

There was no time to reconsider, or indeed to ponder on the full consequences of the deceit in which we were now all involved. Betsi and Daisy took control, and having ascertained that the fire in my room upstairs was lit and burning merrily, they immediately removed me from the kitchen and settled me in to the place that would be my temporary prison. Abel unlocked the front door and stationed himself alongside it, and as the morning passed many other visitors called, to be turned away politely with the same message that had been given to Billy Harries. After a further muttered discussion in the kitchen, the men dispersed, for there were animals to be fed and cowsheds and stables to be mucked out; and Myfanwy and Blodwen had fifteen cows to milk. We women held a conference of war upstairs, keeping our voices low in case anybody in the yard or at the front door should hear us. There were considerable plans to be laid, and practicalities to be addressed, the first of which related to the matter of the death certificate. It was clear that we could not ask Dr George Havard, Daisy's husband, to write it out, for that would be a crime that would result in the revoking of his license and lead to imprisonment. Who else might oblige? We were racking our brains on that matter when I noticed that my beloved grand-daughter Rose was standing in the corner of the room with tears rolling down her cheeks. I got up and walked over to her. I took her in my arms. *"Cariad,"* I said. "What is the meaning of this? Are you not pleased that I am still with you, and that my place in Cilgwyn Churchyard will be unoccupied for a little while yet?"

"Oh Grandmother!" she sobbed. "Of course I am pleased, for you and for the rest of us. But do you realize that my father Brynach, and my brother David, far away across the ocean in America, will now be told that you are dead, and will be forced to grieve because of our conspiracy? We will all have to lie to them, and multiply their misery."

That removed my good humour at a stroke, for in truth I had not yet had a moment for the consideration of such things. I realized now that the lie upon which I was inexorably set would be like an evil octopus, spreading its tentacles across the land and over the ocean, dragging in many who were innocent and who would be harmed in a multitude of ways which could not be foreseen. Brynach and David would be forced to grieve, and their grieving on another continent would be lonely indeed and mixed with guilt, since they would not hear of my death until long after the date of my funeral. My sister Elen would be plunged into misery, also in America, as would my sister Catrin and my brother's widow Nansi, of whom I was very fond. None of them could be told the truth; the risks were too great, and I feared that there were already too many fellow conspirators for me to sleep serenely in the knowledge that leaks were impossible. Catrin and Nansi would attend my funeral, and would weep bitter tears, surrounded by those who would affect grief but who would be in possession of the truth. Theirs would be raw emotions, exposed to an audience of actors. So now I wept with Rose, and at last it was she who managed to smile and who started to wipe away my tears.

"There now, Grandmother," she said. "That's enough. There will be more tears, that's for sure, but my father and brother, and many others, will have to grieve for you at some stage, so maybe it's best for them to get it over and done with now, rather than later. You will recall that I too see things that others do not see, and so I have to support you and respect your wishes if you feel that some destiny awaits you that requires subterfuge on a grand scale. Let's do it, and as long as I live I will not betray you. I love you, *Mam-gu bach*, and can love you better, and keep a little eye on you, if you are alive and kicking........."

A Crime against the Truth

When Blodwen had finished with the milking, and had completed her tasks in the dairy, I set her to ringing the Plas Ingli bell very slowly, for an hour between twelve noon and one of the clock. The baleful sound echoed round the *cwm*, ensuring that those not already in possession of the news of my death would now be fully informed. Betsi walked down to her home at Brithdir to tell her husband Ioan the news of my death and resurrection, and of the conspiracy in which we were now all involved. Abel took the light chaise and drove his aunt Daisy into town, so that she could give the same news to her husband George Havard. They promised to return to the Plas, in full mourning dress, before two o'clock, with their husbands. I prayed that we would get their support, for truly we had need of their skill in planning my escape to a new life somewhere else.

In the short time that I had alone, I forced down a late breakfast of porridge thickly covered with brown sugar, followed by toasted bread and cheese and what seemed like a gallon of tea. Bessie insisted that I should drink it all, and I felt too feeble to disobey her. With the bell ringing out its miserable message, I had an opportunity to ponder on my foolishness. I was very confused -- and so were those around me. Myfanwy and Bessie went about their tasks in the house with frowns upon their faces, intent upon keeping me warm and comfortable but saying very little. Our relationship was suddenly different. How could it be otherwise? My servants and my family appeared to think that there had been a miracle -- and that I had been raised from the dead like Lazarus. They seemed to think that I was, since yesterday, no longer like other mortals. I was in no position to disagree. So was my survival a sign from God that I -- or maybe he --had unfinished business? I was sure of a sign from somewhere, but I was uncertain of God's involvement. I pondered, as best I could, on the Biblical concepts of resurrection, reincarnation, salvation, and redemption and atonement, and wished that I understood them properly. If only I had paid more attention to several hundred boring sermons over the years, I might now be closer to enlightenment..........

Of one thing I was certain. I did not want any talk of miracles in the community at large. I hated the very thought of becoming a celebrity and a source of wonderment, like an exhibit in a freak show. Poor Lazarus must have had a hard time of it after he rose from the dead. But something very strange had happened to me on the mountain, and there remained in my mind's eye a vision during which I looked down on my own body from far above the summit of the mountain, and then saw the mountain bathed in bright light. A flock of white ravens appeared, and a man with a long beard and a kind face, dressed in gold and silver robes, pointed with his staff towards the Plas. What could that mean? It must surely have something to do with my home and family, and my wicked past and the necessity for redemption. I knew that I had a job to do, but I could not for the life of me work out what it might be.

I also thought that I still had enemies in the district, and that it would be better if they, like everybody else, thought me dead. My death and disappearance would also enable the family as a whole to move on unencumbered by an old matriarch like me, and to prosper. I knew that I organized too much, controlled too many aspects of life at the Plas, interfered too much, and was accorded too much respect; therefore my departure, to Heaven or Hell or (as now seemed likely) into a sort of purgatory in some distant place, would be good for family and servants alike. From now on, others could make decisions, determine their own destinies, and put Mistress Martha Morgan out of their minds.

I was still pondering when Betsi and Daisy returned to the Plas with their husbands. The two men, for whom I had the greatest affection and respect, were already fully informed as to the events of the night and the morning of high excitement. When they came into my room they embraced me, and their love was as evident as ever. But needless to say, both of them were thoroughly disapproving of the mad course upon which I had embarked. George, as the only doctor in town and a great pillar of the community, was particularly worried, and feared that any involvement on his part would lead to him being struck from the Royal College practitioners' list for breaking his Hippocratic Oath. I said that I understood his concerns, but reminded him that no crime had been committed by me, or by him, and that I had no wish for anybody to fall foul of the law. I knew that we would all fall foul of the Church, but that was not the same thing as committing a grievous sin. "Is it a sin, or a crime, George, for me to remain alive when I should be dead, or to assume a new identity? I think not. My knowledge of the law is not great, but I think I am right in saying that impersonation is only a crime if it is used as a means to obtain wealth or possessions which belong to others, or which are not rightfully mine. I have no intention of becoming wicked, or obtaining any benefit from what I am led to do."

"Your theology always was something unique, Martha!" grinned George. "But you forget about formalities. There has to be a post-mortem, a death certificate, an inquest and a funeral. Then there is a will to be read out and acted upon. I have to be involved in all of those. Would you like to suggest to me what I might do over the coming weeks and days without jeopardizing my career and my reputation? I suppose I could always retire to my bed, having diagnosed myself as suffering from typhoid fever or some such thing. That would conveniently get me out of the way. "

At that point in the conversation, Daisy intervened, as optimistic and cheerful as ever. "Don't you worry so much, *Cariad*," she said to her husband. "This is surely not an insurmountable problem. Something will come up, just you wait and see."

I had my doubts about that, but there was no time for interminable pondering. My two daughters took control. The first thing they did was to ensure that my appearance was changed as completely as possible. The men were banished from my room, and I was then disguised by having my long white hair trimmed very short and dyed brown with grey streaks. Daisy was the technical expert, and she explained that she had learned a good deal about the arts and crafts of beautification -- and disguise -- during her time in London. While they worked on my hairdressing, they discussed with me the name which I might now assume. "How about Mistress Mary Lazarus?" said Betsi.

"Too obvious, by far," I replied. "I must have an English name, not a Welsh one, if I am to invent a new personality. "Mrs" and not "Mistress" for a start, since things are very modern in England. Mrs Sally Smith or Mrs Ann Brown? *Ach y fi!* No -- I want to use something that links me to this place. I am moved to use my own middle name, which nobody but me knows. I always preferred it to Martha anyway. Then a surname that reminds me of home."

I furrowed my brow for a few minutes, and then exclaimed "Yes! I think I fancy the name and the personality of an elderly widow called Mrs

A Crime against the Truth

Susanna Ravenhill."

"Excellent, Mother!" exclaimed Daisy, as ebullient as ever.

"Ssssshhh, Daisy!" whispered Betsi. "Remember that we must not raise our voices, and neither must there be any laughter in this house. People are coming and going all the time, and the front doorstep is a place of great activity. Abel is dealing with visitors and sympathy as best he can, but people have sharp ears, and there will be speculation as to what is going on inside these four walls."

"Quite right you are," said Daisy. "I am very sorry. Of course, we are grieving, and preparing the body for burial. And that must be done with due respect and reverence."

Betsi nodded. "Thank you, sister. We are agreed. But I also agree that the name of Susanna Ravenhill is as good as any; I cannot think of anything better."

We conducted a consultation in the house, and that was a nightmare which is best not described in detail. Suffice to say that some had second thoughts about the wisdom of my mad plan, and sought to force me into allowing the truth to leak out. I had to argue, and plead, and weep before I obtained full consensus. But at last, when I was utterly exhausted, everybody agreed.

In the middle of the afternoon my coffin (which I had organized in advance from Davy Death) was fetched from town, and he was told by Bessie that his services would not be required any further since she and Betsi would prepare the body and make ready for the funeral. Apparently he was quite relieved, since he was suffering from a heavy chill and looked as if he should have stayed in bed.

Then, around three o'clock, Wilmot and Delilah Gwynne, my dear friends and owners of the Plas Ingli estate, turned up in their carriage, having heard the news. They were let in on my instructions, as were Patty and Jake Nicholas from the Parrog, who arrived at almost the same time. The four of them were greeted in the kitchen by Betsi and Daisy and their husbands. With a certain wicked pleasure I heard the sounds of sobs, and embraces, and conversation from my room upstairs.

I knew that my dear friend Patty would be embracing Daisy, with tears rolling down her cheeks, and that her rough and gentle husband Jake would be standing behind her, rolling his hat in his hands and looking down at his shiny boots, and not knowing what to say.

"Oh, my poor dear things!" sobbed Delilah. "How terrible, how truly terrible! Your beloved mother gone, and so suddenly. Did she suffer? I truly hope not, for she saw quite enough suffering in her long and eventful life........."

"Hush now, beloved!" said Wilmot, in a voice thick with emotion. "This is not the time for eulogies or speculations. Those will come later. So it is true, my dear Betsi and Daisy? Oh dear, oh dear, oh dear. Bad, bad business. My deepest commiserations go with all of you. And we have lost the best and truest friend that any man and wife ever had."

"Please, all of you, no more tears or expressions of sadness," pleaded Daisy. "They are not entirely appropriate in the circumstances........."

There was a long silence. Then Jake found his tongue, and said: "Not appropriate? Whatever do you mean, Mistress Daisy?"

At that point, I saw in my mind's eye that both Daisy and Betsi smiled and motioned to the four new arrivals to follow them along the passage and up the stairs. I heard their heavy footsteps as they ascended and came along the landing towards my room. As they entered I smiled, and Delilah fainted. That caused a considerable commotion, and all available manpower had to be summoned to lift her ample form onto my bed, where Daisy loosened her heavy garments and administered smelling salts. At last she recovered, and all eyes turned from her towards me. "Martha? Is it really you?" asked Patty, in a feeble voice. I suppose that they hardly recognized me, in view of the strange things that had been done to my hair and my complexion by my daughters. But gradually they did come to terms with the fact of my survival or resurrection, and there were more tears and embraces, and even laughter, until Abel ran upstairs and told us off for endangering the whole enterprise. "Please, Grandmother, and all of you!" he spluttered, wagging his finger like a schoolmaster. "There must be no frivolity at all in this house. I beg of you all to remember that there are people back and forth all the time, offering their sympathy and asking if they can help with the animals and in the dairy. They are all remarkably kind, and if I am to carry on telling them a pack of lies, I must at least have a house that is as quiet as death!"

A Crime against the Truth

We apologized in whispers, and determined there and then that I had to get out of the house as quickly as possible. Luckily, once the four new arrivals had heard the story of my coming back to life after being carried off the mountain, and had heard of my determination not to become an object of curiosity or even medical research, they resolved to help me. Wilmot took charge. As a self-made man with a fortune carried west from the copper industry of the Swansea valley, he had a brain as sharp as the Barber of Seville's razor. He moved with amazing facility from grief to the planning of my escape and the deception of the community. Ioan and George, my two sons-in-law, agreed that he was likely to be more dispassionate than they could ever be in the circumstances; and they agreed to accept his guidance and to work with him.

The three men closeted themselves in another of the upstairs rooms for half an hour, while the rest of us had something to eat, and then they emerged to set things in motion. Wilmot seated himself at my desk, portly and ruddy-faced, and if he had had a military uniform I dare say he would have made a passable Napoleon Bonaparte. He put his hands down flat upon my desk, on precisely the spot where I had written thousands upon thousands of words in my diaries over the years. He scanned the room with his eyes, meeting the eyes of all those who watched with bated breath. I realized that he was quite enjoying himself. The old rascal, I thought. At first he said nothing, and then he turned to me. "This is going to be extraordinarily difficult, Martha," he said to me directly. "If we pull it off it will be a miracle on a par with your survival. Too many people know the truth already. How many?"

Daisy helped me out. "Well, in the family me and George, Betsi and Ioan, Rose and Henry, and Abel and his wife Susan. Then among the servants Myfanwy, Bessie, Will, Blodwen and Gerallt. Among Mother's friends Wilmot and Delilah, Patty and Jake, Brendan and Gomer. There must be no secrets in marriage, so Gomer must share the secret with Gwenno. She loves Mother dearly, so her lips will be sealed. And Brendan must tell Mary -- can she be counted on, Mother?"

"I am sure of it, Daisy."

"Very well. She does, after all, owe almost everything she has (including her cottage) to your beneficence and that of Wilmot. That makes, if I am not mistaken, twenty-one fellow conspirators. Then Shemi and Sian must be told, if they do not know the truth already."

"Agreed, Daisy," said I. "Shemi is, after all, a wizard as well as a dear friend. I can keep nothing from him. His contacts in the Otherworld have probably told him the truth already, and I imagine that he will already be on his way to the Plas."

"Twenty-three, Wilmot."

"And then Skiff and his wife Maria. They are faithful friends, and Skiff has such an extensive network of spies that we cannot keep anything from him. In any case, there will be times in the coming months when his contacts will be invaluable to us. He knows the wicked ways of the world better than anybody else. Add them to the list."

"Hum hum. The Group of Twenty-five. I suspected a substantial number, but not that many. Well, it cannot be helped. Do we all have those names in our heads? Nothing must be written down -- is that clear? And there must be no conversations between members of the Group of Twenty-five in the hearing of others -- even sons, daughters, brothers, sisters. Are we agreed?"

Everybody in the room nodded solemnly, and I was encouraged to believe that we might succeed in our enterprise. The conspirators stopped short of a ritual mingling of blood, but all made oaths of complete secrecy, to keep the secret even from their nearest and dearest. They also resolved that if there ever should be a slip of the tongue, or a sighting of me, or any report of my being alive, they should resort to a matter-of-fact explanation that my ghost was abroad, and that it should be left alone, and would eventually find peace. Then Wilmot described in detail what we must do, with only a little discussion here and there. He said that there would be much talk in the district about my death, but assumed that the gossip would be ameliorated by the talk about the earthquake, which might be of more concern at a practical level since some farm animals had been frightened into running away and since there had been some damage to buildings. Some people had been hurt, and had required attention from Dr Havard. Wilmot said that in view of the strange circumstances in which my body had been found and recovered to the Plas, we could expect some interest from the press, and we all agreed on exactly what they should be told. Will had found the body and had called the other five men (Gerallt, Gomer, Abel, Henry and Brendan) who had been searching the mountain since before dawn, following the discovery that I had not returned to the Plas on the previous evening. They had all agreed that I had no pulse, and that I was cold and dead. Abel had gone back to the Plas to fetch a ladder, and all six had helped with the sombre task of carrying the corpse down from the rocky summit. That much was true. And so to the lies. Wilmot said that in view of my prominent position in the community, and the fact that I was greatly loved by the poor people in particular, there would be hundreds who wished to call and pay their last respects. He said that we could not therefore avoid a *gwylnos*, and that the body would have to lie in its coffin in the parlour between now and the funeral, with candles at head and foot and with a constant vigil from all the men of the family and the male servants working to a rota.

I gasped. "Oh my God, Wilmot!" I whispered, with tears on my cheeks. "You mean that you want me to lie in the open coffin and pretend to be dead?"

He smiled like an old dog fox that knows everything. "Not a bit of it, my dear Mistress Morgan!" he chuckled. "We will put it about that you died serenely on the mountain, but that after your death the earthquake caused great rocks to crash down upon your body, inflicting terrible injuries upon it. We will say that your face was most horribly damaged. As a consequence, we will say that the family took the decision to close the coffin so as to avoid distress among those who call to pay their last respects. That would be unusual, but not unheard of. We will say that the family wanted you to be remembered as a beautiful and elegant lady with a perfect complexion............."

We all smiled, and Wilmot had his way on that and assorted other matters. So it was that after dark, the stone wall behind the house was robbed of various convenient stones, weighed to exactly the same as my body weight. The stones were arranged in the coffin, wrapped in old clothes so as to ensure that there would be no rattling and bumping about when it was moved to Cilgwyn Church and eventually interred in the family grave. Then, with no ceremony whatsoever, the lid was nailed down, and the coffin was placed on the table in the parlour. Candles were lit according to the proper procedure, and from that point on Will organized a scheme by which there were always two men present in the room until the day of the funeral. "Funny that," grinned George. "That particular tradition goes back many centuries, and was brought in by our ancestors to ensure that the Devil had no opportunity, between death and burial, to creep in and snatch the body away!"

Suddenly Wilmot took out his pocket watch and glanced at it. "Oh my goodness!" he spluttered. "It's after six of the clock! I must take my carriage and rush back to Dinas. It's pitch black outside, and I hope my carriage lanterns will light the way. There is something I must do, and if I delay it will be too late. I will return within a couple of hours." He turned to Delilah and addressed her. "Will you stay here until I return, my sweet?" he asked. "Will you be all right on your own?"

Delilah giggled and wobbled. "Off you go, dearest," she said, kissing him on the cheek. "Since this place is populated by angels and assorted supernatural powers, I dare say I will be all right."

Wilmot was as good as his word, and was back at the Plas after ninety minutes. He looked extremely pleased with himself , and refused at first to tell us where he had been and what he had achieved. That made us women very irritated, and increased his pleasure. At last, with a great show, he took a piece of paper out of his pocket and waved it in front of our noses before finally presenting it, with a deep bow, to my son-in-law George Havard. George looked at it carefully, and then gasped. "Wilmot, you amaze me!" he said. "Is this genuine?"

"Indeed it is, George. Just as genuine as if you had signed it with your own hand."

"Wilmot and George!" I exploded. "What is all this about? Would you two disreputable fellows kindly explain to the rest of us what is going on here?"

George grinned and passed the piece of paper to me. It was a death certificate with the following words written upon it:

CERTIFICATE AS TO CAUSE OF DEATH
Mistress Martha Morgan of Plas Ingli, Newport
I hereby certify that I was summoned to the residence of said lady on the morning

of 27th of February in the year of our Lord 1855. I found the body of the said lady in the kitchen, to which it had been transported around 9 am following its discovery on the summit of the mountain called Carningli. I conducted a detailed post-mortem examination, and found that although Mistress Morgan had extensive injuries to her face and body there was no bleeding associated with them. I therefore conclude that she died of natural causes in her sleep, in the early hours of 27th February, and that the body was subsequently damaged by rocks dislodged in the earth tremor that occurred at about 2 am.

There appear to be no suspicious circumstances associated with the death, and a number of witnesses have confirmed that the deceased went up onto the mountain of her own free will on the previous evening, as she had done on many occasions before.

Signed
Dr Herbert Figgis MA (Oxon), FRCP
Physician and Medical Practitioner
Currently locum at Dinas Cross, Pembrokeshire

"Wilmot, will you kindly explain?" asked Ioan. "Who is this fellow Figgis? I have never heard of him. Does he really exist?"

"Indeed he does," laughed Wilmot. "He is an old friend of mine, and he is a medical man of many years' standing. In fact, he is retired from active doctoring, but has been in Dinas for a three week period to look after the health of the neighbourhood during the unfortunate indisposition of Dr Wills, whom you all know. He owes me a thing or two, and I know certain things about him, from my time in Swansea, which he would prefer to be kept from the world. It was not too difficult to get him to write down the certificate in accordance with my wishes. Early tomorrow he returns to Swansea, and that was the reason for my hasty exit from this place a while back. If I had left things until the morning, it would have been too late."

"But Wilmot," protested George, "he has now committed a serious medical crime. If the truth should come out, his career as a physician will be destroyed."

"So it will, George. But that would be the least of his problems. He is already retired, and he is slowly dying from the effects of gin consumption over many years. By his own diagnosis, he reckons that he might have a few months left, if he is lucky. He was pleased to help. So now, my dear George, you can simply say to the world that you were unprepared to examine the body of your mother-in-law, on the grounds of the closeness of your relationship. Perfectly normal practice. Splendid! Splendid!"

At this point the assembled company noticed that I was so tired that I could hardly keep my eyes open. Betsi and Daisy decided that it was time for me to be packed off to bed, and they ushered everybody else out of the room. As they left, they all promised to reassemble at 9 o'clock on the following morning, on the basis that the Rector had sent a note threatening to call at eleven, and that I had to be out of the house well before then. All my dear friends embraced me and wished me good night, and as Wilmot departed he whispered in my ear: "Dearest Martha, is this not vastly thrilling, and worthy of a great melodrama in the tradition of *Wuthering Heights*?" He sounded just like an excited ten-year-old about to embark upon a game of pirates and smugglers. I swallowed hard and nodded, wishing at that precise moment to be as far as possible from melodramas. Then Bessie came up from the kitchen and helped me into bed, knowing that I was too tired even to get myself undressed.

So ended the day on which I had died and come to life again as Mrs Susanna Ravenhill, a woman with a mission as yet undefined. I was utterly exhausted, and wanted desperately to sleep, but I knew that this would be my last night in this beloved house, and I could not find any sort of peace. With my mind in a turmoil, I tossed and turned, and paced the floor, and peeped through the shutters at the enigmatic face of the moon, knowing that in the room below mine there was a coffin full of stones, watched over by two of my fellow conspirators in what appeared increasingly to be a dreadful crime against the truth.

2. Deeper and Deeper

On Monday morning those of my fellow conspirators who had not spent the night at the Plas arrived early, to say their farewells. Nobody else was allowed into the house -- not even those kind souls who came without any prompting to help with the animals and the basic tasks around the farmyard. In my room I was dressed in my heaviest and blackest mourning clothes and given a heavy veil, since this was part of our stratagem. For the last time my family and friends referred to me as "Martha" or as "Mistress" and all swore solemnly that henceforth, if ever we should meet, by design or by chance, they would call me "Susanna" or "Mrs Ravenhill." We discussed very briefly the family history of my new persona, which was in truth very sketchy, with much still to be invented. We agreed that I would work it out, and that all would then be duly informed as to who I was, where I had lived, and what I had done with my life -- in case they should ever need to know.

At 10 o'clock promptly, Wilmot's carriage was brought right up to the kitchen door. Quite out of sight of the rest of the world, I was hidden under a blanket and smuggled into its darkened interior. Then I was spirited away, in the company of Rose and Myfanwy, two young ladies who would not be terribly missed from the Plas during the next two hectic days and the forthcoming *gwylnos*. Wilmot drove the carriage himself, and we did not dare to draw back the curtains at any stage of our journey of three hours. We had decided upon Cardigan as our first destination, since that was a place in which I was not well known and since there were many comings and goings of strangers using the port or travelling through by coach and carriage between South Wales and the northern districts. There were many lodging houses used for short stays by people from all over the kingdom. I had to depend entirely upon Wilmot for my survival in a world that was suddenly hostile, in which one false move or a single misplaced word might have led to disaster. I feared that every glance towards me might signal an intent to penetrate my disguise and unravel my web of deceit, and I was very afraid.

But my old friend showed himself once again to be a master of planning. He let me off on Cardigan Bridge, and arranged to meet me back there at two-thirty, by which time he assumed that I would have found lodgings. He knew that if he had delivered me directly to a lodging-house, that would certainly have been noted by the landlady and the neighbours, and the information could then have been passed to others. I wandered into the town, clutching my heavy bag of possessions and noting with some satisfaction that those who passed me in the street were more interested in their own affairs than in mine. At last a small boy approached me. "Lookin' for lodgins, Missis?" he asked in English.

"You are very perceptive, young man. Now why should you make that assumption?"

"You are not local, that's for sure," he grinned. "And if you was out shoppin' you'd be carryin' a shoppin' basket, not that heavy bag. My Aunty Polly is a widow who's got a big house on the Pendre. She had a lodger till a week ago, and then he went off to America. So she's got a room to let, and she can't leave it empty, can she? She'll prefer a lady, since gentlemen drink too much, and smoke, and don't wash of'n enough. For a penny I'll take you to our house."

"That sounds reasonable. For two pennies I will come with you to inspect the premises, if you will carry my bag."

"Agreed, Missis! Let's go then. I've been expectin' you."

I caught my breath. "Expecting me?" I spluttered. "But I did not know I was coming here myself, until just a couple of hours since. Nobody knew it........."

The boy grinned and shrugged his shoulders. "By the way, my name is Merlin, and I'll look after you."

I looked at him closely, and saw that his eyes were as bright as the sun and as old as the stars. I was intrigued, and knew somehow that our destinies were intertwined. Instinctively I trusted him immediately. "What a strange name, young fellow! I have met many Arthurs in my time, but never a Merlin. And why did your parents give you such a name?"

"God only knows, Missis. When I was a baby they was both transported to them colonies for somethin' or other, and I was left with Aunty Polly. She's very old, but she's kind, and life could be worse, couldn't it?"

I had to agree, since I should really have been dead. So Merlin and I chatted as we marched along the High Street and came at last to his aunt's house. I thought it would suit my purpose very well indeed, and after a short interview with Mrs Polly Ifans I agreed her terms and took two rooms at the top of a winding staircase, on the second floor and overlooking the street. That was a major advantage, as was the fact that I could hear footsteps on the stairs should anybody come to visit me or choose to eavesdrop outside my door. Merlin took his tuppence and went off to play with his friends, and as I settled in I tried out my story for the first time. I told Mrs Ifans that I was Susanna Ravenhill from London, recently bereaved by the loss of my husband Jack and left virtually penniless because of the manner in which he had squandered his family fortune. I reassured her by paying for a week in advance and by booking a further week. I explained that I was now seeking Jack's and my own relatives in West Wales, with whom I had had no contact for fifty years or more. The good lady took all of that without batting an eyelid, and even looked disappointed that my story was not more spectacular.

Then I went out again onto the street, telling my landlady that I had already corresponded with certain people who might be able to help me, and now hoped to meet them in town. I met Wilmot, Rose and Myfanwy on the bridge as planned, and took them back to my lodgings, where Wilmot (who claimed to be an old friend from childhood days) put down a bond of five pounds as a guarantee of my *bona fides*. Mrs Ifans left us and returned to her kitchen on the ground floor, and the four of us embarked upon a frantic search for a life story which would be plausible and which might nonetheless defy detailed examination.

I resolved to claim, if pressed, that I was the illegitimate child of Squire Charles Howell of Brawdy and a servant girl, who was sent away to Carmarthen and who was paid an adequate and secret allowance for the rest of her life. That would be a shocking thing to say, and a terrible slander on my own dear father, who would never, never have become involved in a dalliance with a serving wench. I thought about the matter long and hard, and even sought divine guidance; but none came, and in the end I had to make do with my own conscience and the advice of my three dear friends. At last I concluded that in the circumstances dear Papa would forgive me from his place in Heaven. He might even be gently amused, since he had a wicked sense of humour. He would understand that I needed to explain my uncanny likeness to Mistress Martha, now deceased, and also my fluency as a Welsh speaker. I would assume that no other member of the Howell family (including my sisters Elen and Catrin) would have known of this illicit liaison or of my existence. I needed some link with the Plas, since I was sure that I had some unfinished task in the neighbourhood and since I knew that I would be unable to resist the magnetic pull of Carningli and the *cwm*. Martha, as a half-sister, would provide that link.

As to my early life, I resolved to say that I had a good childhood and a modest education, but then became pregnant and eloped to London from Carmarthen at the age of fifteen. I had had no contact with my mother after that. After losing my baby, I was later abandoned by the scoundrel who took me away, and it was some years later that my husband Jack rescued me from the streets of London and married me. He was also from Wales, with family in West Wales, on his mother's side. I will also say that I had two children within the marriage, both of whom died in infancy. I will say that I loved Jack, and that I was now deep in grief following his death. My expedition to Wales was a result of small snippets of information about the Howell family of Brawdy, given to me by my mother and remembered from childhood, and from news of West Wales provided by Pembrokeshire people in London.

Lies, lies, and yet more lies, piled ever higher. At times I literally shook with apprehension, as the edifice of untruths appeared as black and unstable as a mighty slag-heap. But I had to persist, and with Wilmot providing the clear head and the iron will, I pressed on with the creation of my fantastical autobiography.

So I resolved to say that I had discovered through my researches the link with the Morgan family of Plas Ingli, and with my half-sister Martha, but that I had become confused when I discovered that the Master of the Plas Ingli estate was now Wilmot Gwynne of Plas Llanychaer, an old childhood friend. According to my alibi, I wrote to him to say I would arrive in Cardigan on the afternoon of 28 February and asking for a rendezvous on Cardigan Bridge. Wilmot had received my letter and planned to travel with me to the Plas to meet my long-lost half-sister -- but he had brought with him instead the sad news that Martha had died, and had travelled with her grand-daughter Rose and servant Myfanwy to break the news.

I would say that I was so shocked by this turn of events, in the midst of my grief for my own husband, that I could not face any involvement with the family or the Plas until the funeral was over and done with. I would instead shut this new death out of my mind as far as possible, and carry on with my task of looking for clues as to my late husband's roots, in Cardiganshire and Carmarthenshire. Various people who had offered to help me would travel to see me now and then, I would say, in order to ensure that I was well and to keep me informed as to the news.

That much I decided, and I obtained the approval of my three visitors. We rehearsed the story over and again, and they all questioned me on the details of it, to ensure that I could manage detailed interrogation from inquisitive people. During this questioning I invented names for my dead children -- Joshua and Judith -- and decided that Jack and myself had lived in Lambeth in reasonable comfort while he earned a sound but un-spectacular income as a merchant. Rose reminded me -- and I accepted -- that where appropriate I could well claim to have forgotten certain details of my life, since forgetfulness is a part of old age.

With dusk falling, Wilmot said that he must get down to the Red Lion to collect his carriage and his horses, and that he must set off for home immediately. We said our farewells, and off he went. Rose and Myfanwy decided that they would stay with me in Cardigan for one night, since they were obviously worried about my state of exhaustion. They would then travel back to Newport on the post coach next morning, in case they might be needed as witnesses at the Inquest which could be called at short notice. Mrs Ifans was only too happy to make up a couple of extra beds for them, and to give us supper in my larger room, which had an ample table and four chairs. We ate well, and the young people cheered me up considerably before packing me off to bed at nine o'clock. I slept for twelve hours without stirring, and woke to find Rose and Myfanwy up and about, chirping like little sparrows, and organizing a splendid breakfast. "Good morning to you, Mrs Ravenhill!" said Rose. "My goodness, you have been so fast asleep in the midst of all this clanking of dishes and shuffling of feet on the stairs that we thought you must be dead! Another death in the

Deeper and Deeper

family would have been very inconvenient just now........."

We laughed a lot at breakfast, and then they were gone. I was alone for the first time, with my new identity anything but established, and thinking over and again "What have I done? What have I done?" The day was bright and clear, with a freezing wind moaning in from Cardigan Bay. I had to get out into the fresh air, with a view to discovering a little more about the town that might now be my home for weeks, or months. I had no inspiration as to what I might do next, and indeed I expected nothing to happen until the funeral was over and done with, and until that coffin full of stones was safely lowered into the sandy ground of Cilgwyn Church-yard in a few days' time. So I wrapped up well in my mourning coat, with a black hat upon my head, a thick muffler round my neck, and my heavy veil covering my face. Off I went, and spent a happy enough hour or two looking at the shops in town and the sailing ships tied up at the quaysides in the tidal river. I chatted to a few people, and felt increasingly confident that my secret was safe.

Then I began to feel uneasy. At first I did not know why. But then, as I walked, I glanced over my shoulder a few times, increasingly con-vinced that I was being followed. There were many people scurrying about in the streets, and much horse-drawn road traffic as well, so I did not feel in any danger. But my apprehension increased. I think that I caught a glimpse of two men dressed in full-length coats, with hats pulled down over their faces. When I stopped, they stopped, and when I resumed my perambulations they moved on as well. My heart began to beat faster, and I turned towards the Pendre and the safety of my lodgings. I tried an experiment, and slipped into a filthy black alley-way to see if they might saunter past. But they did not, and when I emerged and carried on along the street I glimpsed them again. I was very nervous indeed when I en-tered Mrs Ifans's lodging house. I hurried up the stairs as fast as my old legs would carry me, locked my door behind me, and collapsed into my arm chair until I had recovered my breath and my composure. After some minutes I looked out through the window down onto the street. The two men were on the other side of the road, huddled together and deep in con-versation. There were flurries of dry snow in the air. I was sure that once or twice the men looked up towards my window, causing me to slip behind the curtains lest I should be spotted. I sat on my bed, paralysed with fear, not knowing what to do. I was overwhelmed by desolation.

There was a sudden knock on my door. I managed to croak out an enquiry as to whom it might be.

"It's me, Mrs Ravenhill," said the voice of Merlin. "Can I come in?"

I got up and unlocked the door, and the little fellow came in, scantily dressed and blue with the cold. I parked him by my coal fire and scolded him for not being properly clad on this bitterly cold day.

"I'm sorry," said he, "but I forgot to put my coat on. I've been out workin'."

"Working? You should be in school."

"Too borin'. I go now and then in the hope of somethin' that will make me think, but I'm nearly always bored to tears."

"So what work do you do?"

"Oh, I look after you."

"Is that so? I do not recall asking to be looked after."

"I look after people if they need to be looked after. And you do need it, Mrs Ravenhill. Did you know that you are bein' followed?"

"I suspected it. Those two men standing there, across the street?"

"Correct. They're talkin' in Welsh, but not Cardi Welsh. They're smart, too. They know how to work the streets, and I had a devil of a job to get close. One of them said to the other "I'm sure it's her. I can tell from the walk and the posture, and the way she lifts up her skirts when she steps off a pavement." What do you make of that, Missis?"

I groaned and buried my face in my hands. After only one day away from the Plas, somebody was hunting for me, and now I was sure I had been recognized. I saw my mad scheme collapsing in ignominy, with the fury of the community we had sought to deceive directed at both me and my nearest and dearest. I did not know what to do. Should I invite those mysterious men from the street to come inside and meet me, and discover their purpose? Or should I shut myself in and hope that they would go away? Were they hired thugs associated with some ancient enemies whom I thought I had defeated? Were they opportunists, intent on blackmail? Were they constables alerted to the fact that I had committed a grievous crime? I knew then, beyond doubt, that there were too many who knew my secret -- a few might have kept silence, but twenty-five ....never!

I groaned again. Then heavy footsteps echoed up the stair-well, and I knew that the two strangers had been let into the house and were intent upon confronting me.

"Hell an' damnation!" whispered Merlin. "I told my aunty not to let anybody in. Those fellows must be very convincin'. But don't you worry, Missis. I'll protect you with my life. Just you help me to drag this table over so as to block the door........"

"No no, Merlin. That will not help, and I have no wish for you to be hurt. You must let them in when they knock, and we will soon discover who they are."

The footsteps stopped at the top of the stairs and after a short pause one of the men knocked -- quite discreetly. Five knocks in rapid succession and then two more, with a longer interval between them. I knew instantly who my visitor was.

Relief swept over me like a great ocean wave. "I think it might be an old friend of mine, Merlin," I said. "You need not have any concern for my safety. Will you kindly let those fellows in and then station yourself at the front door of the house, in exchange for two more pennies? Nobody else must be let in -- do you understand?"

"I understand a lot, Missis," said the boy with a grin. He opened the door to let in the two strangers, and took one look at them. "These are different fellows, Missis," he said. "No danger from them." Then he scuttled off down the stairs to take up his station at the front door.

Two big men stood before me, ruddy faced and wrapped up well against the winter weather. One of them was built like an ox, with his face covered in greying whiskers. The other was white haired, slightly stooped, with bushy black eyebrows and a Jewish nose. "Shemi and Skiff!" I scolded. "How dare you frighten me like this? But I should have known that you would come hunting for me, having missed the meetings of the conspirators in the Plas."

There were long embraces, and all three of us shed tears. We three were the best of friends, having had many dealings over fifty years or more. Shemi had started work as a labourer at the Plas before the turn of the century, and had married Sian, one of my favourite servants, before taking up his true vocation as a wizard. He had inherited the wisdom, the skills and the cottage of Joseph Harries of Werndew, the greatest wizard ever to have lived in these parts. He was only a little younger than me, and he was the same age as Skiff Abraham, one-time petty thief and self-made man, and now the wealthiest merchant in the Newport district. Like Shemi, I loved Skiff dearly, having shared many adventures with him over the years, mostly on the wrong side of the law.

At last Shemi found some words. "Mrs Ravenhill, I presume? Delighted to make your acquaintance, madam."

"You are quite correct, sir. And I am delighted to welcome you to my humble abode. Wilmot told you I was in Cardigan?"

"That he did, but very briefly. It would have saved us a good deal of trouble if he had given us your address. But he was in a great hurry, rushing off to get the death certificate for the Inquest."

"That is today?"

"This afternoon, at two of the clock. That need not concern us any longer. That little boy who opened your door, declared us to be safe, and then went off down the stairs.........?"

"He is called Merlin, and he lives here with his aunt. He has appointed himself as my guardian."

"Ah yes, Merlin Ifans. I have heard of him. Remarkable talents, and the next generation after me. He is destined for great things, that boy........."

"Shemi, time is short," interposed Skiff. "You will recall that we have certain matters to discuss, and not very much time."

"Right you are, old friend. Martha -- sorry, Susanna -- whatever encouraged you to follow this mad course when you had been taken down off the mountain?"

"A premonition, Shemi. The strongest one I have ever had. I had to follow it, but it is nonetheless the most foolhardy thing I have ever done. Within the last hour, I was so miserable that I felt like taking my own life."

"That would have been cowardice, Susanna. You, of all people, MUST follow your intuition, and there must be some great purpose to what has happened. Perhaps you will discover it for yourself, and maybe it will be revealed to me, or Rose, or even the lad called Merlin."

"So where were you on Sunday, Shemi, when I needed you?"

Deeper and Deeper

He explained that he and Sian had been away visiting their daughter Molly and her family in St David's for the weekend, but they felt the tremor there at 2 am on the Sunday morning and he knew immediately that something had happened to the mountain and to me. They had rushed back home, but had not arrived until after dark. Picking up on the news that I was dead, Shemi knew, as wizards know things, that I was still alive, and so he had ridden over to the Plas on the Monday morning. He had seen the nailed-down coffin and had received a report from Bessie as to what had transpired. Later he had met Wilmot, and it was his information that had led him and Skiff to Cardigan. Skiff's story was very similar. He had been visiting his daughter Annie when the news of my demise had reached him; but he had really thought me dead until Shemi knocked on his door and whispered the truth.

Then Shemi transformed himself from a friend into a man of science. He sat me down, pulled up a chair opposite me, and insisted that we had to talk through unfinished business. "For example," he asked, "what is your state of health?" He knew, I was sure, that I had been very tired and un-well before climbing up the mountain on Saturday evening and settling down on the summit. I explained that I was still tired, but that my aches and pains had largely disappeared. He examined me and concluded that my heart was sound and that apart from some rheumatism in my joints I was surprisingly fit for a woman of 76 years. He put my exhaustion down to the emotional turmoil associated with the death of my beloved friend Amos Jones less than three weeks before, and the dramatic events that had followed it. That was enough, he said, to have exhausted any woman of half my age.

He then asked me some very silly questions. "Excluding the thumbs, how many fingers do you have?" "If Sunday is the 31st of July, what date is the following Tuesday?" "What is the name of your second daughter?" "What is the name of the great leaning tower in Italy?" and other equally irritating things that made me very angry. Of course I answered them all quickly and correctly, and he murmured "Quite remark-able! Would you not agree, Skiff?" Skiff nodded his assent, and then Shemi admitted that he was testing to see whether my brain was damaged when I became very cold and apparently lifeless on the mountain. "I have heard of an apparently dead person coming back to life three times before, Susanna," he chuckled. "One of them was old Mrs Lewis Mynachlog-ddu, who sat up in her coffin when the bearers banged it into the door-post on the way into the chapel for the funeral service. They still laugh about that on the other side of Mynydd Preseli, although it was probably not funny at the time. It is said that she was a miserable old thing, and that she survived for another three weeks, much to her husband's disgust. When she died for the second time, and came to be carried once again into the chapel in her coffin, Farmer Lewis was heard to say to the bearers, in a very loud whisper, "Gently does it, boys. And for God's sake mind the door-post!"

At that, both he and Skiff bellowed with laughter, and so did I, and so funny did it seem at the time that five minutes later we were still holding our sides and laughing hysterically like small children, with tears rolling down our cheeks. Looking back on it, that was a blessed relief, after the tension and the uncertainty of the previous three days.

When we had recovered our composure, Shemi was able to continue. "I have read something very interesting in my Big Book," he said, "namely that others who have recovered from being dead have gone on to be very soft in the head, and have become no more intelligent than vegetables."

"And do you find me, Wizard Jenkins, to be more intelligent than a potato?"

"At least as intelligent as a turnip, in my estimation, my dear Mrs Ravenhill. I also read an observation in my book that when the body cools gradually, as it might well have done in your case when you went off to sleep on the mountain on a cold and starlit February night, the breathing might stop and the heartbeat might die away to the point where it becomes impossible to discern. *Diawch*! Interesting, is it not? Will and the others who carried you down from the summit saw that your skin was cold and frosted, and they all tested your pulse and found nothing. Quite correct they were, to think you dead. But there must have been a spark of life left in you, and that was fanned into flames when you were brought into the warmth of the Plas Ingli kitchen. I still don't rule out a miracle or supernatural intervention of some sort, but that would be my scientific explanation. Profoundly interesting, would you not agree, Master

Abraham?"

"Quite so, Shemi. And I dare say you will write it all down in that Big Book of yours."

"Correct. Information as valuable as this must not be lost. Susanna, you will be famous in centuries to come in the annals of medical science. There's just one thing you should bear in mind. Your body has just been through the most challenging and stressful episode that anybody can imagine. I therefore expect you to fall seriously ill at some stage -- and when you do you must send for me at once. Will you promise me that?"

I swallowed hard, and nodded. Then Shemi changed direction as rapidly as a rabbit seeking to evade a pack of hounds, and asked what I proposed to do about my sisters Elen and Catrin, and my great friend Mary Jane Stokes, and my sister-in-law Nansi. I said that I had written farewell latters to various of my nearest and dearest, including my son Brynach in America, and that those letters should now be posted off, and accompanied by whatever other messages might be considered appropriate by my daughters Betsi and Daisy. I was committed to the view that there were too many dangers in revealing the truth in writing, even in sealed envelopes, and there were too many people who knew the truth already. Twenty-five, no less. For better or worse, I knew that I had to deceive everybody else. Shemi agreed, and said he would encourage Betsi to write to all of my closest friends and relatives who remained in ignorance.

Again I was close to tears with the realization that my deceit was now likely to split my family down the middle. My beloved Brynach could not be told the truth, and he would have to suffer from the agony of missing the funeral. Rose and Abel were the only two of my grandchildren who were conspirators -- the others (Daisy's three illegitimate children Amy, John and William; Brynach's son David; and Betsi's other two sons Benjamin and Owain) had to be kept in the dark since there were spouses and children with big ears to take into account. William was now in business with Henry and Abel and was by some lucky chance currently in America visiting Brynach and studying the latest developments in farm machinery. Amy and John were in London, Amy living as a stylish hostess and John (married, with one child) practicing as a barrister. Benjamin, married with a little son, was farming at Brithdir, just a short distance from the Plas.

Deeper and Deeper

Owain was away in Hereford, acting as a steward for a small estate. They would all -- apart from William and David in America -- return for the funeral, and would all be misled horribly. If they ever should discover the truth, I thought, they would never forgive me. More to the point, they would never forgive their parents and cousins who had kept a mighty secret from them and who had caused them unnecessary anguish.

When Shemi and Skiff had departed, promising to return soon with other news, I was forced back into the dark loneliness that I had created for myself -- a loneliness that was not in the least ameliorated by the fact that I had to sleep with my demons. They haunted me and taunted me, and in response I had nothing to say, for I still had no idea why I had been spared from death, or why I was involved in this cruel deceit. Was I becoming a demon myself?

On the afternoon of the next day Rose travelled over from Newport as the bearer of bad news. She said that the funeral could not occur until an Inquest had been held, and that although plans had been laid for such a hearing on this very day, it had proved impossible to appoint a new coroner following the resignation of the previous incumbent Will Daniels. So the new date had been set for Thursday 10th March, and on the assumption that the body would then be released for burial, the *gwylnos* had been set for Friday night 11th March and the funeral for the following day, almost two weeks after my alleged death. Letters had gone to the grandchildren who lived far away, and to all other relatives and friends, and Rose said that this delay at least gave some of them a sporting chance of getting to the Plas in time for the funeral.

That was miserable news indeed, and Rose carried with her one other item of news that terrified me. "Do you know, Grandmother," she said with an excited gleam in her eye, "that people have been up onto the mountain in the last couple of days to examine what effects the earthquake might have had. They found that a great chasm had opened up, and within it, when they scrambled down, they found the remains of a human being, with scraps of clothes and ropes and things. They think it is the skeleton of a tall man, and he had the most terrible injuries to the back of his skull, as if he had been struck from behind with immense force. A murder victim, no less, dumped into a crevice in the mountain long ago!

Deeper and Deeper

Close to the body, in some rotten rags, they found a half crown with the date 1795 on it, so the murder cannot have occurred before then. Just think -- a great mystery on the very doorstep of the Plas!"

I thought that I was going to faint, for I knew immediately that the bones were those of Moses Lloyd, the evil manservant who tried to ravish me and kill me on the mountain in the year 1797, shortly after my arrival at the Plas. In defending myself I had managed to kill him, and had dragged his body and dumped it into the deepest crevice I could find among the rocks. How I got out of that situation alive, I will never know. It had quite gone out of my mind, and now here was that monster again, come back to haunt me............

"Grandmother, you are very pale," said Rose. "Are you all right?"

"I think so, *Cariad*. I fear that I am shocked by your news, since there was an evil manservant once, at the Plas, when I was but a slip of a girl. He did the most appalling things during his lifetime, and almost destroyed our family. Then he became a fugitive from the law, and ran off into the night, and was never seen again. Perhaps the bones are his."

"Will you tell me all about him, Grandmother? I'm intrigued."

"One day, Rose, but not now. I am too tired to be digging up old memories. Now then, off you go, or you will be forced to travel home in the dark. Thank you for your company and your news. Give my love to Henry and give little Levi a kiss, if you will, from an old lady."

I held myself together until Rose had gone off down the stairs, and then I wept bitter tears, for I realized that there were still a few people left in the community who were old enough to remember Moses Lloyd, and to deduce that the bones on the mountain were his. Bessie would remember, and draw conclusions, and so would Shemi. They were both present at the Plas when I came down from the mountain, more dead than alive, on that fateful day in August 1797, and when I later refused to explain my injuries. In their eyes I would now not simply be a fugitive and an impostor, but a murder suspect as well.

I fear that my weeping was not as silent as it might have been; and I was unaware that in the street outside there were two armed men watching my window, and that on the landing outside my room there was a small boy with sharp ears, looking after me.

3. The Boy Merlin

Father Time dragged his feet as the first week of my new life came to a close. I wandered about in town now and then, but the cold weather was replaced by a rainy and windy spell typical of February in West Wales, and I was forced to spend much time indoors, waiting for further news. I was cosy enough, and Mrs Ifans was very kind to me, but I did not want too much of her company since she asked too many questions for which I had inadequate answers. So I borrowed some books from her and spent many hours reading, and snoozing in front of my coal fire. Young Merlin popped into my room now and then, and I gave him some lessons in history and geography. I discovered that he had a mind like a sponge, and an extraordinary memory for small details -- just like my friend and mentor Joseph Harries of Werndew, with whom he shared a passing likeness. He had fair hair and bright blue eyes, and features which were sharper than normal for a child. He had freckles on his cheeks and a dimple on his chin. He had an endearing habit of wrinkling up his nose when he was puzzled, outraged or cynical, and I discovered that I was already quite fond of him.

He was also too observant for my peace of mind. One day he said to me quite casually: "Missis, I can't help thinkin' that those people who come to visit you -- Rose and Myfanwy, and the one called Wilmot, and those two fellows off the street -- seem to get on with you remarkably well, considerin' that you ain't met any of them before. Hugs and kisses and all that. A good deal of laughin' I have heard, and weepin' too. And lots of chattin' just like old friends chats to each other........."

"But I do know them quite well, Merlin," I insisted. "I have corresponded with them, and they know that I am very much up and down in my temperament just now, which is what happens after the loss of a loved one. They are trying to cheer me up, and sometimes they succeed in doing that, for which I am eternally grateful. And they are such open and friendly people, unlike the people in London who are always rushing about and minding their own business. Do you understand?"

The boy rolled his eyes, wrinkled his nose and frowned, and gave me a piercing look which indicated that he knew full well that he had just been fed a packet of lies. Then the pair of us laughed together, and we moved on to consider the Battle of Agincourt.

On the first Saturday after my arrival in Cardigan, Mrs Ifans brought up my breakfast and gave me a copy of *The Cambrian* dated 5th March 1855. "See here, Mrs Ravenhill," she said, pointing to something on page four. "*Duw Duw*, there has been a funny business in Newport, and no doubt about it. A singular occurrence, no less. An earthquake, and a dead lady on the mountain, and a murdered skeleton, and six ravens sitting in a row. Here now -- read it for yourself."

With shaking hands I took the newspaper and read the report of my death and the events linked to it.[1] I almost fainted, and my landlady had to give me a glass of water which helped me to recover my equilibrium. "Dear me, Mrs Ravenhill," said she. "You took that very badly, if I may say so. Was it such a terrible tale?"

"Maybe not, Mrs Ifans. But after the death of my own dear husband quite recently, I find it hard to cope with news of deaths and murders and such like. Perhaps, some weeks or months from now, I will find it easier. What do you think?"

"Very likely, Mrs Ravenhill. Grief is a hard thing, as I know from the loss of my own good man. But time is a healer, and you must be patient."

"Thank you Mrs Ifans. You are very kind."

A week after my arrival in Cardigan I began to feel distinctly unwell. It began with hot and cold flushes and a loss of appetite, and within a few hours I felt so weak that I had to go to bed. My landlady realized that I had a high temperature, and offered to call an apothecary in whom she had great faith, but I wanted nothing to do with medical men since I feared that they might investigate my past to a very unwelcome extent. So I said: "Please, Mrs Ifans -- no doctors of any sort. I have had this illness before, and it will pass so long as I keep warm and have plenty to drink."

But it did not pass, and very soon I had a splitting headache and became violently sick. My recollections are hazy as to what happened after that, but Mrs Ifans later told me that I became delirious and drifted in and out of consciousness for two days, insisting whenever I was capable of

---

[1] This report is reproduced on page 397 of *Flying with Angels*

expressing myself that I would not accept any pills or potions. Then I was aware that Shemi the Wizard and George the Physician were at my bedside, seen dimly as through a mist. Mrs Ifans and young Merlin flitted in and out of my room, looking very concerned. Waves of nausea broke over me, and I remember being forced to consume large quantities of liquid including some foul herbal potions conjured up by Shemi. He and George stayed at my bedside, turn by turn, for two days, watching me, ministering to my needs and holding my hand. True healers, both of them. But their power was as nothing compared with that of the boy Merlin, who insisted on holding my hand for a while when I was at my lowest ebb. I was hardly conscious, but suddenly I felt energy coursing through my veins as if my old grey blood had been drained away and replaced with red blood charged with warmth and vigour. My eyes had been closed, but I opened them and met his gaze for a moment. He smiled at me, and then collapsed. Shemi, who was also in the room at the time, gathered him in his arms and laid him on the other bed, and after a few minutes he recovered and went off, somewhat unsteadily, down the stairs. Shemi looked at me, said nothing, and gave the most subtle and knowing of smiles. I returned the smile, and closed my eyes again. We both knew what had happened. For me, it reminded me of the occasions when I had been close to death as a young woman following the loss of my baby and when Joseph Harries, that most wonderful of men, had given me healing derived from somewhere inside and outside of himself. On the occasions of his most intense healing, I had felt renewal, and he had come close to collapse.

Eventually, over the course of twelve hours after that mysterious intervention by Merlin, my fever subsided and my sickness ceased.

"My dear Mrs Ravenhill," said George at last, wiping his brow, "that was a very close run thing. Never have I encountered such a high temperature. You are a very tough lady, no doubt about it."

"It appears that my time has not yet come, Doctor," said I, managing a feeble smile. "The Grim Reaper must be getting very frustrated with these close encounters."

" It appears that your name is not on his list, Madam."

Then somebody stirred on a bed in the corner of the room, and Shemi got to his feet, rubbing his eyes. "Good evening, Susanna," he said.

"You have given us a great fright -- not to mention a great medical challenge -- just as Mistress Martha used to do in the good old days. Now you will recover, and I hope that your recuperation will not take too long. Another day in bed, I think, and then you can be up and about again. Would you agree, George?"

"Yes, Shemi. It's just a pity that this lady is so far from home, and having to depend upon the goodwill of her landlady and young Merlin. She could do with a servant or two to see her back to health."

"What day is it, George?"

"Wednesday. I will stay with you for another twenty-four hours, just in case there should be a setback, but Shemi needs to return to Newport now, I think, before it is too dark. He has a certain urgent matter to attend to tomorrow........."

"May I ask what that might be?"

Shemi spoke for himself. "An important inquest," he said, "relating to the death of a dear friend of mine. I want to be there, just in case there are complications. George wants to be well away from it, for obvious reasons. This particular medical emergency in Cardigan came, from his point of view, at a most convenient time. Correct, George?"

"Yes indeed. I will return home late tomorrow, when the inquest is over and done with. I have a *gwylnos* and a funeral to attend, and they will both require great delicacy and diplomacy on my part, not to mention considerable acting skill. I hope that I -- and certain other individuals -- are up to it. Will you be all right here by yourself, Susanna?"

"I think so, Doctor. I will allow myself to be looked after by Mrs Ifans and her nephew, and will try not to dwell on events elsewhere."

So Shemi collected his horse from the stable round the corner, and went back to Newport as dusk was falling. George gave me his faithful and loving attention till next day, and then off he went too, having done his professional and filial duty. He hoped, as I did, that the inquest had gone off smoothly, and that the family could now proceed with the final arrangements for the funeral and the interment of the coffin full of stones. As Friday afternoon turned into Friday evening, I could think of nothing other than the scene at the Plas, where I knew that there would be a house full of relatives and friends, some of them having travelled a great distance to be there. There would be tears and embraces, and endless talk about Mistress Martha. They would be laughing about her eccentricities, mulling over her virtues and her vices, and recounting episodes from the past sixty years or so, during which time she had been innocent bride, friend, parent and grandparent, employer, lover, estate manager, matriarch, campaigner in just causes, errant old lady, and a lot else besides. Episodes from those years flashed in and out of my mind, and I gave faces to those whom I had met along the way, and put words into their mouths. Six of the clock. How many would be sitting down to supper tonight, in the dining room and in the kitchen? Would they be subdued or ebullient? Would they be sad, and concerned about the morrow? Would my group of twenty-five conspirators be steadfast in their refusal to give anything away, even through the merest hint that I was not inside that coffin on the table in the parlour? Would there be enough food in the pantry to feed all those mouths tonight, and then tomorrow after the funeral, when there might be two hundred people or more calling in after the visit to the churchyard, as a final mark of respect for my memory? Seven of the clock. Who would be washing all those dishes? Bessie and Myfanwy and Blodwen for sure, but who else? Where would all the guests be staying? Who would be taking the final spells of duty as watchmen in the parlour? Will and Gerallt maybe? Would they really be able to stay awake, after the passage of almost two weeks and an interminable succession of spells of duty in the room with the coffin? How many pints of ale would the watchmen have consumed? Was Rose all right, or was she filled with apprehension as the burial drew ever closer? She was too sensitive for her own wellbeing, I thought, and how I loved her and missed her! How I loved all of them! How would I survive without them, stuck here in this spartan little room in Cardigan, with a March gale screaming down the street outside?

"Tears again, Missis?" said a little voice beside me. "I did knock, but I didn't get no response. Forgive me, but I thought I'd better come in anyway, to see if you are all right. Your dinner, if you're ready for it."

"Thank you Merlin. Please put the tray on the table. I'm sorry for my lack of attentiveness, but I was miles away, reminiscing as old people do. And when old people think of people and places from the past, they sometimes weep. Have you had your supper?"

"Thirty minutes ago, Missis. Nice it was, too."

"Will you sit with me while I eat mine? I could do with company."

"All right then. Warmer here, it is, than in the cellar."

I sat at the table and helped myself to a good portion of Mrs Ifans's excellent steak and kidney pie. Between mouthfuls, I turned to Merlin.

"I have been wondering, young man, how it was that Shemi and George turned up here when I fell ill. Did you play any part in that?"

"Of course I did, Mrs Ravenhill. After all, I **am** supposed to be lookin' after you. When your friends Shemi and Skiff came to see you, they took me to one side as they left the house, and gave me a shillin', sayin' that I was to get a message to Mister Skiff's grand house in Newport at the first sign of you being poorly. They said it would be easy to find, just by askin' in the middle of town. A matter of life and death, they said it was. Even before you complained about being unwell, I ran down to Cardigan bridge and stopped the first carriage I could find that was goin' towards Newport. For sixpence, I got a nice ride up in front, next to the driver. Mister Skiff sent messages to Doctor Havard and the wizard, and I got a lift back to Cardigan sittin' behind Shemi on his horse. What a ride, Missis! Twenty minutes, Newport to Cardigan Bridge!"

"But that is impossible, Merlin.........." I looked into his eyes as he spoke, and my voice faded away. So I added "Oh all right then. Nothing is impossible. And thank you for your assistance. If you had waited, it might have been too late."

"It **would** have been too late," said the child, sounding like a hoary old physician for whom there are no secrets left in the world of medicine. "But thank the Lord you are mended now. If I may be so bold as to suggest it, Missis, I think it's time for you to move on."

That took me by surprise, for I had no intention of moving on until I had received full reports of the inquest and the events surrounding the funeral. So I said: "Move on? But my doctors said I must take some days to recover my strength. And I have certain investigations to complete in this area, relating to the family histories of my late husband and myself."

"Suit yourself, Missis. But those two fellows are still prowlin' about outside, and I don't like the look of them. Another thing. My Aunty Polly is gettin' very inquisitive indeed, and I think she might start to spread rumours in town. She's not unkind, but she helps in the Lamb and Flag some afternoons, and when the weather is bad and customers are thin on the ground, she talks and listens."

"Are you suggesting that she knows things about me that she should not know?"

"Well, listen to this, Mrs Ravenhill. When you got ill, and before the wizard and the doctor arrived, you were in a sort of fever and you were talkin' without knowin' what you said. You talked about lots of people when my Aunty and me were in the room, and some names I remember were David, Amos, Owain, Joseph and Brynach. You moaned a lot in your sleep, and said "Oh Brynach, don't leave me! Don't leave me -- I beg of you!" over and again. Another time you sighed like you was in a great passion, and said "Oh, Owain my love, come to me now! Come to me now!" And another time you said "Oh, Amos, what will the deacons think? What will the deacons think?" Very puzzlin', thought my Aunty Polly, for all those names to come bubblin' out of you, but not that of your late husband."

I froze in horror as these revelations were made. The boy continued. "She was mullin' over all of this in the kitchen last night, and she said to me "Was there not something in *The Cambrian* just three weeks back about a clergyman with the name of Amos, most cruelly killed in some wood somewhere or other? It must have been a terrible business -- but surely Mrs Ravenhill cannot have known that fellow, since she is from far away?" I replied to her, I did, that she should not take the ramblins of a person in a fever too seriously, Missis, for at such times, as in dreams, real and imaginary people are all mixed up, and people in the newspapers do become as real as people in your own family. I reminded her that not long since she had told me about a strange dream, and in it she had passionate encounters with Prince Albert and various others, and saw Queen Victoria ridin' on a dragon. Very funny, that is!"

"Thank you, Merlin. I thank the Lord for your quick wit, and hope that you have saved me on this occasion too. Will she talk to others?"

"No knowing, Missis. But she is certainly thinkin', and a thinkin' aunty is a dangerous thing. And by the way, there is somethin' else."

"Oh, no! What is it this time?"

"When you were sweatin' gallons with that fever of yours, there were brown stains on your pillow case, comin' off your hair. I noticed it, and changed the pillow-cases as often as I could without disturbin' you too much, and washed them myself."

"Did your aunty notice?"

"I can't be sure, Missis. She hasn't mentioned it to me, but it's not impossible. And by the way, there's somethin' else too."

By this time I was shivering with apprehension, and I dare say that I was as white a sheet. "Tell me the worst," I groaned.

Merlin looked concerned, but he knew that he had to tell me. "You are bein' followed again, by a third man," he said. "Well, not followed exactly -- bein' observed, more likely. There's this man. He's watchin' the other two fellows as well, and he goes up and down the Pendre every day, watchin' this address very closely and notin' down every arrival and departure in a little notebook. A very tall man, with a smart leather hat on his head and wearin' a full-length black coat and top boots. I bumped into him this mornin', makin' it look accidental. He gave me a fierce look and grumbled at me, Missis, in a funny sort of English accent. I think he's a gentleman, but he's definitely not local."

4. Loose ends

Next morning -- the day of the funeral -- I was on tenterhooks, and I also felt abandoned since I had had no visitors for two days and since I knew nothing of the inquest or *gwylnos*. I could only speculate that all was well. I tried to keep myself cheerful, but I was not yet well enough to venture out onto the street, so I tried to pass the time in reading some of the dreadful works of fiction that Mrs Ifans had inherited from various departing guests over the years. Following Merlin's warning, I peeped through the curtains and out onto the street several times during the morning, and saw a tall man in a long black coat stationed in various places, all of which afforded a view of Mrs Ifans's lodging house. I thought he was one of the men whom I had sighted shortly after my arrival in town, but I could not be sure.

Early in the afternoon Mrs Ifans and Merlin were out in town, and I felt very vulnerable in spite of the fact that the front door was locked. The strange man must have known that I was alone in the house. Possibly he was waiting to observe some movement of the curtains, for next time I dared to peep out he reacted immediately and started across the road towards the front door. He knocked violently on the door, over and again, obviously hoping that I would descend the stairs and open it. But I remained in my room, quite petrified, with my door locked in case he should force an entry and come storming up the stairs. I even struggled to move my heavy table up against the door, so that it would be better able to withstand an assault from the outside. Suddenly the knocking stopped, and there was a great commotion out on the street. A wave of relief swept over me, and I dared to look out through my window. I could not see the door or the doorstep since they were directly below me, but then a cowering man and an angry landlady came into view. I almost felt sorry for the fellow, since Mrs Ifans was berating him in Welsh, using words that are best left off this page, and she was beating him about the head with her umbrella. His hat fell off, and as he bent to pick it up she gave him a mighty kick up the backside which sent him flat on his face in the street. That was enough for him. Without bothering to collect his hat, he scrambled onto his feet and ran off as fast as his long legs would carry him.

Loose Ends

In any other circumstances the scene in the street would have been comical, but when Mrs Ifans and Merlin came up the stairs to my room a few minutes later I was still shaking like a leaf. Mrs Ifans was red-faced with fury. "There now, Mrs Ravenhill *bach*, that knocking and hammering on the door must have given you quite a fright. And you still recuperating from the sickness, too! Bloody cheek! Asking to see "the English lady" and not even knowing your name! At any rate, I will not have strangers hammering on my door like that, and I gave him a piece of my mind and a few gentle blows with my brolly. God knows what he wanted, but I told him he had better go and want it somewhere else. It's a tidy house I keep, and folks banging on doors and disturbing my guests are not welcome here. Now then *bach*, how about a nice cup of tea?"

Without waiting for an answer, she pottered off down the stairs, grumbling to herself about the decline in the manners of the nation. When she had gone, Merlin grinned and said "Close shave, Missis. I think he's harmless enough, but you never know. Did you notice his face? Dark sort of complexion, as if he has been out in the hot sun, even if it is still early spring. Short black hair. Narrow eyes, sort of furtive, glancin' about. And big front teeth like a rabbit. By the way, you might like to look at this." He handed me the tall man's hat, which was covered in mud. I looked at it carefully, and saw that it was made of leather rather than felt, and that it came from France. Inside the rim the words *LeClerc, Paris* were embroidered onto a delicate and discreet label. The stitching and finishing were exquisite. This was a high-class hat if ever I saw one, and I was quite mystified. Merlin had also examined the label, and he said "There ain't many fellows in Cardigan with hats like that, Missis. Can I keep it?"

"It's yours, Merlin. You found it."

"A bit too big for me, it is, but if I grows my hair long and thick I can just about wear it without it fallin' over my eyes. My friends will be very jealous; they won't believe me when I tells them I just found it on the street, but who cares?" He jammed the hat down over his ears, giggled, and ran off down the stairs.

I was so preoccupied with the gentleman with the French hat that I lost track of the time. But then in the middle of the afternoon, at about 3 pm, Merlin came quietly up the stairs again and knocked on my door. I invited him to come in, and he said "Can't stop, Missis. Things to do. But I thought I should tell you that five minutes ago somethin' happened that will make you very relieved. Bye bye." And off he went again, leaving me with my mouth opening and closing and looking like a stranded trout.

It dawned on me then that the funeral was over and done with, and the coffin full of stones was in the ground. How on earth had Merlin come by that news? What an extraordinary child! I don't know why, but I broke down and wept when I should have danced around the room and filled the place with laughter. Mrs Ifans came up and found me sobbing uncontrollably on the bed. "There now, Mrs Ravenhill *bach*," she said calmly. "Here is that cup of tea I promised ages ago, and some nice slices of *bara brith* into the bargain. Just you put that stupid fellow out of your mind." She obviously thought that I was still shocked by the hammering on the front door, and I did not have the heart to disabuse her.

Next day, shortly after noon, Rose and Myfanwy called to see me, and since it was a fine March day with warm sunshine and a gentle breeze from the south, I decided that we could venture out. I was by no means back to my full strength, but thought that I needed the exercise. So the three of us walked, arm in arm, down to the river, and we talked about everything that had happened here and there. We were all dressed in full mourning clothes, so we had to avoid frivolity at all costs. I kept my face covered by my veil, just in case. First, I asked the girls about the inquest.

"Shemi was there," said Rose. "He said that after the week's delay in convening the inquest they have at last found a new coroner. Jonathan Huws, from Mountain West. Quite competent and fair-minded, by all accounts, Mrs Ravenhill. Then there was a jury of ten men from the town. First, they dealt with the death of Mistress Martha Morgan. The Coroner asked if Dr George Havard was present, as he assumed that he would have carried out the post-mortem and signed the certificate of death. Aunty Daisy stood up and explained that in view of the doctor's close relationship with the deceased he had considered it inappropriate to examine the body or to have any involvement in the Inquest. In any case, she said, he had been called to give urgent medical attention to a patient in Cardigan and had not yet returned. 'Then who examined the body?' asked the Coroner. At that point Wilmot stood up and said that he had arranged for a certain

Doctor Figgis, being the only other physician then in the neighbourhood, to perform the lamentable task. 'Never heard of him, sir,' said the Coroner. Then there was an unexpected intervention from the public gallery. 'I can vouch for him, sir,' said Tom Mathias from Dinas, who was no doubt present at Wilmot's invitation. 'An excellent doctor, registered with the Royal College, and doing short term duty in Dinas. He fixed me up good and proper when I was very sick in bed a few weeks back.' 'And is he here?' asked the Coroner. 'I want evidence from him.' Apparently Wilmot stood up again and said 'Sadly, sir, he had to return to Swansea on the completion of his appointment in Dinas. But I have here his signed Certificate of Death.' It was handed over to the Coroner, who examined it minutely before reading it out to the jury. 'This is very irregular,' said he, 'but in the circumstances we have to accept it. Now then, are there any other witnesses to the death of Mistress Morgan?'"

From this point on Myfanwy took up the telling of the tale. "Then, by all accounts, Will, Abel, Gerallt, Gomer, Henry and Brendan all stood up in turn and explained how they had found the body on the top of the mountain after mounting a search at dawn. They all said that the corpse was cold, with no trace of a pulse and no discernible breath. They told how they had carried it down to the Plas on a ladder, and had then placed it on the kitchen table to await a post-mortem examination. 'No suspicious circumstances, Mr Owen?' said the Coroner to Will. 'None at all, sir, apart from the earthquake.' 'Can you confirm that the body was severely damaged by falling rocks and so forth, but that there was no blood?' 'Yes, I can confirm that there was no blood.' The Coroner accepted that, Mrs Ravenhill, and Will never did have to tell a lie! But Master Huws is a very keen and astute fellow, and so he pursued the idea that this might have been a suicide. Several people had to give testimony that Mistress Morgan was in a perfectly sound state of mind, that she wasn't the sort of person to take her own life, and that indeed she had no reason at all to do such a thing. Bessie had to give testimony that Mistress Morgan often went out alone on Carningli, in all seasons and at all times of the day and night, and that she often slept on the mountain in the open air and returned to the Plas in the morning as lively and refreshed as may be imagined. That caused a bit of a stir in the jury and among the members of the public, so we hear, and the Coroner said 'Eccentric behaviour, gentlemen, as you might agree, but entirely in character for the deceased. No other evidence? Very well, gentlemen of the jury, without further guidance from me, I ask you to retire and give your verdict.' Apparently they retired for just a minute or two, and returned with a verdict of death by natural causes. Then the Coroner released the body for burial."

"Excellent, Rose. That must have been a great relief to all concerned in this business."

By this time we were approaching the tidal river, which was flowing in reverse as the flood tide pushed salt water upstream from St Dogmael's and under Cardigan Bridge. There was a scent of spring in the air, and there were birds everywhere -- gulls wheeling and mewing, and oyster-catchers, curlews and other little wading birds on the mud-banks, hopping and scuttling about as the water level inched ever higher and reduced their feeding area. I breathed deeply, and for almost the first time in my new life I felt secure and almost serene in the company of these beautiful young ladies.

"So that was it?" I asked.

"No no, Mrs Ravenhill," said Myfanwy. "That was just the start of the proceedings. Now we get to the really interesting bit. Tell her, Rose."

And so Rose told me, second-hand, what had happened in the second part of the Inquest, when consideration was given to the skeleton found in the deep crevice on the mountain, following the earthquake. This was referred to as "an inquiry into the death of an unknown gentleman some time after 1795."

When Rose said this, she immediately felt the tension in my body, and she recalled our earlier conversation. "I know this is difficult for you, Mrs Ravenhill," she said. "Are you sure that you want me to continue?" I nodded. "Yes please. I have to hear it."

There was a long pause, and I sensed that Rose was suddenly quite distressed. I took her in my arms and whispered into her ear: "What is it, *Cariad*? Is the telling of this too hard to bear?"

"No no, Grandmother. It's not that at all," she sobbed, desperately seeking to keep her voice low. "It's this terrible pretence in which we are all involved! Mrs Ravenhill this, Mrs Ravenhill, that! Will I ever be able to talk to you again as my beloved Grandmother? Sometimes I have to admit to wishing that you really were dead!"

That struck like an arrow to the heart, and for a while I could not respond. I tried to be strong, but my eyes filled with tears. Then Myfanwy came to the rescue and joined us in our embrace. "Now then, Rose," she whispered. "You must, you **must** be brave! We must go through with this, for you know that the Mistress has some great task to complete. It **will** become easier to keep up this pretence with the passing of time -- I promise it! And once the task is done, who knows what joy will follow?"

The three of us gradually recovered our composure and continued with our walk along the river bank. Rose was still shaking, and so Myfanwy took up the narrative relating to the bones on the mountain. The discovery had apparently been made initially by some small boys from town, who had collected the bones up and thrown them into a sack. They had given them to Billy Pinder, one of the local constables, who had berated them for 'destroying evidence of a possible dastardly crime.' The constable had then climbed the mountain with the boys and various other inquisitive adults, and they had climbed down into the crevice and recovered scraps of clothing, some bits of rope, two iron pots and three pans, all badly rusted, a leather bucket and a leather mug, a knife, the remains of some woollen blankets, and a pair of men's boots. There were some ashes and charred bits of firewood, some rabbit bones and some chicken bones. All of these items had been assembled in the constable's office and examined by the Mayor and various others. Apparently they had asked Shemi, as the most astute sleuth in the district, to examine the bones and the other items, but he had declined to help, on the grounds that he was much preoccupied with helping the Morgan family of Plas Ingli, following the sad death of Mistress Martha. So they drew certain conclusions of their own, which were reported to the inquest by the Mayor. They concluded that the possessions were those of a gentleman, since the boots were of good quality, and there were traces of fine embroidery on the waistcoat. The belt had a silver buckle, and the knife had a carved ivory handle. From the presence of the pots and pans and other signs of domesticity it had to be concluded that the deceased gentleman had been living rough on the mountain, maybe in the open and maybe in one of the little caves among the boulders on the southern slopes. But how was it that the bones and all of the other things came to be at the bottom of a deep crevice? Constable Pinder apparently gave evidence that there were lots of stones on top of the human and other remains, suggesting that everything (including the body of the deceased) had been tipped into the crevice and had then been deliberately covered with stones so as to hide evidence of a crime. At this suggestion of murder, said Myfanwy, there was a murmur of anticipation and excitement in the public gallery.

I knew what was coming next, and thought that I had had enough emotional upheavals for one afternoon. I felt myself shivering, although in truth it was a warm enough afternoon, with daffodils nodding and gleaming in the sunshine. Rose, who was stronger now, took up the tale again. According to her information, she said, the Coroner then asked for evidence relating to the human remains.

"And who gave that evidence?" I asked weakly. "Not your Uncle George, I hope?"

"No, Mrs Ravenhill," she said, giving great emphasis to the name. "He was asked and refused, so Billy Blood gave evidence instead."

"Billy Blood? What on earth could a common butcher say on such matters?"

"It's not so absurd as you might think, madam. Butchers know about bones, and killing and such things. And remember that he is also a part-time surgeon, who has performed amputations in the past, with a modest survival rate."

I moaned. "Oh my God! So what did he say?"

"By all accounts he was very competent. He said that the bones were those of a tall man, probably scattered about as the body decomposed by the depradations of rats and foxes. Many of the bones had the signs of being gnawed by animals, and there were signs of gnawing on the leather bucket as well."

"So the body was consumed by vermin?"

"That is what he suggested."

"A perfectly fitting end for such a monster," I said bitterly, losing my self-control for a moment and causing Myfanwy to catch her breath.

Rose, who knew of my interest in the matter, continued. "Then he came to the skull. He said that the back of the skull had been smashed by a blow of very great force from behind, and that that was probably the cause of death. The other interesting thing about the skull of the deceased was that the two front teeth were missing; that, thought Billy Blood, might give a clue to his identity. The evidence being thus concluded, the Coroner asked whether any person present might have any idea as to the name of the deceased -- a tall gentleman with his front teeth missing, who might have lived rough on the mountain some time after 1795, that being the date of the most recent coin found with the remains."

"Should Rose continue, Mrs Ravenhill?" asked Myfanwy. I nodded.

"For some time, so I hear, there was silence in the room, but then a very old man got to his feet. It turned out to be Benjamin Mathias, who used to be a cobbler in town and who once did duty as a petty constable, before the turn of the century. Now he was well into his eighties. 'I have something to say, Johnny,' he blurted out. 'Now then, Benny,' said the Coroner. 'This is a formal inquest. Kindly refer to me as "sir" or "Mr Huws". Pray continue.' 'Very well, Sir Johnny. I think them bits and pieces of bones belonged to a fellow called Moses Lloyd, son of old Squire Lloyd of Cwmgloyn. Everybody knew that he was cut out of his father's will and was penniless. A right bastard he was, if you will forgive the expression, your Honour. He caused mayhem locally, thieving and whoring, and once he smashed up the bar room of the Black Lion in a drunken rage. I was the constable at the time, and I remember it well, so I do. I had him in the lock-up. In the French invasion he ran away when others fought, so he was as yellow as a field of mustard. In the end I recall a warrant out for his arrest, for insulting a magistrate and for some more thieving. He worked for a while for the Morganses of Plas Ingli, he did, but God only knows how they had the patience to put up with him. The lazy bugger never did a decent day's work in his life. He lost his two front teeth when he was beat up by some lads from the Parrog. There must have been fifty people in town who had every reason to murder him, Sir Johnny, for he had debts everywhere, and I know for a fact that there were four wives seduced and money stolen from Arthur Lord and Billy.........'"

At that point, said Rose, the Coroner pulled him up short and thanked him. "Then he said something like this: 'We are not here to speculate about motives or possible culprits, and this is not a court of law. All we have to do is establish a cause of death and facilitate the burial of the remains. I must draw these proceedings to a close. I give this guidance to the jury. We have some evidence suggesting that the deceased met his death a long time ago, and that he was the subject of a violent attack. You must decide whether murder was committed. You also have some evidence that this person might have been one Moses Lloyd of Cwmgloyn. I also ask you to determine whether this deceased person should have a Christian burial in sanctified ground, or whether he should be consigned to a pauper's grave. Kindly retire and reach your verdict.'"

So, said Rose, the jury left the room and returned after half an hour of deliberations. The foreman announced the decision that the deceased person, possibly one Moses Lloyd of Cwmgloyn, was unlawfully killed by a person or persons unknown some time around the year 1798. It was their decision that interment in a pauper's grave would be appropriate in this case, unless anybody came forward with an offer to meet the costs of a burial in hallowed ground. The Coroner thanked the jurors and dismissed them, and Rector Llewelyn Thomas said that he would seek to arrange an appropriate burial. The bones were then replaced in the wooden box which had been used for carrying them around.

"So there we are, Mrs Ravenhill," said Rose, with her equilibrium now restored. "Those present said that they had seldom had a more interesting afternoon's entertainment, and all were impressed with the new coroner's common-sense approach, in contrast to the corrupt and scandalous behaviour of his predecessor. Afterwards, there was much talk in town about Mistress Martha and about the villainous Moses Lloyd."

She looked at me, and I knew that she wanted to know more. So we found a bench by the river, and we sat there in the sunshine. I told the two young ladies that I had vowed long ago that the truth about what happened on the mountain in August 1798 would never, never pass the lips of Mistress Martha Morgan. But now that she was dead, Mrs Susanna Ravenhill might, in her stead, describe those terrible events.

So over the next hour or so I told them all about Moses Lloyd and myself, about how he had taken me captive in a cave on the mountain and had attempted to ravish me, and about how I had somehow saved myself and brought about his sudden death. Then I told them how I had cleansed the cave, disposed of the body and all his possessions, and finally staggered and crawled back to the Plas, more dead than alive. I also told them about my written confession, without saying where it was. "So you see, Rose and Myfanwy, Mistress Morgan of Plas Ingli was the one who committed the murder, and she had to live with that terrible knowledge until the day that she went to her grave."

The two girls saw through my veil that there were tears rolling down my cheeks, and I saw that they were weeping too. They both embraced me, and then Myfanwy said: "But Mrs Ravenhill, if a death occurs in the course of self-defence, that is surely not murder? No court in the land would have convicted Mistress Martha, had they been given the evidence."

"But don't you see, Myfanwy?" I sobbed. "I have analysed my motives endlessly over the years, and have concluded that at the critical moment I **wanted** to kill Moses Lloyd. I hid all the evidence of his death, and said nothing........"

"Careful, Mrs Ravenhill," whispered Rose, with a twinkle in her eye. "What was it we discussed ten minutes ago? Passers-by have ears. No more first person, if you please. Don't you mean **she** hid all the evidence?"

"I'm sorry -- you are right. I am very emotional just now. Give me a moment, if you will."

I breathed deeply, dabbed my eyes and blew my nose. Then I continued. "Mistress Morgan wanted to cleanse her cave, since that was her secret and sacred place. She managed to do that, although she was at the very edge of her endurance. But the attempts to dispose of the body and all other traces of the man and the crime might well have been taken by a jury as a sign of guilt, and it is quite possible that Martha would have been sent to the gallows as a result."

"Never!" exclaimed Rose. "Extenuating circumstances!"

"You forget, Rose, that the application of the law was a very corrupt business when today's old ladies were young. The magistrates were all gentry, and some of them were cronies of Moses Lloyd. There is absolutely no guarantee that the lady involved would have had a fair trial. But let's cheer ourselves up. It was all a long time ago, and everything is resolved. One day, when I have gone to my maker, you might like to tell this morbid story to your children, if they are tough enough to hear it......."

We laughed, and mopped our cheeks, and continued on our promenade along the river. We still had much to talk about, and I wanted to know all about the *gwylnos* and the funeral; but all three of us wanted to chat about the weather, and the daffodils, and the cheerful spring birdsong for a while, after the heavy and emotional matters recently discussed. We walked in silence, and had not gone very far when Merlin popped out from behind a large tree trunk. He looked quite absurd, with the defeated spy's French hat upon his head. "Afternoon, Missis! Afternoon, ladies!" he grinned. "Nice day for it!"

"Very pleasant indeed, Merlin. And you look very silly with that hat on your head."

"Appearances can be deceptive, Missis. News for you. You know that fellow who sort of gave me the hat? Well, he's still in town, stayin' in lodgins near the Mwldan. He calls hisself a businessman, and he's from London. He speaks French quite well, and he sends letters written in bad French to somebody in London, and written in bad English to somebody in Fishguard. I'll soon have their names for you. He don't seem to have any friends, and he keeps to hisself. He drinks in the Rose and Crown every evenin'. He's pretty miserable most of the time, and looks as if he would rather be somewhere else. So he has a job to do -- watchin' you, Missis, if I'm not mistook. And his name is Iago Woodward."

"Where is he now, Merlin?"

"Behind that tree by the green boat, at the edge of the water. He would be listenin' to you now, if he could get close enough."

And off the lad skipped, down towards the green boat at the edge of the water. "The little devil!" I said to Rose and Myfanwy. "Look at him! He's intent on provoking my enemy by flaunting that hat a few yards from where he's hiding!" True enough, and as we watched Iago sprang from behind the tree and made a grab for the hat. But Merlin was too quick for him, and was off like a flash along the muddy river bank, leaping from stone to stone and avoiding all the mud. Iago was not so clever, and he had his eyes on the hat, so that he soon lost his footing on some mud and went straight into the water, with legs and arms flailing. It was not very deep, but it was deep enough and smelly enough to do severe damage to his dignity, and the miserable fellow dragged himself back to the footpath soaked to the skin and covered in thick slime from head to toe. In a state of high dudgeon he trudged back towards town, glaring at all the passers-by who were out for their afternoon strolls in the sun.

That cheered us up enormously, and when we had recovered our composure we returned to the lodgings. I knew that I could not stay in Cardigan any longer, since Iago Woodward -- be he clown or hired assassin -- would catch up with me eventually. So I pleaded with Rose and Myfanwy to arrange for me to be moved somewhere else, preferably on the morrow. They appreciated my concerns, but said that if proper plans were to be laid, at least two clear days would be needed. They said that they would arrange for me to be collected around 8 pm on the following Thursday, when Iago would be off duty, downing a few jars of ale in the Rose and Crown. Rose suggested that I should not announce my departure in advance to my landlady or anybody else. I had, after all, now stayed with Mrs Ifans for two weeks already, and that was all I had committed to.

Then the two girls were off, on the afternoon stagecoach to Newport. I ambled gently back towards my lodgings, and was surprised to find that the front door was open. I entered the front passageway, and shouted for Mrs Ifans, but there was no reply -- nor did I really expect one, for it was one of her afternoons in the Lamb and Flag. I knew that something had happened, and that somebody had been into the house with evil intent.

With my heart beating wildly, I climbed the stairs, and saw that the door to my room, which had been locked, was swinging loosely on its hinges. Somehow it had been opened, apparently without any damage being done, by somebody who knew all about breaking and entering. Maybe he had picked the lock, or maybe taken Mrs Ifans's master key from the kitchen? I was afraid that somebody was waiting for me inside the room, out of sight, and I froze, too terrified to enter. At last, with no sound coming from within, I did step inside, hardly daring to breathe. There was nobody there, but the room was in chaos. The blankets had been pulled off the bed, clothes were scattered everywhere, and the chest in which I kept my personal things had been tipped over. My most intimate garments had been trampled on the floor. I had very little in the way of necklaces and earrings, but those few small things which had been in my little jewellery box had been tipped out onto the bed. Nothing, as far as I could see at first, had been stolen, and I thanked my lucky stars that I had not left in my room any personal papers or letters that might have been incriminating. Now I felt not only scared out of my wits, but also defiled. Whose grubby hands had rummaged through my clothes and my most personal possessions, and stripped away my privacy? Emotion drove away rational thought, and I was not even capable of speculating on who might have been responsible for this outrage.

At first I was so shocked that I simply collapsed onto my couch in the middle of the chaos and did nothing. But I realized that if Mrs Ifans should get to know of this invasion of her lodging house, she would certainly call the constables, and that was the last thing I wanted. So I first of all descended the stairs and closed the front door, in case she should turn up and think there was something amiss. Having puffed back upstairs again as fast as my aching joints would permit, I frantically started to tidy up the mess. I made up the bed again, put all my clothes back in their correct places, and got the place back to more or less its original condition. When I was just about to relax and to congratulate myself on a job well done, I noticed something dangling in the window, hanging from the curtain rail on a piece of string. It was my little bottle of brown hair dye. On its label were the words "Huws Bros, High Class Pharmacists, Newport Pembs." Now my mood changed from shock to despair, with the realization that while Iago Woodward had been trailing us along the river bank, an accomplice had planned and executed this assault upon my lodgings. Furthermore, these shadowy operators now knew me to be an impostor with dyed hair, and knew that I had a link with Newport.

Mrs Ifans was back before long, and I do not think she suspected that there had been anything amiss in her lodging house. She certainly said nothing to me. But I knew that things had taken a very serious turn, and I spent the whole evening contemplating my future. I had two options -- to flee in terror, or to show these men (however many of them there might have been) that I would not be intimidated. I really had no choice but to breathe deeply, reinforce my nerves with iron, and choose the latter course.

I had two days to endure, during which time I had to stay clear of the chief spy and his accomplices and avoid getting into trouble. The first day passed pleasantly enough in the company of young Merlin. I gave him a lesson on the Civil War in the morning, and as payment he gave me a guided tour of the town in the afternoon, taking in the prison, the castle (very ruinous) and assorted dignified buildings. As expected, Woodward shadowed us but could never get very close, and Merlin made sure that we never went anywhere that was thinly populated, shadowy or dangerous. The agent of darkness never got half a chance to attack us or even to over-hear our conversation -- and even if he had, he would have learned far more about the town than about me. But in the evening, when I was alone in my room, I did become very preoccupied with the spy, and on mulling things over I came to the view that he had to be a sort of special constable who had been alerted -- possibly by a traitor in my Group of Twenty-five fellow conspirators, or possibly by a slip of the tongue or something over-heard -- to the fact that I had falsified my own death. He was waiting for me to make a false move, so that his suspicions might be confirmed, or he was looking for an opportunity to interrogate me prior to making an arrest. I knew that if I was questioned at length by an expert I would not be able to maintain my play-acting for very long, and that he would very quickly find huge holes in my fabricated life history. I tried to convince myself that his links with France were unimportant -- after all, many educated people spoke French, and many had visited Paris and bought fine clothes and hats while they were there. But if he were reporting to the authorities in London, it might be convenient to communicate in French, so as to avoid the possibility of letters being intercepted or read by uneducated persons without authority. Even with good seals, we all knew that letters sent in the post were never entirely safe.

I went to bed that night feeling utterly miserable, convinced that my freedom was about to come to an end and that my insane enterprise would collapse around my ears, probably on the morrow. I could not sleep, and in the small hours I conceived a further mad plan which would certainly have been instantly stamped upon by any of my fellow conspirators, had they been consulted. But they were in Newport and Dinas and assorted other places in North Pembrokeshire, and I was all alone in Cardigan. So I determined to carry it through as a last act of defiance. On looking back, I now think that what came into my head was guidance from somewhere --

not the profound guidance I was looking for, relating to my destiny, but at any rate something far better than introspection and inactivity.

On a bright and calm morning I rose early, and told Mrs Ifans at breakfast time that I was minded do some shopping. I said that I was also intent upon certain investigations into my family history which might take me out of town. So off I went at eight o'clock with a wicker basket over my arm, and a promise that I would return by dinner time. There was no sign of Iago when I stepped out onto the street, and I concluded that he would not be on duty until 9 o'clock at the earliest. I was cautious nonetheless, and after walking along the High Street and crossing Cardigan Bridge, I turned near the warehouse and strode off towards St Dogmael's. A big ship was being unloaded at the quayside, and there was much noise and activity, with horses and carts coming and going, and merchants and seamen rushing about. Just in case I was being followed I turned a corner, dodged into an alleyway and waited in the shadows. Sure enough, after a couple of minutes a tall man with a woollen frock coat and muffler walked past, hesitated as he realized that he had lost sight of me, and then walked on more quickly up the winding hill towards the village. I knew it was Woodward, dressed in new or borrowed clothes following his ignominious descent into the river. I waited till he was out of sight, and then, with my heart racing, I doubled back and crossed the bridge into town.

I turned into Stryd y Castell and entered Billings Superior Gentlemen's Outfitters just a couple of minutes after it opened for the day. Half an hour later I came out again, carrying in my basket a parcel containing a long black cloak, a heavy black muffler, and a wide-brimmed black felt hat. I bought some hot pies, cheese and fruit from a market stall. Then, without further ado, I hired a covered chaise and instructed the driver to head for Newport, telling him that I would need him for the whole day, and that he would be required to wait for me for a couple of hours while I attended to certain business. He was a young fellow called Bobby who had never been west of Eglwyswrw before, so the trip was an adventure for him. As we trotted along, I sat quietly inside the chaise, dressed in my mourning clothes and with my veil over my face. I felt a sort of quiet satisfaction, since I knew that I would not be followed in this enterprise by my enemy, who would hopefully be spending an unproductive day hunting for me in the streets of St Dogmael's. After an hour or so I caught my first glimpses of my beloved mountain, prominent on the western skyline, and looking for all the world like a mighty volcano about to erupt. In reality it is quite a little mountain, barely over eleven hundred feet high, but therein lies a part of its charm and its magic.

As I made my plans I entered a state of calm resolution spiced with just a little apprehension. What I was about to do was, after all, very risky indeed. There was virtually no traffic on the road, and we reached Newport before 11 o'clock. I asked the driver to continue through the town and to turn left up the Bedd Morris road. He needed my instructions in order to reach the old standing stone at the highest point on the road to Pontfaen. According to legend, it is the place where a notorious robber called Morris was captured, hung and buried. There, in the middle of a wild moorland with no sign of human habitation, I alighted from the chaise with my parcel and told Bobby to wait for two hours. I gave him the larger part of my picnic supplies, and told him that I was going to visit a relative who lived in a very remote cottage which could only be reached on foot. He released the horse from the chaise, wiped it down after the long journey, and tethered it to the standing stone. Then he settled down in the spring sunshine to eat his lunch, to listen to the skylarks, and to read a penny dreadful.

I walked eastwards along the mountain track towards Carningli, filling my lungs with the sweet fresh mountain air and obtaining a temporary release from my imprisonment within the persona of Mrs Susanna Ravenhill. There was no sign of any other human being, and there were very few sheep on the mountain since I knew that they would be down in the fields of Dolrannog, Penrhiw and the Mountain West farms for the duration of the lambing season. A few shaggy mountain ponies, which I recognized as belonging to Gelli, moved reluctantly out of my way as I walked past. When I reached Carn Edward, a prominent crag of bluestone with great boulders scattered around it, I disappeared among the rocks with my basket, dressed as an old woman in mourning, and emerged a few minutes later as a mysterious figure draped in a long black cloak, with a muffler over my face, and with a wide-brimmed black hat upon my head. I continued along the footpath, just out of sight of the Plas and the cottages and farms of Cilgwyn, with invisible skylarks carolling in the sunshine high above my head. At last I reached the rocky outcrops of the mountain itself, and followed the track that led into the tumbledown old fort inhabited by Druids and other ancient people many centuries ago. The approach to the summit was easy from this side -- a great deal easier than the steep ascent from the Plas, which lay to the south.

I suddenly realized that I was enjoying myself. True, life might become difficult if I was spotted by somebody or -- even worse -- apprehended by somebody who might be out and about on the mountain in the middle of the day. But I thought that if I was to meet anybody, it would most likely be Will, Gerallt or one of the other Plas Ingli servants, and since they were fellow conspirators I would be content to reveal my identity if circumstances allowed. Otherwise, I was well protected by my disguise, which was calculated to give me the appearance of the Nightwalker, that mysterious figure who had walked upon the mountain many years ago and who had caused me, and many others, a good deal of distress. He (for it was a man, and not a ghost or a devil dressed in that long black cloak) had wandered about on the mountain, watching the Plas and reserving his closest attention for me personally, sometimes making frequent appearances over weeks, and then disappearing for months on end. At last, so concerned had people become about his hauntings that some local squires had even organized a hunt with horses and hounds, but he was never found; and in the end he had revealed himself to me, shortly before his death, as Iestyn Price, the natural father of my adopted son Brynach. He had loved me from afar, but he was a tragic and reclusive figure, terribly disfigured because of a wartime accident with an exploding cannon, who had every reason to hide away from the prying eyes and crude judgments of the world. But there were, I knew, still dim memories of the Nightwalker in the community, and those old enough to remember him still thought of him as a ghost. My own grandchildren certainly knew about him, having picked up greatly exaggerated tales of him flying through the air and appearing and disappearing at will. I recall that when he was young, Abel recounted for me a most remarkable tale of the Nightwalker flying over the mountain on a wild evening towards a red sunset, revealing through his long tail and prominent horns that he was really Satan out and about doing devillish things. I smiled as I recalled his wide-eyed boyish wonderment and his relish in the telling of the tale, as I accepted all his nonsense with grandmotherly good grace. I thought that if I was spotted, it would be most likely that my observer, being local and well-informed about local phantoms, would run away in a state of panic -- and that suited me well enough.

The old blue rocks, encrusted with lichens and mosses, smelt warm and even welcoming as I followed the twisting path to the summit. I was too warm for comfort in my heavy disguise, but I knew that I had to keep my cloak tightly wrapped about me, my hat pulled down over my eyes, and my muffler over my face. When I reached the grassy patch near the summit I was ecstatic. I was at home again, on my mountain, beneath a spring sun, with the world beneath my feet. Was this heaven, or was I still bound to the earth?

But then my mood was transformed, as memories flooded into my mind: of the occasions when I had come here with my children at sunrise on Easter Sunday for the scattering of the Easter Water; of flying kites and winter gales; of love-making with my wonderful husband David, who died too young; of chance encounters with Owain Laugharne and Amos Jones, both now dead; of picnics with my grandchildren on balmy August afternoons; of the fateful evening, just over a fortnight ago, when I had lain just here beneath the cold crisp stars and fallen asleep, content that my life was at an end. How could I put all of that out of my mind in some idiotic attempt to "be" somebody else? Should I now attempt to empty my head and my heart of all the things that gave Martha Morgan life -- her virtues and her vices, her mannerisms and ways of speaking, her foibles and her little secrets, her grand designs and high aspirations? Impossible! How, I thought, could I scrub away my love for my grandchildren and my children, and even for my servants and friends? Impossible! Could I ever meet them face to face again without demonstrating my affection and concern for them, or acknowledging, through words and gestures and glances, the bonds which gave us our strength and which were unique to the Morgan family of Plas Ingli? Impossible! It was all very well for me to have made plans, and to have talked of theoretical situations with my fellow conspirators shortly after my miraculous recovery in the kitchen of the Plas, but how would I cope with encounters in the real world? Could I come face to face in public or in private with my little great-grandson Levi, the child of Rose and Henry, without wanting to embrace him, or hold him on my knee? I could not.

As I wiped away my tears on the hem of my black cloak, I knew, without any feeling of arrogance, that the Plas, a place inhabited by angels, was at least partly my creation. Could I now turn my back on it, and pretend that it did not exist? Impossible! Some of my friends, in their innocence, were mourning for me still, and I felt more acutely than ever the outrage that I had committed against them. I felt a black, terrible despair, and I was overwhelmed by the thought that I had committed a cold, cruel and calculating act of deception on people who had done nothing to deserve it. I knew that towards them, and towards all those who had walked from the Plas to Cilgwyn Church in Martha Morgan's funeral procession, I should have shown nothing but respect and affection. Now, in pursuit of I knew not what, I had lost everything -- family, friends, possessions, home, security, and even identity. I was penniless, and dependent upon the charity of others, and especially upon Wilmot. I could not presume that his generosity would last for ever. I would never again be able to socialise publicly and comfortably with my own family and friends. I realized that I missed Bessie dreadfully, and longed to sit down by the Plas Ingli kitchen fireside and to talk to her of old times. Worst of all, I would never again be able to walk freely and openly on the slopes of Carningli, or talk to the ravens, or listen to the skylarks.

And who was I now? A phantom, a fantasy, with a name dreamt up in a moment of madness and a history invented as one might invent a bedtime story for a small child. I felt that I had no more substance than a wisp of sea mist curling over the summit of the mountain on a summers day, to be melted away by the heat of the sun. Oh, that I could take the place of those stones in the coffin in Cilgwyn Churchyard! Oh, that I could join David, Owain, Iestyn, Joseph, Caradoc and Amos in the warm embrace of the Good Lord in his heaven! Six good men who had loved Martha Morgan of Plas Ingli in spite of her many vices and her strange and childish changes of mood, her moments of panic and indecision, and her predisposition to mistrust those who should be trusted. Martha Morgan -- who was she, and where was she now? My head was spinning, and I felt sick.

Loose Ends

Then in the midst of this black and terrifying episode I opened my eyes and saw that the sun was still shining, and I heard that the skylarks were still singing their praises of the God that gave them life and music. And there, just a few feet from me, perched in a row on the highest summit rock of the mountain, sat six ravens. They were black and beautiful, and they watched me unblinkingly and impassively. They knew who I was, even if I did not, and they were back on the mountain as they had been, according to reports, on the morning of my reported death. I knew that when other people walked on the mountain and invaded their kingdom they were cautious and even irritated, flying about and giving vent to their feelings with that strange and unlovely combination of calls that I had grown to know and love. I think I even understood them. These angels who guarded the mountain said to me, without making a sound, that I was still Martha Morgan, that I was still loved and capable of loving, and that I still had work to do. So as they watched me I got up from the ground, brushed the mud off my cloak, and decided that I might as well enjoy being alive. I thanked them for their kind intervention in my affairs, and peeped over the edge of the bluestone crag down towards the Plas. The old place looked as comfortable and familiar as ever. Will and Gerallt were working in the farmyard and others whom I could not recognize from a distance were harrowing and planting in the fields of Penrhiw, Gelli and Dolrannog. Two small children were running around in the farmyard. I did not recognize them, and thought they might be the grandchildren of Wilmot and Delilah. One of the sheepdogs was barking. Blodwen, thick-set and ungainly in her movements, came out of the dairy and fetched a bucket of water from the big tank fed from the sacred spring of St Brynach. My mind turned to sacred things, and I remembered that this mountain was holy, and deserving of my respect and reverence. It was, after all, my cathedral, and the place where I worshipped, as others worshipped in the cathedrals of St David's, and Canterbury, and Salisbury. And at the heart of my cathedral, I had my cave, used long ago by St Brynach, its location known only by one person now living -- namely my alter ego, Mistress Martha Morgan of Plas Ingli.

The cave! That was where the body of my beloved Amos Jones, saint and preacher, had been laid to rest, with its entrance then sealed by a great boulder. And the earthquake! What might that have done to the cave? Might it now be open to the elements, allowing the rats and the foxes to consume his body as they had consumed the body of Moses Lloyd? In a brief panic I looked around me and saw that the mountain summit had been rearranged, exactly as mentioned in *The Cambrian* and as described by my friends. Some of the summit crags had split open, and there were boulders and sharp-edged stones lying around on the grass which had previously been clean and unsullied. Those were, I supposed, the boulders reputed to have damaged the body and the face of the corpse collected from the summit by Will and the others early on that fateful Sunday morning when Martha died and Susanna was born. So I climbed down on the southern side of the summit, to discover that everything had changed. The gaps between the rocks, the little ledges and gullies which had previously led me to the cave on innumerable occasions were no longer there, having been replaced by a topography that was entirely new. Systematically I searched back and forth, hopping from one large stone to another. I discovered that at the age of 76 I was not as agile as I used to be, and that was a cause of some mild irritation. My joints ached, and my balance was not as good as it had been. Several times I had to haul myself up from one rock to another, like an intrepid mountaineer. That was painful, with rheumatism in my fingers. Three times I sent boulders -- which were precariously balanced after the earthquake -- crashing down into deep crevasses. Once I thought I should crash down too, and had to stop to recover my composure and to ensure that the noise created by my misadventure had not carried down the hill to the Plas. I pressed on, and at last I found the site of the cave. It was no longer there, and it appeared that it had collapsed, sealing the wasted body of Amos into the warm and solid body of the mountain. The entrance boulder was still there, recognizable in shape and colour but tipped onto its side.

Nearby there was a fearsome chasm, newly opened up. I peered into its depths, and could just make out a pile of stones. This must be the place, I thought, where those small boys had found the bones of Moses Lloyd and the few possessions that had given the clues as to his death. Surprisingly, I was unmoved by this discovery, and felt that my memories of that fearsome episode on the mountain when I was but a slip of a girl, and even the recent events connected with the inquest, were now consigned to the dust-heap of history. They would trouble me no more.

As the sun slipped down towards Pen Dinas I walked back to Carn Edward, removed my Nightwalker disguise, and struggled back into my bothersome petticoats and widow's weeds. Then, transformed into Mrs Ravenhill, with my black bonnet and crepe veil in position, I continued to Bedd Morris and the waiting chaise. The driver was fast asleep in the rays of the setting sun, and his pony was grazing contentedly at the side of the road. "Any passers-by, Bobby?" I asked. "Not one, Mrs Ravenhill," said he. "Never have I seen such a lonely place, to be sure. But it has been very pleasant in the sunshine, and I always enjoys being paid for doing nothing. And your visit to those people? Successful and interesting, I dare say?"

"Very pleasant indeed, thank you, Bobby. All was well, and it was good to see them again."

By dusk we were back at Cardigan Bridge, where I paid Bobby his dues and thanked him for his services before walking back to my lodgings. Later on, over my well-deserved supper, I felt a sort of satisfaction that I had renewed my contract with the place which truly has possession of my heart. I also knew that I could now leave the Plas and the mountain behind me and make a new life elsewhere.

My complacency was upset when young Merlin poked his head round the door and said "Evenin' Missis. Nice day in the country?"

"Whatever to you mean, Merlin? I do not admit to being anywhere other than in Cardigan."

"Indeed, Missis? Then why the mud on the hem of your skirt, and the shoes with sheep-shit on them, and why the bits of heather caught up in your wicker basket? That means you've been up a mountain, if I am not mistook. And Charlie is not best pleased that you gave him the slip, so I hear. You must be more careful, Missis, if you are to keep out of trouble." He wagged his finger at me and disappeared down the stairs.

I had been careless, and I repented over my pudding. In fact I had been very careless indeed, for earlier on in the day I had also been seen upon the mountain by several sharp-eyed people, including a man who was to become a formidable and implacable enemy.

5. Tactical Retreat

Next day my old joints protested violently against that long walk on the mountain, and particularly against all the clambering I had done amongst the craggy rocks. So I decided to wait quietly in my lodgings until the time came for me to be collected and moved on to some safer place. There was a change in the weather too, and as the wind swung round to the east and the temperature plunged down towards freezing, I knew that snow was on the way. The daffodils would be buried by nightfall, I thought.

As the day wore on, I quietly assembled my meagre belongings so that I could leave quickly when my carriage arrived. I peeped out from behind my curtains occasionally, and saw that Iago was on station as usual, dressed once again in his own attire but with an undistinguished floppy felt hat upon his head. But then I was greatly surprised when he was joined by another man , and after what appeared to be a short altercation the two of them disappeared. After lunch I noticed this new man wandering up and down the street, making his presence much more obvious than his predecessor had done. He was also dressed in a full-length black coat, and he had a fine leather hat on his head, identical to that which was now in the possession of young Merlin. Messrs LeClerc de Paris had clearly done a tidy trade in leather hats, I thought. Maybe they were specially designed for spies belonging to some sinister organization.......?

I was disturbed in my reverie by footsteps on the stairs. I knew that they belonged to Merlin. He knocked at my door -- five times in quick succession, followed by two further knocks with a longer interval. "Shemi's knock," I thought. "Is there nothing that this child does not observe?" I invited him to enter, and thought of reprimanding him for being so presumptuous and provocative, but when I saw his grinning freckled face I had to forgive all his sins. "Hot news, Missis," he said. "Iago's gone -- on the coach back to Fishguard. Him and another fellow had a big row in the Rose and Crown, and he's in trouble 'cause you gave him the slip yesterday. The other fellow's name is Silas Reynolds -- he's the one Iago has been writin' letters to in Fishguard. He's now booked in to the same lodgins on the Mwldan that Iago was in. And by the way, like

Iago this new one is armed to the teeth -- a pair of pistols and a big knife."

I groaned. "Oh no! Do they know where I was yesterday, Merlin?"

"That I couldn't say, Missis. But I knows, of course."

"You are very impertinent, Merlin. And how do you know?"

He broke into his infectious grin again. "A very easy matter, Missis," said he. "I have noticed that you likes to be anonymous, with that veil over your face all the time, and black clothes and all that. So I thought that if you wanted to go anywhere out of town, you would hire a covered chaise, from somewhere down by the river. My mate Afan saw you down there yesterday mornin', carryin' a basket and a parcel. There's only two fellows down near the quay with covered chaises. One is Rufus Williams and the other is Bobby Reed. I asked Rufus and it wasn't him. So I asked Bobby, and he told me all about your nice trip to that mountain near Newport."

"Merlin, you know too much."

"It's not me you need to worry about, Missis. It's them other fellows with guns who are after you. By the way, the letters that Iago sent to London were for a Jonas Harry in South Kensington. A friend, Missis?"

"I have never heard of him, Merlin. There was a Harry family in Newport, and they were all merchants with pretensions. Not very nice people, and all dead now. I suppose he might be a relative."

"I see that you are about to leave, Missis."

"Oh, and what leads you to that conclusion?"

"Your bag is on the bed. People always puts their bags on the bed when they are about to leave."

I looked at him, and realized that this strange child with the freckled face and the tousled hair was insinuating himself into my heart. I could not lie to him. "Yes, Merlin. I expect to be collected this evening, when that fellow outside is off duty."

"It's just as well, Missis. They are gettin' too close for comfort, and Silas Reynolds may not be as cautious as Iago was. Then there's that other fellow too. He's still around -- God knows what he's up to."

It dawned on me that I was going to be lonely without this cheeky child who lived in the cellar. So I stood up and opened my arms to him, and he ran into my embrace. I had tears in my eyes. "I shall miss you, Merlin," I whispered into his fair hair.

"I'll miss you too, Missis. You are like a sort of special old aunty, and that feels good. But we'll meet again, and before very long. I knows it. Just you take care now. You have a job to do."

"Oh indeed?" I stepped back from him, held his hands in mine and looked into his clear blue eyes. "And what might that be?"

"Somethin' to do with that mountain you visited yesterday, Missis. And watch out for a funny old castle, too."

At dusk I was on my way from Cardigan to an unknown destination, having said my farewells to Mrs Ifans and Merlin and having made a more than ample contribution to the family budget with a request that it should be used for Merlin's education. Mrs Ifans had agreed to that, and promised that she would hire a special tutor in the light of the boy's extraordinary intelligence. I travelled in Wilmot's carriage, with a driver and one other servant in attendance outside, and inside in the company of Wilmot himself, Shemi and Betsi. The four of us cuddled up and tried to keep warm. The two fellows in the driving seat must have been bitterly cold, in spite of their heavy coats, coachmen's hats and thick scarves. We saw no sunset as we travelled, since the sky was the colour of lead and since there were flurries of snow in the air. Wilmot would not at first tell me where we were heading, but I realized that we were still north of the River Teifi, on the Carmarthen road. "Surely we are not going to Carmarthen, Wilmot?" I asked. "With darkness coming on, and a blizzard too, if I am not very much mistaken, we may not get much further than Newcastle Emlyn."

"Then we had better stop there, Mrs Ravenhill!" said Wilmot. "I think we can decide upon that, since there is no chance that we will be followed on such a night. I have had three alternative plans. But Newcastle Emlyn it must be -- a small and friendly town, far enough from Newport to keep you out of trouble."

"Trouble, Wilmot? I specialize in keeping out of trouble."

"Then why, my dear Mrs Ravenhill, did you make an expedition to Carningli yesterday?" asked Shemi, with a grin on his face.

"How did you know that, Shemi?"

"Daisy, who was walking up to the Plas during the afternoon, saw the Nightwalker on the summit and on the southern slopes among the rocks. When I called later on, she told me about it. That particular phantom has not been seen for thirty years or more. Daisy recalls seeing it as a child, and hearing tales about it."

"I remember it too," said Betsi. "My mother was very scared of it, and thought it must be the devil, come to take Brynach away from her."

"Quite so," said Shemi. "When Daisy reported her observations to me, Susanna, I knew immediately that it was you, since you would not be able to resist another visit to the mountain before being whisked off to foreign parts. I didn't think you would risk such an enterprise so soon after your illness, but it seems that you are a very determined lady......."

"Can we please talk about other things?" I asked. "I want to know about the *gwylnos* and the funeral. Rose and Myfanwy told me about the two inquests, but I am in the dark as to what followed."

So between them, Wilmot, Betsi and Shemi told me, as we travelled in the gathering gloom, what had transpired. The *gwylnos*, they said, had gone off smoothly after the release of the coffin for burial. Will, George, Gerallt and several other men had kept watch over it, as they had done since it was filled with stones. My sister Catrin had travelled over from Castlebythe with her husband James, and they had stayed at the Plas, together with my sister-in-law Nansi from Haverfordwest, who was very frail and distressed. My dear friend Mary Jane also came and stayed at the Plas -- and by all accounts she was very calm and supportive, helping out about the place in spite of the fact that she was also decrepit in her old age. She had remarked upon the fact that the atmosphere in the Plas was serene and even good-humoured, and not at all as sombre and dark as she had expected. Betsi and the others had explained that the long delay between Martha's death and the funeral had allowed family and servants to do their grieving in peace, and to move on. In any case, they said, Martha had had a good death, and was it not more appropriate in the circumstances to cele-brate her life rather than mourn her death over and again with every pass-ing day? The visitors, of whom there were hundreds, were given a similar explanation of the remarkable state of equilibrium which prevailed within the Plas, and by all accounts they accepted that with good grace, paid their last respects to the coffin, and then enjoyed the abundant refreshments which our remarkable Bessie had organized, with Wilmot's unstinting help. He, after all, was the real owner and Master of Plas Ingli, and after the passing of Mistress Martha it was he who was responsible for all the decisions beneath its roof, and all of its expenditures.

I asked about the attendance of various friends and acquaintances, and was gratified to learn that they had all been to pay their last respects either at the *gwylnos* or on some earlier occasion. "And the *gwylnos* itself, in the dining room and kitchen? Good-humoured and convivial, I hope?

"Oh yes!" said Wilmot. "The best anybody could remember. The feast was truly remarkable, coming at the end of a long hard winter. Bessie, Blodwen and Myfanwy performed miracles. And the singing! Never heard better! We got through six barrels of ale, and apparently the noise at the Plas could be heard over the hill in Brynberian!"

"Humph! Spare me the details."

"Oh, we gave your apologies, Susanna," grinned Shemi.

"Whatever do you mean?" I asked sharply.

"We announced the apologies of many absent friends who had written or sent condolences through others. Among those missing, we mentioned Brynach, David, and William in America, of course, for they were sorely missed -- and probably not yet even in possession of the sad news. We dropped in a mention of a certain Mrs Susanna Ravenhill, a distant relative who was currently indisposed but who hoped to visit and pay her respects on some future occasion. Nobody batted an eyelid -- not even Catrin, the only one who might know distant relatives on your side of the family. But she is getting very whimsical and forgetful in her old age."

"Thank God for that," said I. "The last thing I want just now is a sister with a mind as sharp as a new-stropped razor."

They told me about the funeral. It had been the biggest seen in Cilgwyn for many a long year. All of the immediate family, children and spouses were there, together with the grandchildren and great-grandchildren, cousins and second cousins and their families, tenants and their families, and labourers from far and wide who had worked at the Plas or helped with the harvests over the years. Then there were squires and their wives from far and wide, people with whom the Plas had done business over the years, the Mayor and the freemen of the town, the members of the Court Leet, and most of the local shopkeepers and merchants. It was notable, said Betsi, that many of those who had been my enemies over the years had also turned out -- which might be taken as a sign of reconciliation or opportunism, depending on how cynical one might be. Even the Lord Marcher, Sir Mervyn Lloyd, had turned out, in spite of the fact that I had done little in my lifetime to curry favour with him and had even caused him a great deal of trouble at various times. The funeral procession was three hundred yards long, said Wilmot, his eyes glowing with admiration. "If my funeral procession is half as long as that," he said, "I will be well pleased, for that would signify true acceptance by the community."

My eyes were moist with tears, but I wanted to hear it all so that I could put it behind me. Wilmot described the funeral at Cilgwyn Church, held with the doors and the windows open because only about a quarter of those present could be accommodated inside. He said that so large was the party of chief mourners (the Morganses of Plas Ingli and many other places besides) that there was a scramble for the remaining seats in the church; and it was more by luck than judgment that the Lord Marcher and his lady, and the Mayor and his lady were accommodated. On a fine afternoon, said Wilmot, there was lusty singing which, on account of the great numbers collected outside beneath the trees and in the open, echoed around the *cwm* in a fashion that was very moving for all who experienced it. The eulogy from Rector Llewelyn Thomas was as generous as could be, containing many references to Mistress Martha's espousal of good causes, her assistance readily given to the paupers and other poor people of the parish, and her famous hospitality at the Plas which had left many in the day's congregation with full bellies and sore heads. There were some oblique references to Martha's brushes with the law and her conflicts with assorted squires which had led several of them to the gallows, and there was a rather too direct reference to her fall from grace in the company of the reverend gentleman called Amos Jones. "But all in all, with all things considered," the Rector had concluded, "the life of Mistress Martha was a life lived to the full, and it must be said that her eccentricities and her occasional errors of judgement were greatly outweighed by her beauty, her zest for life, and her compassion. She ran her estate with truly amazing skill and delicacy. She was a strong, passionate woman, and the Newport and Cilgwyn that we know today are kinder, and gentler, and more honest places than they were before she arrived in our midst. We thank God for the gift of her life, and as we lay her to rest alongside her beloved husband David in the Morgan family tomb, we celebrate her life and rejoice that she is now with her angels."

By the end of this narrative I had been reduced to a quivering wreck, and I could not hold back my tears for another moment. So I sobbed uncontrollably as Betsi put her arms around me and as the coach bumped its way in the darkness towards Cenarth, very slowly indeed. At last I was able to exert a measure of control over my emotions, and after wiping my cheeks and blowing my nose I said: "I'm sorry, dear friends. That was too much for me. I am humbled, and know not what to say........."

"Say nothing, Mother," said Betsi, forgetting that she was supposed to call me Susanna. "No further words are needed, but now you know -- if you did not know it before -- of the love and esteem which you have earned in the community. That's the end of the story. The interment went ahead without further ado. There were emotional scenes at the graveside which we will not go into. And then another catering triumph from Bessie back at the Plas." She grinned, and if it had not been so dim in the carriage I would have seen the twinkle in her eye as she added: "Of course, most of those who came to the funeral were there so as to avoid a good day's work and so as to enjoy the Plas Ingli refreshments!"

"True, true," intoned Wilmot, sounding like a pontificating pastor. Then I realized that he was teasing me, and the tension was released as all four of us roared with laughter.

When we arrived in Newcastle Emlyn the snow, which had been threatening us for the whole journey, was becoming a real problem for our horses and our driver, for the feeble candle lanterns fixed to the sides of the coach were not capable of penetrating the swirling whiteness in which we were enveloped. Even with the assistance of a lantern-carrying servant on foot ahead of the coach, our progress had slowed to a snail's pace. One of the horses hated snow, and was very difficult to control. So we were relieved to arrive safely at the Emlyn Arms, where Wilmot made the decision that we must all stay for the night. The inn was an old-fashioned place with draughty corridors, creaking stairs and low ceilings, and because of the ominous weather we were the only travellers there; but the landlord made us all welcome, and with roaring log fires in all the rooms we were cosy enough as the blizzard caught up with us and raged about outside like a beast that was not allowed to enter. We were given a good supper in a large room which served as public bar and dining room combined, and since there were a few local fellows downing their ales around the fireplace and flapping their ears, we had to be very careful in our conversation. We also had to assume that the two young girls who served us discreetly and politely had big ears and loose tongues. But the situation gave us a good opportunity to do a little play-acting, and to the credit of my fellow conspirators I was always referred to as Susanna.

We had no opportunity to talk about the fact that I was being followed by three different men during my time in Cardigan, but since I later shared a room with Betsi I was able to tell her all about the episodes involving Iago Woodward and Silas Reynolds. I told her of the break-in and the chaos caused in my room by an unknown intruder. I also told her of my suspicions that somebody called Jonas Harry might be behind the spying activity, and of my fears that I might be apprehended at any moment. Betsi became desperately worried at this news, and promised to pass all the details on to Wilmot and Shemi on the way home. "I hope to God that they have not tracked you here, Mother," she said. "Like you, I can only assume that their intentions are to reveal your true identity, and that they might be armed constables from some special law enforcing unit. In that respect, they might see their objectives as honourable, and designed to uphold the law. So I doubt that they would actually hurt you. On the other hand......."

"They might take me at gun-point into custody for interrogation? I have thought of that myself."

"That's a possibility. But I was about to say that they may be criminals who specialize in blackmail. If they know -- or even suspect -- your true identity they may use violence, kidnap you, hold you prisoner somewhere and then seek to blackmail all of us who are part of the conspiracy."

I groaned and buried my face in my hands. "Oh my God!" I said. "That would be a truly appalling scenario, Betsi. And I am sensible enough to know that the blackmailing would not affect the likes of Bessie, Shemi and even Brendan, since they have no money. The ones who would be assailed with demands for money would be you and Ioan, Daisy and her husband George Havard, Skiff Abraham and especially Wilmot and Delilah, since you are the ones who have resources and reputations."

"True, Mother. But now we are all into this pit too deeply to climb out smelling of roses. God knows that I have wanted to be out of it several times, when I have been awake in the dark hours of the night, staring at the black ceiling. But in the light of day Daisy, whose resolve is as solid as the mountain, has pulled me back in each time. So now we will just have to keep you two steps ahead of the people who are trying to find you, and preferably far away from the Plas and Carningli. Rest assured that we will all do what we can."

Next morning, the blizzard had passed through and we woke to find a dazzling snow-covered landscape with a cloudless sky and a blazing sun. Such is the way with March blizzards. By the time we had finished breakfast, the snow had turned to slush, and the roads were becoming passable again. In the company of Wilmot (who had organized matters in advance) I walked to one of the back streets and settled into the lodging house of Mrs Lizzie Elkins. She had only one room, and it was reserved for me, Mrs Susanna Ravenhill, a lady from London intent on doing some local studies into the family origins of herself and her late husband. Then Wilmot and the others were gone in their carriage, splashing along on the rutted road to Boncath and Newport, and leaving me on my own once more.

Two days later Mrs Elkins brought me a copy of the last *Carmarthen Times* with my breakfast. It contained an obituary and a report of my own funeral. There were full details of the chief mourners and other notable persons who had turned out, and a report of the eulogy from the Rector. The remarkable constraint shown by certain members of the family was remarked upon -- with obvious admiration. Then I turned over a few pages, idly scanning the news of events great and small, and came across a report which reminded me that even if Martha Morgan was dead, the consequences of her actions in the last weeks of her life were still making the news. The report said that the Spring Assizes had started in Haverfordwest , with Squire Dafydd Laugharne and Squire Thomas Watkins charged with the murders of Master Elijah Collins and Rev Amos Jones. The report continued: *The trial is expected to last two days. This is a most exceptional case which is attracting interest throughout the land. First, it is most unusual for a single member of the gentry, let alone two, to face the hangman's noose. Second, it is believed that Master Collins died almost ten years since, and that the crime which caused his untimely death was discovered only after painstaking work by the authorities, using the most modern scientific methods. And third, it is a most appalling thing, and indeed a mark of these lawless times, that the other victim should have been a respected minister of religion, strung up by the neck and left to die in a dark and lonely wood in the vicinity of Newport. It is believed that the accused squires were active in the Society of Sea Serjeants, which was reputed to have wielded great influence in the town of Newport some years since; and it is further believed by our very reliable sources in that district that the two victims were vehemently opposed to the activities of that shadowy and evil organization. The brutality of the men responsible for the two murders is hardly to be credited, especially since the accused are both magistrates and substantial landowners. They are therefore supposedly gentlemen, brought up to behave with sensibility and due respect for the law, for the Church, and for their fellow men. If these men are guilty of the heinous crimes with which they are charged (and far be it from us to suggest that they are, until justice is done) what chance is there that those less fortunate in their circumstances, and lacking in education, finance and manners, will henceforth respect the law and live according to the precepts of our Lord?*

I was almost petrified when I read these words, and I knew that Wilmot, Shemi, Henry and many others would have to give evidence at the trial, which would probably leave them all exhausted. There was but one compensation -- the trial would certainly be the big talking point across West Wales for days and maybe weeks to come, therefore making it less likely that my own conspiracy would be uncovered.

Over the course of the day I could think of nothing but the trial of Watkins and Laugharne, and I relived the horrors of the days surrounding the death of my dear and virtuous friend Amos. As I walked the streets of the town and tried to enjoy the sunshine as it reasserted its control after the spring blizzard, an image of Amos and his torturers was fixed stubbornly in my head. He had truly been too good a man to die -- but he had also been too good, from the viewpoint of those who were evil, to be allowed to live. So he had been slaughtered without mercy, having diverted attention onto himself in order to save me. I started to think again about the Society of Sea Serjeants -- an organization built upon extortion, brutality and intimidation which had members in Ireland and Wales and which had, at one time, virtually ruled Newport. I had thought that all the members had been accounted for; but perhaps some of them were still out there, in the merchant houses and on the estates of the district, skulking in the shadows, intent upon continuing their activities and obtaining revenge upon the Morgans of Plas Ingli, who had brought them to their knees? I knew that they had spies and sympathizers everywhere -- had they somehow obtained information about my survival, and might they be behind some plan to blackmail Wilmot, George, Skiff and others? That would be a much more vicious and carefully planned campaign, I knew, than one organized by one or two opportunists.

One name kept on coming back into my head -- Jonas Harry. He might be in London, and he might be controlling the likes of Iago Woodward and Silas Reynolds, but surely -- inevitably -- he had to be related to Jacob Harry of Newport who had been a key member of the Society of Sea Serjeants and who had been lynched in Ireland last year? Might this new Harry be carrying on an ancient family feud, or seeking revenge for the death of his relative? If so, he could be a dangerous man indeed.

Later in the week, when my mood had lightened somewhat and when I had become familiar with the streets of my new home town, Rose arrived on the mail coach, intent upon staying for two days. Mrs Elkins put an extra bed for her into my room. I was delighted to see the sweet girl, and we spent many hours out on the streets and in the lodgings in animated conversation. She carried with her much news and gossip, which I was delighted to hear. I felt somewhat more relaxed than hitherto, having seen no sign of spies and having observed no undue interest from the good people of the town in my credentials or my history.

Rose told me that Wilkins Legal had called at the Plas a couple of days earlier and had summoned all of the family to attend -- for the reading of my will. I recalled that it was a very small and simple document, since Plas Ingli and the old estate, and several of its farms, were now in the possession of my friend Wilmot Gwynne, having passed out of the family a decade or so earlier. I had remained -- in name only -- as Mistress of the Plas Ingli estate only because of the generosity of Wilmot, who saw it as a capital asset and who was not minded to manage it himself. My worldly assets consisted of a small sum of money in the Black Ox bank, another small sum in a box under the bed, and some clothes and items within the house. According to Rose, Master Wilkins had quietly and efficiently arranged for the disbursement of £250 each to Betsi, Brynach and Daisy and £50 to my grandchildren according to my wishes, and also for the distribution of my personal effects -- furniture, jewellery, silver cutlery, china, clothes and hats, again as specified. I should not have been surprised by the news of the reading of the will, but I found it a profoundly depressing experience, probably because it marked the severance of the last link between my old life and the one which I had now chosen for myself. My clothes, given away, and now being worn by servants or poor people in the town........ my beautiful German china set, handed down by my paternal grandfather to my father, and given to me and David as a wedding present, and now in Betsi's home instead.... my writing desk, used for the writing of my diaries and my letters over a period of more than 50 years, now removed to the house of George and Daisy in town..... my library of books, greatly loved, now scattered to the four corners of the earth.......

"More tears, Susanna?" said Rose, with her arms around me.

"Are you surprised, Rose? The last slender thread between me and the Plas has just been cut by a blunt instrument."

Then, with my head upon Rose's shoulder, I saw through my tears that she was wearing my favourite pearl necklace, which I had bequeathed to her in my will. Rose had been waiting for me to react, and she smiled as only an angel can smile. She said: "I wondered how long it would take you to notice!" and without another word, in a touching and beautiful gesture, she took it off and fastened it round my neck. That caused me to break down and hang onto my grand-daughter like a small child in distress. She made light of it, but when I was on my own, a little later in the day, I experienced a cold terror as I realized how much weeping I had done since the day of my reported death. I felt that I had lost not just my identity and my history, but also my family and possessions, and my fighting spirit. I felt that I was a nobody, destined to drift through what might remain of my life with no clear purpose, no opportunities for pleasure, and no freedom to express myself as I might wish, either through my clothes or my conversation or my activities. Money was not a problem, since Wilmot and Betsi and the family had promised that I would want for nothing, but where could I go, and what could I do, if I was being hunted down by men who wanted to bring down some sort of retribution for my sins upon my head and upon the heads of my nearest and dearest?

I resolved to make the most of the rest of Rose's stay, and she was very protective and very understanding of my precarious state of mind. We walked arm in arm round the streets and along the river beneath the ramparts of the castle, reinforcing our strong and mysterious bond which had existed between us ever since she had been a little girl without a mother. Although I was still dressed in mourning clothes and kept my wretched crepe veil over my face, we contrived to laugh a good deal. That was something which I needed. Then, on the very morning of her departure, she told me very quietly over breakfast that she had had a powerful premonition of a threat greater than anything previously to have been encountered in the neighbourhood of Newport and Cilgwyn. I pressed her -- who or what was threatened? Family or friends? Rose said that in her vision she only saw the mountain -- so she assumed that everybody and everything in the district was under threat.

"Disease? Famine? Some great natural disaster for which God will get the blame? And will all be well, Rose?"

"It will," she nodded. "At great cost -- but I saw no loss of life."

That gave me some reassurance, since news came through in the afternoon, after Rose's departure, that in the Spring Assizes Laugharne and Watkins had been found guilty of two murders and had been sentenced to death. I knew that was inevitable, and that their crimes and the punishment to come were a consequence of their own wickedness. I knew that they would not get the Queen's Mercy. But I still felt responsible in some measure for sending another two men to the gallows, to add to an already long list, and that did nothing to improve my spirits. With Rose gone, I was alone again, and desperately lonely.

I was confined to my lodgings by another spell of bad weather as the month came to a close, but then the sun came out again, and I ventured out. I spent the next few days giving cock and bull stories about the life history of Mrs Susanna Ravenhill to the people whom I met, and I started to feel more comfortable with my new identity. I indulged in some experiments relating to a change in my personality as well -- pretending on one day to be absent-minded and vague, and on another to be short-tempered and thoroughly unpleasant. But I found that very difficult, and decided that I would be better off, in establishing new relationships, by behaving more or less as I had always behaved to others. Play acting can only be taken so far. Surreptitiously, when Mrs Elkins was out for a whole day, I renewed the brown dye on my hair, since I had noticed that the old dye was wearing thin. I visited churchyards, claiming that I was hunting for the graves of my relatives. That was a very fascinating occupation, for graveyards are full of poignant information about livelihoods and diseases, not to mention poetic epitaphs. The people whom I met while I was out and about were almost too kind, and kept on interfering. I was mildly irritated, since they all wanted to help me to recover from the loss of my dear husband Jack and to trace my long-lost relatives. One old gentleman, who thought of himself as an expert on all the local family histories, even interrogated me at great length, in order to help me the better. That kept me on my toes, and kept me alert, but I had to cover my confusion on occasion with the excuse that my memory was failing..

Then came a bombshell. Somebody (possibly the old gentleman) put a notice in *The Cambrian* on 26th March, to the effect that *"A warm welcome is extended to Mrs Susanna Ravenhill from London, who has come to the district for a short visit in spite of the inclement winter weather with a view to discovering more about the antecedents of her late husband Jack. She will no doubt be delighted to receive news at her lodgings, 15 Porth-y-Castell, from any person who may be able to help her in her researches."* The notice was shown to me by Mrs Elkins, who commented on the kindness and sensitivity of local people, and their instinct for helping others. I swallowed hard and nodded "Yes indeed, Mrs Elkins. I am touched by such concern for my welfare." But in reality I was horrified and furious, and I became convinced that I would now receive visits from constables, busybodies and probably my enemies too.

On the very next day, on a quiet Sunday morning, I peeped from behind my lace curtains, as I had become accustomed to doing, and saw a tall man in a well-cut three-quarter length coat across the street. My eyes were not as sharp as they had been in my prime, but I did not think I recognized him. I was quite sure that the man was not Iago Woodward or

Silas Reynolds. But I was very scared. I spent the day indoors, in a state of very deep gloom and introspection, and I knew that even if I was not arrested or abducted I could not continue to live like this, fearing every shadow and every unusual sound, looking over my shoulder every time I went out, and peeping obsessively from behind my curtains every half hour to see if I was being spied upon. I thought that I was being given a new life when I woke up on the kitchen table of the Plas after my night on the mountain. In my more miserable moments thereafter I had thought that I might have to put up with a sort of purgatory for a while, but this was far, far worse than the purgatory imagined by the Catholics. I was now living in a black hell, and I cared not whether it was created by paranoia or by a real and imminent threat. I was terrified that I might spiral down into a state of despair as deep and long-lasting as that which I experienced as a young woman after the loss of my first baby. So, gripped by a cold fear, I sat down and penned the following letter, three times:

15 Porth-y-Castell, Newcastle Emlyn, 27th day of March 1855
Mrs Ravenhill, late of London, will be grateful if Master and Mistress Rhys of Brithdir, Doctor and Mrs Havard of Newport, and Master and Mistress Gwynne of Plas Llanychaer will attend at the Emlyn Arms in Newcastle Emlyn on Friday 1st April at 12 noon for a conference to discuss MOST URGENT matters.
With kindest regards. Susanna Ravenhill (Mrs)

Mrs Elkins posted it off next morning to the three addresses, and I resigned myself to being a prisoner in my lodgings for four days until my dear friends arrived. I did not even dare to think that they would not come, or that my letters might go astray. On the next day I fear that my melancholy mood was perfectly obvious to Mrs Elkins, who encouraged me to "talk things through, and not keep them all bottled up." That was the last thing I wanted to do, and I kept the lid on the bottle. Not for the first time, I started to think of the means by which I might end my life.

On the 29th day of March there was a knock on the outside door, and Mrs Elkins came up to my room. "There is a gentleman here to see you, Ma'am," she said. "He has a uniform on, and says he is here on official business. He refuses to go away, and he has a warrant. Shall I let him in?"

6. A Tightening Net

Mrs Elkins stood silently, waiting for my reply. I was terrified, but in truth I had no option but to allow the man to come up to my room. He turned out to be a short red-faced man dressed in a police uniform made for somebody several sizes smaller.

"Mistress Ravenhill? Yes?"

I stood and gave a little curtsey. Then I did my best to look as tall and elegant as a Dowager Duchess, and my terror was alleviated somewhat when I noticed that the constable looked very nervous indeed. I could have reduced his nervousness by inviting him to speak in Welsh, but I chose not to, since a conversation in English would allow me to retain a degree of superiority.

"Delighted to make your acquaintance, Madam," said he, in English. "Sergeant Dafydd Gruffydd of the Cardiganshire Constabulary." As he spoke he shuffled about like a man who had just sat upon an ant-hill, and he cleared his throat frequently. "I am here, you understand, Madam, at the request and instruction of -- ahem -- Squire Edward Lewis, who is the most senior and the least junior magistrate in these parts. You know of him, I dare say?"

"I do not have that pleasure, sir. What can I do for you?"

"Well, Madam, if it do not cause you too much inconvenience or discomfort, I am here -- ahem --to make certain enquiries about you -- without, you understand, prying too deeply into your circumstances and conditions, which must understandably remain private and non-public, if you do see my meaning."

"I am not sure that I do, Sergeant. What do you want to know?"

"If I may make so bold, Madam, without prying too deeply, and putting things in the most delicate and indeed sensitive way possible, it would be helpful to me if you would be so kind as to tell me, without of course divulging or passing on anything of a private or confidential nature, just a little bit about your -- ahem -- connections and antecedents."

"I fully understand, Sergeant. I am puzzled, sir, because I thought that we lived in a free country, in which law-abiding folk might travel about the countryside without let or hindrance, and without being interrogated by the forces of law and order."

Sergeant Gruffydd became very discomfited and looked at his boots for a minute or so, while being very uncertain what to do with his hands. "Quite so, Madam. You are quite correct, and far be it from me to impose upon you or indeed burden you in a manner which might be offensive to you or which might cause you to think that I do overstep the mark; but the Squire asked me, in the most diplomatic and gentlemanly fashion, you understand, to undertake a gentle investigation as to your conditions and circumstances............"

"Your delicacy does you credit, Sergeant, as does your mastery of the English language. Let me assure you that my circumstances are perfectly healthy, and that I will not cause a charge upon the Poor Rate by staying for a little while in your community. Indeed, I might even contribute a little to the local economy."

"You are very kind, Madam, and I am glad to hear it. But it is incumbent upon me, in the course of my duty, which I do seek to fulfill to the best of my humble ability, to suggest to you, Madam, without causing offence, you understand, that it is the carefully considered view of the Squire, who feels his magisterial responsibilities most keenly, that you may not in actual fact be what you seem to be."

"Whatever do you mean, Sergeant? It seems to me that you have made, in a roundabout sort of way, a most serious accusation. I am already in mourning, as you might have observed, and now you have compounded my grief. Do you understand that this might be a matter to be reported to my solicitor?"

The sergeant became very agitated. "No no, please, Madam. I beg you not to misconstrue the meaning of what I do say. I have no wish or desire to intrude, encroach or intervene, or to wound your sensitivities. Let me explain........"

"I wish you would, Sergeant. If I could just have it established what this is all about, my damaged sensitivities might be somewhat healed."

"Oh dear. I was supposed to keep this quiet, Madam, but I do suppose I had better tell you, on the grounds that your sensitivities and sensibilities are in need of restoration. Some weeks back an elderly lady was in town, she was, dressed in a most elegant fashion and speaking as a countess or a princess might speak. She stayed in the Black Swan and ran up considerable bills in various respectable and worthy establishments, and then all of a sudden, Madam -- nay, in the blink of an eye -- she entirely disappeared and was gone, owing no less than thirty-five pounds! And nobody knows whereunto she has gone, Madam, be it east, west, north or south. A bad business, Madam, as I'm sure you will agree. A great scandal indeed. So as you will perceive and appreciate, Madam, the Squire is rightly very suspicious -- in a gentlemanly sort of way, you understand -- about fine ladies who turn up in town in the middle of snow-storms and start looking for lost relatives............"

Suddenly I could not resist roaring with laughter. "Oh my goodness, Sergeant! I see it all! And indeed I appreciate the deep sense of duty which resides in the breasts of Squire Lewis and yourself. Very commendable. I congratulate you."

I decided that I might as well now try out my story. "Please sit down, Sergeant," I said. "I feel intimidated when you tower over me like that. Now, let me see if I can put your mind at rest. My name is Mrs Susanna Ravenhill, as I think you know. I have lived in London for the past sixty years. My dear husband Jack died some weeks back, and having no family to sustain me I experienced great difficulties in coming to terms with my new situation............." It was time for a little play-acting, so I took out my kerchief with a great display, and proceeded to wipe my eyes and blow my nose very theatrically. To my intense gratification, the Sergeant was visibly moved.

"Dear Madam, pray do not upset yourself. I do appreciate that the memory of such recent and raw events must be deeply disturbing to you, not to say upsetting. Can I get you a glass of water or some other refreshing or restorative liquid?"

"No no, Sergeant. I will be all right in a moment." After a suitable interval, I continued: "I was left with a modest fortune, and pondered on what to do next. Then I was taken with a great urge to get out of the grime and the smoke of London and to seek to find any relatives of my husband or myself in West Wales, if any of them should still be alive. My husband had relatives in Carmarthenshire and Cardiganshire, and I came originally from the western part of Pembrokeshire. I will not go into the details of my birth, for it is something of which I am not very proud. Do you get my meaning?"

The dear man nodded sympathetically, and I continued. "My father came from a good family not far from St David's. My mother was a servant. I know that I have several half-sisters, Sergeant, but I know not if they will acknowledge me............" Now I was beginning to enjoy this play-acting business, and at this point my voice broke with emotion, causing the Sergeant to look very embarrassed.

"May I share this with you, Sergeant, although it is a most sensitive matter?"

"My lips are sealed, Madam."

"My poor mother was sent away and supported by the man who was my father, but I was denied the security, and the family, which were rightly mine. When I was but a slip of a girl I was swept off my feet by a scoundrel who declared that he loved me and would give me the glamour and wealth that I craved in the great city of London. I was little more than a plaything for him, Sergeant..........."

"A very bad business, Mistress."

"To continue. He abandoned me after two years, and it was my great fortune shortly thereafter to meet my husband Jack. He was much older than I, and he was in business in the city, but he loved me and promised to keep me safe and to provide for me. What was I to do? I was so young, lost in that great city full of thieves and charlatans! Oh, he was a good man, Sergeant, and how I came to love him! We had good times and bad times, sir. We had two children, a little girl and a little boy, but they both died in infancy........"

Once again I wiped my eyes and blew my nose, and rocked back and forth in a paroxysm of grief. At last I looked up and noticed that the Sergeant was sitting transfixed, with tears running down his cheeks. "Please, Sergeant," I pleaded. "You must not upset yourself. Here, borrow my handkerchief."

He wiped his eyes with my handkerchief. "Thank you, Madam. You are very kind."

"That was all a very long time ago, and since then there has been great happiness............"

There was a knock on the door, and Mrs Elkins returned, looking perplexed. "Please excuse me, Madam," she said, "and excuse me, Sergeant Gruffydd, but there is a gentleman down below -- a tall gentleman in a long coat, with a big sort of hat -- who wishes to speak privately with the Sergeant."

"Who, me?"

"Yes, you, sir."

"Well, blow me down! Who can that be? Excuse me, Madam, for just a moment. I will return very shortly, and as soon as maybe."

He went downstairs, and my good humour disappeared at a stroke. After a few minutes he returned.

"Well, Sergeant?" I asked. "Does your friend wish to see me too?"

"No, Madam. He has gone again, and indeed departed. It appears that the rest of your story will not be necessary or essential, and that I shall have to manage without hearing it. A great pity, if I do say so, Madam, since it was a truly appalling and moving narrative on the basis of which I do extend to you my deepest sympathy and condolences. Madam Ravenhill, the gentleman who just called, who was not a gentleman of my earlier acquaintance, and was indeed a stranger to me, presented me with certain credentials and indicated, on the highest authority -- and I do use that term advisedly, Madam -- that my investigations need be pursued no further. I am reassured, and am indeed confident in my reassurance, that you are exactly what you seem to be, as of course I knew from the very beginning and start of things. I do assure you that I had not a shadow of doubt about it, Madam, and that the Squire will be delighted -- and indeed pleased -- to know of it."

"You are a credit to your profession, Sergeant. Please be assured that I have enjoyed our conversation, and give my greetings to the Squire."

"So without further ado or procrastination on my part, dear Madam, I will leave you to get on with the business of the day, and will take my leave and go on my way. Farewell, and good day to you, Madam!"

He bowed, kissed my offered hand, and clattered off down the stairs, leaving me shaking like a leaf. When I had recovered, I tried to find an explanation as to why one of the spies had encouraged Sergeant Gruffydd

-- with some force, it seemed to me -- to terminate our interview. The Sergeant had said he did not know the man, so could he have been a magistrate, or some senior police officer? Was he a gentleman? I was very confused, since young Merlin, in Cardigan, had assured me that Iago and Silas were rough fellows who used language that no squire or magistrate would use. I got nowhere with my deliberations.

On the appointed day, April 1st, my six invited visitors arrived in Wilmot's carriage, just a little late. We all met for lunch in an upstairs room which I had hired in the Emlyn Arms Hotel -- and to which I had made my way by a tortuous route just in case I was being followed. I wanted no serving girls flitting in and out of the room, so once we were all installed, I left strict instructions that I would serve the food myself and that we were not to be disturbed.

It was indeed a mighty relief for me to see them all again, after my wild imaginings and swings of mood of the last week. We exchanged news of no great import for a while, as as we dished out the food. Then I was about to tell them excitedly about the visit of Sergeant Gruffydd when I heard a small sound from the door leading to the back staircase. I motioned to Ioan, at which he crept up, flung the door open and grabbed somebody who was listening outside -- a scruffy urchin of no more then ten years old. Ioan threatened to thrash him, and got the boy to admit that he was a stable lad in the hotel, and that he had been paid ten shillings to eavesdrop on the meeting by a tall gentlemen dressed in a cloak. "And who is he, child?" Ioan hissed.

"Never seen him before, sir, I promise!"

"English or Welsh?"

"Can't say, sir. Neither, I think. He sounded sort of foreign."

Ioan sent him packing, telling him to inform his benefactor, whoever he was, that this was private meeting on family matters that were of no concern to anybody else. "And by the way," he added ominously, "if I hear so much as a fluttering moth or a scuttling mouse within a mile of this room until we are done with our private discussions, my boy, your master will have my report, and so will the constables. And a thrashing will be the least of your problems. Away with you!"

"You know that I have been followed?" I asked miserably. "From the

A Tightening Net

Plas to Cardigan, and thence to Newcastle Emlyn, somehow or other in spite of Wilmot's precautions and the threatening blizzard on that journey. As Rose knows, I have seen the same man on many occasions, and once he had the effrontery to knock on the door of my lodgings and ask to see me. His name is Iago Woodward, and he is not a gentleman. There's another fellow spying on me too, called Silas Reynolds, and quite possibly a third. I think all three are armed. Somebody has betrayed us!"

"No no, Susanna," said Wilmot. "That is impossible. We all love you far too much for that, and we all have too much to lose. Betrayal is out of the question."

"But there always were too many people who know the truth............"

"Twenty-five people can keep a secret just as well as two, Mrs Ravenhill."

"That may be, but with all those people going about their lives and talking to others, there is a heightened chance of a slip of the tongue, or a tight lip loosened by alcohol, or a conversation overheard."

"True, Susanna," said George. "But is it also not possible that the person who has been following you has been protecting your interests, rather than seeking to harm them?"

"If so, he might be so kind as to put me in the picture, instead of doing his best to frighten me out of my wits at frequent intervals...... And by the way, do you know that I have been interviewed by the police?"

"What?" said Betsi, with concern writ large on her face. "Oh my goodness -- what do they know?"

"Very little, I think, apart from my cock and bull story. But I feel like a hunted animal. There are far too many people taking an interest in my whereabouts and my credentials. That's my own fault, I suppose, for hunting for the records of my non-existent relatives and ancestors."

Then I showed them the little item from the *Carmarthen Times*, which I had torn out and kept. Wilmot said "Oh dear, oh dear" and Delilah moaned.

"My dear friends," I continued, "something is afoot, and I am at a loss to know what it is..............."

From this point on, our meeting became a very sombre one -- and although the others sought to put a brave face on things, I sensed that they knew more than they would admit to, which caused me great concern. I bewailed the fact that I had involved so many of my loved ones in my conspiracy, and said I was quite convinced that my secret could not now be kept for much longer. More to the point, I admitted to my dear friends that I still did not know why I had been spared, and that I doubted my own capacity to maintain the pretence of my death for much longer.

Wilmot tried to be cheerful, and reported that the Plas, having now reverted to the Gwynne family with no encumbrances, had to be occupied and used. He said he had installed his second son Joshua as Master of the Plas Ingli estate. He had a hard-working and lovely wife called Jane and two small children aged two and five. They were already in residence, he said. "Yes, I am aware of that, dear Wilmot," I said with what I hoped was an enigmatic smile. Wilmot raised his eyebrows, but did not comment further. He said that he would retain ownership of the estate for the time being. He and Delilah would stay at Llanychaer -- and his eldest son Samson would stay on at Tumble, near Swansea, running the family business in smelting. Gerallt, Myfanwy and Blodwen would remain in employment. Will had agreed to continue as head man at the Plas, he said with delight, although he was getting rather old and stiff, helping the new master who was very naive in farming matters.

"So are we all when we start," I said. "I am sure the old Mistress of the Plas, if she were still alive, would wish them all the very best, and would send them her love."

Betsi and Daisy said that the family all approved of these arrangements, and reported that Bessie had now chosen to retire, and had already moved to lodgings on the Parrog with Patty, where she could spend the rest of her days living in reasonable comfort on her small savings. She had not been well, said Daisy, but she was bearing up and sent her kind regards to Mrs Ravenhill. She was settling in to life by the sea, and promised to write quite soon. I realized then just how much I missed my beloved Bessie -- faithful servant and closest and dearest of friends, with whom I had shared my most intimate thoughts, and discussed my most intractable problems, ever since my arrival at the Plas in 1796. How I longed to walk with her, arm in arm, chatting as we had done on countless occasions over a span of almost 60 years...............

A Tightening Net

But this was no time for reveries, and I had certain decisions to announce. I said that with life returning to normal at the Plas, I now had to force myself to break my emotional ties with the place, and with the mountain. I said that it was now my destiny to seek to spread goodwill and to make recompense for the hurt that I had caused to others during my life.

"Rubbish, Susanna!" said Delilah, who had thus far been very quiet. "You give us a travesty of what you have done down through the years! If only you could have heard the Rector's eulogy at the funeral, and the comments about you from the hundreds who came to the Plas before and during the *gwylnos*, you would be in no doubt at all about your reputation as a kind, loving and generous lady. If you have hurt some -- as do we all -- you have brought balm to many, many more........."

"Thank you, dear Delilah," I replied. "You are, as ever, very kind. But I am not intent on fishing for compliments -- I am too old for that. I must do penance for the crimes which only I know about -- they are my secrets, and will remain so. I have sent too many men to the gallows, and others, like poor Ceredig ap Tomos and my beloved Amos, went to premature graves because of me. Do not, I beg of you, seek to absolve me of my responsibility in those matters. Only God can do that. My sins have been many -- arrogance, pride, deviousness, untruthfulness, and particularly vengeance. The last has been my single greatest sin and is now the greatest cross for me to bear -- and somehow I must learn forgiveness and humility. And I vow that I will never again be the cause of any violence towards any other human being."

"How can you say such a thing, Susanna?" said Daisy. "You do not control the destinies or the passions of others. Any one of us can unwittingly set in motion trains of events which lead to violence. Even Christ caused violence and the deaths of untold thousands in the Crusades, because men twisted his message of love into a message of war and retribution. You are deluded if you think that saintly behaviour by one person makes saints of other people."

"You are right, Daisy. But please allow me to try, for that is what I wish to do."

Then I announced that I would accept no more charity from Wilmot -- I said that he had helped me too much already, since the collapse of the

Plas Ingli estate ten years since. I knew, as we all knew, that times were tough for the small estates -- and I said that he and Delilah had their own family to think of. They protested that looking after me was no more than any friend would do -- but then Betsi and Daisy surprised me -- and Wilmot and Delilah -- by handing me £500 in cash -- the very money handed to them by Wilkins Legal as a result of my will. They insisted that I must take it. I could hardly believe it, and wept while they smiled.

Ioan then admitted to me that my letter dated 27 March had been intercepted and read by somebody else. When it was delivered to Brithdir the seal had been broken and crudely repaired. The delivery boy had claimed, upon being accused of a criminal act, that it was like that when it came into his possession, having previously been handled by two other delivery men en route.

We were all now very worried, and my friends became even more worried when I said that I suspected one Jonas Harry of being behind some campaign to harm me, interrogate me, or abduct me. When I mentioned that name, I noticed that Wilmot and George exchanged the most fleeting of glances. All who were present in the room knew that blackmail could destroy them. So we discussed what I now needed to do. The men agreed that I must go far away, at least for a few months, in order to grow into my new identity and hopefully to throw off my pursuers. The women were less certain, for they knew how lonely I would be. But I assured the family that I would keep them informed of my whereabouts. I said that my letters would always be short and unemotional and would be signed as "Mrs S Ravenhill." We agreed that all letters must be destroyed as soon as they were received and read. My daughters said that I should shortly get out of mourning dress and face the real world without a veil. But, said they, in spite of my having left my old clothes behind at the Plas, I must beware of dressing flamboyantly in bright blue or red, the colours favoured by Mistress Martha. I must keep my hair dyed, and keep it short. Women are too observant, said Daisy, and too suspicious........ and I was pleased that on the occasion of the meeting I had decided not to wear that beautiful pearl necklace recently given back to me by Rose.

Wilmot smiled and said "We are all in this together, my dear Mrs Ravenhill, and we might as well be discreet, and do as little as possible to cause tongues to wag ." He suddenly produced some papers and handed them to me. They referred to a Susanna Ravenhill of Trefach, Swansea. I was mystified, until he explained with a crafty grin upon his face that this was a property which he owned and for which he had made out a fictional "tenancy agreement."

"But so far away, Wilmot? What if I am forced to show this to somebody, and am asked to describe the area where I supposedly live?"

"You will think of something, Susanna. And the risk is much smaller than that involved in giving you an address in Puncheston or Brynberian -- any suspicious fellow who wanted to check on your credentials could do it in half a day, even without a horse or a carriage. And as for Trefach, Swansea, there must be fifty places of that name in my fair town, making it almost impossible for anybody to find the one which you have supposedly taken a lease on. And in view of your great age, Mrs Ravenhill, you are probably pretty unsure of where it is yourself, having just come down from London. Perfect, don't you think? And a very jolly subterfuge!"

He roared with laughter and slapped his knees, as he was wont to do on all jovial occasions. Delilah was as surprised as I, and squealed in her admiration for her husband. Her bosom, already considerable, swelled with pride. "Dearest man," she gushed. "You are truly a genius!"

Wilmot also gave me various documents including recommendations, forged letters from fictional relatives, receipts and invoices from imaginary shops, bank papers and so forth. I was amazed.

"Where on earth did you get all of this material, Wilmot?" I asked, with my eyes wide.

He winked. "I have been in business for a long time, Martha. There are a good many people -- some of them very unsavoury fellows indeed -- who owe me favours...... and our friend Skiff is very helpful too."

That was just the start of it. He had opened a bank account in my name in the Carmarthen branch of the Lewis Bank, and asked for my signature on a bank document. I signed as Mrs S Ravenhill. That made me very worried, since forgery (a capital offence) was thus added to my list of crimes -- but on thinking about it I had no alternative if I was to survive more or less independently out in the wicked world. As Wilmot explained, I had to have a bank account as well as an identity so that I could remit funds and draw upon them as needed. With Wilmot's advice I decided to keep £100 and to bank the other £400 for the time being.

Finally Wilmot produced a pair of heavy horn-rimmed spectacles, very different in appearance from those which I normally used for reading. The lenses were the same as those which I currently used -- and indeed they had been taken from one of the old pairs of spectacles found among my possessions at the Plas. He also handed me another pair of heavy spectacles for use when I was out and about, and advised me to use them.

George insisted on paying for the hire of the room and for the meal. And then my dear friends left me to decide for myself where to go and what to do next. I promised to inform them as soon as decisions had been made. As they climbed back into their carriage Ioan promised, under his breath, that he would investigate and deal with the strange men who had been following me. I thanked him, and wondered how on earth he would find them, let alone deal with them, since he would be in Newport and they would be skulking, in all probability, round the next corner in Newcastle Emlyn. But I begged him, if he should catch up with them somewhere, not to resort to violence against them, and to that, he reluctantly agreed.

When I walked back from the Emlyn Arms to my lodgings, I saw the stable lad running off down a back street, and I knew that I was still being watched and followed by the forces of darkness.

7. The CelestialEmpire

I decided suddenly, without informing anybody else, that I would go to Cardiff to help the poor, and maybe to do some private tuition in order to keep myself alive, if funds should run low. I also thought that I might be able to throw off the armed men who were on my trail.

I remained indoors all day, packing my bag and hoping that I could induce boredom in the men outside. Next morning, before dawn, I paid Mrs Elkins and walked out of town on the Carmarthen road, assuming that spies would not yet be out and about. I enjoyed an early breakfast in the White Hart Inn, which I knew was a stopping point for the early morning stage coach to Carmarthen, and at 8 o'clock I was safely away, in the company of two other passengers. In Carmarthen I took a light lunch and then caught the train to Cardiff, and felt that at long last I could relax.

Cardiff had changed out of all recognition since my last visit, and was now a bustling place crossed by roads and railway lines carrying coal and iron from the pits and great industries to the north down to the docks. The streets were crowded and the shops and inns were busy. I took a room in a little guest house near the docks which was used by respectable people newly arrived in the town, and for some days I wandered about, getting the feel of the place and learning to know some of the locals. I had never seen such a community of all colours and all creeds, and although the air was thick with smoke and poverty, and the smells on the streets did not exactly remind me of a Pembrokeshire springtime clifftop, there was a raw energy about the place which was intoxicating and challenging. I began, in a strange way, to enjoy myself.

I had not forgotten that it was my penance for past sins to help the thousands of poor people who swarmed in the streets; and as the days passed, I gradually discovered which of the local gentry were involved in good works. I met several gallant and high-principled ladies and offered to help them in their endeavours, and they accepted without question my story about bereavement and about my need to do good works among the poor, so as to "give something back" to those on whose sweat-covered backs and bowed shoulders my late husband's fortune had been built.

So for the rest of the month of April most of my daylight hours were spent in the Workhouse and the Prison. Before gaining entry to those places, I needed to prove my credentials, and my forged papers came in very handy. They were truly terrible institutions, filled with the dregs of humanity who had been condemned to lives of misery, hunger and deprivation thanks to either their own shortcomings or the slingshots of fortune. Some of them were unpleasant individuals who had sunk into crimes of the most appalling nature and who were now paying the price that must be paid for evil. Others were incarcerated following mishaps or dreadful miscarriages of justice. My heart went out to them, and while I did my best to minister to their needs, I could not do much to alleviate their distress or to intercede on their behalf with the authorities. I got to know some of them very well indeed, and because I knew Welsh better than most of the other ladies in my little circle, and I suppose because I was older and tougher than they, I found a little niche for myself as a representative of those who had come from the country districts of Wales and who spoke no English. They seemed to find some relief just from talking to me, and relating their tragic tales. I helped in the distribution of food at mealtimes. I ministered to the sick, and rediscovered my aptitude for healing. And I wrote letters for those who could not write, and posted them off to their loved ones in all corners of the globe. I even wrote letters to Africa, and posted them off, on behalf of a little group of negro prisoners in the gaol, although I never was sure that the recipients would be able to read English, or indeed read at all. I used my powers of persuasion to convince various tailors and dressmakers to give me offcuts and old garments, which I turned into passable items of clothing for those who were dressed in filthy rags. Although my hands were giving me a good deal of rheumatic pain, I found that I could still stitch and knit. To my delight I found that I could also still play the harp, and when I found an old instrument in a back room of the Workhouse I obtained permission (after much aggravation) from the Master and the Overseer of the Poor to give little performances for the inhabitants and to bring a little light into the dark corners of that foul place.

All this activity gave me a new lease of life, and was a merciful release for body and soul after the weeks of hiding from thugs in Cardigan and Newcastle Emlyn. I felt younger and healthier, and above all I felt free.

The Celestial Empire

On several occasions I had to suppress the instinct to try and reform this, that and everything; and I did that by reminding myself that any proposals put to the authorities would involve more contacts with magistrates and other notable persons, and more publicity in the press, both of which would bring me unwelcome attention. So I tried to remain anonymous, and found that anonymity was actually quite pleasant. Every night I went to bed exhausted, and slept as only the just can sleep. Sometimes I became over-tired, and decided upon a day reading in my lodgings, or a day down at the Docks, watching the comings and goings of the ships; and on those occasions I simply sent messages to my fellow charitable workers to say that I would not be on duty again until such and such a date. They were perfectly accommodating, since in any case we worked to no fixed schedules, and I put in many more days of work than they. On several occasions I wrote to my friends and family to assure them that all was well, taking care not to reveal my address. I did not even tell them that I was in Cardiff, and described my present home only as "a growing place based upon industry, far away to the east." This meant that I could receive no messages from them, but I took out a subscription to *The Cambrian*, and that provided me with snippets of news about the happenings in and around Newport.

I felt fulfilled in doing my good works, and although I missed my family and friends, and my beloved Plas, activity kept my mind busy and my feelings of loneliness and loss under control. But I was appalled by the degradation and exploitation of the poor people caught up in the crushing jaws of industry, and the manner in which many previously honest shopkeepers and merchants were corrupted by their dreams of wealth and power, just as the great entrepreneurs and iron-masters were. This was certainly a city of hard work and respectability, populated for the most part by good people; but within my sphere of interest I saw cruelty and greed everywhere. I often thought that the captains of industry were rich beyond the wildest dreams of the poor, but that sensibility and nobility were attributes which they might never understand, let alone attain. Some of the most powerful men in Cardiff knowingly turned their workers into beasts who, when they were cast aside by industry because of injury or the vicissitudes of the market place, prowled the streets like hungry tigers and took their revenge upon innocent passers-by. Ironically, the wives of the captains of industry then went out onto the streets and helped the victims through their charitable works, without ever seeing the connections. The poor people themselves joined this charade, bowing and scraping and tugging at their forelocks, and thanking the "good ladies" for providing modest relief from the misery into which the "good lords" had dumped them. Indeed, those good ladies obtained admiring mentions in the newspapers, enhancing their reputations as benefactors and as "the new nobility," notable because of their largesse. Where newspaper reporters did not report these charitable works, the good ladies actually placed notices in the papers themselves, drawing attention to their latest soup kitchens or schemes for the alleviation of poverty and ignorance. I saw the consequences of murder, rape, robbery and extortion, and mindless violence associated with the consumption of ale in prodigious quantities. The churches and chapels (of which there were many) were thriving, and their members did what they could to encourage virtue, but they could do little in the face of the sheer scale of social deprivation and malaise. The petty crimes of my little Newport and the hamlet of Cilgwyn paled into insignificance alongside the misdemeanours of those who made crime into a profession in Cardiff. In my rural paradise I had remained largely ignorant of the savagery inflicted upon human beings by the monsters called iron and coal, and the trades and industries which they spawned.

Then I realized that in mulling over the inhumanity shown by men towards other men, I was in a glasshouse throwing stones. Had not my own father invested in industry, and made a good fortune from those investments, and passed on some of his earnings to me at the Plas when he died? Was my own son Brynach not involved in buying and selling the products industry in America, giving me much maternal pride as he accumulated wealth and gave security to his children David and Rose? And my good friend Wilmot -- was he not a man who had made his fortune from industry, in the filthy and dangerous copper smelters of the Swansea valley, and was it not his money that had saved the Plas and kept me alive for a decade or more? I resolved to keep my outrage under control, and to try to stop throwing stones..............

When I had been in Cardiff for about a month, I met up with a feisty woman named Lady Charlotte Guest, a widow whose husband Sir John had been one of the great ironmasters. She said that she had heard of my good works and my inexhaustible energy, and I found it hard to convince her that I was old, and that my reserves of energy and enthusiasm were anything but inexhaustible. She was herself a veritable whirlwind of energy and good intentions, speaking at a ferocious pace in a strange and affected way. But I liked her, and knew immediately that she was honest. "Mrs Ravenhill," she said, "I have heard from other ladies of your talent for winning the sympathy of the poor, and of your skill in healing bodies and souls. I also hear that you are a fluent Welsh speaker. It so happens that I am about to depart for Merthyr Tydfil and Dowlais, where there is deprivation on such a scale as to make Cardiff appear to be a paradise. I need you there. Will you come with me?"

"Madam, you flatter me. But I am a woman of very modest means, and a journey to Merthyr Tydfil will involve planning and expense. I can just afford the modest guest house which is my current home, while I am away from my normal rented accommodation near Swansea............."

"Think no more about it, Mrs Ravenhill. You will travel with me in my coach, which I use in preference to my railway. I will pick you up at your lodgings at ten in the morning. You need not think about accommodation. I will ensure that you are comfortable, at no cost to yourself. Help me in my latest scheme, if you will, with no obligation. I have absolutely no wish to take advantage of your goodwill, or to tire you out by loading you with responsibilities. Give whatever time you can spare, and if you wish to return to Swansea at any stage I will be perfectly understanding. Those of us involved in charitable works know that every hour freely given out of the best of motives is a gift from heaven."

I thought that that last statement involved a degree of hyperbole, but I could not help smiling, and of course I agreed to go with her. After all, I had no ties in Cardiff, and I had nothing to lose. Merthyr Tydfil would give me a new place, a new challenge, and a new opportunity to do penance for my past misdemeanours.

Next morning Lady Charlotte's grand coach collected me from my guest house, and I left no forwarding address. On our journey we spent four hours in convivial conversation, during which I learnt a great deal more about her than she learnt about me. But that suited both of us, since for all her charitable instincts Lady Charlotte enjoyed talking about her wealth and her status. I was amazed to learn that following the death of her husband, she was having to raise her ten children alone. She was herself now in charge of the greatest iron-making enterprise in the world, with an income measured in hundreds of thousands of pounds each year, and with the destinies of thousands of workers in her hands. She personally placed orders for ship's cargoes of iron ore from Sweden, Spain and elsewhere, and trainloads of coal and limestone; and together with one or two other ironmasters like Sir Robert Crawshay who owned the blast furnaces at Cyfartha, she effectively controlled the world price of iron. Perhaps because she was so powerful, she also had enemies, and those whom she hated with particular passion were the Butes of Cardiff. I learned later never to mention them to her, for fear of bringing on a fit of apoplexy.

We passed stretches of canals busy with laden barges carrying pig iron, iron rails and coal to Cardiff and Barry, railway lines with neverending queues of steam engines and trucks, and coal mines and spoil heaps in profusion. Parts of the valley were still green, but the pervading colour was black, black, black. We travelled through Pontypridd and approached Aberdare Junction, where Lady Charlotte told me of no less than sixteen locks on the Glamorganshire Canal within a distance of one mile. I was duly impressed, not just because of the engineering involved but also because of the thought that there must truly have been great fortunes at stake, for such works to have been contemplated, paid for and built in the first place. We stopped for a splendid lunch in the Swan at Aberdare Junction, which my hostess appeared to own, and spent rather too long there, indulging ourselves. I had to be very careful with the red wine, lest my tongue should be loosened. Then we skirted round the great canal basin where barges assembled and manoeuvred in their hundreds, and pressed on up the Taff Valley, on a road which became worse and worse as we headed north. Here the valley was very steep, but I was amazed to find that canal, railway and road ascended more or less in parallel. Then the cloud base descended and it started to rain, and I felt that an ominous gloom was settling onto the world and all its inhabitants. Lady Charlotte read my expression and picked up on my mood. "Come now, Mrs Ravenhill," she chortled. "I see that all this blackness is making you miser-

able. I can assure you that up above, on the high ridges between these val-
leys, the white grass still blows in the wind and the heather still blooms,
and there are still skylarks in the sky. You are looking, down here in the
valley, at the colour of money, and it is a colour that attracts both the rich
and the poor. It will be the colour of this place for maybe a century, and
then it will be gone, and the greenery of grass and trees will return. I
guarantee it."

Then, as we reached the head of the valley at dusk, and the landscape opened out into a sort of undulating plateau, I was confronted by the
most amazing sight. The sky was glowing in the far west as the setting sun
illuminated the base of the lowering clouds, but this was as nothing compared with the red inferno that revealed itself to the north, maybe five
miles away. It was as if the sky and the land had been joined together
seamlessly, and that the whole of this vast canvas had been set alight. I
could see no actual flames, but the glow was a fearsome one, and I was
very afraid that some great disaster was afflicting the area. Again my
colleague laughed. "I see that this is all new to you, Madam," she said.
"That crimson glow is also the colour of money. What you are looking at is
the glow that comes from the blast furnace slag and the coke oven ash
when tipping is in progress out on the mountain side. There is fire everywhere -- in the coke ovens, in the furnaces and forges, in the calcining kilns
and boiler house, and in the refineries. There are five or six ironworks in
the vicinity of Merthyr Tydfil, some owned by me and others by competitors including Crawshay, and they are here because ironstone, coal and
limestone were all, years ago, to be had within a short compass. This is
now the greatest concentration of smelting activities anywhere in the
world, and it will make Wales great. In the day-time you do not see the
glow; but at night, especially if one of the furnaces has recently been in
blast, the sparks and the steam and the veritable inferno of the slag heaps
are truly magnificent! More thrilling by far than the most vivid sunset! I
met a lady once who had seen a great volcano in Italy erupting, and she
said that the molten rivers around Dowlais were more spectacular than the
rivers of lava that she had seen on the side of that burning mountain."

As we drew nearer, with Lady Charlotte nodding off on the seat
opposite, I was struck not just by the red glow which illuminated

everything, but also by the smell of the noxious fumes that rolled down from the iron works into the valley, and the roar of the furnaces as they went into blast. If Dante's Inferno should be set anywhere on God's earth, I thought, it should be here. Then I smiled to myself as I realized that here, in this place of fire and brimstone, I was destined to do my penance. Chance, or the hand of destiny? It mattered not -- whatever came next, I would cope to the best of my ability.

Lady Charlotte installed me in a cottage which she owned on the edge of Dowlais, maybe half a mile from Dowlais House. There was even a housekeeper -- a young lady called Maggie who was not as sweet as she looked, having learnt how to survive on the streets of this burgeoning and vibrant town of 30,000 people, built on coal and iron. Free accommodation and food, and a personal servant to boot! I was so pleased with myself that I wrote a brief note to Daisy and Betsi saying I was now near Merthyr Tyd-fil, living very comfortably indeed. In retrospect, that letter was a mistake.

Over the weeks that followed I became a member of a little group of wealthy ladies whose pet project was the education of the women and girls who had come to this place in the company of their husbands and fathers or who had travelled alone, escaping from rural poverty in Ireland or rural Wales and attracted -- in their naivety and ignorance -- by the prospect of wealth and comfort. Most of the women provided cheap casual labour around the brickworks, mines, furnaces and slag heaps; those who were regularly in work were as tough as the men, working seven 12-hour days in every week, out in the open and in all weathers. They lived a life more suited to savages than to the fair sex, and in truth many of them dressed and looked like men. They earned (if they were lucky) maybe eight shillings a week if they were fit and determined, but with the realities of child bearing, their monthly bleeding times and then the change of life, their capacity for earning was very erratic . Then there were those who were unable to find work even on the iron-ore patches or in the breaking of limestone. There were hundreds of them, and we managed to teach a few of them to read and write, and to rescue even fewer of them from the streets.

Many young girls were sucked into prostitution or petty crime, or into degrading work in the ale-houses which were springing up everywhere and which were dens of vice, seldom if ever visited by the police.

The Celestial Empire

Before I saw for myself what was happening in Merthyr, I had assumed that girls as young as sixteen were somehow forced into prostitution by poverty or starvation, and that the whores were at the very bottom of the social scale. But I had to revise that view. The "nymphs" were better off, better dressed, and better fed than those who subsisted on piece work, for they could earn in a day what a respectable piece worker could earn in a month. They were protected by husbands, brothers or "bullies" who took a cut from their incomes for services provided. They were whores by choice, and in the places which they called home, they enjoyed considerable status. The good people of church and chapel did their best to provide safe places, medical help and education for those who wanted to escape, because they were brutalized or ill, but relatively few were attracted by the gospel, and there was a great gulf between those who were devout and seeking salvation for their souls, and those who jeered at the hymn singing and sermonizing of Bethesda, Ebeneser, Tabor and Horeb. My colleagues and I operated in this gulf, sometimes supported and appreciated, and often given abuse by those who stood on the banks on either side.

Lady Charlotte was right -- the deprivation on the back streets of Merthyr Tydfil was far, far worse than anything I had seen in Cardiff. I had not seen anything like it since my visit to Ireland at the height -- or should I say the depth? -- of the Irish Potato Famine, more than a decade before. In some districts there were not even proper streets. In the district officially named Ponty-storehouse, but known to everybody as "China", between the Cyfartha Works and the iron bridge over the Taff, I found a veritable labyrynth of hovels clustered together more or less randomly, and separated by narrow alleyways. The hovels, called "the cellars", were mostly in a stinking ditch between the roadway and the mighty piles of slag and cinders from the nearby coke ovens which were prominent features of this landscape of Hell. The places inhabited by human beings were made of rough stone blocks, stolen bricks, pieces of solid slag, broken wooden beams, sheets of tin and old bits of canvas. In many hovels there were no windows. Grubby faces peered out at me from the spaces which should have held doors. The stinking pig-sties at the Plas were better built, cleaner and drier. Here and there I glimpsed the interiors of these hovels, and saw broken-down beds and flimsy bits of furniture that passed for tables and chairs. Some hovels, hardly bigger than a *ty bach*, held extended families of maybe ten or twelve people, waking and sleeping in rotation. The local police sergeant told me that about 1,500 people lived here.

And thinking of excrement, it was everywhere, thick underfoot when the weather was dry, and running in slimy stinking streams when it was wet. In the more organized of the alleyways, it was scraped into piles which also contained food scraps and other domestic detritus. Every time I visited China it covered my boots and soaked the hems of my skirts, and I carried it back with me to my lodgings, much to the disgust of my house-keeper. There was no water to be had anywhere near the hovels, and no sanitation. The river was not far away, but that was filthy too. There were rats everywhere, scuttling about even in broad daylight. It followed that disease was rife, and almost every hovel housed at least one invalid, suffering from a lack of nutrition, or scurvy, or even cholera or typhus. Then there were the casualties of the iron industry -- men and women who had lost limbs or other parts of their bodies, people blinded by splashes of red hot metal or scalded by cinders, or simply scorched by proximity to white-hot flames. Some of the injuries which I saw were quite horrendous, and led to slow and miserable deaths. I tried to minister to those who had fresh injuries, and managed to obtain a modest supply of dressings and oint-ments through the good offices of Lady Charlotte; but I had no formal medical training, and in truth my efforts at healing met with very limited success. Looking back, I can only feel a limited satisfaction that my loving attention brought some succour to the sufferers and their families, and reminded them that they were not entirely forgotten by the world. I had to arrange for the removal of many bodies from these hovels, and for the visi-tations of pastors and doctors -- but they were too thin on the ground to cope with the real extent of human misery in China, and in any case they hated going there. But I had some successes, particularly in obtaining compensation of a few shillings a week from Lady Charlotte and the other ironmasters in the form of small pensions for injured workers.

Above the cellars of China, and elsewhere too, there were great cinder tips which gave off acrid fumes and occasionally burst into flames for reasons that I could not fathom. They were fed from the coke ovens and blast furnaces, and they covered more land than the iron works and housing areas combined. One or two of the older and cooler cinder tips held communities of troglodytes; homeless children had excavated tunnels and caves inside them, where they felt warm and safe. Safe from adult robbers and thugs, maybe. But God only knows how many of them were suffocated by fumes or crushed when their tunnels collapsed on top of them. Many of the boys belonged to a class known as "the Rodneys" and they survived on begging and petty thieving, sometimes on their own account and sometimes under the control of older and experienced criminals. They measured their status by the number of times they had been arrested and convicted; and they had no respect either for the police or the magistrates. I saw some of them in court, where they postured and bragged, swore at the magistrates and took pleasure in demonstrating that they were beyond control and beyond redemption. They actually seemed to enjoy their short spells in gaol, for there they were able to luxuriate in clean clothes, dry accommodation, and food in their bellies.

There was smoke in the air all of the time, and at intervals one of the Penydarren or Cyfartha blast furnaces would roar like a dragon and make the ground shake, as if there was some great earth tremor a mile down towards the centre of the earth. There were other sounds in the air which never stopped, day or night -- a rattling of heavy chains, and a ceaseless thudding and tapping of hammers, some driven by great machines with wheels, and others wielded by sweating craftsmen. These skilled men, employed in the puddling, shingling and rolling plants, worked without their shirts in temperatures and fumes from which normal human beings would long since have fled. When a furnace was tapped, molten iron flowed in incandescent streams, flashing and sparking and giving those of us who could look and wonder from a distance the most extraordinary displays of changing lights and colours.

I visited China often, seeking to encourage young girls to join our classes and to learn how to read and write, thereby greatly enhancing their chances of finding reliable work as shop assistants, housemaids or even as servants in the inns and guest houses of Merthyr and Dowlais. I tried to convince those of them who worked as nymphs that their relatively comfortable lifestyle could not be maintained, for they were breaking the law every day, and would inevitably be pulled in by the police, prosecuted and transported. I tried to convince them that they would not always be pretty enough to enjoy the protection of their bullies, or to attract customers wealthy enough to pay a shilling a session. Without seeking to judge them for their immorality, I told them that one of my best friends had been a prostitute, but was now, as a result of her own determination, the wife of a wealthy trader. Sometimes I succeeded in my exhortations, but more often I failed. I counted it as a minor miracle that on my visits I was never physically harmed or robbed. I came to believe that my angels were providing me with their familiar protection, for on many occasions I had to sidle my way through street brawls, dances and processions of drunken labourers, gangs of street urchins and gaggles of abusive beggars. Sometimes I was rescued from dangerous situations by tough old women who saw everything and imposed their own law and order on the community in which they lived -- and it **was** a community of a sort, for in the depths of the filth and the squalor I saw many acts of kindness, loyalty and self-sacrifice as people sought to overcome their deprivation and to lift themselves into a better life in which they might have food in their bellies and real coins (instead of ironworks tokens) in their pockets.

On one occasion something happened which I do not fully understand to this day. Around dusk, at the end of a difficult afternoon during which I had seen a mother and her newborn baby die, I was walking through China towards the arch which led to the Penydarren Road. This archway was always guarded by Rodneys, in case the police should appear. Most of the urchins knew me, and normally they gave me a cheery greeting and let me through. But on this evening they were accompanied by some older boys who had obviously been drinking, and they started to taunt me and to throw stones at me. I could not understand it, and I became very afraid. I was already exhausted because of the traumas of my afternoon in a miserable hovel, and I did not have the energy either to speed my steps towards safety or to berate the boys for their lack of respect. A stone hit me on the temple. I felt blood running down my cheek. I fear that I became giddy and fell to my knees on the dusty trackway, with the taunts and the jeers of the boys swirling around my head and rising to a climax inside and outside my head. Suddenly I was aware that the boys were transfixed, and silent; and as I looked around me I saw that they were

140

holding their ears as if they were being deafened by some unbearable noise, and at the same time trying to cover their eyes from some intolerably bright light. I could hear nothing, and see nothing untoward. Then they all turned on their heels, and ran away. I climbed to my feet and looked around me, and saw a fair-haired child standing about twenty yards away, beside one of the great brick supports that held up the bridge. He was smiling. It was Merlin -- of that I have no doubt. But as I looked he faded away and then disappeared into thin air. "Merlin?" I asked. "Is that you?" But there was no reply, and no sign of life apart from a few rats on the river bank. I shook myself down and walked on, with my mind racing, and I reached my lodgings without any further incident. I asked Maggie to find some dressings for the cut on my temple. "Cut, Mrs Ravenhill?" said she, examining my skin and looking bemused. "What cut?"

The women of China became the focus of my attentions, but I got to know some of the men too. They were rough characters, but they accorded me a good deal of respect. In particular, I helped two fellows called Twm and Ianto, just released after serving a sentence for affray and drunk and disorderly behaviour. They had grizzled chins and cauliflower ears, and they were both built like bulldogs. They were both skilled puddlers, but they had been involved in union activities some years since, and had been blacklisted by all of the ironmasters. Now, unable to work at their trade, they were too old to be Rodneys and too inefficient to be bullies. They returned to China one day when I was there, to find their hovels and their families gone. I never did find out what happened to their nearest and dearest, but assumed that they had had to make way for a new heap of cinders. I saw the sparks of decency in both of these poor men, and found temporary shelter for them. Next day I found work for them too, in the extensive stables where Lady Guest kept her barge horses.

Strangely, although I was angered by what I experienced in this, the most horrid place on earth, I kept my good health and my enthusiasm for the work initiated by Lady Charlotte, and found after a while that I had obtained a reputation as a ministering angel among the members of her social circle. I met them often, in grand parties in Dowlais House (called "Ty Mawr" by the workers), where I suppose I stood out from the crowd because of my sombre and plain dresses and my lack of jewellery. Now and then I managed to reduce these exotic ladies to tears with my "tales of China." They had never heard of the place, and one elderly lady actually fainted when I described the conditions there in graphic detail. The word "excrement" was not often used in the dining room of that particular mansion. I encouraged these refined and well-protected ladies, while they were in a state of shock, to use their female wiles to obtain from their husbands, the ironmasters and the big squires and the managers and agents, commitments to build more homes and to improve the lot of those on whose sweat and blood their empires were founded. I cannot be sure of it, but I think that my stratagem met with some success.

My relationship with Lady Charlotte went up and down, and I became very uneasy with her easy acceptance of the poverty and squalor suffered by those whom she employed. She appeared as cold as ice, and very seldom showed any emotion. She loved publicity and luxuriated in her elevated status as a noblewoman. She had a strong social conscience -- of that there was no doubt -- and she saw herself as a benign provider of labour and wealth for a vast force of workers. However, she was dismissive of the political activists who grumbled and schemed in her ironworks, and was thoroughly intolerant of those who requested higher wages or cheaper tools, and who sought to follow up the past work of the Chartist lodges by organizing unions for the defence of workers' rights. She dealt with strikes and deputations more ruthlessly than her husband had done before her, and I saw several lockouts and violent confrontations between sacked workers and the police in my short time in Dowlais. She would not improve the safety measures in the most dangerous parts of her works, because new barriers and fenders would "cost too much." She was a stout defender of the "slow payment" system, although I argued with her often that the payment of workers at intervals of 90 days left them no better off than slaves or serfs, utterly under the control of their employers. It was better than the old truck system, in which workers were paid in tokens that could only be spent in company shops -- but only just.

True, Lady Charlotte devoted time to charitable works, and encouraged me and other ladies to alleviate suffering and to embark upon educational and other well-intentioned projects where we could, but more than once I felt that she was exploiting my goodwill and that of others. I told her on several occasions -- perhaps unfairly -- that her charitable works were no better than gestures, designed to demonstrate her role as a benefactor and to improve her standing in the eyes of the press and the politicians. Once she objected very violently to my words, and I thought that our friendship was at an end; but she knew that what I said contained more than a grain of truth, and that I was the only one who dared to say what many thought. After all, she could have ameliorated the poverty of her workers at a stroke by diverting just a small proportion of the payments that went to her directors into expenditures on housing, schools, sanitation and water supplies. She did a little in that regard (and indeed built a library near Dowlais House), but not enough. She chose to feed on venison, salmon and honeyed ham, and to give champagne by the gallon to her wealthy guests while the people of Dowlais froze in the winter winds that whipped across that bleak plateau, and starved and rotted to death from their ironworks injuries. But she chose to keep me as a friend, and I suspect that she needed me more than I needed her. On several occasions I received favourable mentions in the local newspapers, with her name alongside mine, and I knew that the reports had been instigated by her.

I should have known that I was living on borrowed time, especially since, in my work in China, I sought to maintain good relations with the police, the ironmasters (including Crawshay of Cyfartha) and with the bullies, nymphs and Rodneys who ruled (if that is the right word) the cellars and filthy alleyways beneath the slopes of the cinder tips. I was moving in and out of China with too much ease and too much confidence, and I should have learnt from the stone-throwing incident near the arch that my good works were not universally appreciated. One day, I was on my knees inside one of the hovels, trying to alleviate the agony of a poor man who had lost a foot when the molten metal from a sand mould beneath number six furnace overflowed. His crime was that he was Irish, and there were many people in China who hated the Irish, for they worked too hard and drank too much. Without warning, I was grabbed from behind, dragged outside and flung to the ground. Then I was picked up and pushed against a wall, held by two ruffians, with a third standing in front of me, holding the tip of a very large knife against my throat. Now for a real death, I thought, with a full ration of terror and pain............

8. Palace of Treasures

The knife touched my skin, and I felt a trickle of blood running from my neck onto the front of my dress. Trying desperately to retain my composure, I looked at my three captors, but did not recognize any of them.

"Is this her, Jammy?" said one, in Welsh.

"It is indeed," said Jammy. "Seen her around. She's a spy for Napier and the bloody police."

"How dare you?" I demanded, speaking in Welsh and taking the three of them by surprise. "I spy for nobody. I seek only to help those who are suffering, regardless of race or creed."

"So, Welsh are we? Fancy that. By whose leave are you here?"

"I need no leave, sir. I demand that you let me go at once!"

"You don't have my leave, and this is my patch, Missis."

Then another one spoke. "That bloody sergeant came with his mates and took Bobsy Edwards last night. He's before the magistrates today. Somebody knew where he was, that's for sure. Ain't that right, Missis?"

"Bobsy Edwards?" said I. "I have never heard of him. So why should I know where he lives?"

"Too much talk here, Jammy. Nobody comes on our patch without our leave. Let's cut the bitch and dump her -- somebody that loves her can pick her up and cart her off to the morgue or the police station."

All three of them looked as if they were tiring of this conversation, and I was petrified. I knew that these men, the chief bullies on their own patch, had certainly killed before and would have no compunction with killing again, even if for no particular reason other than the maintenance of their own status. They would not be in the least bit concerned that they had an advantage of three to one over a defenceless old woman. Suddenly I spotted a massive shadow through the corner of my eye, and the hand that had been holding the knife was smashed down by a stave which was the thickness of a man's arm.

"What the bloody hell are you bastards doing here?" roared a deep bass voice. "I thought I told you to stay the other side of the iron bridge?"

"She's a spy, boss," whined Jammy, nursing his damaged arm, with tears in his eyes.

"She's no more a spy than you are the King of India," said the big man. "How can she be a spy when she've only just come here and don't know nobody? And she's old, for Christ's sake! Old women like her don't go round spying!" Then he lowered his voice to a whisper. "You three, if you are not across that bridge in the next two minutes, I'll come after you and skin you with my own hands. And if you ever turn up in China again, I'll carve you up and feed you to the rats. God help me, so I will!"

The three ruffians skidded and stumbled away with terror on their faces, and that was the last I ever saw of them. I was shaking like a leaf, and I fear that my legs collapsed under me. The big man picked me up as if I was a little doll, and carried me for maybe fifty yards through the maze of alleyways before entering what looked like a typical hovel.

Once inside, he put me down on a low bed, and tenderly dabbed at the little cut on my throat with a damp cloth. Gradually my eyes became accustomed to the dim light. I was amazed, for this place was several times larger than any other Chinese hovel I had ever seen, and it even had a table, five or six beautiful upholstered chairs, and other items of furniture including a splendid mahogany long case clock, a glass-fronted bookcase, and what appeared to be a Sheraton rosewood side cabinet. There were porcelain vases, bronze statuettes, delicate cut glass wine decanters and a multitude of ornaments of all shapes and sizes, perched precariously on every flattish surface available. The floor was dry, and the place smelt of incense rather than excrement. The walls were covered with opulent wall hangings and tapestries, and there was a huge oil painting of some iron-master or other which acted as a sort of partition or internal wall. On the other side of the oil painting, I could see steam rising, and I heard a woman singing, not very musically, to the accompaniment of splashing sounds and the gurgles and giggles of a small baby. My amazement seemed to amuse my rescuer, for he roared with laughter, with a bellow deep enough to split a blast furnace from top to bottom.

"Ha! Missis Ravenhill!" he chortled. "You are amused, if I am not mistook, by the domestic pleasures of my little palace?"

At last I found my voice. "I am amazed, sir, and I do not mind admitting it. I have not been inside such a cellar before, and your refinement is to be admired. But I have to thank you, sir, for I am convinced that you have saved my life........"

"Think nothing of it, Madam. Those bastards have caused no end of trouble in China in recent weeks, and it was time for me to show who is in charge. My Rodneys have been following them all day, and knew they were out to pick up a scapegoat and to carve it up as a sacrifice. Your bad luck to have been in the wrong place at the wrong time."

I managed to grin. "I am far too old and tough to be a sacrificial goat. And your name, sir.......?"

"John Wylde, Emperor of China, at your service."

"And the good lady behind the oil painting? Your wife, I assume?"

"Not good, not a lady, and not my wife, Missis. But she is the Empress, and her name is Mags Williams. And she's a hell of a fine mother, to boot."

"I have heard of you, your majesty. And I have heard of your Empress too -- she's the one who controls the girls in the Shanghai Arms?"

"You are well informed, Missis. Napier, that scheming bastard of a Chief Constable, calls it a house of ill repute, but Mags says it is a very respectable establishment, a place of repose and refreshment for gentlemen of discernment. She is in the business of providing a valuable service, and I give her a little assistance in the matter of protection. Without the likes of Mags and me, Missis, the bloody economy would be in bad shape and the world would be a miserable place."

He gleamed, and bellowed with laughter once again. Now I was able to take in his appearance, which was as extraordinary as his dwelling. He must have been six feet and six inches in height, and the ceiling of the "palace" was too low for him to stand erect. He had a smooth chin and a very eccentric black droopy moustache which, I assumed, was an imitation of something he had seen on a portrait of a real Chinese emperor. He wore a green silk smoking jacket, and on his head he wore a little red hat with a tassel attached. He was a portly fellow, and his military trousers were held up by a belt with a massive silver buckle. On his feet he wore shiny black boots, no doubt acquired in the course of some encounter with the military.

I thought I had better not discuss the role of brothels in the local economy and in the provision of happiness, so I changed the subject. "So why did you rescue me, sir? You could have left me to my fate; and as you know from your Rodneys and your bullies, I see it as part of my function in life to encourage nymphs -- and maybe even some of those belonging to Mags -- to seek education and a better life."

"That's what we all want, Missis -- a better life. The girls don't stay pretty for very long, and then what are they to do? Grovel about on the iron-ore patches with their soft hands, or wade knee-deep in clay at the brickworks? Two of the old girls from the Bridge Inn did that, and they were dead inside a fortnight. Mags! Come out here with little Billy, and meet Missis Ravenhill!"

"Coming, *Cariad*, you old bugger!" shouted Mags, and a minute later she emerged from behind the oil painting carrying a very pretty child who was maybe six months old. "Good day to you, Missis," she said, without the slightest trace of deference. "I heard your chattering. Rescued you, did he? Oh yes, he's a very chivalrous fellow. If he weren't the Emperor of China, he'd be King Arthur, and we wouldn't be able to squeeze into this palace because of the bloody big round table he'd have in the middle of the floor." Then she laughed too, causing her voluptuous body to ripple and wobble beneath a loose Chinese silk gown that covered some parts of it, and revealing that most of her front teeth were missing. Her red cheeks glowed, and I judged her to be maybe thirty-five years old, and nowadays more interested in motherhood than whoring. Young Billy gurgled with delight, and I noticed that he was pink and well fed.

Suddenly the mood changed, and Mags said to John: "Well, Johnny, you going to ask her?"

The Emperor thought for a moment, and then said: "Well, bugger me, I might as well." He turned to me, approached and sat on a very delicate chair next to the bed on which I was still reclining. He twirled his moustaches with dextrous, greasy fingers. I noticed that he had dark eyes, and that like his moll he had more gaps than teeth in his mouth. I wondered idly what it must be like to kiss a mouth like that, but then banished the thought when I became aware of the alcohol on his breath. "Mistress, it was my pleasure to rescue you today from those bastards. There was no plan to it, you understand. It just happened. But all's fair in love and war. You owe me something, perhaps?"

There were alarm bells inside my head, and I could not see where this might lead. "Well, your majesty, I am certainly greatly indebted to you for getting me out of a tight corner........"

"You think I'm after your money?"

"Well, sir, that was after all a strange question to ask a lady."

"Never fear, Missis Ravenhill. I don't want for money. What I want -- and what Mags wants -- is to get out of this hell-hole. Will you help us?"

I was thoroughly taken aback, but there were still alarm bells inside my head. "Do you mean," I asked, "that you want me to help you to evade the police and get out of China?"

"Not at all," said Mags. "We could walk out of here any time, and Cap'n Napier wouldn't be able to touch us. Ain't that right, Johnny?"

"Correct you are, my sweet. We are not stupid, Mistress. There is nothing Napier would like better than to get us two onto a transportation ship. But they wouldn't dare to come near this palace of ours, right in the middle of the cellars, even if they had a contingent of fifteen policemen. And they can't tie anything on either of us. That's what bullies and Rodneys are for -- they do the thimble-rigging and the thieving and the bits of necessary blackmail on the fancy men who come to visit our nymphs and would prefer their wives not to know. We are always two or three stages removed from the dirty work. No -- evading the law is not our problem."

"So what is the problem? Why don't you just take your baby and move on?"

"Because we want to go and settle in America, Missis, where we can make a good life."

"But you are the wealthiest man in the whole of China, Johnny. May I call you that?"

"If I can call you Susanna."

"Very well. Can you not afford to pay for a passage?"

"We need at least fifty pounds, Susanna, to get from here to Cardigan and then on to Liverpool and New York. And another fifty pounds for a piece of land that my brother, who is over there already, says is a piece of paradise. I fancy paradise, Mistress, after twenty years in this hell-hole."

"But our total savings are twenty pounds, Mistress," said Mags. Then she gestured around her, to all the furniture and wall hangings. "And all of this will have to be left behind, and cannot be sold........."

"Stolen?"

"What do you think? Every item has come from one or other of the grand houses in this district. Dowlais House, Cyfartha Castle, Penyard House, and all the others. If any of it was to be put up for sale, or even taken out of China on a cart, Napier's men would be onto us like a flash, and then it would not just be a matter of transportation. Half of these things have come from the houses of the magistrates! That means the gallows, for sure, for anybody who has touched them."

The three of us sat in silence for a while, and I was aware that I felt sorry for them. I tried to remonstrate with myself, for I knew that these two people were responsible for much of the thieving and thuggery that caused despair in and beyond China, and which caused outrage in the *Merthyr Guardian* and in the chapels and churches of the district. How many murders had they had a hand in? How many Rodneys, bullies and nymphs did they directly control? I wondered what the answers to my questions might be, but I did not ask them. Instead, I reminded myself that the inhabitants of China were ruled over, and protected by, this man with his immense bulk and soft heart, and that this voluptuous lady provided better working conditions and better wages for the unskilled, than the Crawshays and Guests of this world. Crime was a profession and a way of life, involving the redistribution of wealth from those who probably could afford to part with some of their assets and towards those whose needs were desperate indeed. I still felt sorry for them......

"You are thinking a great deal, Susanna."

"So I am, Johnny. I have to admit to mixed feelings about Emperors. A friend of mine knew another Emperor once, when he went away from here and into West Wales."

"Not that filthy pig Shoni Sgubor Fawr?"

"The very same. He is dead now. He was not a nice man."

"He was as bad as they come, Susanna. He lived in this very palace. He was a killer, I know it for a fact. The best thing that ever happened to China was when that policeman beat the shit out of him in a bare-knuckle fight, and he could not hold his head up after that. So he went off to cause mayhem elsewhere. He killed an old woman once, somewhere near

Palace of Treasures

Llanelli. Bastard! Bastard!"
  "And have you killed, Johnny?"
  "Never! Never, Mistress. I swear it on the life of my little Billy. I have bashed in a few heads, and put a few fellows into bed looking the worse for wear, but it was all in innocent fun, and that's the Gospel truth."
  "He's right, Susanna," added Mags. "Soft as a little kitten he is, in spite of that big body and that voice like the thunderings of doom, and the threats of mayhem."
  "Very well. I believe you, and I'll try to help you in repayment of my debt. Now then -- that picture that you use as a screen for your bathroom. Lord Crawshay, if I am not mistaken?"
  "Correct, Susanna. The old master -- grandfather to the present Sir Robert. Painted around 1790, I think. That mad bugger Jenkin Rhys, the smartest Rodney I ever saw, pinched it from Cyfartha Castle for a £5 bet, six months since. God knows how he got it out of there, what with all them battlements and guard dogs and things. He gave it to me, since his cellar was too small to take it. Very kind of him, I'm sure. I have hardly slept since. Come to think of it, I think I'll take it up onto the cinder tip tonight and send it up in flames. I'll be glad to get shot of it."
  "Don't do that, Johnny. I happen to know that there is a £300 reward out for its recovery. It is -- or was -- the prize possession of the Crawshays, and they want it back. I live only a mile away. Tonight I will come under the Jackson Bridge arch, in a carriage, and I will stop here at 8 o'clock prompt. The police patrol doesn't come out until later, so we should be unobserved except by those from whom you have nothing to fear. Wrap the painting up well, and get it into my carriage. Back at my lodgings, I will clean it up as best I can, and take it to Cyfartha Castle tomorrow. The Crawshays will be beside themselves with delight, and I will be something of a heroine. They will ask me where I got it, and I will simply say that I came across it during my charitable works in a certain poor district. They will happily pay me the £300, and I will say that it will all be devoted to helping the poor and the infirm. That will give them an extra glow of pleasure. Then I'll pass the cash to you, and everybody will be happy."
  So it was all agreed, and so it came to pass. My plans worked perfectly, with Johnny's careful cooperation. On the return of the painting I

was given a very splendid dinner by Sir Robert and Lady Crawshay, and on the next day (before the police were aware that the painting had been recovered) I called in at the Emperor's Palace and handed £300 over to Mags and Johnny. They both wept, and in truth so did I. Later Chief Constable Napier, whom I knew to be an arrogant and officious little man, came to interview me personally as to the theft and recovery of the painting, but I told him that a word out of place from me would prejudice not only my good works in the district, but also those of my fellow sisters in charity. He swore and he grumbled, but at last he had to accept the sense of what I was saying, and he agreed that I would henceforth not be disturbed any more by either himself or any of his officers.

A week later, I heard that Mags and Johnny were gone, leaving a vacuum which would no doubt be filled by some other up-and-coming bully and his moll. They were well out of it, I thought, for the days of the Chinese Empire were numbered. With every week that passed, the condemnation of the lawlessness of China became louder in the press and in the more upright parts of the community, and Napier and his police force became more courageous and adept at targeting the chief criminals and taking them off the streets. Prosecutions forced some of the most notorious brothels to close. There were more and more court cases, and more and more transportations. I could see that the iron works which fed both the respectable economy and the criminal economy of China would decline as steel replaced pig iron and as more and more competition came from new works and new processes on the Welsh coast and in Sweden, Germany, Russia and elsewhere; and when that happened, workers would drift away, taking with them the money that kept the whores in business. I tried to imagine China without the cinder tips, the cellars, and the piles of excrement, but as a place of tidy houses and Victorian respectability; it was difficult to make the picture in my mind, but I knew that it had to come, and that nobody would grieve for the passing of the Empire. By that time, I hoped, Mags and Johnny would be happily breeding and tilling the land in Paradise, USA.

9. A Glimmer of Light

One evening, about a week after the departure of the Emperor and the Empress from China, there was a knock on my door, and my housekeeper announced "Mistress Ravenhill, there is a tall gentleman dressed in a long black coat to see you, and he has two of the roughest fellows in town as his companions. I don't like the look of them one little bit. Shall I let them in?"

I was terrified, but I nodded. With the excitement of the Empire and the stolen painting, I had forgotten about the mysterious armed men who had been on my trail. I thought I was finally rid of them. But no. If this was to be my moment of destiny, I thought, so be it. Perhaps I had now done my penance, and it was time for a final reckoning.

I was greatly surprised when my friends Twm and Ianto marched into my room. Between them they held a tall man whom I did not recognize, with his hands tied behind his back. Ianto was holding a knife to his throat. The prisoner was thoroughly dishevelled, and had a cut lip and bruises to his face. One of his eyes was very swollen, and was well on the way to being closed, and black into the bargain. His coat was covered in mud. "This fellow has been snooping about, Mistress Ravenhill," said Twm, "and asking too many questions into the bargain. He've bin following you for days. He's clearly up to no good."

"And you have been watching him?"

"Us and others, Mistress. Protecting you, we have been, as instructed by the Emperor before he went off to pastures new. He gave Twm and me £10 each for doing the job. Better pay than in the bloody Guest stables."

I sighed, and thanked heaven for the Celestial Emperor. "And why, Twm, do you think this fellow's up to no good?"

"Well, Mistress, he had these in his pocket." Twm handed me four folded documents. I was bemused, and opened them carefully. They proved to be maps of Carningli, the Common, and the adjacent estates, with the barony land marked in red. I was lost for words.

"Maps, Mistress," advised Ianto, "but not from these parts. Distant parts of Wales, if we are not mistaken. Shall we slit his throat now and dump him in the Taff? Or we could throw him into a blast furnace........"

"Good God, no! I thank you, Twm and Ianto, for your noble intentions. But who are you, sir, and what do you mean by following me around? Am I some sort of threat to you, as I see out my declining years in charitable pursuits? I hope you do not seek to rob me, since, from the look of your attire, your assets are considerably greater than mine."

"Far from it, Mistress Ravenhill," said the stranger, in a voice that was difficult to interpret because of his cut lip, but which I thought to contain a hint of a cultured Irish lilt. "It was foolish of me to allow myself to be apprehended by your fierce friends, but you may take it from me that it is my business to protect you."

Twm and Ianto roared with laughter. "A funny manner of protecting he has, Mistress," said Twm, "by lurking in corners and asking questions. Irish he is, Mistress -- they are a bad lot, but I dare say there are one or two Irish buggers who are less bad than the others."

Ianto added his judgement. "But he is a seriously bad bugger, Mrs Ravenhill, I'll wager. He had this in his belt........." He produced a long sheathed knife, and gave it to me.

I gave the Irishman what I hoped was a withering look. "Is this what you use when you are protecting me, sir?" I demanded. "If, so, I do not approve. I abhor violence."

"The weapon, Madam, is my means of defence. This is a rough place, and you are pursued by rough men."

"My dear sir! This is preposterous! I know virtually nobody in this place, and nobody knows I am here!"

"Well, I know it, Madam. I have my ways of knowing. But I admit to being surprised that others knew it as well. At any rate, I have followed those who have been trailing you."

"Why should I believe a word of this?"

"I think we should definitely slit his throat, and dump him in the river, or preferably in number five furnace," said Ianto. "A nasty Irish bastard, if ever I saw one."

"Yes indeed," said Twm. "And a smooth tongue, into the bargain."

"Diawch! Never heard a smoother one, Mistress, in all my years of dealing with magistrates and other vermin." said Ianto. "Now then, all this talking is leaving me very exhausted, Mistress............ justice must be swiftly dispensed, as a policeman said to me once, may he rest in peace."

"Hold on, if you please, gentlemen! Now sir, who are you?"

"My name is Donal."

"Are you the man who encouraged Sergeant Gruffydd to leave me in peace in Newcastle Emlyn?"

"It was my pleasure," he smiled.

"And were you shadowing me in Cardigan as well?"

"Again, it was my pleasure. Now then. Does the name O'Connell mean anything to you?"

I perceived that this might be a trap. So I scrutinised the fellow's face, and read nothing in it. "I fear not, sir," I said at last. "There are probably many O'Connells in Ireland, and quite a few in Merthyr Tydfil."

"And one at Garfeth, too, who is indebted to a relative of yours."

I narrowed my eyes, and wondered how much this man knew. I swallowed hard. "Is blackmail your business, sir?"

"Certainly not, Mistress Ravenhill! Blackmail is a sordid business, always accompanied by avarice, mayhem and in most cases death. I leave blackmail to idiots."

It was time to find out what was really going on. So I said: "Twm and Ianto, will you please leave us, and ask young Maggie down below to give you some tea and something to eat. Mr Donal and I will also appreciate some refreshments. And I need some warm water and a clean cloth, to tidy up his face as best I can. Take the knife, please, and I will be obliged if you will wait in case I have any cause to summon you to my rescue............"

The two rough fellows looked suspicious, but reluctantly did as they were asked. Over the course of the next hour I dressed Donal's wounds, and derived some simple pleasure from it, for although he was somewhat damaged he was a very attractive man with strong features and beautiful eyes. While I worked, we talked, and we continued to talk over refreshments. I discovered that he was a relative of Brendan O'Connell, to whom in a previous incarnation I had given the cottage at Garfeth in 1848.

"Mistress, my cousin Brendan became aware of certain activity in the district some months since," he said. "He is an honest and peaceful fellow, and refuses to be involved in anything troublesome, but he has sharp ears and good contacts. Certain strangers have been asking questions in the district, and others have been set to closely observe six estates around the mountain, including Llannerch, Llanychaer, and Plas Ingli......."

"Those owned by Master Wilmot Gwynne, in other words."

He smiled. "For a stranger to these parts, you are very well informed, Mrs Ravenhill."

"I listen to things, and I am a fast learner, sir. I count Wilmot Gwynne as a friend, albeit one of recent acquaintance. I have met him now and then, in Cardigan and other places. He chooses to give me his support. Now then -- to these mysterious fellows. I assume we are talking of Iago Woodward and Silas Reynolds?"

He nodded, and I continued. "Do they belong to the Society of Sea Serjeants, which I understand to have caused great distress in and around Newport in the past? "

"Nothing to do with them, Mrs Ravenhill. According to my contacts, the SSS is finished, thanks to a certain Mistress of Plas Ingli and a gentleman called Amos Jones, who was a dear friend and neighbour to cousin Brendan. And good riddance to those who orchestrated its operations, and those who played the fiddles. They were idiots, obsessed with feuding, revenge and even murder. People like those belong in the last century, not this one. No no, these fellows are much more sophisticated. Some of them come from Swansea."

"Very strange. Do they work for Jonas Harry?"

He started in surprise, and had clearly not expected me to know that name. Then he gave a little smile and said: "I assume so."

"Have they had past dealings with Master Gwynne?"

"That I do not know. Now, to the maps. Yesterday I apprehended one of the fellows who has been following you, down by the river, close to his lodgings. He has prominent front teeth, like a rabbit. A little search of his person revealed some interesting things, including one hundred and ten pounds, a small compass and the maps which are now in your possession. There were also some letters, which I have left at my lodgings. I will prefer to keep those private for the time being, if you do not mind."

"A compass? Was this fellow a mariner?" The stranger shrugged. "And a hundred and ten pounds? That's a great deal of money..."

"For buying information and paying for services, Mistress. Every well-connected criminal has a budget. You should know it, from your dealings in China. Dirty money. I thought it best to relieve him of it, for the good of the community."

"I have not the slightest idea what is going on here, sir. I might be inclined to think that you mean me no harm, but I am mystified by one thing -- why did you pay a servant boy in Newcastle Emlyn to spy on my meeting with various people from the Newport district?"

"Ah, that was another tall man with a long black coat, Mistress. A friend of the one who kindly gave me the map and the other things. Very clumsy of him to hire a naive serving-boy. I observed it all, and was greatly entertained when the child came rushing out onto the street as if he had a red-hot iron attached to his shirt-tails! A lot has happened since then, and you have led all of us a merry dance."

I buried my head in my hands, convinced that there were now too many people who knew too much. To my surprise, the stranger put his hand on my shoulder in reassurance. "Do not worry, Madam. I have already told you that it is my purpose to protect you."

"Are you then a guardian angel, sir?"

"Far from it, Madam. Shall we say that I am a free spirit who acts in the interests of my countrymen and of those whom we count as friends. I have no interest in prying into areas which are none of my business."

"Then may I ask who gives you instructions?"

"I think it best, for your sake, that I do not answer that question just now. But I have a certain interest in the activities of Jonas Harry of Swansea and South Kensington."

"You are very diplomatic, sir. So what did you find out from the fellow from whom you obtained these interesting items?"

"Not very much, I am afraid. When I had relieved him of his possessions, and held my knife to his throat, he blurted out: "That there Mistress Ravenhill -- she is not what she seems! Take it from me, sir, she is not what she seems!" I think I knew it already, but I wanted to confirm who pays him, and what for. But then his friend came looking for him, so I whispered into his ear that if I should ever see him or his fellow spy again, I would arrange for both of them to be killed. I pushed him into the Taff and retired gracefully, leaving him to be rescued by his colleague. That was quite entertaining, since neither of them could swim. But they climbed out of the water in the end, wet and slimy but otherwise unharmed. Feeling quite pleased with myself, I went home and had supper.

"Today I came up here and took up my observation post again, in the coal-yard across the road. I was just pondering whether I should knock on your door and introduce myself. That was when your friends Twm and Ianto jumped on me, proving that I am just as incompetent as my enemies. Damned undignified, Madam -- and I dare say I will take a long time to recover my self-esteem. You know the rest."

I smiled, and then became serious. "May I call you Donal?"

"Please do, Madam."

"Donal, what do you know about me?"

"Why, that you are just what you seem to be, Mrs Ravenhill. An elegant and beautiful lady with eyes that have, I surmise, sent many gentlemen mad with passion, and who has known a good deal of pain and pleasure over a long and fruitful life."

"You are very kind. Is that all?"

"That you come from London, and speak surprisingly fluent Welsh. And that your presence in Cardigan, Newcastle Emlyn and Cardiff has generated considerable traffic originating from the Newport district."

"It is clear to me that you have spoken to landladies and that you have also read *The Cambrian*. You probably wonder why I keep on moving from one place to another?"

"Indeed I do."

"Let us say, Donal, that I am a restless soul, and that as I approach the end of a long life I am on a quest. There are certain things which I regret from the past, which I now seek to put right. I keep on moving on partly because I am afraid, and partly because am searching for evidence relating to my roots and the roots of those whom I love. I have discovered a loose and yet very precious link to a close family which now seeks to support me, in spite of the tragedy which has recently struck Plas Ingli. To their eternal credit, there are a number of good people from Cilgwyn who might have been preoccupied with the process of grieving for the dead, but who consider it more worthwhile to help the living. That extremely unwelcome notice in *The Cambrian* was meant to help me, but it was profoundly embarrassing, and made me very angry."

"I can quite understand your displeasure, Madam. I feel that I begin to know you. You are a lady, and I consider myself a gentleman. Indeed, I once owned an estate in County Cork until events -- and certain near neighbours of mine -- conspired to take it from me..............that damned Hunger!" He looked away, and said nothing for a while. And then he said: "Would you take offence if I call you Susanna?"

"Not at all. If you tell me that your name is Donal, and I tell you that mine is Susanna, we have the foundation for mutual trust."

"And will you take offence if I say that I am concerned about your circumstances, and give you most of the money which I have confiscated?"

"I will be greatly offended, sir! And I can assure you that my present circumstances are not as precarious as you may assume..........." But I fear that I cannot have sounded very convincing, and Donal smiled and pressed into my hand a bundle of paper money, which I could not refuse. I knew that I needed it, for my own bank resources were beginning to look precariously low. I sighed and put the money under a cushion. "You are very kind, sir," I said with tears in my eyes. "But I hope you expect nothing in return, for I truly have nothing to give........."

"I expect nothing, for the money was not mine. I suspect that it rightly belongs to the poor. Shall we call it a contribution towards your charitable works in China? I have watched your efforts from a little distance, and have immeasurable admiration for what you do."

Suddenly I felt exhausted. I said: "Forgive me, Donal, but I am very tired. I can hardly keep my eyes open, and I have a thoroughly unpleasant headache. I fear that I am feeling my age........."

He bowed. "I am sorry, Susanna, that I have disturbed your quiet evening. Please keep the maps, which I assume to be safe in your possession. In fact, I have a feeling that you will use them more effectively in the cause of justice than I might do, since you have better contacts. Those fellows whom I left in the river know that I have them, but they will not know I have passed them to you. But do you think you could convince those two friends of yours to give me a stay of execution, and to give my knife back?"

A Glimmer of Light

"I will call them up. But where can you be contacted if I need you?"

"Just write to me care of Brendan, at Garfeth in Cilgwyn, near the church. I am sometimes out of the country, but messages will find me."

"And the two men who have been following me?"

"There are at least three. I doubt that you will see them again in this neighbourhood. They will have left town by now, having lost their maps and their money, and without their compass they will not now know which way to turn. More to the point, their cover has been blown away, and I have threatened to kill them. Merthyr Tydfil is a rough place, and men disappear all the time. I suspect that they have gone back to Swansea very frightened, and that they will not trouble us for some considerable time."

I called up Twm and Ianto and told them that Donal was the friend of a friend, and that he meant me no harm. They both rubbed their grizzled chins and nodded. They gave him back his knife, and he dug into the lining of his coat and gave each of them a five pound note. They were staggered, and the three of them went off into the night as bosom friends. I watched from the window as they walked down the street, chatting and gesticulating, and illuminated by the flames of three furnaces in blast.

That night I went to bed with my mind racing. What on earth was going on? Why did Donal wish to protect me? He was a very striking and intelligent man -- but who was he? How did he know where to find me? And the spies -- how much did they actually know? Did they want to hurt me, or was blackmail their business? If so, who did they wish to blackmail? Donal's information had not helped me on that point. Then there was the Swansea connection. I had a suspicion that the real target of the spies, and maybe of their leader Jonas Harry, was Wilmot, and not me......... and I had a deep concern that my conspiracy was now going to harm the dear friend who had helped me more than any other.

I looked at the maps, and noticed that all of the enclosures of recent years were marked on them, together with the names of the main landowners. The name Wilmot Gwynne was underlined in red ink. And all over the maps there were numbers which seemed to have no relation to anything else. Were massive enclosures of the common being planned, and might that explain why Harry's men had had contacts with the Lord Marcher? I drifted off into a fitful sleep, more confused than ever.

10. Salvation

Some days later, around the end of the month of May, I returned as usual to my cottage after a day in China. I was soaking and steaming in my tin bath, and enjoying the scent of soap suds and lavender oil. Suddenly there was a great commotion downstairs, and I heard raised female voices. Maggie came upstairs considerably flustered, and said: "Mrs Ravenhill, there is a Mrs Daisy Havard to see you. I told her you were not receiving visitors, and that in any case you were in the bath after a hard day's work, but she refuses to go away. What shall I do?"

"Good Lord, Maggie! Mrs Havard? How can that be? Please give her a cup of tea and some scones -- she will need refreshment after a long journey. Send her up in ten minutes, when I have finished my bath."

So it was that I met my dear daughter again in this most unexpected of places. When Maggie had left us, we embraced, and there were tears. I was delighted to see her and to have the chance to catch up on all the news of home. But I quickly perceived that she was not interested in gossip, and was agitated and even angry with me.

"My dear Mrs Ravenhill, you are quite incorrigible!" she blurted out. "What do you mean by galavanting about without keeping us informed? Here am I, rushing about all over South Wales, and never finding anybody who has heard of you or knows where you are!"

"But Daisy, was that not our objective? If I am proving elusive, then I am rather pleased with myself!"

"Yes yes. But do you know that I have been to Cardiff, and home again, only to find your recent letter waiting for me, causing me to set off on a new journey straight away, to this foul town of fire and brimstone! It's a horrid smelly place..........."

"It is truly not so bad as you think. And there are good people here, as everywhere else. But why the urgency, Daisy? I have work to do here, as a sort of penance, and my job is not yet done.........."

Daisy looked at me carefully, and then said that I had lost weight (which was true), that I had lost the colour in my cheeks (also true), and that I was wearing myself out on charitable works (which was probably also true). She said that she feared greatly for my health and safety, and I thanked her for her concern. Then she smiled, calmed down and gave me another embrace. She said: "Now, my dear Mrs Ravenhill, do you want the good news first, or the bad?

"I think the bad, since I am more accustomed to dealing with it."

Daisy fished into the depths of her bag, and pulled out a large envelope with crude handwriting on it. It said: *To Missis Ravenhill at the hows of Doctor Jorje, from Merlin.* Inside it there was a smaller envelope, addressed to Jonas Harry Esquire at the Royal Oak Inn, Fishguard.

"Good God!" I exclaimed. "Young Merlin has managed to intercept a letter to Harry! And Harry is in Fishguard! I thought he was in South Kensington, or at home in Swansea......."

"Apparently not, Mrs Ravenhill. He appears to enjoy travelling. Open the letter and read it -- I have already done so, in case it needed attention. But I thought I had better leave things to you."

So I opened the letter and read as follows:

Ty Coch, Mwldan, Cardigan
25th March 1855

Dear Master Harry
There's sorry I am that I lost track of that woman in town that day in Cardigan. Carless of me, and I got the message from Silas that you was not best plesed. But she is a tricky one, that one. And she knows we are watchin her, and takes precaw-shons. And there's a bloody kid making a nusance of hisself as well. He pinched my hat, and caused me certan indignites.

To the bisness in hand. I am back in town and Jeremy tells me that she've gon without trace. Can't find her anywere. I grabbed the kid and gave him a hell of a beatin, partly because he pinched my hat, but he wouldn't say nothin. I don't think he knows where she've gone, Boss.

As to the figure you saw on the mountain, dressed all in black. You said the locals call him The Nitewaker. As to your suspishons that it was not a him at all, but actully this bloody woman, up to no good and takin certan mesurments, you are quite rite. Upon your instrucshons I checkd all the tailors and whatnot in town, with some cockanbul story abot my old ant gettin me the wrong size of hat, and there she were in the lists of Billins Shop, listed as buyin a big black hat, a cloke and a mufler -- all perficly adekwate for coverin her up to look like a Nite-waker.

So that solvs that mistry, Boss. If I was you I would get her out of the way as quick as possibl, before she dos more damidge to you plans. She's too bloody smart, that one. Jes tell me where she is, and I will do the job for you, no charge, becos of the mistak I made in Cardigan.

Tell me your instrucshons.

Yours etc

Iago Woodward

I closed the letter and moaned. "Oh, this is truly terrible, Daisy! This monster Iago has beaten up a child -- and a very special one at that -- just in order to get information as to my whereabouts. Jonas Harry himself must have seen me on the mountain, and now he knows it was me. God only knows what he was doing there. And it is also clear from Iago's words that he wants to get rid of me, as compensation to his boss for losing track of me in Cardigan. He sounds more like a professional killer than a run-of-the-mill thug. He is bound to catch up with me eventually............"

Daisy put her hand onto my shoulder, as a mother might console a small child. "Things are not as bad as you might think, Susanna. Remember that this letter is very old -- it was written about five weeks ago. It has been in my possession since early April, and I would have given it to you earlier if only I had known where you were to be found in Cardiff or Merthyr Tydfil. Also, it was never delivered -- so that would have caused some confusion and possibly recrimination in the ranks. I imagine that by now Iago will have passed this information to Jonas Harry, either in writing or in person, but I think in the meantime you have probably left them far behind." She smiled suddenly. "And there's another thing -- since Iago is clearly incompetent, Harry might well have sent him packing by now!"

I was horrified. "You are pleased about that, Daisy? I would rather have Iago Woodward on my trail under strict orders from his boss, than as an unemployed assassin with a pistol in his belt and vengeance in his mind. If he has been given marching orders, Daisy, remember that he will blame me, and me alone, for his misfortune and his lost earnings."

"Pure speculation, Mrs Ravenhill. Now then, to the good news. I bring your salvation."

I was not listening to her words, for I was obsessed with dark thoughts about Iago Woodward. Also, I wanted to tell her about Donal, and Sergeant Gruffydd, and the spies and the maps. "Daisy, I am involved in a great mystery here. Some very strange things have happened," I explained, "and you must be the first to know of them!"

My dear daughter was clearly not interested. "All in good time, dear lady," she said with a grin on her face. "First of all, look at this!"

She handed me a letter. "Oh no! Not another one!" I grumbled. "Have I not read enough literature for one day?"

Then I looked at it. It was from my sister Elen in New York, written and posted on 26th February and greatly delayed en route by storms in the Atlantic. "You had better sit down before you read it," said Daisy, still smiling. I obeyed instructions, and read as follows:

New York, 26th February 1855

My Dearest Martha,
I received your letter, written shortly after Christmas, in which you described for me some of the sad happenings in and around your beloved Plas Ingli. I trust that you and Amos are well, and that you have been able to defeat those evil men connected to the wretched Society of Sea Serjeants........

At this point I froze, and tears welled up in my eyes as I realized that when she wrote the letter Elen did not even know that Amos was dead, let alone knowing of my own sad demise. That dear man had been murdered on 12th February -- a fortnight before Elen put pen to paper --by those very men referred to in the letter. "Daisy, you were grinning a moment ago," I whispered. "I can hardly credit it."

She came over and put her arm around me. "I am very sorry, Mother," she said. "That was crass of me, and I beg your forgiveness. I had forgotten how the letter started. Take a moment if you will, and then read on."

So I composed myself and continued:
I am old and infirm now, and know not how much more time I have on this

Earth. But I have the great pleasure of seeing my son Brynach and my grandson David every so often, and they are thriving. Brynach is a mighty merchant now, and it is my pleasure that having given him a little help at the beginning of his time in this great country, he has put the disappointments of his time in Wales behind him and has blossomed. He is a fine upstanding young man with a reputation for honesty and probity, and that is down at least in part to your own wise and tender upbringing. I love him dearly, as I know you do.

I have been thinking a lot about the past and about the future. The one thing that has impressed me more than anything I have ever experienced is the knowledge that when you could have kept the secret of my childbearing and Brynach's birth to yourself, you chose to tell him the truth -- in the full knowledge that you, his adoptive mother, would then lose him to his natural mother. He could not, in the circumstances of the day, resist the desire to meet me and to make a new life far from the place in which -- in his eyes at least -- he had failed. He lost the Plas, and in so doing he lost almost all of his self-esteem. What that loss must have meant to you, dearest sister, God only knows, given your passion for every square inch of its land and for every stone and blade of grass upon it.

Your beloved family has lost its pride and has been scattered to the four winds. You personally have lost your home, your savings, your estate, and your only surviving son. For a decade you have battled on, and in your letters you have given me a picture in vivid words of a life lived to the full, with joy and sadness in equal measure. My dear Martha, my love for you is unbounded, and with all my children safe and secure, and well provided for in my will, I have one further task to fulfill.

I am resolved to make some sort of recompense for the events of the past and for the burdens you have carried without complaint. It is my most urgent desire to give you some comfort in your declining years. God knows that you deserve it. I have therefore written out a cheque for £4,000 for you and you alone, and I enclose it for you to spend as you will. Cash it as soon as may be. Your instinct will be to give it to your children or your grandchildren, but I want you -- indeed I beg you -- to spend it on yourself, and to do something entirely frivolous. Beloved sister, write soon and tell me what you will do!

I have more news, but that will wait. I am as excited as a small child -- I cannot resist the desire to send the cheque and this letter off with the mail directly, so as to reach you at the earliest possible moment.

Salvation

I long to hear from you, and send the warmest greetings of my children and
of Brynach and David in particular.
Give my warm regards to Amos and to all of your family
Your loving sister
Elen

I sat white-faced and shaking for several minutes after completing my reading of the letter. Then I read it again, and did not know whether to laugh or cry.

"Well, Mrs Ravenhill?" said Daisy. "Shall I tell you more?"

"Please do, Daisy," I managed to whisper.

So my daughter explained. The letter had been delivered to the Plas on 1st April, after she and George and the four others had left for our meeting at the Red Lion Hotel in Newcastle Emlyn. On being given the letter next day, she and Betsi had thought it prudent to read it and to pass it on immediately to Wilkins Legal since it contained a substantial cheque made out personally to Martha which was to be cashed "as soon as may be" at any branch of the British and American Bank. Since Martha was alive when it was made out, Master Wilkins said it was legally a part of her estate. So, said Daisy, using his power of attorney, and with the bank fully informed of all relevant circumstances, he had cashed the cheque on 3rd April and put the money into his safe. He had then signalled his intent to distribute the money equally between herself, Betsi and Brynach. This was in line with the wishes relating to the distribution of cash assets as expressed in my will.

"But then there was a problem," said Daisy. "The will had already been read out, some time in March, and all of your known possessions had already been disbursed. Betsi, Wilkins and I were rather sure that Brynach would not want his share of the money sent by Aunt Elen. But it would have been improper to act without his instructions. So Wilkins wrote to him in the middle of April to ask what he should do. About ten days ago we received his reply. He reported that he was in rude financial health and said that he wished his share of the bequest to go to me and Betsi. He also confirmed that he had spoken to his mother and obtained her blessing. Since then I have been trying to find you."

Daisy then dug deeply into her leather travelling bag and extracted a brown paper parcel tied up with string. "Open it, Mrs Ravenhill!" she invited, with her eyes gleaming. I did just that, and almost fell off my chair when I found that it contained a huge quantity of bank notes.

"A nice round £4,000," said my daughter.

"Daisy!" I remonstrated. "Is this real money? If so, you are mad to have carried it with you like this. What if some dastardly fellow with a pistol had waylaid you?

"My dear Susanna, Dick Turpin was in his grave long since," laughed Daisy. "This is all yours. Aunt Elen intended it for you. You deserve it, and you shall have it. Betsi and I are immovable on the point. Some weeks back we wrote to our aunt, explaining the legal position of the gift, and telling her that our family solicitor had added the money to your estate and had distributed it according to the terms of the will. Elen is a very wealthy woman. We know from Brynach's letter that she is content with what has now been done, but is of course distraught in the knowledge that both Amos and her sister Martha are dead........."

"She has been fully informed about my death and about the disbursement?"

"Of course," said Daisy, with exasperation in her voice. "You are very slow today, and clearly need a holiday. Elen knows everything, apart from the fact that you are alive. She will have received your farewell letter written prior to your night on the mountain long since, in addition to other letters from Betsi and me giving the sad details of your reported death, and the funeral and so forth. She is also in receipt of your obituaries, and various press reports on the funeral."

"And there are no further encumbrances?"

"No, no and no again. Believe me, dear lady, the money is yours, with the full agreement of all concerned and in accordance with the law. Betsi and I have chosen to give our bequest to a lady called Mrs Susanna Ravenhill. Wilkins Legal does not know that, nor does he need to. And what we have done is of no concern to either Brynach or your sister Elen, since they both believe you to be dead.

Suddenly I was a wealthy woman. Even in the best years of the Plas, when corn prices had been high and when we had lived in great comfort, I had never had so much cash at my disposal. As the full significance of this fact sank in, I was literally rendered speechless, but when I recovered I was at a loss what to do. I had assumed it to be my destiny to see out my days doing good works among the poor and hungry in the slums of Merthyr Tydfil, as a penance for past sins, and I explained this to Daisy.

"Rubbish, Mother!" said Daisy. "If divine intervention is involved, then this is a gift of manna from heaven for one who has made a good contract with humanity, and has kept faith. And enough talk of penance, if you please. You have lived a good life while others have lived theirs in timidity and fear; and if God has anything to do with it, this is your reward and your salvation. I will not brook any further argument or pro-crastination. It is yours, and you WILL enjoy it! Now then, let us put your affairs in order here, and write certain letters to your confederates. You must say your farewells. Then I will help you to pack your bags, and we will be gone."

Daisy stayed for a day while I went for one last time to China to say my tearful farewells, explaining to those poor distressed people in their hovels that I had been forced to accept that I needed a holiday. They wept, and thanked me for what I had done, and understood. I wrote letters to my charitable colleagues and called in at Lady Charlotte's mansion, where I explained to her that I had become exhausted by my work and had to return to Swansea to recover my strength. She too understood, and in say-ing farewell she gave me a beautiful ruby ring as a token of her thanks and her affection for me. It had the letters CEG engraved on the back of it. I was very touched, and left that grand place with tears in my eyes.

I gave £10 to my housekeeper Maggie, and then we climbed up onto our hired carriage. We planned to take the high road towards Hirwaun, and our route took us past Penydarren, Jackson's Bridge and the entrance to China. I was looking out of the window idly, and as I caught my last glimpse of the filthy hovels that I had come to know if not to love, I saw a tousle-haired child standing beneath the slope of the great Penydarren Cinder Tip. It was Merlin. He smiled, and waved, and then he was gone from my view as the carriage rattled round a corner. I was mystified, as I had been on our earlier encounter. Was it really Merlin I had seen, or some sort of phantom? I said nothing to Daisy, but I felt a calm reassurance that the little fellow was safe and relatively unharmed after the beating which he had apparently received from Iago Woodward. We rattled on down the Vale of Neath, and in Neath we took the train to Carmarthen. There I put all of my money into my bank account, causing the bank manager considerable alarm. We took very comfortable lodgings, ate the best meals that money could buy in that modest and unpretentious town, and made plans. I did not know whether there were any spies on my trail -- and for the first time in months, I truly did not care.........

As a consequence of my long discussions with Daisy, I decided to travel abroad on a long and epic Grand Tour. There were places I had always dreamed of visiting, and things that I had always dreamed of doing. Afterwards, I would write down my adventures as a great saga. I also decided that I wanted to go in the company of Bessie, my servant and housekeeper at the Plas for more years than I cared to remember, but also my oldest friend and confidante. Daisy left me to return home, and promised to ask her whether she was healthy enough to come, and indeed inclined to undertake a considerable adventure for somebody who had never been outside West Wales before.

Various letters were exchanged over the course of ten days, and much to my delight, Bessie agreed to accompany me. Although she was older than me by a couple of years, and was somewhat stiffer in the joints as a result of constant hard work, she took the view (at least, this was how she expressed it in writing) that this sudden invitation from an unknown lady was a reward from heaven for a lifetime in service. So the word was put about in town that Bessie had been invited by Martha's long-lost half-sister to accompany her on a European tour as her companion, and that she had accepted. We set a departure date of 16th June, and I enjoyed a couple of days of shopping for dresses and hats that might suit all occasions and all climes.

A week before I was due to embark on my grand tour, the sun rose in a blaze of glory and I knew it was going to be a very hot day. I was overcome by a mood of restless excitement. I was expecting no visitors, and contemplated yet another day of wandering round the streets of Carmarthen. More shopping, maybe -- was there anything I had forgotten? Then I realized that if anything should happen to me on my travels --

through accident or a decline in my health, or through Iago Woodward catching up with me and putting a pistol shot through my heart, I might never see my beloved Carningli in June again. I decided therefore to make one last trip to my mountain and to thank the angels for the good fortune which had recently attended me. I packed my Nightwalker disguise into a bag, took the early morning train to Clarbeston Road, and hired a covered chaise to take me up over the mountain. When we got nearer to Mynydd Preseli, I saw, to my intense disappointment, that it was a drizzly day with low cloud. Such is the way with mountains, I thought. But I urged my driver to press on, and we arrived in Cilgwyn just as the cloud started to melt away, and as the sun tried to break through.

Not far from Waun Isaf, having checked that there was nobody else on the road, I jumped off the carriage and instructed the driver to meet me in three hours' time at Bedd Morris. He was no doubt happy with the prospect of a little interval in the Black Lion or down on the Parrog. Then I donned my disguise, left my bag behind a wall, and walked up onto the mountain. Most of the time I was lost in the drifting and wispy cloud, but I was entranced -- as ever -- with the early summer flowers and the sound of skylarks. I have to admit to feeling my age, and I walked very slowly, standing still every time the mist rolled away and drinking in the beauty of the mountain and the *cwm*. I skirted round the steepest slopes which were littered with great boulders, following sheep tracks through the bracken and climbing gradually into the area covered with fresh green bilberry, heather and early flowering furze. At last I reached the western end of the crags and walked through the tumbledown fortifications towards the familiarity of the summit.

I was almost on the summit when I heard voices. I did not know what to do, but one does not stop being inquisitive just because one is old, so I crept up quietly behind one of the the summit crags and peeped out. There were two men dressed in tweed jackets and and felt hats, deep in discussion. I did not recognize either of them. They were no more than twenty yards from my hiding place. They had a map with them, and they were doing something and marking the map. There was much pointing and gesticulating, and sometimes they seemed to be concentrating on the south side of the summit and sometimes on the north. Then they folded up the map, and one of the men put it into his pocket. I was petrified lest they should walk towards me and discover my hiding place, but luckily they walked north and descended by the steep path that led to Newport. The cloud drifted back in again, and I hurried off the summit and along the path leading to Bedd Morris. As on my previous visit, I took off my cloak, muffler and wide-brimmed hat at Carn Edward and carried them under my arm in a bundle. I was only a little late, and the chaise was waiting for me. I kept myself hidden as the chaise passed through Newport. On the Cilgwyn Road I collected my bag from behind the hedge, and we made great haste back to Clarbeston Road. I paid off the driver and thanked him for his efforts, and was just in time to catch the evening train back to Carmarthen. As my carriage hurtled and rattled eastwards, drawn by one of those steaming monsters, my mind was racing in parallel. Who on earth were these men, and what were they doing?

Next day Bessie packed her bags and travelled to Carmarthen, in the company of Betsi and Daisy, with Ioan driving the carriage. I greeted them all warmly at the entrance of my lodgings, and we exchanged news. As for Bessie, I was overjoyed to see her, and I think that feeling was mutual. As we embraced, we both wept. After a convivial lunch at my expense (that was a luxury indeed, for all of us) I asked Betsi if she might be travelling into Cardigan with Ioan on the next market day, with the buying or selling of stock in mind. She replied that she might well do that, next Saturday. I was greatly relieved, and asked her if she would be kind enough to call in at my old lodgings on the Pendre and enquire after the health of young Merlin. I told her that I had a great affection for the child, and that I was concerned about him since he had been beaten up by Iago Woodward because of the assistance he had given me. She said she would be very happy to do that, and I gave her £10 to pass across to Mrs Ifans, for the child's continuing education.

My daughters decided that henceforth they would refer to me in writing as "Aunt Susanna" on the grounds that my distant and theoretical link with their deceased mother Martha had now been widely publicized and was known to a good many people. I agreed to keep them informed as to our continental wanderings, and to give them addresses where possible, so that they might write to me. Then I said my farewells to my daughters and to Ioan, and they set off for home.

I talked with Bessie far into the night, and I told her everything that had happened to me since my reported death. She told me of all the changes at the Plas, which I was able to accept with equanimity. Over the next few days we read travel books and consulted maps, and we made our plans. Dear Bessie had hardly any clothes, and so we did more shopping, giggling like small girls as she tried on this and that, and eventually we found bonnets and dresses that made her look very pretty, and half her age. We ate in the best restaurants in town, and I believe that I started to put back onto my body those pounds which I had lost in Cardiff and China.

One day Shemi turned up at my lodgings without warning, and over a splendid lunch in the Duke of Wellington he and I enjoyed a long talk. He knew all there was to know about the spies, and confirmed that Iago Woodward was still making occasional appearances in Newport. He said that he drank in the Black Lion with the fellow called Silas Reynolds, and assumed that they were waiting for me to turn up in town. He confirmed that they had been seen more than once visiting the castle. Shemi knew about the letter written by Iago and intercepted by Merlin, and said he doubted that Iago would try to kill me, as I was more valuable alive. "Thank you very much, Shemi," I said. "I am reassured. I wonder what I'm worth?"

My favourite wizard also told me that he had news of Merlin. The child had indeed taken a beating from Iago, but he was as tough as all the other street children of Cardigan, and was now fully recovered and as mischievous as ever. That news was a great relief to me. I asked Shemi whether Merlin could possibly have been in Merthyr Tydfil during the past weeks, keeping a friendly eye on me. "Not that I know of, Susanna," said he. "But he is an extraordinary child, and for the likes of him, nothing is impossible........."

As we chatted on, I became convinced that Shemi also knew the cultivated Irishman called Donal, although he would not admit it; and I was led to conclude that somehow Wilmot, Shemi and Donal were working together, probably for the protection of Wilmot's estates. Later on we returned to my lodgings and I gave Shemi the bag with the black cloak, muffler and wide-brimmed hat in it, as a present from the latest incarnation of the Nightwalker. I knew that I would not need them again, but I had a feeling that he might find them useful. He knew of course that I had used the garments on the mountain prior to my departure from Cardigan in March, but he had warned me not to use them again because of the risks involved. "Oh dear, Mrs Ravenhill," he said, rolling his eyes. "Splashes of mud on the cloak. And still not properly dry. As I thought. Never fear -- I will look after them until you return, and will try to keep them clean."

Then I went to the chest of drawers in the corner of my room and took out the maps which I had obtained from Twm and Ianto. I gave them to Shemi and asked him to look after them. I was sure that they would be safer with him than they would be in the possession of two elderly ladies travelling about all over Europe. He took one look at the maps, and said "Where on earth did you get these from? Mrs Ravenhill, you are almost as amazing as your half sister Martha Morgan." Then he studied them in more detail, and said: "Yes indeed, as I thought. Exactly as I thought........." But he would not elaborate further.

On the day before our departure for France Wilmot and Delilah called to say farewell, carrying greetings from Will and the other servants, Rose and Henry and all of our fellow conspirators. We enjoyed a good lunch together, and it was my pleasure (for a change) to pay for it. Later on, while Delilah chatted to Bessie on a bench in the park, I asked Wilmot to accompany me on a walk along the river. He was wheezing and puffing at the slightest exertion, but was otherwise apparently full of the joys of spring. He offered me his arm, and I accepted it. We exchanged snippets of news, and then I asked him out of the blue whether he had any enemies from his days in Swansea. His good humour disappeared at a stroke, and a shadow came over his face. "Why, Susanna," he protested. "What a strange question!"

"Not strange at all, but deadly serious, Wilmot."

"I dare say that all businessmen have enemies, Susanna. As I have said many times before, in business there are some winners but many losers. Swansea was a rough place, twenty years ago. I have always acted with propriety, but yes, there are times when I have beaten jealous men to deals on plant, transport, and purchases of copper ore, and have thereby damaged their prospects. Some of them might therefore have viewed me as an enemy. But I have never sought to harm another man, I can assure you of that."

"I accept that, dear friend. But is there any man who has a particular reason to hate you?"

He thought for a while, and then said: "Yes, Martha. The only other person who knows this is Delilah. There is a certain Squire called Jonas Harry who has estates and coal mines around Gorseinon.........."

"Not related, by any chance, to the Harry family of Newport, who have been enemies of mine since the day I arrived at the Plas?"

"I fear so, Martha. He is a cousin of Jacob Harry, who was lynched in Ireland a couple of years ago for unspeakable crimes against the starving Irish. The two men were very close -- and I believe that they shared certain business interests."

We walked on, and I was deep in thought. "May I ask why he hates you?"

"Probably because I beat him to various capital purchases, refused to join his consortium for the fixing of copper prices, and consequently made my fortune through signing contracts which he and his confederates assumed were theirs for the taking. I made lower profits than he might have done, but I still made a great deal of money, Susanna. In the meantime, he lost a great deal."

"But he is still involved in industry?"

"Very much so -- when I defeated him, I fear his pride was hurt more than his pocket. Since then he has made a great fortune, and owns at least five coal mines and two copper smelters. His mansion on the Mumbles is something to behold!"

"Then what is the point of continuing his hatred? Does he not know that you have retired from industry, that you are in poor health, and that you have moved to the country to live out your days as a gentleman?"

"Of course he knows all of that. But it seems to me that hatred is the fuel that drives him. And he knows that I played a not insignificant role in the downfall of the Society of Sea Serjeants and in the consequent death of his cousin."

"But that wretched man was entirely responsible for the actions that led to his terrible death! You had absolutely no involvement in it!"

"That may be, Susanna, but hatred clouds logic.........."

"Will he try to harm you?"

"No no, I do not believe so. He is not so stupid. But I have a letter in my safe in which he vows that he will see me crawl into a pauper's grave."

"But that is a threat. Wilmot! You must show it to the magistrates and obtain an order from the court........"

"Good gracious me, dear lady!" he laughed. "People use more violent language than that every day of the week, verbally and in writing! Do you not read your newspapers?"

I had to accept the point. Then I asked: "Does he covet your estates?"

"I admit that he does. He has written to me several times, offering a pittance. I have told him repeatedly that the estates are not for sale in any circumstances or for any price that he might like to name. He is no farmer and no gentleman -- I am at a loss as to what he should want the land for. But land appreciates faster than money in the bank. I know that, and so does he. The wealth of the nation is increasing just now, and good little estates are hard to come by. That is all by the way -- to tell the truth, finance is not a consideration as far as I am concerned. As I get older, my heart grows stronger than my mind, and I admit to a growing fondness for the mountain and for the Plas, my dear friend!" And he gave me a little kiss.

"That is a relief, Wilmot. I could not bear to see the estate changing hands again, now that it is back on its feet. Thinking of predators, what role might the Lord Marcher have in the perpetration of Harry's plans? I hear that his men have been seen visiting the castle."

"I am aware of those visits. The Lord Marcher is no great friend of mine. It is said that the Barony covers more than 30,000 acres hereabouts, and Sir Thomas owns all of the common lands on the mountain. He is also in debt, having invested heavily in a monstrous fairy palace at Bronwydd in Cardiganshire and having taken on the restoration of the castle in Newport.........."

"Using borrowed money?"

"I believe so. It's possible that he wants to dispose of much of the common as a means of raising funds. Perhaps Harry is the prospective purchaser."

"But the enclosure and sale of the common would cause a revolution, Wilmot!" I spluttered.

He smiled and patted my hand. "Now then, dear lady," he said, "we had better not get too involved in wild speculation. In due course, we may have some facts to work with; but for the moment, I urge you not to become too agitated."

I had to agree with him, and promised to keep my imagination under control. Then I said: "Wilmot, my biggest fear, arising from my moment of insanity on the morning after my alleged death, is that my secret will come into the possession of an enemy -- let us say Squire Harry -- and that you will be blackmailed into disposing of the estates for a figure which will leave you destitute."

"That has occurred to me, Susanna. But I am taking certain measures to guard against the eventuality."

"I am glad to hear it. And do you know that you are being followed? That fellow strolling along fifty yards behind us, with a rather elegant leather hat, is a man whom I recognize. He has accomplices, of that I am certain, and I suspect that some of them are shadowing you very closely indeed. Our shadowy friend probably took the same train as you from Haverfordwest to Carmarthen."

"You are very perceptive, my dear friend. Yes, I am aware of what is going on, and again you must accept that I do not feel terribly threatened. If they want my estates, they are more likely to get them with me alive and unharmed than with me dead and my assets distributed among my heirs. So they may spy on me, but they will not hurt me."

"What about Delilah? Does she know about these spies? And might she not be more at risk than you? These men could even kidnap her and hold her to ransom, as a means of obtaining your estates!"

Wilmot roared with laughter, and his eyes gleamed. "My goodness, Mistress Ravenhill! You are in a very melodramatic frame of mind today, if I may say so! Yes, Delilah knows about the spies. But kidnap and ransom? Impossible! It would take ten men to kidnap her, and if they tried to contain her she would pull down the pillars of their temple, with or without her golden locks! No no -- impossible!"

"Very well, Wilmot. Do you share my view that the threat will be considerably lessened if I simply disappear for a year and leave your enemies, and mine, on the wrong side of the English Channel?"

"You are very wise, Susanna. And much as I will be sad to see you go, I think you are probably right in assuming that an absence would be beneficial to us all. I have it on good authority that Jonas Harry is angry with you. And I beg you to think of your own health -- you have been through death and transfiguration, and I have heard all about your charitable works in Merthyr Tydfil and Cardiff. You must be exhausted. You need a very long holiday, and a good deal of pampering. Enjoy your new fortune, and know that wherever you go on your Grand Tour you carry with you the blessings of all of us who know the truth."

Later on, when we had said farewell and Wilmot and Delilah had taken their late afternoon train back to Haverfordwest, we noticed that at least one of the spies went west on the same train. Bessie and I returned to our lodgings and organized our travelling trunks and bags. Very early next morning, just as it was getting light, we took the first train to Paddington, before any of Harry's local spies were awake.

11. Transfiguration

A few days later we were in France, travelling as Mrs Ravenhill and Mrs Walter. I insisted from the beginning that there would be no mistress/maid relationship -- we were to travel as two old friends, equal in all things apart from the fact that I was paying. There was no friction between us, and indeed we knew each other so well that we sailed through our travels with a fair following wind and with virtually no debate as to whether to do this or that. I was as comfortable with Bessie as I might have been with a husband of fifty years' standing, and indeed I thought on many occasions that female company was preferable, at least for ladies of our mature age. As we travelled we reminisced a great deal, and the further we travelled from home, the more nostalgic we became. But we had a wonderful time.

During our first passage through Paris, Bessie found a letter from Will on the bottom of one of her bags, which she had clean forgotten to give me. At the top of the letter "Dear Mistress Martha" was crossed out, and replaced with "My dear Mrs Ravenhill" rather too prominently for comfort. This is what the letter said:

12th day of June 1855
I write to wish you all the best for your travels in foreign parts, and trust that the insects and poisnous creatures which are, I am relaibly informed, Mistress, very prodigious, will not prove to be too disturbing to your ladylike comforts.

I have to tell you of a very strange thing. Rather, two very strange things. The first very strange thing is that there have been men on the mountain sevral times in recent weeks. Gerallt has seen them, and so have I, and we do hear say that Williams Gelli and Jenkins Penrhiw have also seen them. They creep about most furtively, and try to hide out of sight, but our eyes are sharp and their brains are a bit slow. I saw them once through my spyglass. They have maps, and they seem to be mesuring things. We think that they might be official gentlemen making maps for the goverment, but then surely they would knock on doors and talk to people? Maybe they are mesuring the common and the grazing. There have been strangers in town too, keeping very much to themselves. Four of them. Jake has

Transfiguration

seen them lurking about on the Parrog. Sombody also saw them making a visit to the castle, so perhaps they are friends of that stuffed-up Lord Marcher.

Now to the other very strange thing, Mistress! You will be very entertained by this, I warrant! The Nightwalker has been seen again on the mountain! Not once, but twice. The first time was some weeks back, some days after your funral, I think it was, when eight diffrent people to the best of my knowlege saw the Nightwalker on the mountain, moving about very slowly and somtimes standing still for a long time, just observing things. Just like in those good old days, Mistress, when you were so scared of him!

Then just yesterday, there he was again! A cloudy and drizzly sort of a day it was, with the low cloud coming and going, and the sun trying to come through. Just standing there, he was, observing things, here and there on the south side of the mountain, and then also spotted in a little break in the cloud, right on the summit. I saw him, and so did Myfanwy and Gerallt, and so did half a dozen others. Mistress Jane also saw him, and came over all frantic, and wept and wailed about ghosts and hauntings and such like. Very sensitive, she is, Mistress, and not at all used to the ways of the country. We explained to her at great length that the Nightwalker may indeed be an apirition, but we said he had been seen on the mountain oftentimes before, in the good old days, and that he never did any harm to nobody. (Apart from harming your equilibryum greatly, Mistress, if I am not much mistaken!) We said she should not worry her pretty head about it, but she is much shaken and stirred.

So it is out and about, all over the place, that the mountain is haunted. And a fellow I met in town today says that it is not the Nightwalker at all, but the Ghost of Mistress Martha up there among the rocks that she loved so well. I nodded, and said that was a very logical thing to think. Now is that not very entertayning, Mistress? Oh dear, I mean Mrs Ravenhill. Write to us now and then, if you will, and report your prodigious adventures.

We are all well, and it is a jolly thing (but the tantrums are very tiring for an old fellow such as me) to have two small children in the house again. If we get news of where you are, we will send reports of the harvest and the sheep dipping and such like. The hay is looking good, and will be a week earlier than last year.

I remain Your ever faithful servant
William Owen
PS look out for bears and scorpions, and bandits

Transfiguration

I read the letter aloud for Bessie. Then I put it on the fire. "Dear Will!" I sighed. "How I miss him, and Gerallt and Myfanwy! What a kind and genuine man! But I thank my lucky stars that you forgot to give me this letter till now, Bessie, and I thank my guardian angel that it did not fall into the wrong hands. If it had done, I fear that our little game would have come to a premature end.........You really did forget to give me the letter before now?" Bessie smiled enigmatically, and shrugged. "Old age, Mistress," she said.

"Please, Bessie. Not "Mistress" but "Susanna". I see that we have much work to do on the matter of identity. You must try, or we will get into deep trouble, both of us." Bessie smiled and nodded. There was a long pause, and then she added:

"And the Nightwalker, Susanna. Nothing at all to do with you, I suppose?" I smiled and let her draw her own conclusions.

"Ah, my dear friend!" she said, rolling her eyes to heaven. "You and your secrets! You are truly just as bad as your half sister."

As we travelled about, we were two gentlewomen with effectively no limit on our funds. My bank manager in Carmarthen had been very kind before our departure, and had arranged for currency to be made available to me from various banks across Europe. For about a year, from June 1855 to May 1856, we travelled all over Europe, starting in Paris, travelling by train or on the best coaches, and staying in the most luxurious hotels. We spoke Welsh all the time, except when I had to use English or French. We ate so well that we both put on weight, and we drank too much too. Sometimes we laughed so much that we overstepped the bounds of decorum and attracted disapproving glances from certain prim and proper people. But people with money are always forgiven, as I discovered at a very early stage.

We were especially blessed in our travels because Daisy had written introductions for Mrs Susanna Ravenhill, her "beloved aunt", for counts and princes in every country we visited. I was amazed by the extent of her contacts, and concluded that in her days as a London courtesan she must have got to know all of the top people in Europe, or at least those who wore breeches rather than dresses and who attended the English court. Many of those great counts and princes had undoubtedly been met between the sheets; and others were casual acquaintances about whom she knew more than perhaps she should. So doors opened miraculously everywhere, and we were feted and feasted, and shown sights which ordinary travellers never see. We roamed about in castles and palaces which were strictly guarded private residences, and saw at close quarters many great works of art in private collections. We visited grand opera houses and theatres, and had our fill of musical and other entertainments. For me, the high point was a most moving performance of La Traviata in Venice, to which we were invited by a very charming count and his lady. We hired guides as and when necessary, and sometimes travelled with other companions if we found their company convivial. Three gentlemen fell in love with Bessie (or so they said) but only two fell in love with me, which was very bad for my self-esteem. We became drunk on culture, and every now and then we escaped from the clutches of the nobility and hired simple lodgings in places with wonderful views of mountain or coast, and spent a few days sitting in the shade, reading and snoozing. So the weeks and months passed in unadulterated pleasure. Both of us were blissfully happy. We travelled from Paris to Brussels, into Germany, Austria and Switzerland in the summer, and then went on over the Alps in the autumn to enjoy Venice and Florence in January and February, and then Naples and Rome in the spring. In April we took a sea passage to Cartagena, and embarked upon the final leg of our journey to Granada, Seville, Lisbon, Madrid, and Barcelona. Finally we moved north again, into France, staying in Marseilles, Limoges and finally Paris for the second time.

On 27th February Bessie and I were in Florence, and we had a private party for just the two of us, involving the consumption of a good deal of champagne, to celebrate the first anniversary of my death and transfiguration. I remember it well, for we sat on a hotel balcony by the river Arno, with the most wonderful view of the Ponte Vecchio caught in the light of the setting sun.

There were various troubles in Europe as we travelled, but we managed to steer clear of revolutions and battles, and discovered that two old ladies travelling together can always get help since they threaten nobody and bring out the kinder side of people's nature. Even fierce soldiers and frontier guards treated us with great courtesy and respect. I insisted on

Transfiguration

visiting many of the places described for me long ago by Owain, the wonderful man whom I should have married long ago, and never did. He had travelled here, there and everywhere during his wanderings in 1807-1822, and now, after the passage of many years, I even found some people who remembered him.

In our idle moments, as we travelled, we spent many jolly hours inventing more details for the life of Mrs Susanna Ravenhill and her husband Jack, creating details about the children, places of residence, Jack's career, family events and so forth. As the months passed, I became more and more comfortable with my new name and my new history.

One day, when we were in Italy, Bessie decided to discusses the findings of the Inquest relating to the mystery man who was found on Carningli after the earthquake. She knew of course that the body was indeed that of Moses Lloyd, as suggested by the Coroner at the Inquest back in March of the previous year. She recalled the occasion when I had crawled back to the Plas, more dead than alive, in August 1797, and asked whether that was the consequence of a deadly encounter with Moses. I decided to tell her everything, as I had already told Rose. I saw no need, at this late stage in my life, for secrecy. As I spoke I relived the horror of the occasion and became very emotional, and Bessie needed to console me as only a dear friend can do.

On another day, in Seville, I told Bessie about the strange encounter with the man called Donal in Merthyr Tydfil, and about the men who were following me. I told her of the money, the pocket compass and the maps taken from the spies, and now handed over into the safe keeping of Shemi. Of course we made a link with the contents of Will's letter, and agreed that two and two should make four, but in truth neither of us could make head or tail of what was going on. We speculated on whether Donal or the spies working for Jonas Harry knew my true identity. Maybe they just suspected it, and were seeking confirmation? But why? Were the spies seeking to blackmail the family or Wilmot, and possibly take control of the estate? I recalled my conversation with Wilmot by the river in Carmarthen, and then forgot all about it.........

Weariness was beginning to affect us by the time we reached Limoges in France and took up a brief residence with a French count whom we had met in Venice. When we were shown to our room, a letter was waiting for me on the dressing table. It was from Wilmot, and read as follows:

Plas Llanychaer, 15th day of March 1856

My Dear Mrs Ravenhill,
I trust that this finds you well and happy. Please give my greetings also to Mistress Bessie, your excellent and valued companion. Delilah and myself are as well as may be expected at the end of a hard winter, with much snow. We envy you as you enjoy the delights of sunshine and high culture in exotic places, and follow your messages with interest, consulting our maps and following your route as best we can, and seeking to imagine your adventures.

Now I have a confession to make. I thought I should hold back on it until you are home again, for fear of spoiling your enjoyment of foreign parts, but Delilah (who is always right) counsels me to inform you of the situation as early as may be, so that you may take action as appropriate. I am writing this letter away from home, and will personally deliver it to the post, for fear that it might otherwise be intercepted.

I have been betrayed. Following our resolution to treat certain information concerning your good self as utterly secret, and not to be revealed to any other living soul, I have systematically destroyed all letters received from you and have never kept copies of letters sent by my good self. But I have committed certain information to the pages of my appointments book, which is always kept under lock and key in a desk drawer in my office. I have entered up such things as "SR, c/o Mrs Ifans, 29 Pendre, Cardigan, until further notice" and "SR, Hotel de la Rosette, Rue St Germain, Paris, June 12 -29, 1855" -- information as provided in your letters -- so as to keep in touch. But woe is me, idiot and trusting fellow that I am! Unknown to me, our housemaid (who has been taught to read and write by none other than Delilah) has been in possession of a spare key to my desk, and has, I fear, been examining the contents of my appointments book as far back as the troubled time surrounding the death of our dear friend Amos. I found her out the other day, having become suspicious of her on account of a certain friendship which she has developed for a man whom I have cause to mistrust. That man is called Silas Reynolds, who has in the past spent time in Fishguard. I set a little trap for her, and caught her in the act of examining my book. I sent her packing straight away, but I could get little out of her since she has been well trained by her accomplices. She appeared to be more frightened of them than she was of me in a fury! God only knows what information she has passed on, and what damage is done.

My dear lady, I can only apologize with all my heart for this most lamentable development! I have looked back over my entries over the past year or more, and since most of the entries are about your movements and addresses, and not your personal details or family history, I hope that your secret is still safe. I cannot be certain. But I fear that wicked people who may seek to harm you -- and who certainly hate me -- may have been in possession of information as to all of your movements, and may therefore have been spying on you and delving into your affairs. I recall that last time we met -- in Carmarthen -- I gave you certain information and you warned me about spies, and I can only hope that you will have exercised due caution in all of your dealings since then.

My deepest apologies, madam, for this turn of events. I now pray that you and Bessie are safe, and that you will remain safe until you return to this district.

With warm and affectionate greetings from Delilah and myself,
Your friend
Wilmot Gwynne

I was shocked by this, but not entirely surprised, since I had long since come to the view that information about my whereabouts had been leaking out from somebody's private papers. I was saddened more for Wilmot's sake than my own. I talked over this development at great length with Bessie, and at least we now knew how it was that I had been followed and spied upon in South Wales in the months after my reported death.

Neither of us had spotted any spies, or felt threatened, during our travels. But now that home was almost in sight over the horizon, both Bessie and I resolved to look after each other as necessary, and to take certain basic precautions, just in case..........

12. Moment of Truth

It was a delight to be in Maytime Paris again, with blossoms on the trees and spring smiles upon the faces of the inhabitants. It was our intention to stay for two weeks, prior to travelling by rail to Calais for the Channel crossing. We stayed in the same hotel as before. Each afternoon Bessie took a siesta while I walked in the streets, enjoying the warmth of the sunshine and looking at people.

I was strolling along one of the little back streets not far from our hotel, without a care in the world, when I suddenly noticed a very discreet shop with the following words in white lettering on a black background, painted upon a sign above a bow window: LeClerc de Paris. That rang a bell, and I peered through the dusty glass into the darkened interior. I could see nothing apart from a few elegant hats, not very tastefully arranged, together with a scatter of handwritten notes that might have been testimonials from satisfied customers. I was intrigued, and without stopping to think about my safety I decided to pop inside in order to satisfy my curiosity.

Just then a gentleman stepped in front of me, doffed his hat and gave a deep French bow. "Mrs Ravenhill?" he asked, with a voice more English than French. Without thinking I said "Yes sir, that is my name." Immediately two other men took me by the elbows and hurried me through an open door next to the door of the LeClerc shop. I swear that when that happened my feet were off the ground. The man who had spoken followed behind and closed the door. It was all done so quickly, silently and smoothly that passers-by would not even have thought there was anything amiss. I was immediately very frightened, but knew that there was no point in screaming or struggling. So I tried to keep calm, and to collect my thoughts. I was ushered into a small room which reeked of tobacco smoke. It was dimly lit, and the blinds were drawn. The men released me, and I was motioned to sit down on a sofa. I did so, and the three men who had grabbed me off the street retired and closed the door.

My eyes gradually adjusted to the light, and after removing my unnecessary spectacles I saw that I was faced by a slim man who was immaculately dressed in green trousers and a red smoking jacket. He was sitting in a deep arm-chair in front of the window, so that his face was in shadow. He did not get up. He wore heavy spectacles with tinted lenses, and he had shiny black hair greased with macassar, and an extravagant mustache. He was smoking a briar pipe and using foul tobacco.

"Sir, this is an outrage!" I stormed. "I know not who you are, or what your intentions are, but you are no gentleman. Gentlemen do not abduct elderly ladies off the street in broad daylight......."

The man held his hand up and stopped me in full flow. "Calm yourself, Madam. I mean you no harm. So, Mrs Ravenhill, we meet at last. I have been hoping to make your acquaintance since March of last year, but you have been very elusive. A merry widow indeed, claiming to be grieving and penniless, but enjoying the best that Europe has to offer!"

"What do you mean, sir? And who are you?"

"My apologies, Madam. Jonas Harry of Plas Glas, on the Mumbles, at your service."

"At my service! Sir, your place of residence may be fit for a gentleman, but your behaviour is that of a common criminal. I insist that you release me immediately!"

There was a long pause while he looked at me levelly, and took a few puffs on his disgusting pipe. "Now then, Madam, your temper appears to be as fiery as that of your late half sister, if indeed you had one. I beg you to be calm, and to hear me out. I think I can indeed be of service to you, and that we have -- shall we say -- mutual interests. Now then -- you know of me, I think?"

"Yours is not a name familiar to me, sir."

He scowled, and then laughed. "Come now, Mrs Ravenhill! Do not try to upset me. Everybody knows my name! I venture to suggest that I am very well known in the circles in which we both move. Perhaps, then, you have heard say of my relatives from Newport, who were well known in business circles?"

On that point, I thought it best to remain silent. "Dear me, this is very difficult," said Harry, after a while. "I perceive that you are not a great conversationalist. So much time spent over the last year speaking Welsh with your dear friend Bessie that you have forgotten how to converse in civilized English?"

I looked up sharply, and he reacted immediately. "Ha! A response! And how did I know that? Because I make it my business to know things, Madam, and spare no expense in finding the information I need."

There was another long silence, and at last I said: "So what is your purpose, Master Harry, in bringing me to this place?"

"I have brought you here today, Madam, because I now know everything," said he with a self-satisfied grin.

"Well, I trust that you have benefited from your great knowledge of absolutely everything, sir, and that your superior intelligence has made you a very wise man."

Suddenly the smile was wiped off his face. "Do not play games with me, Mrs Ravenhill! I do not take kindly to sarcasm. Let me make myself clear. I know that you are not what you seem."

I swallowed hard, expecting the moment of truth. "Then, sir, what am I other than an old lady who has nothing more to lose in life, and no fear of death?"

"Very well. I will put my cards on the table." He laid down his pipe on an ash-tray. Then he leaned forward, allowing some light to fall onto his face. I saw that he had a sallow complexion and sunken cheeks, and I speculated that his spectacles and heavy mustache were used to promote the image of a vain man who considered himself mysterious and even omnipotent. I was intrigued, and he continued.

"For a start, Madam, your disguise was apparent to me from the earliest days of my surveillance. You colour your hair with brown dye bought in Newport, and you use spectacles which have ordinary glass in them instead of lenses. Haha! Now why on earth should an elderly woman go to such lengths to hide her true features? I would appreciate enlightenment."

He smiled in triumph, picked up his pipe and puffed on it contentedly. I felt my temper rise. "Sir, have you never before met a woman? Do you know a single woman who does not seek to enhance her appearance in public? Does not your good wife -- I assume that you have one -- spend an unconscionable amount of time, to your great irritation, in front of her dressing table, tidying her hair, fixing her eyelashes, patting on her rouge and applying her mascara? Does she not wear stays to narrow her waist and lift her bosom? I assure you, sir, that as one gets older it is even more essential to put considerable effort into the business of enhancement. I happen to like my hair this colour, and I think that my spectacles make me appear intelligent and even erudite. I find that this helps to earn respect among gentlemen. Now then, sir, no more of this nonsense, if you please. I now wish to return to my hotel."

"Not so fast, madam. You have a sharp brain and a smooth tongue, and I like that in a woman. Let us continue, then, to my next point. There is of course no such person as Mrs Susanna Ravenhill. My men have spoken to many landladies, and other persons of your acquaintance, and the story of your life appears to be nothing but a tissue of lies! Husband Jack, now deceased, residence in London, the loss of two children in infancy, a fortune made in business, and a search for the roots of your family and his -- balderdash, Mrs Ravenhill!"

"How dare you, sir! You talk of most sensitive matters and strike at the deepest part of a woman's soul! How then do you come to this scandalous conclusion?"

"Through the most painstaking research. We could not do much in the checking of your credentials last spring, since you led us a merry dance across South Wales, but since your departure for Europe my men have undertaken the most extensive research of all the public records. Neither you nor your fictitious husband Jack can be found anywhere, in London or in West Wales. Nothing in the Census returns, or on the tax records, or in the registers of births and deaths, or in the records of business enterprise! There now! What do you say to that?"

I decided at that point that I would not go down without a fight, and I felt an old fire rekindling itself in my belly. "Sir, shall we assume that everything which I have said is perfectly true, except for the name? I would not be the first person, or the last, to feel it expedient, at a certain time of my life, and for reasons of my own, to use an assumed identity. You may have done it yourself, in certain business dealings. I believe that in this country, among the writers of melodramatic fiction, it is called a *nom de plume,* and in England and Wales a pseudonym? Would it help if I should refer to myself as Mrs Jenny Smith, or Mrs Abigail Brown?"

Harry looked non-plussed. He growled and had to admit defeat on that particular line. Then he looked at his pipe, which had gone out. He filled it with fresh tobacco, lit it up and inhaled the foul smoke. "Very well, Mistress Abigail Smith, I perceive that we are not going to get very far on this line of enquiry either. So let me continue to use the language of this fair city and, without doing anything to harm you, administer my *coup de grace*. I know all about the wicked conspiracy in which you are very deeply involved."

"I have no idea what you are talking about, Master Harry. Please enlighten me."

"You are very resolute in your denials and your evasions, Mrs Ravenhill -- or whoever you may be. I find that intensely irritating, and my patience is sorely tried." I did my best to look as innocent as a little girl of four years old, thus irritating him even more. "As you are fully aware, Madam, I compete in business matters with Squire Gwynne of Plas Llanychaer -- shall we say that he and I have clashed swords more than once in the past, in the county of Glamorgan? It has therefore been in my interest to watch him closely over the past few years. One has to know what one's competitors are doing. Following that messy business with the preacher, brought about by those idiots in the Society of Sea Serjeants, things became very confusing in Newport, and even more chaotic when that Mistress of Plas Ingli died. There were so many comings and goings between Plas Llanychaer and Plas Ingli that my men became quite giddy. But on the very afternoon of Mistress Morgan's death, when grieving and consolation should be the order of the day, off went Wilmot Gwynne in his exotic red carriage to Cardigan. Most suspicious, would you not agree?"

"Quite so, Mr Harry. One has to wonder what was going on."

"I'll tell you what was going on, Mrs Abigail Smith! He was coming to see you! With Martha Morgan dead, and the Plas Ingli estate thus freed of encumbrances, he had to move fast. At first we did not know who you were, but then it became clearer and clearer as we watched you. All that mourning and grieving -- my men felt quite sorry for you. And you were very good, I have to say, at acting out your hunt for relatives and moving on before we could obtain information. But it was clear to me from the beginning that negotiations were in progress between Gwynne and yourself relating to the future development of his three estates. I knew that his capital assets were not big enough for him to go it alone -- so he needed financial backers, and preferably big ones. Then you kept on receiving visits from the doctor and his wife, and from Rhys Brithdir, and various others -- all members of the Morgan clan. Correct, Mrs Smith?"

"I will not confirm or deny anything, sir."

"Haha! An admission of guilt at last! With all those great shows of affection, I was fooled for a while into thinking that you really were a long-lost half sister of Mistress Morgan, and that it was your intention to buy back the old family estate from Gwynne. That would explain all the meetings with the family. But why all the secrecy? And why the sudden move from Cardigan to Newcastle Emlyn? We had a devil of a job keeping track of you -- partly because of a spell of snowy weather, as I recall -- and only traced you to Newcastle Emlyn after that helpful newspaper announcement appeared. Why, if you were a long-lost relative, did you not immediately come to Newport to stay at the Plas, or with one of the daughters, or even at Plas Llanychaer? I thought at first that that was because you were all conspiring to keep the delicate negotiations out of the sight of inquisitive neighbours or other likely purchasers. But I am no fool, Mrs Ravenhill!. I began to suspect that the half sister story was nothing but a fantasy, and having found out Mistress Martha's birthplace I sent one of my men to Brawdy to check the parish records of births and deaths. There never was a half sister, Mrs Smith! There! What do you make of that?"

"You amaze me, sir."

"Then you made two very bad mistakes, Madam, which might have fooled a man of lesser intellect than myself."

"Indeed? Pray explain yourself, sir."

"First mistake. On at least two occasions, to the best of my knowledge, you have been up on that mountain, undertaking certain activities which lesser men will not have understood. But I know well enough what you were up to, Mrs Brown! Oh yes! And dressed up as the mysterious Nightwalker, to boot! I saw you once myself! Very impressive, and indeed when I saw you that time on the mountain, when I was up there doing certain investigations of my own, you gave me quite a shock. It took me a little while to get to the bottom of your cunning plan, and to obtain confirmation of your purchase of the clothes and hat, and your hired carriages and so forth. But I have good men working for me, Mrs Brown........."

"And some incompetent ones as well, Mr Harry."

He glared at me for a moment, and continued. "Why did you have to do all of that yourself? You went to a great deal of trouble, for a lady of mature years who might have been expected to stay in her lodgings in a comfortable armchair. But I worked out that like all of the most powerful and successful business people in the land, you trust no-one and base your judgements on your own observations. You were no doubt following up earlier studies done by others, and wished to confirm certain matters with your own eyes."

"I admit to nothing, sir."

"On the matter of geology, Madam, do you like rocks?"

That was a surprising question, and for a moment I was taken aback. But then I said: "I have to admit, sir, to being fascinated by rocks ever since I was a small child. I once had a very pretty collection of pebbles."

"Aha! I thought so! Now then. Second mistake. After your play-acting in West Wales, you suddenly disappeared off to Cardiff, causing great confusion in Plas Ingli, Plas Llanychaer and indeed in my humble dwelling on the Mumbles. When we caught up with you, you were playing the part of the distressed noblewoman in Cardiff, living in the simplest of lodgings and helping the poor and sick! At first I could not work it out. Then I obtained reports that you had been seen in the company of Mistress Wayne, Lady Guest and other members of the wealthiest families in South Wales, and I perceived that through your charitable works you were worming your way into the drawing rooms of those who hold almost all of the power and influence in Glamorgan." He slammed his fist down onto the armrest of his chair, like a petulant child, and shouted: "Even I have not been permitted into those drawing rooms, Mrs Smith!"

"I am sure yours is just as comfortable, sir."

"Very true, Madam, but that is not the point. You even went to Merthyr Tydfil, a place where very serious wealth is to be found in the families of the Guests, the Crawshays and others. It was reported to me that you had been given more or less free access to Dowlais House! Then you were given a grand dinner by the Crawshays, in Cyfartha Castle, no less! So at last I perceived that you were in the process of obtaining commitments for substantial sums of money, from the richest families in the land. I was in the process of deciding what to do next when those idiots who were on your trail were intercepted by some Irish fellow. God knows what he was up to. No matter -- they came back to Swansea with their tails between their legs and minus certain items that belonged to me. That made me very angry indeed. Let me tell you that I am not very pleasant when I am angry, Mrs Brown."

"That I can well believe, sir."

"Well, in the event their incompetence did not matter too much, because on the very next day you abandoned your pretence of poverty and suddenly became a very wealthy woman again. First class train tickets, new clothes, and the best rooms in Carmarthen! And a very elaborate new ruby ring upon your finger, spotted by one of my men through his spyglass. I see that you have it on your finger as we speak. Show it to me, if you please."

"I will not do anything of the sort, sir! It is a very precious thing, Master Harry, and not just because of its monetary value. It was a gift from a dear friend. I never take it off my finger."

"Please, Madam. It is beneath my dignity to steal rings from ladies, and I have no wish to use violence............"

He held out one hand in front of him and patted the palm with his other hand. I knew that he could call in his men at any moment, and that they could easily remove the ring by force. So I reluctantly slipped it off my finger, got up from my chair and put it into his cold hand. Without a word he leaned over and adjusted the blinds so as to admit a little more light from the outside world, and he examined the ring minutely, holding it just a few inches in front of his nose. "Ah yes," he said at last. "Very nice. An excellent stone. And CEG engraved on the back. Charlotte Elizabeth Guest. All is explained." With that, he gestured to me again to rise and take the ring from him, and I had to struggle once more from the sofa to do so. He then returned the blinds to their previous position, plunging the room into its accustomed gloom, as if he abhorred the brightness of the sun. I had resented his bad manners as soon as I had entered the room, for he had not risen to his feet. And now he remained embedded in his plush armchair and expected me to jump up and down from my sofa like a serving wench, delivering and fetching my ruby ring. My hackles were high to start with, and now they were raised even higher. But I managed to keep my mouth shut.

"Where were we?" he said. "Ah yes, your sudden change of fortune in the town of Carmarthen. My men were amazed when they observed the lavish luncheons and suppers attended by your accomplices from the Newport district! No expense spared! No doubt you paid the bills. But their behaviour was quite disgraceful, Madam, though I say it myself, for they were all supposed to be in deep mourning following the death of Mistress Martha. A little more decorum might not have come amiss."

"I take that point sir, and am touched by your sensibility."

"To continue. And then, in a great flurry of activity, you make plans to go off to the continent with another old lady from Newport who was a faithful retainer of the Morgan family. Mrs Ravenhill's Grand Tour, they called it! No doubt to celebrate the completion of your business deals, Mistress -- and the last person to see you before you went off to Paddington was none other than Gwynne! One of my men saw the pair of you wandering by the river, arm in arm, making plans. He even gave you a kiss! A nice little deal, sealed with a kiss! Very touching."

At this point I became quite convinced that Jonas Harry was as mad as a hatter, which probably explained his interest in LeClerc de Paris, makers of fine gentlemen's headwear. I smiled to myself at my little joke, and thankfully he did not appear to notice.

"Once you were on the Continent, I tracked you for a while, but then gave up on it and decided to wait for you to come home. Not all of us can afford the Grand Tour, Madam, or afford to send fellows chasing after you from one capital city to another. And some of us have work to do. I know you have stayed in certain grand houses and at least four castles, and have visited a few more counts and princes with capital to spare, who might be looking for a sound investment in South Wales. But I knew that you were coming back to Paris, and knew where you would stay, so I thought that a little interview would be appropriate, well away from that fellow Gwynne and the Morgan family............."

Knowing very well by now what the answer was, I asked: "And how did you know when and where I would be in Paris, sir?"

"Ah, that would be telling. Shall we say that I have my sources, and very reliable they are."

"I know more about them than you might suppose, sir. Now then. You have told me a very long story, which I will not bother to dispute. But that cannot have been your reason for intercepting me. I would be glad to know why you have gone to all this trouble."

"Ha! We are getting somewhere, Madam. You are old and frail, but I have to say that your intelligence -- and your ability to lay false trails and to act coolly under pressure -- are mightily impressive. I am full of admiration. I wish I knew more about your contacts, and about the scale of your activities. All in good time. But just now I think that you and I could work well together, for the good of the people of Wales."

"Is that a proposition, sir?"

"In a manner of speaking. I cannot see why you choose to work with that fellow Gwynne, who is ill, and whose mind is addled with too much country air. I assure you that I know much more about the manner in which finance works, and about the great projects that are suited to the modern world."

"And you are working with Sir Thomas Lloyd, the Lord Marcher, no doubt under the pretext that your plans will bring great benefits to the community?"

"I don't deny it. Your information is sound, Mrs Smith. I am very impressed."

I judged that the time was right for me to move over onto the offensive. "You realize, Mr Harry, that I have been greatly inconvenienced by the armed thugs whom you have hired to follow me and threaten me over the course of many months?"

"As I have explained, Madam, I deemed it necessary. It was not my intention that you should feel threatened."

"Not your intention?! Frankly, sir, I do not believe you. That fellow Iago sought to frighten the living daylights out of me in Cardigan, and another of your men actually ransacked my lodgings. I thought that I might get a bullet in my brain or a knife in my back at any moment. Not very subtle, Mr Harry -- considering that you see yourself as a man of sophistication and sensitivity."

Jonas Harry squirmed in his deep chair, and wiped his brow. "Well, Madam," he muttered at last, "perhaps Iago and the others could have been more invisible. They are not very delicate fellows............'

"So,will you now call these thugs off Master Gwynne and myself?" I asked, drawing myself up to my full sitting height.

"If you wish it, Madam."

"I take that as a promise. Do not betray me, sir. I do not take kindly to those who say one thing and do another. Now then, Mr Harry. I'm intrigued by your familiarity with Paris and by your connection with the hat firm of LeClerc. Will you tell me more?"

He laughed. "I am in Paris very frequently, Mrs Smith, when I am not in my London office, or at home in the Mumbles. I find it convenient to use the financial facilities of this fine city, for reasons that should be obvious to you. And I am Monsieur leClerc! What do you think of that? A nom de plume is, as you say, a very fine thing in certain circumstances. I actually do employ three good men who make fine hats, and so we are a very proper and well-established commercial concern. I find my French bankers very cooperative......."

"I quite understand, sir. Where can I contact you?"

"The time for subterfuge is past, Madam, and my plans have all been set in motion, while you have been away. Just write to me at Plas Glas. I expect to be at home in three days' time."

"Now sir, will you be so kind as to tell me the time?"

"Twenty-five minutes after three, Mrs Smith."

I stood up. "Then I will be obliged if you will ask your thugs to release me back onto the street. Bessie is under strict instructions, today and every day, to alert the gendarmes if I am not back on the premises by half past three."

Harry slapped his knees and roared with laughter. "Oh my goodness, you have a fine sense of humour, Mrs Brown! I like it! As if the gendarmes would miss an old lady who is a few minutes late for her afternoon tea! Very good indeed!"

"You may laugh, sir, but the minutes are ticking away. You might have observed, if you had been more fastidious, that when I am in Paris I always use hotels that are next door to gendarmeries. And I always make a point of getting to know the gendarmes personally; I find that they are exceptionally kind to wealthy old ladies who move in the right circles."

A minute later, I was on the street again, walking back towards my hotel and feeling very smug. As I entered the hotel foyer, I was accosted by a tall and very handsome man with a bushy beard, who gave a deep bow. I did not recognize the beard, but I did recognize the eyes. It was my mysterious Irish friend.

"Why, Donal!" I said. "How good it is to see you! I observe that you have recovered well from the injuries inflicted upon you by Twm and Ianto. What on earth are you doing here?"

"Looking after you, as ever, Mrs Ravenhill. I saw that those bastards had grabbed you, and I was very worried. Have they harmed you or forced you into any indiscretions?"

"No no. I assure you that I am perfectly all right. In fact, I have had a most entertaining time, talking with a silly fellow over matters of mutual concern. I declare that I have never felt better."

He looked relieved, and I continued. "Now then, I would count it an honour if you will come upstairs to my suite, and meet Bessie, and join us old ladies for afternoon tea and pastries."

In the very interesting conversation which followed, I did not at first press Donal as to his real identity or affiliations, nor did he press me on mine. But after we had talked for a while, Bessie told me with her eyes that he was honest, and I decided to trust him. I did not reveal my identity, but I told him almost everything I knew about Wilmot Gwynne and Jonas Harry, and about what had transpired in the smoke-filled room. Donal decided to trust me too, and told me what his real purpose was in following Harry's men and in protecting me. We talked far into the night, and made plans.

13. Bolt from the Blue

After a year away, with only occasional news from home, both Bessie and I were suffering from *hiraeth*. Truly we had seen enough of castles and palaces, and had grown weary of travelling through landscapes which we had initially considered fascinating. We had attended too many operas and had admired too many wondrous works of art. Now we both longed for the fresh sea air of the Parrog, and the wide sky over the summit of Carningli, and the unpretentious comforts of our little town of Newport. Only three days before we were due to leave Paris for Calais and home, Bessie's health took a turn for the worse, and I wanted to get her home where she could receive good attention from my son-in-law George Havard and from Shemi, who between them made a formidable medical team. Now I realized that I would have to live the part of Susanna Ravenhill, half sister of Mistress Martha, in the full light of day, and in a familiar environment. This would be my ultimate test.

One day in late May we travelled by train from Paddington to Carmarthen, and thence to Narberth. We took the best room in the King George Hotel, and were joined there on the following day by Daisy and George, Betsi and Ioan. We six had a great reunion, and I treated them all to a splendid supper and to a night's accommodation in the grand style. For me it was a late birthday celebration, and I felt wealthy, having been informed by my bank manager that I still had more than £2,000 in my bank account. I had not previously appreciated the full extent of the free hospitality and free transport which had been given to us on the continent, partly as a result of Daisy's apparently endless list of counts and princes who had, almost without exception, proved to be remarkably generous. So I gave Daisy an extra warm embrace, and she winked in that devilish way of hers, and we all fell about laughing. I wanted to know all the news, and some of it was given to me over our interminable and excellent meal. They all called me Aunt Susanna, and I realized that I was now, well over a year after my reported death, quite comfortable with that label.

All of my own relatives were thriving, said Betsi and Daisy, but Wilmot's son Joshua and his wife Jane were not proving to be very popular at Plas Ingli. They were petulant and disorganized, and were thoroughly bored. The children were ill-behaved, and three nursemaids had come and gone in less than a year. Myfanwy had also left after being very badly treated by the new mistress. Will and Gerallt had both complained to Wilmot, said Ioan, and had threatened to leave within the month if things did not improve.

"Is this recent news, Ioan?"I asked.

"Just last week, Aunt Susanna. Wilmot is at his wit's end, and the worry is not improving his state of health."

On pressing further, I discovered that Wilmot had been confined to bed on several occasions over the past year, and appeared to be distracted by weighty business matters. George thought there was a rift between father and son. I was greatly saddened by this news -- and by the thought that the Plas, once a House of Angels, should now be a place racked by dissension and ill-will.

"I met Wilmot just two weeks since," said Betsi. "He is seldom seen in town. He looked haggard, and he has lost his good humour.............."

"Oh, no!" I moaned. "I cannot imagine dear Wilmot without his good humour. He is the most jovial fellow I have ever met -- and the life and soul of every party! I wonder if I can help him in some way?"

I left matters there, but I knew in my heart that Wilmot's misery must have something to do with Harry and his plans. I determined to find out more on my return to the district.

After breakfast next morning the members of my family left me in Narberth, and took Bessie back to Newport with a view to settling her into her lodgings with Patty and Jake, and giving her proper medical attention. Before they left, they promised that they would "lay the foundations" for the arrival of Aunt Susanna in Newport, and said that they had already organized accommodation for me, in the cottage called Brynglas in Cilgwyn -- a place which had a better view of the mountain than any other residence in the district. I knew it, and was delighted.

I arrived quietly in Cilgwyn some days later by hired carriage, and presented myself at Brithdir, the residence of Betsi and Ioan. With very little fuss, I gave my greetings and then went with Myfanwy (who was now -- much to my delight -- to work for me) to settle into Brynglas. I had forgotten what a sweet cottage it was, placed quite high up on the eastern side of the *cwm*, with Carningli dominating the western skyline. The Plas was within easy walking distance, but even closer was Tycanol Wood, a place of particularly vivid memories which I preferred, for the moment, to keep at the back of my mind. On the slope above the house was the big farm of Cilgwyn Mawr, which in my days at the Plas I had often coveted but never managed to buy; and on the summit of this prominent ridge were the beautiful rocks of Carnedd Meibion Owen, blue and cool and lichen-encrusted, and reputed to be the petrified remains of the last giants to have lived in the neighbourhood. I determined that if I needed exercise and fresh air, those rocks should be my destination for the time being, for I did not want my routines and my passions to be identical to those of Mistress Martha.

It was early June, and a time of clear skies, and high sun, and mellow light. I chose for my bedroom a little room on the west side of the cottage with a single window which gave me a perfect view of Carningli and the Plas. On my first morning I woke at five o'clock to find that it was already light and that I had missed most of the dawn chorus; I grumbled to myself and resolved to wake earlier on the morrow. I got out of bed and pulled aside my curtains, and saw before me the great bulk of the mountain bathed in the most beautiful golden light. I had never seen anything like it, for I had never before looked at the mountain from this angle, so early on a summer morning. It took my breath away. There was not a cloud in the sky, and not even a whisper of wind. I felt that the whole world was holding its breath. High on the slope of the mountain the Plas, that beloved and lovely place where my heart resided and where angels dwelt, gleamed in a sacred whiteness that made it look more like a church or a shrine than a working farm. Below it the lower fields and indeed the whole of the basin of the *cwm* were invisible, lost in an early morning gossamer blanket of mist which moved about with infinite slowness and began to dissolve as I watched. A column of smoke, hardly visible, rose straight from the kitchen chimney and eventually disappeared high above the mountain summit. Somewhere -- I think it was at Brithdir -- a border collie barked. A cock crowed somewhere else, and I realized from the strange choked ending to its serenade that it was the Plas Ingli cock which I had hated ever since it had first attacked me. Was that monstrous creature still alive, when it should have been consigned to the pot long ago? Time passed, and the gold that burnished the mountain turned to silver. Had I really had the temerity to insult this place by wishing to be somewhere else? With the full realization that I was at home again, I became aware that tears were streaming down my cheeks.............

"Breakfast time, Mistress! It's eight o'clock!" shouted Myfanwy up the stairs.

For some days Myfanwy and I enjoyed ourselves in the cottage and went nowhere. There was plenty to do, since the place had stood empty for almost two years following the death of the last member of the Gwilym family. We brushed and dusted and polished, moved furniture about, made curtains and sorted out linen and sheets and blankets. I sent orders to various shopkeepers in town, and received deliveries of china and glassware, cutlery and wooden bowls and platters, meats and vegetables, bread and pastries, fruits and preserves, cheeses and pickles, and all the other things needed for a well-stocked pantry. I ordered in some good wines, and barrels of cider and ale. The cupboard had not exactly been bare when I arrived, for Ioan and Betsi had kindly taken care to stock it with essentials like flour, dried fruits, spices and sugar and salt. Gradually I put my stamp upon the place, and once there were flowers in the vases and food in the cupboards Myfanwy and I began to feel quite homely and cosy. Somehow or other, several of my favourite ornaments from the Plas, which had been distributed to family members following the reading of my will, took up residence at Brynglas. So a favourite ebony statuette which had gone to Betsi appeared on the mantelpiece of the dining room; a lovely crystal decanter which had gone to Daisy took pride of place in my glass cabinet; and a carved wooden fruit bowl given to me long ago by Owain and passed on to Rose now miraculously reappeared on the sideboard in the little parlour. I was a little concerned at first that these personal effects might be recognized by strangers or neighbours who were not part of the conspiracy -- but I need not have worried, for people are in truth a great deal less observant than one might think.

One day I went for a walk among the giant rocks of Carnedd Meibion Owen, and on another I dared to enter Tycanol Wood. That was a place of undimmed memories, where I had lain in the arms of my husband David on many occasions; where I had allowed my passions to get the better of me in the presence of my last love, the preacher Amos Jones; where I had found the rotting corpse of the poor woman who loved Amos, and who could not bear to see him in the arms of someone else; and where Amos had been strung up in a tree and left to die. Wonderful memories, and terrible ones, from the final pages of the journals of Martha Morgan. Much to my surprise, I coped. As I walked, there were certain spots which I knew I would never again visit, but I found new places instead, beside the gnarled and fantastical oak trees with their intertwined branches, and beneath the whispering canopy of fresh oak leaves, and behind moss-covered rocks, and in hidden dells dappled with sunlight. I put my memories away, and tried to see the wood as a small child might see it, as a place of shy elves and dancing fairies.

Visitors came to see me -- in a trickle at first and then in a flood, and in the course of my first week almost all of my fellow conspirators called to give me their greetings and to find out about my adventures in foreign parts. The older ones -- whether or not any blood relationship was claimed as a part of our subterfuge -- called me "Aunt Susanna," and the younger ones, like my beloved Rose and my other grandson Abel, called me "Great Aunt Susanna." That gave me great pleasure, and pulled me once again into the bosom of the family from which I had departed in mysterious circumstances. The only conspirators who did not come were Wilmot and Delilah, who sent their apologies and explained that they were both suffering from summer chills. I am not sure that I believed that. My visitors all brought welcoming gifts with them -- barrels of salted herrings, eggs and chickens, hams and sausages, cakes and scones, cans of milk and pots of cream. These gestures were greatly appreciated, for over the course of a fortnight a considerable amount of catering was required, and I felt that my visitors could not just be received and cursorily sent away again. I wanted to spend time with all of them, and they wanted to spend time with me and Myfanwy; and the cottage which had stood empty and cold came to life again, and echoed with laughter, animated conversation and the clinking of glasses and the homely sound of cutlery on china.

At last I plucked up the courage to go into town with Myfanwy, dreading the fact that I would meet many people on the street whom I would know but who would themselves not know Mrs Susanna Ravenhill. I was convinced that they would all recognize me in spite of my short brown hair and my horn-rimmed spectacles. I need not have worried. Myfanwy was quite wonderful, and whenever we came face to face with a familiar person she immediately said something like this: "Good day to you, Mrs Shinkins. Nice weather we are having. May I introduce to you my new employer, Mrs Ravenhill, a distant relation to the late Mistress Martha? She has lately been travelling abroad, and has taken up residence at Brynglas." We enjoyed many convivial conversations on the pavements and in the shops, and between us Myfanwy and I managed to cope with all the questions which were directed at us in a perfectly easy manner. After an hour or so, Myfanwy noticed that I was getting tired, no doubt because of the amount of nervous energy I was having to invest in these random encounters, and she took me home.

The hay harvest was in full swing, and the time came for the field in front of Brynglas to be cut. It was owned by Billy Lewis Cilgwyn Mawr, and he called in on the day before the harvesters were due, to introduce himself and to warn me that there would be several days of frantic activity on my very doorstep. He was a short man with a ruddy face, extravagant side whiskers and intelligent eyes; I knew him perfectly well, of course, and I thanked my lucky stars that he was not so intelligent as to see through my disguise. I said I was delighted to meet him, and over a cup of tea I said that I would be only too happy to assist if at all possible with looking after the harvesters. "*Duw Duw*, Mrs Ravenhill!" he said. "It's good to have one of the old generation of Morganses back in the district! Things are not the same, with those young Gwynnes in the Plas."

"My dear Mr Lewis," said I. "I am entirely unrelated to the Morganses, and only half related to the Howells of Brawdy. I am a half sister to the late Mistress Martha, conceived, I am sorry to say, in circumstances which had better not be described."

"I am sworn to secrecy, Madam. Wealthy squires always were too liberal with their oats. But dammo, your voice is just like Mistress Martha's, deep and strong, but a bit older, and that's good enough for me to welcome you as a good lady. If you have half her blood and half her spirit, we are well blessed by your arrival."

Next day the men with their gleaming scythes moved in early, before the dew was off the grass. I thought they were a little too early, but dared not say so. Will was one of the harvesters, as was Gerallt, and Gomer, and a dozen or so of the labourers from the surrounding farms, all of whom had worked for me at the Plas in the past. I introduced myself, and they all bowed and touched their caps and bade me welcome to their community. I was very touched. Soon they were striding across the field, one step at a time, in a staggered row, with their lethal blades flashing in the sunlight. The tall sweet grass, enriched by a thousand varieties of summer flowers and herbs, fell in swathes before them, to be raked back by the women who followed at a safe distance. I could not resist joining in, and raked away alongside the servant girls from Cilgwyn Mawr and Fachongle, singing a traditional carol which set the rhythm for the harvesters. "Well I never!" said Polly Griffin from Fachongle Ganol. "You are clever, Mrs Ravenhill, knowing that song of ours! We thought it was just local!"

Luckily I had my wits about me. I laughed and said: " No no, Polly. It's known elsewhere as well -- I remember it from my childhood in Carmarthen, where my mother used to help in the hayfields to earn some extra money." I got away with it, but the incident reminded me that I could not drop my guard for a moment.

It was so hot in the open field beneath a beating sun that I soon felt my age and had to retreat. In truth I was also afraid that I might perspire so much beneath my straw hat that my hair dye might start to run and cause me embarrassment. The other women and girls laughed and let me go, and were happy enough that I then assisted with the laying out of the harvest picnic beneath a mighty oak tree on the southern edge of the field. At noon Billy Lewis's head man, who was Lord of the Harvest, signalled a stop to the harvesting, and the men, who were close to the point of exhaustion, stopped to catch their breath, leaning, heads down, on their scythe handles. I looked at their gleaming shirtless torsos, and in spite of my great age a thrill ran up and down my spine. I may have a new name and a new history, I thought, but thank God I am still a woman. I exchanged glances with Myfanwy, who was also helping; she smiled and winked, and I blushed like a twelve-year-old. Thirty-five people sat down on the grass to bread and salty butter, cheese, slices of ham, pickled onions and a host of other good things washed down with copious quantities of cider. Afterwards some of the men snatched forty winks, flat on their backs in the deepest shade; and then the Lord of the Harvest gave a great shout, and within five minutes the blades were flashing again and the songs of the women were echoing around the hedgerows and treetops.

That evening, with the harvest done and the field of cut grass below my window smelling better than heaven, I went to bed in a state of blessed contentment.

Three days later a ragged urchin appeared at my door, carrying a small bag of possessions. I did not recognize him at first, but then I realized that it was Merlin. He immediately ran into my arms, and as I embraced him my joy disappeared as I realized that he was sobbing. "Why, Merlin," I said. "I am overjoyed to see you, but why the tears? Whatever is the matter?"

Ten-year-old boys do not enjoy weeping, and he did his best to fight back his tears. He sniffled and choked, and wiped his freckled cheeks. "My Aunty Polly is dead, Missis."

"Oh, no!" I exclaimed, and gathered him once again into my arms. At last I continued: "You poor child! She was a strong and feisty woman, as I recall, and not very old. When did this happen?"

"Ten days ago, Missis. She's already in her grave. She got apoplexy, I think, and I found her dead on the floor in the kitchen. I tried to bring her back, but my powers are not strong enough, Missis......."

He said that quite unselfconsciously, and I looked at him in amazement. He continued. "She didn't own the house, and she owed money on the rent. The man that owns it took it back and threw me out. They wanted to put me in the Workhouse, so I ran away. I knew I would find you somewhere around Newport, with a nice view of the mountain........"

I embraced him again, and both of us wept. Then we managed to compose ourselves, and I said: "No relatives, Merlin?"

"Not a single one, that I know of, Missis."

"Then you will come to live with me, for the time being. I will have to send a message to the Overseer of the Poor in Cardigan, in case they come hunting for you, and there may be some complicated formalities to go through, but we will see what we can do."

The poor child managed to smile through his tears, and Myfanwy and I took him into the house, washed him and fed him, and found a space for him in the attic which we later fitted out with a bed and some simple furnishings. When he had cheered up and settled in, we three talked at great length, for we had much to talk about. In one conversation, a few days after his arrival, I asked him casually whether he had ever been to Merthyr Tydfil. "Never, Missis," he said with an enigmatic smile. "But in my dreams I did once go to China, and had tea with the Emperor."

About a fortnight after my arrival at Brynglas, Rector Llewelyn Thomas arrived without warning. No doubt he had heard about the rich widow who had just taken the cottage, and thought it necessary to intro-duce himself and extend a welcome to a potential benefactor. Perhaps his motives were entirely altruistic, and indeed my feelings for him were already modified, to some degree, by the kind words which he had report-edly used in the eulogy at my funeral and as the coffin of stones had gone into the ground. I became somewhat flustered when Myfanwy announced his arrival and called me down from my room, but thereafter we gave a good account of ourselves, and over tea and scones I became quite relaxed and confident in my new persona. I think I managed to converse in a perfectly level fashion, and did not once cause him to raise his bushy eye-brows in surprise.

Then I noticed that he was twitching like a nervous schoolboy, and that he had some important news to impart. Arising out of nothing in particular, he said: "Yes indeed, Mrs Ravenhill. You will find this a small but exciting community. There are good people here, and wise men to pro-vide leadership. Sadly, we have lost trade since the arrival of the railway in Haverfordwest, and if you go to town you will observe that the ware-houses are by no means full, and that the estuary becomes more and more silted up. I fear we will lose more trade when the railway reaches Fishguard and Cardigan, as it will within ten years, if I am not much mis-taken. But all is not lost, and there is optimism in the air. The plans to which I am privy, and which are shortly to be announced will, I am sure, restore Newport to its accustomed pre-eminent position among the Cardigan Bay sea-ports."

"Indeed, sir? The town seems to me to be quite pre-eminent enough as it is."

"No, no. The future lies in industry, Mrs Ravenhill, as you will know, since I believe your late husband had dealings with iron and coal and manufactories. And you will know that the fortune which supports the Plas Ingli estate was made by Master Gwynne through the smelting of copper. The little estates cannot survive without such enterprise."

"Oh but they can, sir, since the nation will always need food, on the hoof or in the fields, and it is down to the squires and the estates to provide it. The likes of Master Lewis, just up the hill, and the family of my half sister at the Plas, have shown down through the decades that they can put good, cheap food onto the market and look after the community and the land into the bargain."

"My dear Mrs Ravenhill, those days are gone." said he, shaking his head. Then he looked round furtively, for fear that he might be overheard, leaned forward conspiratorially, and continued in a voice not much louder than a whisper. "I refer to the great plans now being made, with the active involvement of our most excellent Lord Marcher, for the growth on the Parrog of a great new port. It was a new port once before, Madam, you understand, when the Norman invader came. Now it will be reborn and resurrected!" His voice became louder as his body was filled with excitement. "My goodness yes," he enthused, "with a breakwater half a mile long, and wharves and warehouses. I have it on the highest authority, although it is not yet common knowledge in the town, that the iron smelter will go where the sand dunes now stand, and........"

I almost fainted, in spite of the fact that I was already sitting down. "Dear me, Mrs Ravenhill," said Rector Thomas. "May I fetch you some water? You appear to be excessively surprised. Do I take it, therefore, that you are not familiar with the wonderful plans that are being talked of for that horrid mountain.........?"

14. Council of War

Myfanwy ushered the Rector out, and I tried to digest the information which he had fed to me. At first I was in a state of shock, but after a while I regained the power of speech. I asked Myfanwy what on earth the fellow had been talking about. She had no idea, so I sent her her to fetch Rose and Henry, who lived not far away, at Trefelin near Cilgwyn Bridge. Henry was out at work, but Rose hurried back with Myfanwy, and confirmed that she too was quite in the dark. "If Henry had known anything about new ports, warehouses and ironworks, he would certainly have told me," she said. "He prides himself on having his ear close to the ground. He is, after all, an engineer himself, and knows all about iron prices and such like." Then I recalled that he and my grandsons Abel and William had set up a forge and engineering workshop not far away at Dolbont, where they were making ploughs, seed drills and other machines. If they had heard nothing from their trading contacts, this was a tight secret indeed, and probably the Rector had given something away that was not yet due for announcement.

Further investigations got me nowhere, but it was not long before the truth emerged. Next day, after the delivery of the post, Daisy called to see me, with a grim expression on her face. She had in her hand a letter and a parliamentary announcement sent by her son John from London. It referred to a Bill shortly to come before Parliament for the setting up of a new company called the Carningli Stone Company, with provisions for the enclosure of virtually all the common land on the mountain, and for associated port developments incorporating a crushing plant, grading machinery and storage hoppers on the Parrog. There was also a mention of the removal of the sand dunes of the Bennet, to facilitate the development of certain manufacturing activities, to be connected to the port by a mineral railway. The sponsors of the Bill were Jonas Harry Esquire and the Lord Marcher of Newport; and five other subscribers (all of them Members of Parliament) were listed. There was little further detail. In his letter, John said "Dear Mama, if Grandmother had been alive to see this announcement, she would surely have shouted "Over my dead body!" As it is, she will probably turn in her grave."

Feeling more dismal than ever, I immediately sat down and copied all the details of the parliamentary announcement and sent them in a sealed envelope to Donal, care of Brendan at Garfeth. I gave the envelope to Merlin, and having described for him the route he must follow, trusted him to make the delivery. I did not know where my mysterious and dashing Irish friend was at the time, having had no recent contact with him; I assumed that he was probably in London or Swansea, tracking Jonas Harry. I also urged him to come to Newport with all possible haste, since matters were clearly coming to a head. I did not know at that moment whether the Bill was just a speculative one; as Daisy reminded me, there were many such, particularly associated with railway developments, which never led to anything solid. But other Bills were enacted and did allow developments to happen, with or without the support of the communities likely to be affected. I looked again at the date on the Parliamentary Notice, and saw that there were only five days to the parliamentary debate.

I then invited Ioan and Betsi, Daisy and George, Shemi and Sian, and Wilmot and Delilah to dinner on the following day for a council of war. For a start, I was desperate to find out who knew what. More importantly, I wanted us to agree a strategy for fighting this monstrous proposal. I was now not so worried about spies, since Harry had promised me -- somewhat reluctantly -- in Paris that he would call them off.

They all came, and I gave a special welcome to Wilmot and Delilah, who both looked weary and ill. I was concerned for their welfare, and determined to talk to them later, alone if possible. After we had eaten a simple dinner of three courses, we got down to work. Daisy read out John's letter and the cutting attached to it. Ioan and Betsi said they knew nothing more, apart from the fact that men had been seen on the mountain at intervals over a year or more, attracting a certain amount of speculation. George, as a burgess and member of the Court Leet, who should have been informed about any great plans for the town, knew just a little more. He said that while the Lord Marcher had recently been renovating the castle (which had previously been ruinous and quite uninhabitable) he had let it be known in town that he had "certain plans for the restoration of the port" without elaborating any further. He had also told the burgesses at a meeting some months back that he was looking to bring great benefits to the community through new commercial activities which were still in the process of development. For a few days there had been speculation in town, with most people broadly enthusiastic, on the grounds that the economy needed to be revitalized. But then it had gone quiet again, and he and everybody else had assumed that this was just another expression of good intentions, like many others over the years, which had no substance to it.

"But what about the boulder which the Rector threw into the pond yesterday, creating waves which almost knocked me over?" I asked. "He was very specific, and talked of breakwaters, wharves, railways and ironworks. There was no mention in the Parliamentary Announcement of ironworks -- just "certain manufacturing activities". Was he speaking out of turn, and does he hold other privileged information?"

"Maybe, Aunt Susanna," said George. "He is a great crony of the Lord Marcher, and also an inveterate gossip. He may well have heard things. But I imagine that the Lord Marcher would not be best pleased if he were to find that those of us in this room now know more than we should."

Shemi and Wilmot knew a very great deal more than the Rector, and it transpired that they had been waiting for my return before bringing their information to more general attention. Some weeks back, they said, they had thought of writing to me, but had then decided that they did not want to alarm me or disturb my Grand Tour with unwelcome news. They also speculated that because of his privileged position as a barrister in and out of Parliament almost every day, John had spotted an announcement of a Bill long before it was likely to be reported in the press. They assumed that there must be a plan to announce the project within the next few weeks.

"So, Wilmot," I said, "not for the first time, we will have to turn to you for enlightenment. May I first tell you everything I know?"

"Please do, Susanna."

"First, I know that Jonas Harry hates you, Wilmot, with a frightening vehemence, and will do almost anything to defeat you and thwart whatever plans you may have. Second, he wants your estates, for reasons which become clearer by the day. He also wants the other estates around the mountain, and which have associated commoners' rights. He has followed me everywhere, because of the information provided by that wretched serving girl at Plas Llanychaer. I take it that we all know about that?"

We all nodded, and Wilmot became flushed, and started to apologize again. I put my hand on his arm and said: "No no, Wilmot. That betrayal could have afflicted any one of us. Anyway, in a strange sort of way, it might have helped our cause. And I am almost certain that Harry does not know my identity. I have met him, and we have a certain rapport."

Wilmot looked alarmed. I laughed, put my arms around his neck and gave him a kiss. "Don't you worry, my dear Wilmot. I love you far too much to do anything that might harm you or yours. We all have a lot to lose here if anything goes wrong. Just you trust me. To resume. Harry is quite convinced that Wilmot has elaborate plans for the mountain and the common, and he also suspects that the owner of these two good little estates knows more about certain things than he does. Correct, Wilmot?"

Wilmot looked weary. "Correct, Martha. That fellow must lead a miserable life, suspecting everybody and everything. I give you my word, all of you, that I have no plans for the mountain, or the port, or the common. Nor am I in any sort of business relationship with anybody who does. As you all know, I have always fought for the continuation of commoners' rights, and have resisted enclosures. And I love the mountain, and will not see it harmed. But I will admit to you, between these four walls, that cash is tight, that copper prices have fallen, and that I have been finding it a struggle to maintain the estates. I have been talking to certain parties about loans and possible partnership arrangements, not with a view to financing some mad industrial project, but because I simply wish the estates to survive."

We all understood. There was a sympathetic silence, and then Ioan asked: "So Harry has found out about these approaches of yours, Wilmot, and has assumed that you are seeking capital in order to turn Newport into a sort of industrial heartland for West Wales?"

"I suspect so, Ioan. He has more or less accused me of that, in talking to mutual acquaintances, and that has been reported back to me. I have actually written to the fellow to say that I have no further interests in industry, having left all that behind me in Swansea under the control of my son Samson, but he refuses to believe me."

The poor fellow looked utterly dejected. "What more can I do?" he pleaded, as Delilah took his hand and held it tight.

Then George said: "And if copper prices are falling, presumably Harry's industrial empire is also in trouble?"

"Indeed it is," said Wilmot. "He has always invested his profits and kept little in reserve. Some of his investments -- for example in that absurd palace of his on the Mumbles -- have been foolish in the extreme. So now his instinct is to invest his way out of trouble again, in competition with a non-existent project of mine! I fear that the man is probably mad........."

"I think I concur in that, Wilmot," I said. "But what is he doing in bed with Sir Mervyn Lloyd, the Lord Marcher? Unlikely bedfellows, as I think you might agree........."

"Remember, Susanna, that Sir Mervyn is a very large landowner with estates in Cardiganshire and Carmarthenshire as well as Pembroke-shire. He also has industrial interests. I suspect that he and Harry are both Freemasons, intent upon a little mutual back-scratching."

"Why should Sir Mervyn now come back to Newport and start re-pairing his castle, which has stood in ruins for centuries?" asked Ioan. "I have been pondering on that for some little time, and now it becomes clear. He is a vain fellow, as we are all aware. Not content with the bowing and scraping of deferential local people, I think he wants to gaze down from the battlements on his new port and his smoking factories, just like Crawshay in Cyfartha and Guest in Dowlais!"

"No no, Ioan," I insisted. "Vanity cannot drive a scheme as vast as this. There must be much more to it than that............. "

Shemi, who had remained unusually quiet and thoughtful thus far, now intervened. "Let me assist, dear friends. I have been looking and listening, and have been collecting little dregs of information from here, there and everywhere. Some of the men who have come here from the Swansea district have been thugs and spies, well trained to remain tight-lipped even when their tongues have been lubricated in the Black Lion. They have not stood out from the crowd in any particular, since there are scores of passing sailors, merchants, craftsmen and itinerant labourers prowling around in Newport and on the Parrog at any one time -- particularly in the summer. The ones who caught my eye, round about Eastertime of last year, were the professional men, carrying maps and measuring things. Some of them came in their own carriages. They worked quite surreptitiously, sometimes in bad weather so as to avoid observation, but there was no doubt as to what they were up to............"

"Did you know at the time," I asked, "that these men were working for Jonas Harry?"

"I suspected it, but I was not certain. To continue. I would have given a fortune for one of their maps, but they were incredibly careful with them. Then, more than a year ago, just before you went off on your Grand Tour, Susanna, you presented me with a set of their maps, kindly obtained by a mutual acquaintance of ours from one of Harry's spies. I examined them carefully, but still could not work out their full importance. Then I heard from my friend that he had obtained from the same fellow a compass, and suddenly everything became clear! In the summer and autumn, those same fellows were back again, and I surmised that they were repeating the same work, following the loss of the first set of maps. I imagine that their noble leader was not a happy fellow, and that his scheme was set back by at least six months. "

"It may be clear to you, my dear Shemi, what the nature of this great scheme may be, but I am perfectly mystified!" said Delilah, who liked a good mystery. "Is this not wonderfully thrilling?" She glowed and wobbled with excitement, and the rest of us scowled.

"Several of the maps have got pencil lines on them," said Shemi, "and numbers scribbled here and there. Some of the lines on the maps are compass bearings, my friends, and some of the numbers are compass readings. Other lines are intended to indicate the routes of new roadways and mineral lines, and possibly overhead cables or Blondins intended for the transport of bulky materials. And then the final set of numbers relates to the distances covered by these various routes, as an aid to estimating construction costs. So there we have it -- the veins and arteries of the Carningli Stone Company."

Everybody in the room was stunned. Then Betsi said: "But this seems to be a giant project, Shemi, if you are right. We know something of it already, of course, from that cutting sent by Daisy's son John, with mentions of a new port with a crushing plant, grading machinery and storage hoppers on the Parrog. But where will those things go, and what will happen to the houses, warehouses and fishermen's cottages?"

"It can be taken as read that the existing buildings will all have to go," said Shemi, "to make room for these new structures. It is obvious from the maps that the shoreline from the Parrog towards the mouth of the estuary is the place where the new quay will be built, and where stone will be exported. There will also have to be adequate storage space for the storage of limestone and coal which will be imported."

"Coal and limestone? But what for, Shemi?" asks Daisy.

"For the iron smelters, Daisy, which I have suspected to be a part of the plan and which have now been confirmed as a result of a loose tongue."

"That would, I fear, make perfect sense," said Wilmot, to an audience of petrified listeners. "For iron smelting you need iron ore, coal and limestone. And very substantial buildings. Those buildings could not, I think, be built entirely of slate slabs from the sea quarries along the cliffs, but they could easily be built of stone from the mountain. Some of the sea quarries could provide the roofing materials. Coal and limestone already come into Newport, in small quantities, to feed the lime kilns. There would be a need for bigger ships and preferably for deepwater berths accessible at all states of the tide. That means the river would have to be diverted, and that there would have to be a huge dredging project along the western side of the estuary and probably a breakwater at least half a mile long out in the bay. As for the iron works, I can well understand why it needs to be across the river. Iron works are filthy, disgusting things, and if one is to be built in Newport it needs to be downwind or east of the town, in a position where the Lord Marcher can see it but not smell it."

"And how large would this iron works be, Wilmot?'" asked Ioan.

"I am not an expert in iron smelting, but I should have thought that there would have to be an output of at least 4,000 tons of pig iron every year for the project to make sense. That would be a small plant in comparison to those of Merthyr Tydfil and other great centres of the iron industry, but quite large enough to change this little town of ours for ever and to kill all the greenery for miles around."

"But why have these mad entrepreneurs called their company the Carningli Stone Company?"

"Well, if I was a mad entrepreneur, the first thing I would go for would be the stone from the mountain. I would anticipate at least one large quarry on the Newport side of the mountain, and possibly others as well on the south and east sides. They would carry stone down to the port by mineral railway and on overhead cable transporters. Very easy -- all downhill. The best bluestone -- which is wonderfully hard and magnificently coloured when fresh -- would be sold as a prime building stone, and the rest would be crushed. Remember that they have planned for a crushing plant and for storage bins and hoppers. At a guess, I would say that the crushed stone will probably go into Ireland for use in the road building programme instigated by the government."

Perhaps I should not have been so surprised. I was in a deep state of shock as I listened to all of this. And there was one thing which I still did not not understand. "My dear friends who know about such things," I said, "you have mentioned the importation of coal and limestone -- presumably from Milford Haven or South Pembrokeshire. But you have not mentioned iron ore or ironstone. That will have to be imported as well, meaning that all three of the essential ingredients for pig iron production will have to be brought in by ship. Surely that is not sensible? I know, from my time in Merthyr Tydfil, that all great iron and steel enterprises are located where at least one of the three essential ingredients is plentiful. At Dowlais and Cyfartha they had all three in the neighbourhood, just waiting to be dug out of the ground..........."

"You are very perceptive, Susanna," said Wilmot. "That is a sound rule, and it is hardly ever broken. I am mystified myself. All I can assume is that these men with grand designs are attracted by the location of Newport, on the far west coast of Wales. That gives this place a great advantage over the ironworks at Merthyr Tydfil and Ebbw Vale, which are a long way inland and have high transport costs. Land leases, canal and rail charges are going up all the time. Perhaps they see a future market for iron in Ireland, and see that they can sell into it from Newport in Pembrokeshire at an advantageous price."

"Let me enlighten you," said Shemi, having strung us along for long enough. "Nobody this evening has wondered why the fellows working for Harry and the Lord Marcher have been playing about with compasses. The answer is that they have been measuring compass deviations, and recording these on their maps. On the mountain there are certain places where the needle does not point north, but points somewhere else instead -- and in one spot it spins about and does not know where it should come to rest. I have observed this phenomenon myself, and so have many others. Some say that these anomalies indicate that the mountain is sacred, but for a scientist they indicate that the mountain is full of iron........."

We all stared at him with our mouths open, incapable of words.

He continued. "Iron is the only mineral that affects compasses in this way. Sadly, my friends, the conclusion has to be that the Carningli Stone Company intends to take out the surface stone to start with, and to then remove the heart of the mountain to feed its blast furnaces. The mountain is after all not very big, not much more than a thousand feet high and maybe half a mile from one side to the other. The only conclusion I can come to is that Carningli will be removed in its entirety."

I felt that my heart had been turned to ice, and I suspect that all of us in the room were similarly afflicted.

Before any of us could say anything more, Myfanwy knocked and came in. "Mistress," she said, "My brother Gerallt has just come back from town with certain news. A notice has gone up on the church door saying that next week, at seven of the clock on Thursday evening, there will be a public meeting in the Church Chapel at which the Lord Marcher, accompanied by certain scientists and experts in the matter of industry, will inform the people about exciting developments designed to alleviate poverty and bring great wealth to the town. I thought that you might like to know."

All of us in the room were white-faced and in a state of shock. I did not tell the others, but I knew now what my destiny was, and why I had been spared from the grave. I also knew why I had been guided to China, and encouraged to wade through human excrement, and forced to watch men die in agony from the effects of molten iron, and allowed to see what industry and greed do to people who cannot defend themselves.

I stood up and faced everybody, shaking with passion, and said: "My friends, if your conclusions are sound, and if these evil men truly plan to desecrate this sacred mountain and to destroy this beloved place in the name of progress, I swear before you and before God that I will stop them with my bare hands. If I fail in my enterprise, and if this diabolical scheme does go ahead, it will, quite literally, be over my dead body."

15. Atonement

The meeting went on far into the night. It was four in the morning when I got to sleep, and the eastern sky was already lightening. I slept fitfully, and in my dreams I was assaulted by beggars, orphans, maimed iron-workers, convicts and lunatics. I saw half faces and limbless bodies, eyes blinded by white heat and torsos eaten away by splashes of iron. Street urchins laughed at me, screamed at me, abused me, and tore at my clothes. Others threw their pathetic scraps of food into my face. A treadmill spun before my eyes, and I was inside it, trapped, trapped....... Drop-hammers clattered out a mad rhythm and furnaces went into blast. Dowlais tokens clattered down out of the sky onto the roof of Cardiff Prison, smashing the slates into slivers, and the prison turned into a hovel, and the hovel turned into a Workhouse, and that turned into a filthy bar in Penydarren, which turned into a brothel in one of the back alleys of Dowlais. The ground shook and thundered now, as a thousand furnaces went into blast, filling the sky with sparks and pouring streams of molten iron down into China, consuming hovels and alleyways and turning screaming children into vapour. Then I saw the brothel again, and Lady Charlotte Guest walked out of it, face painted like a whore, with her breasts bared, and grinning at me, and waving her red ruby ring before me on a chain. More whores joined her. They had fat legs and big hips and quivering breasts, and they turned into honey-eyed hams which were placed before a row of slavering ironmasters lined up along the big dining table in Dowlais House. The captains of industry leered at me and danced a mad Irish jig around me, going faster and faster, and at last whirling with such abandon that their fine clothes flew off them and they turned into skeletons, which then crumbled into small pieces, which in turn blew about like dust in the wind, and fell to the ground, and turned into cinders, stinking of sulphur and glowing red and orange in the blackness of Hell. I ran to escape from the flames, and slipped in a stream of human excrement, and found that I could not rise to my feet again. I started to sink in this foul slimy morass, up to my thighs, and then my waist, and then my neck, and as I sank out of sight it entered my throat, and I could not breathe..........

I woke with a start, covered in perspiration, with my sheets scattered around me, to find that Myfanwy was calmly drawing my curtains to reveal the brightness of another lovely June day. "Bad dream, Mistress?" she asked in a level voice.

"You could say that," I replied, still gasping for breath. "Myfanwy, is there still a real world outside that window?"

"Yes indeed. The mountain is looking as pretty as ever, I am pleased to say. The mist is just clearing."

I ate breakfast with Merlin and Myfanwy, and was pleased to see that the two of them were developing a fine relationship like that of a little brother and a big sister. The boy was growing tall and strong, and he was beginning to recover his spirit after the tragedy which had recently befallen him. That cheered me up, and banished my nightmare to the rubbish pile where it belonged. This poor child must be given a future, I thought, like all the other children of this district -- and that future should not -- would not -- be one dominated by sulphurous fumes, a blackened countryside, and the exploitation and humiliation of honest working people. By mid-morning I was possessed of a rock-solid resolve, and I had made plans for my atonement.

I sat down at the dressing table in my bedroom, and composed a long letter to Jonas Harry at Plas Glas on the Mumbles. It took me two hours to write, because the rheumatism in my right hand was very bothersome. I wrote that I had seen the notice of the Thursday public meeting in Newport and trusted that he might be present together with the other main shareholders for the occasion. I also assumed, and expressed this in writing, that they might all come to town on the Wednesday for preparatory discussions, and that they would all stay with the Lord Marcher in the newly refurbished castle. I wrote that I had also seen the Parliamentary announcement, obtained through "one of my sources." I declared that I was familiar with almost all aspects of the project as it had been designed, through other contacts whom I declined to name, and that I was familiar with the project maps. I knew that this would get him growling, and also suspecting that some of his partners had been loose with their tongues. Then I thought that I might make the most of Harry's mad idea that I was a closet geologist, and added that I was in possession of certain "detailed and most fascinating geological information about the mountain". Further-more, I confirmed that I was in possession of two confidential reports relating to smelting developments in the Guest iron works in Dowlais, Merthyr Tydfil, which would halve the amount of limestone required in pig iron production and allow the use of lower-grade iron ores. I also wrote that I was the holder of information on new steel making methods, involving certain additives to the smelting mix, based on confidential documents illegally obtained from the Krupps works in Germany.

Poppycock, all of it, but desperate times need desperate measures......

I also declared in my letter that I was aware that Wilmot Gwynne was in declining health, and that his plans for the mountain had not pro-gressed as far as he had anticipated. I expressed concern that the capital which Gwynne had promised -- to go with the funding committed by my own consortium of financiers -- would not materialize, leaving me with considerable assets but no viable project. I wrote that I was considering an alternative project in South Pembrokeshire, not far from the Vickerman smelter at Kilgetty, but that on balance I would prefer to invest in the New-port area, "in view of the great love for the local countryside which I have developed since my arrival." I doubted that he would see the irony in that statement.

I wrote that in view of the difficulties being experienced by Wilmot Gwynne, I now thought that I could secure the sale of his three estates for a total figure of £35,685, representing a recent valuation.

Finally, I asked whether £600,000 might be an appropriate figure by way of investment, bearing in mind that I would require a predicted annual return of at least 10% in order to secure the commitment of my confederates in Glamorgan and on the continent.

It was all rubbish, but I knew full well that Harry would rise to the bait, and would arrange a meeting in the castle on Wednesday evening, come hell or high water.

I sent off the letter, elaborately sealed "SR" with the invaluable assis-tance of my friend Skiff Abraham, by special messenger to Plas Glas, Mumbles. I insisted that the rider should hand the letter only to Harry in person, and that he should wait for a reply. The man arrived back next morning, having used six horses and having ridden a total of 150 miles. He was exhausted, and I paid him twice the asking rate. He brought this message from Harry:

Plas Glas, Mumbles
17th June 1856
My Dear Mrs Ravenhill
I acknowledge receipt of your most interesting letter. I am so pleased that as a result of our pleasant conversation in Paris we should now have established a constructive working relationship, and that you foresee certain benefits as arising out of cooperation. I will consult with colleagues and reply within 3 days regarding your proposal. The strong must stick together always, Madam, if they are not to become weak.
    Yours etc
    Jonas Harry Esq

He is on the hook, I thought. Sure enough, next day I received another message from him by express delivery, confirming that a meeting of the shareholders of the Carningli Stone Company would take place on Wednesday in Newport Castle, and extending an invitation for me to attend as an observer. "As an observer!" I thought. "Very kind of them, to be sure. I think it just possible, when I have done my observing, that they might like me to say one or two things about iron and money as well........."

On Monday morning, shortly after breakfast, one of the Lord Marcher's servants rode up to Brynglas with a very grand invitation to dinner in the castle on Wednesday, preceded by drinks at 7 o'clock. I knew that I had a very short time available to me to do some serious work, so I immediately asked Abel if he would kindly take me in the Brithdir chaise to Plas Llanychaer. I needed to talk to Wilmot and to my grandson in great depth, since they knew about smelting, and iron ore and coal prices, and the workings of the market place. As we drove along, Abel teased me because I could not sit still in the chaise and because I could not stop talking; but in truth I was possessed of a sort of mad energy, similar to that which I had felt before at various stages in my life, arising out of the knowledge that I was coming to a great challenge and a great victory. That was my instinct, and I hoped desperately that I was not deluding myself.

Atonement

When I got to Plas Llanychaer Wilmot and Delilah were sitting in the garden drinking tea, in the shade of an apple tree. There were two men with them -- Donal O'Connell and my old friend Shemi. "A warm welcome to you, Susanna, and to you, Abel!" said Wilmot, getting to his feet and sounding a good deal more sprightly than on our last meeting.

"Why, this is a miracle!" said I. "The very people to whom I wish to talk -- and whom I feared might be scattered about elsewhere, minding their own business."

"We were expecting you, Mrs Ravenhill," said Shemi, grinning mischievously behind his bushy beard.

"But that's absurd, Shemi. I didn't know I was coming myself, until about two hours ago!"

"Let's put it down to anticipation," said Shemi.

So we talked and planned, and I received a very intensive and exhausting course in all manner of things about which I had previously been entirely ignorant. Wilmot produced newspaper reports on share prices and investments and the like, and various trade journals read by men who smelt ores and make metal. And Donal placed before me certain financial information which I found fascinating and even shocking. We all stayed at the Plas for the night, for there was so much work to do; and it was not until late on the Tuesday that I felt well enough prepared to take on Harry and his confederates in Newport Castle. I went home exhausted, and managed to get a good night's sleep.

Early on Wednesday morning, I decided to go for a walk on the mountain. I took Merlin with me, and he was excellent company, talking non-stop, asking a multitude of questions, and observing little things that I, in a lifetime of observing, had missed. It was a perfect spring day, and for the first time in my new incarnation I did not have to hide, or act furtively, or resort to my ominous disguise. Merlin and I reached the summit, and he knew instinctively that he must now stop chatting and allow me to lose myself in my own thoughts. We sat on the blue rocks on the summit, holding hands, in complete silence. About half an hour passed as we gazed down at the Plas, and across the *cwm* to the distant moors of Mynydd Preseli, and to the north down on the sleepy town of Newport and far out across the placid waters of Cardigan Bay. This was a new experience for

Merlin, and he appeared to be greatly moved by the spirit of the place. A single raven appeared, wheeling high in the sky above us. Merlin lay on his back on the grass and watched it, as it went higher and higher, circling over the mountain, until we could see it no longer. The real world intruded when Will saw us from a distance and walked up for a chat. He had been looking for some stray lambs, lost somewhere among the crags and the boulders. We embraced and I introduced him to Merlin. Then we talked about the Plas, and I was pleased that Will referred to me as "Aunt Susanna" just as my own family members were getting used to doing. Will said he was desperately worried about the planned developments in Newport and the Parrog, but I was now feeling increasingly confident of our prospects, and I told him that the Lord Marcher would not have his way without a great fight.

At five minutes to seven, I was delivered to the Castle gatehouse by Abel, in as much style as we could muster. I was very worried indeed, but I knew that this meeting would decide not only my destiny but that of the whole of the Newport district. As I walked the short distance to the great door of the refurbished residence, I breathed deeply and saw in my mind's eye the breeze rustling the rushes on the estuary, and the tide flooding in with little slaps and ripples, and I heard the sounds of curlews and oyster-catchers. I saw the gulls wheeling around the herring boats as they came in on the tide towards the waiting fish-wives of the Parrog. I saw the sleeping town on a crisp winters night, with a full moon sailing high over the silhouette of Carningli. I saw Market Street on market day, filled to over-flowing with cattle and pigs and people, the air resonating with the sounds of town and country, and with familiarity and conviviality the main products on display. I saw the white grasses of the sand dunes, and the tall pine trees whispering on the edges of the churchyard..............

"Welcome to you, Mistress Ravenhill!" said a booming voice, bringing me back to the real world. The Lord Marcher and his lady were at the door. I curtseyed and he bowed, and after introducing me to his wife Henrietta he offered me his arm and led me inside. He was a big noisy man, oozing self-confidence and thoroughly used to looking down on everybody with whom he came in contact. But his manners were impeccable. He led me into a large room with a high vaulted ceiling. It was not too grand, and was sparsely furnished with a few tapestries and some ancient oak dressers, chests and chairs. There were no family portraits on the walls, and no statues or other ornaments. There were one or two small carpets on the floor, which was made of local black slate slabs. It was more like a refurbished castle than a home, and more like a second or third home than a primary place of residence. But I knew anyway that Sir Mervyn lived in his Gothic castle at Bronwydd in Cardiganshire by preference, and that his commitment to Newport was marginal at best.

I was introduced to five rather grand gentlemen, whom I had never met before. But their names were familiar from the Parliamentary Announcement sent from London by John; they were all Members of Parliament, and all potential shareholders in the Carningli Stone Company. We made small talk for a little while, and drinks were served. I was immediately impressed by the smug self-satisfaction displayed by each one of them; these were obviously men used to the exercise of power, but I was confirmed in my belief that men who were in partnership with crooked businessman like Harry were probably crooked themselves, or else very naive. I suspected that their egos were probably bigger than their fortunes. I wondered where Jonas Harry was, but then I was greatly surprised when he was carried into the room by the very men who grabbed me on the street in Paris. They settled him into a chair facing the window, and I was relieved to see that he had left his disgusting pipe behind, possibly in Paris. But in the brighter light of a Newport summer evening, and without his heavy spectacles, he looked desperately ill, with a pale complexion, sunken cheeks and eyes that lacked vigour. I was genuinely moved when I saw him. "I am so sorry, sir, to see your disability," I said. "Last time we met, I fear that I resented your lack of gentlemanly manners since you did not rise when I entered the room, or when I left. I apologize for that shortcoming on my part, and trust that you will forgive me."

"Entirely forgotten, Madam," said he, in a shallow voice. "And since we are apologizing, I have to say that I also much regret the somewhat discourteous manner ......" at which point he coughed, and then fought for breath "..... in which we encouraged you to attend for an interview with me. George and Jeremy, my friends, might have been more diplomatic."

"Never fear, sir. I look back on that episode with amusement, and indeed I was not in the least bit harmed by the encounter."

When George and Jeremy had left their master, we continued to chat about London, and Paris, and the state of the weather, and the latest news from Westminster. I think I held my own. We enjoyed an excellent champagne, and I was interested to observe that they all consumed far more than I did. I lied that for health reasons I was under orders to restrict my alcohol consumption to two glasses, on very special occasions only. This was such an occasion, I reported, to general merriment. Eight against one, I thought; not very good odds. But I felt as bright as a new sovereign, and I was well prepared.

At dinner, I had a close shave when the Lady Marcher said: "Mrs Ravenhill, that necklace is an uncommonly fine one, I must say. The only time I have seen such a necklace before, with fine cream-coloured pearls culminating in a wonderful pink pearl flanked by two blacks, was on the neck of the late Mistress Martha Morgan, of Plas Ingli, before that family fell on hard times. One of a pair, perhaps?"

I was taken aback, but recovered quickly: "I cannot tell a lie, Madam. It is the very same one, bequeathed by my late half-sister to her grand-daughter Rose and then given to me, her old aunt, by that charming young lady as a gesture of affection. I am inordinately fond of it."

At the end of an excellent meal, Sir Mervyn decided that it was time to get down to work. I was half expecting a preliminary meeting, at which I was permitted to observe but not comment, but he got straight to the point. "Now then, Mrs Ravenhill," he said. "I have heard a great deal about your expertise in financial matters, and indeed in the field of iron smelting. Most surprising and welcome skills for a woman, if I may say so! Lady Charlotte Guest had better look to her laurels! Truly you must be a most emancipated lady, and your arrival in our little community will be welcomed by all."

"You are very kind, sir. I know Lady Charlotte well, and I hope that I may have learned something from her."

After that, there was an elaborate game of cat and mouse. They tried to prise information out of me, and I let out just enough to impress them that I knew what I was talking about. The five MPs had very little to say, and I quickly gained the impression that they were there to provide finance and respectability, but that they would rather have been at Epsom Races. Having consumed a great deal more alcohol than I, they very quickly became bored by talk of slag, blast furnaces and iron ore percentages once they had ascertained that I was no fool. I thanked my lucky stars for that time in China and Dowlais. That left the Lord Marcher and Jonas Harry as the ones doing the talking and driving the project forward. The former was bluff and noisy, but not very well informed; but Harry was every inch the businessman, and in spite of his infirmities his mind was sharp. I wondered whether this mad project of his was actually keeping him alive. The men pressed me to reveal the "confidential information" mentioned in my long letter of some days earlier, but I left them in no doubt that I would not divulge anything about new iron- or steel-making processes and so forth until I was in possession of the financial information I needed.

I moved the discussion on from iron to stone, and said that I had customers for building stone and roadstone. "What prices per ton are you building into your budget, gentlemen?" I asked. When Harry told me, I raised my eyebrows, and he noticed my response, for the figures were wildly inflated. So I then pressed them for the assumed prices which they might get for pig iron from the Newport smelter, and found that those were wildly inflated too. I did not say so, but I was already aware that the projected income per annum from the business was twice as high as anything that could reasonably be expected in the real world. I did suggest that their projections were "optimistic", but the gentlemen simply shrugged their shoulders. Harry said, with a grin on his face: "As you will know, Mrs Ravenhill, all is fair in love, war and business."

Having obtained their respect, I continued to press them, and discovered that the project they were planning was based upon a host of extraordinary and unrealistic assumptions. They needed £1.3 million but had only raised £400,000 (£100,000 each from Harry and the Lord Marcher, and £200,000 in total from the other five). They had further promises of £300,000 if £1 million could be demonstrated in firm share sales -- so I knew immediately that I was the key to the whole enterprise, having dangled a carrot worth £600,000 in front of them in my letter. I had been briefed by Wilmot to press the Lord Marcher on his shareholding, since it was known that he was already deeply in debt following the building of his fairy castle at Bronwydd. So I pressed him, and would not be diverted. He was at first irritated by my impertinence, but kept his self-control; and at last he admitted that in order to raise the necessary funds he would have to mortgage Newport Castle, and also sell 25 farms and holdings on and around the mountain to the Carningli Stone Company for a few pounds each. Their full value would then be recorded and incorporated as company assets. "So you plan, sir, to sell worthless properties to the company and pretend that they are substantial liquid assets?"I asked. "Is that not something that might be referred to as false accounting?"

"Humph, I am advised,Madam, that that is entirely in order."

"Do the tenants know? Have they been given the opportunity in the past to purchase the properties they have lived in for generations, and improved bit by bit?"

"No, no," said the Lord Marcher, with his blood pressure rising. "If I sell to them, and then invite them to sell on to the company, obviously the price of every single property will rise, and that could make a difference of tens of thousands of pounds. And some of them might decide not to sell. That would certainly affect the viability of the project. I will simply terminate their leases and tell them that the properties have to be demolished in the name of progress."

"And do you anticipate that they will be happy with that, sir?"

"They will be very unhappy, Mrs Ravenhill, but I will be even more unhappy if this project fails to come to fruition. I prefer to be happy, so as to deal with the complaints of my tenants in a firm and decisive fashion."

"And the commoners' rights?"

"They will be dealt with when our Bill is enacted. Once it is through Parliament, the whole mountain will become enclosed land, where development is allowed and indeed encouraged by our government. That will involve a further Bill, which is currently being drafted. The farmers and tenants who currently have grazing and other rights can shout and scream as much as they like, but they will have no defence against our plans."

Harry then added that, of course, their Bill would have gone through Parliament on that very day, probably unopposed. The other six gentlemen thought this was all very entertaining, and I was amazed that in their ebullience they seemed to be so blissfully unaware of the fact they they were all involved in a gigantic confidence trick. Harry certainly knew that the scheme was corrupt from top to bottom, but I could not work out whether the others were capable of rational thought. Maybe they thought that ALL business deals were like this.........

I had heard enough. I announced that it was late, and that Abel would collect me at ten o'clock. Then I said: "Your proposals are of interest, gentlemen, although I have concerns about certain aspects of them. I should now like to ask you for a copy of your Business Proposal, so that I can inform myself as to the financing and small details, in advance of tomorrow's meeting. I wish to show it to my business advisers."

Harry and the Lord Marcher exchanged glances. "I fear that that will not be possible, Mrs Ravenhill. It is strictly confidential, and might find its way into the hands of competitors."

"Sir, if, as you say, your Bill has been enacted in Parliament today, there are no competitors. Wilmot Gwynne is already out of the way. And on the matter of confidence, if I am to be your major shareholder, and if I am not allowed to examine your calculations, I might as well bid you good night and be gone."

"Please don't be hasty, Mrs Ravenhill! I quite see your point. Of course you may have it until tomorrow. Your advisers are here, in Newport, Madam, and not in London?"

"They are indeed. Messrs Jenkins, Owen and Rhys. Excellent people. You will have heard of them. I like to keep them close to me at all times, sir, so as to facilitate rapid decisions. It's the only way to operate."

Then, I said, if I was satisfied, and if my advisors concurred, I would in all probability wish to make an announcement at the meeting on the morrow, allowing the Directors then to confirm that all of the finance was in place and that there were no practical obstacles in the way of the project, whatever the local objections may have been.

Ten minutes later I was on my way home in the chaise, exhausted but elated. I had in my bag a copy of the Stone Company's Proposal, having ascertained that there was only one other. I read through it by candle light when I got home to Brynglas, and I was amazed. Then I collapsed into bed, knowing that the morrow would be the day of destiny for my landscape, my community, and my alter ego.

16. Confrontation

At 11 o'clock on another wonderful June morning, visitors began to arrive at Brynglas. There was no great need for secrecy, since I was not being watched; and even if Harry's spies had been gazing down at us from the Carningli summit or from Carnedd Meibion Owen, and had seen the arrival at my cottage of a succession of chaises and gigs, and gentlemen on horseback, they would not have been surprised, for had I not committed myself to consultations on the Business Proposal? Shemi came early, and was followed by Ioan and Betsi, George and Daisy, and Wilmot and Delilah. Most of my fellow conspirators came and went as the day went on. Donal came down from Garfeth with Brendan, and I had a long private conversation with them. Throughout the day we all sat in the garden, in animated conversation, as the hot sun rose to its zenith and then slipped down again westwards, with Myfanwy and Merlin running in and out with long drinks of fruit cordial and food as required. What we enjoyed was effectively an extended picnic in the shade of my garden trees, but there was not much laughter, for very serious matters were being debated. There were grim faces on all sides, and I was very worried, for I knew that everything now revolved around me, and I feared that at any moment, in a very public forum, my true identity might be revealed. It needed just one slip of the tongue from one of my friends whose discretion thus far had been exemplary. And how much about me did Harry really know? In the time that had elapsed since our meeting in Paris, his men had had time to do a great deal more research; and if I went onto the offensive, might he then produce his trump card and announce to a packed hall that I was not Mrs Susanna Ravenhill at all, but Mistress Martha Morgan? That would cause such a commotion that all attention might be diverted from the plans of the Carningli Stone Company, allowing them to slip through unopposed.

In mid afternoon a small deputation of men arrived on foot. They were fishermen from the Parrog, and they asked to speak to me in private. I recognized two or three of them, but of course pretended that they were strangers to me. "Mrs Ravenhill?" asked their leader, one Tomas Wills who lived not far from Patty and Jake. I confirmed my identity, and he continued. "We have come to wish you well, Missis," he said. "Patty and Jake tells us that you have a certain interest in stopping these mad plans for the estuary and the mountain. Talking in town, we have been, and people are greatly afeared. Hundreds will march in the streets if this goes through, and I shouldn't be surprised if the castle is attacked. The Lord Marcher, miserable bugger, don't listen to nobody and thinks he can do what he likes just because he owns much of the land hereabouts. He don't even live here most of the time, Missis. Patty and various others have organized a petition, and they have eleven hundred signatures on it, just in the course of the last week since the news came out."

"Wonderful! Will you present this petition at the meeting?"

"That we will, Missis. Then there are other plans too that we can share with you. If these bastards get permission from the Queen to go ahead, and it looks as if work will start, we have fifty people who will build *ty unnos* cottages on the common, using that ancient law of Hywel Dda. You know about that old law, Missis?" I nodded. "A good one it is, too. There will be another fifty hovels built on the sand dunes and on the Barony land down on the Parrog. They will put them just where the smelter is supposed to go, and the crushing plant, and all the other big installations and railway lines and so forth. We haven't seen no maps, but the Rector has been yapping like a daft puppy, and we can work things out. We are not stupid. There will be all hell to pay if the Lord Marcher tries to get his people to move the squatters off by force, for they have rights, indeed, and will defend themselves using the law. Wilkins Legal has advised us, and says that could take years. Is that not a very jolly thing, Missis?"

"Very jolly indeed, Tomas. This is all good to know."

"One last thing, Missis," said another man whom I did not know. "If they try to bring in dredgers and so forth, we will block the river mouth with fishing boats. And if they want labour, nobody will give it. And if they then bring in navvies from Ireland or wherever, nobody will give them accommodation, and nobody will sell them food. The publicans have said, indeed, that they will not even sell them drinks."

Then Tomas sidled up to me and whispered in my ear: "And we also have the makings of an underground army of saboteurs, Missis."

"Good God! You realize that you will not get public support for that? I personally would speak out against anything that might involve damage to life and limb."

"No no," said Tomas. "Do not misunderstand me. No hurt to anybody. But I was in the wars against Napoleon, and so were several of the other older men in town. Some of us old soldiers and seamen are getting stiff in the joints, but our brains still work, and we know all about explosives and where to get them.........."

"Thank you Tomas. I would prefer not to know any more. Your news is greatly encouraging, and it's good to know that a mighty protest is building up. Some of us are taking a slightly more diplomatic approach, and hope that that might succeed, but if all else fails, the way may open up for you and your friends to act as appropriate."

They grinned, and all offered me their big rough hands, and through handshakes I received their goodwill and gave them in return my blessing. Then they returned to town to continue with their plotting.

One man who did not call at Brynglas during the day was Abel, for he was waiting -- with the Brithdir chaise -- at Haverfordwest railway station for the arrival of the first train from London.

The big meeting in the Church Chapel was packed out, with people crowding outside and peering through the windows. In theory, it was an open meeting, but as soon as I arrived I saw that there were several rows of town burgesses in the front, no doubt at the invitation of the Lord Marcher. They were mostly small traders and small farmers who would put their hands up when required, for they owed a great deal (including their status in the community) to Sir Mervyn's patronage, and they had no doubt all been thoroughly briefed as to the merits of the plans for the town. Then there was a sizable flock of faithful church-goers, shepherded by the Rector. Their votes could be counted on too. And in a rare alliance, they were joined by perhaps forty members of the Nonconformist chapels in town, from Bethesda, Tabernacle and Ebeneser, no doubt also convinced of the merits of industrial "progress" and seeing the plans of the Stone Company as a means of promoting hard work, thrift and assorted other virtues. I wondered if any of them had ever seen the real impact of industry on men's lives, or if any of them had ever heard of China. Eager anticipation

Confrontation

was in the air. This was not going to be easy.................

But as I took my place towards the front of the hall, flanked by George and Ioan, I reminded myself that outside there was a jeering crowd, burning a straw effigy of the Lord Marcher. And about twenty black-faced men dressed in female garb were on station -- just in case the *Ceffyl Pren* should be needed. The constables were nowhere to be seen, having absented themselves as soon as they scented a whiff of trouble in the air.

The Lord Marcher strode into the hall, looking as imperious as ever, flanked by his five gentlemen shareholders. George and Jeremy arrived, carrying a frail Jonas Harry. They took him to the front and settled him into a deep chair specially brought down from the castle. The rest of us had to sit on benches, tightly packed. I noticed that Iago Woodward, Silas Reynolds and one other man were also standing at the back of the hall, trying (with not much success) to look intimidating. I looked at the faces of the shareholders of the Carningli Stone Company, and saw in them apprehension if not fear; indeed, they would have been idiots if they had not already picked up on the disquiet in the town, and if they had not recognized the threatening behaviour of the black-faced men outside the door. There was chaos for a while, as yet more people tried to push into the hall and as the Lord Marcher's servants tried to stop them. We all had to squeeze in yet more tightly. The seven directors of the company were crushed up at one end of the room, but at least they had chairs, and the Lord Marcher invited me to join them. I accepted the invitation, causing a wave of murmured speculations to wash across the assembled company. Was this the Mrs Ravenhill people had been talking about? What on earth was **she** doing here?

The Lord Marcher took the chair and opened the meeting. He took it upon himself to give the outline of Carningli Stone Company proposals, more or less in accordance with what we already knew. There was much jeering and laughter from the start, to which he appeared impervious. "You will be aware, ladies and gentlemen," he said smoothly, "that there is not another smelter anywhere on the coast of Cardigan Bay or indeed anywhere in Pembrokeshire, apart from the little one at Kilgetty which is too far inland to be a success. We have here a deep-water harbour, sheltered from the south-westerlies which are the bane of other ports. We have a wondrous source of bluestone within a mile of the sea -- and there is nowhere to compete with it anywhere on Cardigan Bay. There is nothing in the way to prevent the efficient transport of the stone from the quarries to the port installations........"

"Apart from my paddock!" shouted somebody.

"And my house and garden!" shouted somebody else.

The Lord Marcher was momentarily ruffled, but pressed on. "We have markets for stone and slate only a little distance away, in Wexford and Waterford. And the most wonderful feature of the whole plan, ladies and gentlemen, is the iron mountain which we call Carningli. We do not believe there is anything like it in the whole of the British Isles -- eight million tons of iron ore, again less than a mile from the coast, available at very little cost to feed the Newport blast-furnaces, and indeed others across the globe which might wish to take advantage of a superior product at a most competitive price."

"Very competitive indeed," said Jonas Harry, nodding vigorously.

The Lord Marcher continued. "Ladies and gentlemen, we are most privileged to have with us today three scientific colleagues, whom I now ask to identify themselves ...."

Three men whom I did not recognize stood up a few rows from the back of the hall, and bowed, to the jeers of the crowd. We never did discover what sort of "scientists" they were, and many of us suspected that they were simply henchmen of Jonas Harry, brought in to increase the impact of the Lord Marcher's theatrical performance.

"These great experts have confirmed our findings and our calculations. In short, we have stone, and iron ore, of unparalleled quality. So, ladies and gentlemen, to conclude before I invite questions, there will be great benefits for all. Jobs in abundance, opportunities for local men to become experts in the craft of iron making, new schools for the little ones, new houses for the work-force (not in the same places as at present, you understand, but a little way removed), and wealth on a scale unimagined heretofore. And this wealth will bring in new shops, new facilities, and -- dare I say it -- new places of worship and recreation. The only slight inconvenience, as I see it, ladies and gentlemen, will be the necessity to relocate a small number of houses.........."

Confrontation

"You mean demolish, not relocate!" shouted my friend Jake.

"How many? There are thirty on the Parrog alone -- those and how many others?" asked Skiff, in a perfectly level and controlled voice.

"Yes, Mr Abraham, thirty, and maybe a few more in town. But many of these properties in town are old, damp and draughty. The new houses which we plan will be of the highest quality, built to exacting modern standards. And all who are required to move will be amply recompensed and commodiously accommodated elsewhere, so nobody will suffer........"

There was uproar. Questions were shouted from all directions. What about the common and the commoners? What about the fishing rights on the estuary? Where would all the workers come from? And what about the mountain? Does Sir Mervyn not realize that the mountain is a sacred place, blessed by St Brynach and inhabited to this day by angels?

Then my friend Tomas strode to the front of the hall, accompanied by another man. They carried between them a large paper parcel, and in spite of the protests of Sir Mervyn they dumped in on the table in front of him. "Eleven hundred signatures!" announced Tomas. "Not one of them wants your bloody quarries and your iron works, so take them away and put them somewhere else, if you please!" Then they stamped back to their seats, waving their fists in the air, with wild cheering in their ears.

Shemi Wizard stood up. He was dressed in his full regalia, including a long white cloak and a tall green pointed hat which I had not seen before. Half-way up it there was a wreath of the most beautiful summer flowers, no doubt picked and arranged by his wife Sian. He looked much taller than his six feet four inches, and with his great bushy beard he looked like a giant, or something straight out of the Mabinogion. Lady Charlotte Guest, the translator of that great work, would have been pleased. He had no staff with him, but he carried a bunch of oak saplings in full leaf. There was another cheer, for he was a man greatly loved as a defender of the poor and as a scourge of the pompous. Here we go, I thought -- time for a splendid theatrical entertainment from a doughty defender of nature and the countryside. I settled back into my chair, trying not to smile.

He waited patiently till he had complete silence in the room. "Sir, you call yourself Lord Marcher," he said, in a low voice, "and presume on the basis of some out-moded law to tell us what to do, where to go, and how we may lead our lives. Because you own land, you presume to do with it what you will, regardless of the consequences for others." As he continued his voice began to rise in pitch and volume. "Sir, have you no sense of the spirit of this place? Have you placed no value upon the whisper of a rising tide upon the sand, or the song of the skylark, or the scent of the furze upon a May day? If you had trod upon the mountain on this very morning, sir, you would have come down refreshed and renewed, and would have instantly confined this insane plan to the rubbish heap! Instead, you and your cronies -- whoever they are -- have been closeted in your dusty castle, counting tons of metal and charges of dynamite and volumes of rock and piles of golden sovereigns! What sort of lives do you lead, sir, and what sort of world do you want? Whoever your cronies may be, I see it in their eyes and their mode of dress that their future lives will **not** be lived here, enveloped in choking dust, with the rising sun blotted out by noxious fumes and with their ears assaulted by explosions on the mountain, and the thunder of furnaces in blast, day and night!"

The Lord Marcher became more and more agitated as Shemi gave his performance. "Be quiet, sir!" he said at last. "You are making outrageous accusations, and indulging in wild flights of fancy.........."

"Flights of fancy, sir?" roared Shemi, jabbing his finger towards him. "Have you ever been to Penydarren, or Cyfartha, or Dowlais? Have you waded through the shit in the alleys of the place they call China?"

"I am chairing this meeting!" shouted the Lord Marcher, drawing himself up to his full height. He was certainly imposing, but not as imposing -- or as colourful -- as Shemi. "I have not given you leave to speak!"

"Let him speak! Let him speak!" shouted the crowd, and at last Sir Mervyn had to sit down wearily.

Shemi continued. "I do not need your permission, and I do not recognize your authority, sir! There are those who doff their hats to you in the street, and count it a great blessing should you purchase a loaf of bread from them, or provide a day's work for them in your garden. Not I -- I am a freeman, and choose to defer only to those whom I respect. And you, sir, have done nothing to earn that respect! You have clearly not spent enough time in this place. If you had, you would know that the mountain which you plan to destroy is protected by spirits! One of these spirits is called the

Confrontation

Nightwalker. How many of those here present have seen him?" "I have!" "I have!" "Last year!" "Just the other day!" "Last evening!" "This very morning!" came the shouts from all over the hall.

"It is said that he is the ghost of some gentleman who many years ago committed some dreadful deed upon the mountain, and that he will place his mark upon any man who so much as takes a single stone from the slopes. A single stone, ladies and gentleman! How much greater then is the curse that shall fall upon the shoulders of he who should dare to build a railway upon the mountain.......?

"Amen!" shouted the crowd, as if they were in the middle of a great revivalist meeting.

" ..... or hack a black quarry into its gentle flanks........?"

"Amen! Amen!"

"..... or take away the summit, the part closest to heaven, to make crushed stone, to sell for thirty silver pieces.......?"

There was another even bigger roar, as some of the audience rose to their feet and the five MPs sank deeper into their chairs. I looked at Harry, and he looked like death. I had to grin, for here was Shemi, an avowed atheist, using the techniques of an evangelical preacher, and using choice references from the Bible to boot.

"But these men are not content with that, ladies and gentlemen, for they want to dig into the very centre of the mountain, and to take out its **bleeding heart**!" The townspeople in the room roared, and clapped their hands, and stamped their feet. The wizard held up his hand and waited for silence. Then he started again, with his voice no more than a whisper but rising almost imperceptibly to the climax which we all knew would come. "My dear friends, take it from me that every stone -- every stone -- that has iron in it will be taken and crushed.....and burnt in the hellish fiery furnaces which these men plan to build on the sandy dunes where we have all played as children! The mountain -- this wild and lovely place, this sacred Mount of Angels -- will be levelled, and the high places made plain! The golden furze and the purple heather -- gone for ever! No place, in the world which these men want, for ravens or skylarks or buzzards! No place for our children to hide among the rocks or to gather bilberries upon a summer day! No place for the cutting of turf or rushes! No white grasses whispering in the wind, and no place to breathe. Ladies and gentlemen, no silence.......... no silence .... and no peace." There was another long pause in his oration, and complete silence in the hall. I noticed that even the Lord Marcher was holding his breath, as if he was bewitched. Then came the whisper again, and the crescendo: "Oh, dreadful, dreadful indeed will be the retribution visited upon those who would do these things, for they will surely be cursed to their dying day by the just spirits which guard this mountain. Let these men of vile intent repent now at their leisure, in their castles and their mansions, for, my friends, if they do not, they will surely repent in hell, in this generation and indeed to the sixth generation in the years to come! Amen!"

There was thunderous applause and cheering from the crowd, and Shemi sat down. My old friend Amos, that beloved preacher and pastor, who used *hwyl* in his sermons as others used butter on their bread, would have been proud of him.

It was clear at this stage that the Lord Marcher had lost control of the situation, and he turned to Jonas Harry for help. People did not know him, and because of his disability they quietened down, accorded him some respect, and gave him an opportunity to speak. He spoke in a very quiet voice, and it was clear to me that he was not capable of speaking any louder. "Ladies and gentlemen," he said, "we have heard a good deal of invective here today, and that does not help us to assess, rationally and coolly, the merits of our proposal. This plan, if it comes to fruition, will be a godsend for the town and its inhabitants. I promise you that. There will be some disruption for a year or two, but nobody will suffer. Compensation will be generous. We have most excellent and reputable financial backers in the shape of the five gentlemen who sit with me here today, and others who wish to remain anonymous. I also dare to hope that Mrs Ravenhill will put her considerable resources behind the project. She is in possession of all the facts, and perhaps she will say something shortly. But whether you like it or not, ladies and gentlemen, and whether or not this excellent lady chooses to give us her support, this project will go ahead, since yesterday we have it on good authority that a Bill for the initiation of the project was enacted in Parliament."

There was a stunned silence in the room, and then a disturbance at the entrance to the hall. "Wrong, sir!" said a voice. It was my grandson John, who had been rushed to the meeting from Haverfordwest by Abel, having taken the morning train from Paddington. Everybody turned as he spoke. "I was in Parliament yesterday, and I can report that the Bill was rejected unanimously by the House on the advice of the law officers, on the grounds that it was deeply flawed according to the statutes, and inadequately supported by the necessary financial information."

Sir Mervyn, Jonas Harry and the five MPs looked as if they had all been hit by a dead haddock. The MPs had clearly told their confederates that everything in Westminster was fixed; but they had not reckoned with Daisy's contacts. I had not been aware of it, but Daisy and George had written on the 15th day of June to John in London and also to certain contacts in the House of Commons, asking for a little help in delaying or killing the Bill, on any pretext that could be devised. George had suggested that according to the ancient statutes relating to the Barony, the correct procedures had not been followed; and he had sent a petition to this effect, countersigned by the requisite number of burgesses and certified as valid by Wilkins Legal.

The mood of the meeting changed again, and everybody started talking at once. Then there was another voice -- this time it was Wilkins Legal himself. "I have in my possession, sir, a Business Proposal for the said Carningli Stone Company, which contains financial projections and details of funding arrangements which are grossly fraudulent. The document is signed by the seven gentlemen who sit before you in this hall. Should this project go ahead, I would have no option, on behalf of my client Squire Wilmot Gwynne, to institute legal proceedings against all seven." He then pointed straight at Sir Mervyn and added: "That includes you, sir, notwithstanding your elevated position as Lord Marcher of the Barony of Cemais."

There was another great cheer, and the Lord Marcher aged ten years as we all looked at him. The Lady Marcher, who was sitting at the side of the hall, looked as if she might faint at any moment. Wilkins held up his hand and waited until he had silence. "However, my client instructs that if this project is abandoned forthwith, with written guarantees from all the gentlemen involved that they will never resurrect it in any shape or form, he will burn this document and take no further action. That, in my view, is a most worthy and gentlemanly act, and deserving of commendation."

Then there was another voice from the back of the hall. It was Donal, flanked by Twm and Ianto, resplendent in uniforms. I was amazed. What on earth were those two rough friends of mine doing in Newport? "Ladies and gentlemen," said my Irish friend, standing tall and proud, and looking very handsome, "today I call myself Donal O'Connor, and tomorrow I might call myself something different. I have the honour of working for Her Majesty's Government, here and in Ireland, under the instructions of the Prime Minister, to whom I report. I work for the Commission for Propriety in Public Affairs, set up by Lord Palmerston to eliminate corruption in government and in corporate matters. Recently it has been my pleasure to work with two special constables, Mr Twm Bevans and Mr Ianto Morys, who have been assiduous in their collection of evidence."

Twm and Ianto, looking very wonderful already in their smart uniforms, grew several inches as I looked at them, and gave radiant gap-toothed smiles to the assembled company.

Donal continued. "For the last two years I have been following with great interest the business dealings of this gentlemen, namely Mr Jonas Harry of Plas Glas, Mumbles, who in spite of his disability has been a devious and determined opponent. He is, ladies and gentlemen, a common criminal. He has consistently misrepresented his profits for the avoidance of tax, and has broken the laws of the land in the conduct of his businesses on no less than fifteen occasions according to my latest count. He operates mostly in this country, out of an office in South Kensington, but he keeps his funds in France. Conspiracy, fraud, blackmail, intimidation, assault and false accounting are included among his crimes. I have a witness statement as to his methods from the orphan called Merlin Ifans, only ten years old but beaten up without mercy by the man who now stands at the back of the hall, one Iago Woodward, who works for Mr Harry." At this, there was an ominous growl from the townspeople in the hall, and I thought that I would not like to be in that particular thug's shoes when the meeting ended. I looked at him. His face was pale, and there was fear in his eyes. Donal pressed on. "Then I come to Mrs Susanna Ravenhill. This frail lady who sits before you, and is newly come to this district, had to suffer gross intrusions of her privacy as she was spied upon and hunted down over the course of a year or more, simply because Mr Harry thought she was a friend of Squire Wilmot Gwynne. Take note that her only crime, ladies and gentlemen, was to be a casual acquaintance of a business rival. We have in our possession a letter written by Mr Woodward to Mr Harry, dated 25th March 1855, making it clear that they actually considered the possibility of murdering this innocent and harmless elderly lady, who was herself a grieving widow.........."

There were gasps from around the hall. "Then, when Mr Harry and his colleagues realized that Mrs Ravenhill was in possession of a small fortune, they sought to suck her into their mad project, since they needed further backers. The Lord Marcher even invited her to the Castle last evening, and wined her and dined her, in their attempts to convince her to buy a substantial shareholding."

"Disgraceful!" "Bastards!" "How dare they!" and "Outrageous!" came shouts from the hall.

"That is a gross misrepresentation, sir!" said Jonas Harry, but his voice was so weak that hardly anybody heard him.

"The good lady sits with these scoundrels before you today," said Donal, "as they anticipate a positive announcement from her. I hope to God that she has not already been led astray and has paid good money for worthless shares, for if she has, I fear she will never recover it. I hope that through my modest intervention we have saved her from making a dreadful mistake." He caught my eye, and I smiled. "Now then, the bad news for Mr Harry is that if I institute proceedings he will probably be incarcerated at Her Majesty's pleasure for the rest of his natural life. The good news for him is that because the Commission is a new body, and not yet familiar in business circles, the Government is prepared, in its wisdom, to allow amnesties to miscreants who will agree with me on how their tax debts will be settled, how their affairs will be regulated in the future, and how their finances will henceforth be reported. I require written confirmation of your willingness in this matter, Master Harry. Before this assembled company, do I have your agreement to a signature?"

"Sign it, Harry! Sign it, Harry!" shouted the crowd. He looked even paler than he had done at the beginning of the meeting, and his eyes had the look of a cornered rabbit about them. "I will sign it, sir," he moaned. "It appears that I have no option......." At that, there was a further great cheer in the hall.

Then there was another voice, which I heard with great surprise. It was Rose's husband Henry. "One last word, sir, if I may. My name is Henry Evans of Trefelin, and I bring a message from the new owner of the Plas Ingli estate. He wishes it to be placed on record that he will not allow any wayleaves across his land for any industrial purpose; nor will he allow any interference with his common land rights or those of his tenants; nor will he allow any interference with his fishing rights on the estuary, which might be occasioned by any interference with the course or the flow of the river, or with any structures that might be placed in the river or adjacent to it, or which might be occasioned by the release of noxious substances into the river water. He has also purchased, on this very day, three properties on the Parrog waterfront, and a further three properties on land known as Mountain East, located in a row along the contour and somewhat above the castle. He says that he will in no circumstances offer these for sale to any other person or company, and will insist on the maintenance of all his rights of access and all other rights attached to those properties, including the right to live peacefully and without outside disturbance. That disturbance will include dust and explosions connected with quarrying operations. Again, he says that he will absolutely forbid any crossing of his land by roadways, tramways or overhead cables designed for any industrial purpose. Shall I continue, sir?"

"No, no, I think we have probably heard enough," moaned the Lord Marcher. "It would appear that our project is dead in the water, for a multitude of reasons."

There was another resounding cheer from the audience, inside and outside the hall. Sir Mervyn had a look of resignation and weariness on his face, but he managed a feeble smile. He held up his hand and continued. "And pray, Mr Evans,who is this formidable new land-owner about to bless us with his presence?"

"His name, sir, is Master Brynach Morgan, my father-in-law and son of the late Mistress Martha Morgan."

17. Reconciliation

When the announcement was made to the effect that my son had just purchased the Plas Ingli estate, I fear that I collapsed, and had to be resuscitated and carried home. I have to this day no recollection of anything else that happened in the public meeting called by the now-defunct Carningli Stone Company. That does not matter too much, since by all accounts the meeting then broke up in disarray, with crowds spilling out onto the grassy verges at the side of the church, and with a chaotic party started spontaneously on the streets. It went on, so they say, into the small hours, with Shemi providing entertainment in the form of magic tricks.

I am told that there was much talk in the town for days afterwards about this mysterious lady called Mrs Susanna Ravenhill, who had been saved from a dreadful fate -- and possibly bankruptcy -- by the sleuthing and timely intervention of Donal O'Connell. It was put about that my collapse was down to lack of air in the stuffy hall, tight corsets, and a realization that I had almost been dragged down by villains. That was good enough, by all accounts, to satisfy everybody. Only a few knew of my own role in the downfall of Jonas Harry and his colleagues, but I did not mind about that, since all I wanted anyway was a low profile in the neighbourhood, and a quiet life. I was utterly amazed that, through some strange coalescence of good fortune and good planning by my friends, I had been spared from speaking a single word at the meeting. Daisy and Betsi both teased me without mercy afterwards, when we were alone, saying that it was the first time in my two lives that I had gone through a whole meeting without interfering and causing trouble. Looking back over the years, I think they were probably correct.

On the very next day, by all accounts, there was a long meeting in the Castle, attended by Wilmot Gwynne, all of the directors of the Carningli Stone Company, and Donal O'Connell and Wilkins Legal. I am not party to exactly what transpired, but I have it on good authority that various documents were signed, that certain binding commitments were made, and that the company was formally wound up by all the shareholders. The Lord and Lady Marcher then went off to their distant estates in a huff, vowing never to visit Newport again. They would be back, of course, but the arrogant and condescending Sir Mervyn had been brought low by Shemi's verbal assault and was now also widely suspected of corruption. I could have confirmed that, since I knew the details, but thought that nothing would be gained by revealing them. The other directors of the company, considerably out of pocket, disappeared back to London and the peace and quiet of the House of Commons. Patty saw them leaving Newport in the Lord Marcher's coach, with faces as black as thunder.

Iago Woodward and Silas Reynolds left town in a hurry, and will probably never be seen again. The other three members of Harry's gang stayed behind -- they were at least loyal to their employer, who would, in his increasingly pathetic state, have been quite lost without them. He was now a broken man, and I could not help but feel sorry for him. Donal would not allow him to retreat to his palace on the Mumbles where he might lick his wounds; he wanted extended interviews, since his investigations were not yet complete, and part of the amnesty offered to the miserable fellow was based upon full revelations of all his shadowy business contacts. That would take time. So Harry moved into the Black Lion for a few days, having by all accounts been evicted from the Castle. Twm and Ianto, thoroughly enjoying their new-found status, made sure that he did not escape. Without his power and his mad dreams he seemed to have shrunk in size, and he became very morose. I suspect that he was also bankrupt, since whatever Donal's charitable intentions might have been, they did not extend to the forgiveness of financial crimes against the state. The man had to recover all his monies from France, and he had enormous bills to pay. Donal told me that the sum total of his unpaid invoices was about twice that of his assets.

Wilmot's health took a turn for the better now that Jonas Harry was off his back and now that his prime estate had been sold. Perhaps his illness had all been in the mind. He told me with delight that the sale of Plas Ingli was a very fair one, which resolved all his financial difficulties. In a move of great magnanimity, he offered the hand of friendship to his erstwhile enemy Jonas Harry, and that offer was accepted. He moved him out of the Black Lion and into Plas Llanychaer, and somehow found space for his three manservants as well. Shemi also showed that he was a man who knew the meaning of magnanimity. He had whispered and roared at the public meeting with the sole intention of bringing Jonas Harry's precarious scheme crashing down about his ears; but having achieved that, he showed considerable generosity towards his victim and offered to treat Harry for his disability. He examined him and conducted tests which seemed to others to smack more of magic than of science; and then he gave him various herbal potions to drink, designed to have an efficacious effect upon the nervous system.

Around mid-July, something extraordinary happened. Donal formally released Jonas Harry, having completed his investigations. The Irishman came to visit me at Brynglas, and we embraced and said a fond farewell, for I had come to have a great liking for him as an honest and attractive man, and a gentleman to boot. We drank tea together in the garden, and I asked him where he was off to next. He smiled enigmatically and showed me an envelope with an elaborate seal upon it. "From Lord Palmerston," he said. "London for my next task, following up certain irregularities in South Kensington." Then Ianto and Twm turned up as well, to say their farewells. They had news for me. Having finished their spell as special constables, they had received their full payment from Donal and were also intent on setting off for London, with a friend from Merthyr Tydfil, to set up business as coal merchants. I gave them £100 each to help them to get the business going, and they gave me hugs fit to burst my stays before they went on their way.

As if that was not enough for one day, Shemi then turned up in Wilmot's carriage, with Jonas Harry and his three servants. "Myfanwy, please put the kettle on and make some more tea!" I shouted. "We have more visitors!" We talked for a while, and enjoyed tea and scones in the shade. I found Harry to be much changed; he admitted that he was bankrupt, but hoped that he might be able to keep Plas Glas, and he said that he was giving up all of his business activities and would henceforth remain close to home, devoting his time to charitable works. I was not sure I believed that, but at least he would not be breaking the laws of the land and spreading mayhem. Then Shemi said: "Susanna, I have to admit that I've not come to see you at all. Where's young Merlin?"

"Why, he is up at Cilgwyn Mawr, helping in the dairy. He will come back if I ring the bell."

So I rang the bell, and ten minutes later the boy came running, with his fresh complexion ruddy from the exercise. "Well, Grandma Susanna," he panted. "Trouble is it? Or is it time for lunch?"

"Neither, Merlin. We have visitors who wish to see you. But since you are always hungry, I will see what we can do in the matter of food."

I went into the kitchen to organize a light lunch with Myfanwy, leaving Shemi and the other visitors to talk to Merlin. Ten minutes passed. When I came out again, carrying a tray laden with food and drink, I almost dropped it in surprise, for Jonas Harry was standing up, unsupported, with tears streaming down his face. Merlin and Shemi were embracing, and the three manservants were dancing a jig around the lawn. Shemi would not let Harry try to walk, and said that the muscles in his legs were so wasted that he might fall and do himself great harm. "This will take a long time, Jonas," he said. "You will have to exercise those legs very carefully and persistently for several weeks, but I will show you what you have to do. In about a week you can take some steps, supported by your good friends here. Then you will need crutches once you become independent. I predict that by Christmas you will be able to throw the crutches away."

What a lunch we enjoyed! Jonas Harry was giggling and laughing like a small child, and his servants behaved as if a great load had been taken from them, which indeed it had. I noticed that Shemi was lost in thought for much of the time, and that Merlin was exhausted. That child has a wonderful and mysterious skill, I thought, and he is the next in a line of great wizards in this district. I knew that one day he would be a greater healer than Joseph Harries.

A week later Jonas and his men returned to Plas Glas, and as predicted by Shemi, the man who had been my implacable enemy was walking freely in time to carry the flaming plum pudding to his Christmas table.

And what of my beloved Bessie? At the time of the great events described in the last chapter she was still poorly, and being nursed with great devotion by Patty and her family in their house on the Parrog. She recovered, and in truth her condition was probably brought on by sheer exhaustion, occasioned by the extent of our travels abroad, or by too much opera, or too much red wine. I visited her often, and felt guilty on that account; but she said over and again that the expedition to foreign parts, in my company, was the most wonderful thing she had done in her life, and that she would not have missed it for all the world. I believed her.

One day, while walking arm in arm with Bessie along the estuary, I asked her if she might be interested in working with me on this memoir. She knew that my rheumatic right hand was making writing very difficult, and so we devised a plan whereby I would dictate and she would write. Subsequently we have spent many happy hours -- indeed many happy days and weeks -- together over the course of more than a year, reminiscing and committing this tale to paper. Now we approach Christmas in the year 1857. The task is almost done, and when it is ready, maybe next spring, I might travel up to London with Daisy to see if I can find a publisher. Indeed, she is encouraging me to seek the publication of my fantastical memoir. She says that a certain publishing house owned by Messrs Jebson and Pickersniff is reputable and relatively generous in the matter of royalties. Truly I do not need the money, but however much more time is left to me on this earth, I wish to remain independent, and pay my way.

I have written to all of the villains in the story, and they have all given their consent, for a memoir about the saving of the mountain and the defeat of the Carningli Stone Company. They have asked that certain elements of the tale should be disguised, and I have respected their wishes. They do not come out of it too badly, and after all, none of them has been as evil as Attila the Hun or Genghis Khan. And in this gentle adventure nobody has died, and in truth nobody has been greatly harmed.

What my correspondence has not revealed to anybody else with a role in this tale is the secret of my true identity. That will, I think, be a surprise for many if this memoir should be published. In the way of things I think it most likely that this book will be published after my death. And what will I do if a publisher, in his wisdom, wishes to rush it into print and turn it into a great publishing success while I am still alive? Then I will have to face the music. There will be anger, and even fury, among those who have been misled; but I think I might be quite relieved about that, since I will be able to resume my own identity. Will I then have to live out my days incarcerated in some foul prison? I hope not, for I think I have committed no crime, and I have not sought to benefit from the impersonation of someone else. I am old, and increasingly frail. And I hope that if I should end up in court, the likes of Donal and Wilmot might speak for me, and argue that I have made my atonement. I trust that my misdemeanours are more than balanced by the manner in which I fought for my people and my beloved mountain, and brought a wicked conspiracy to light.

My bank account in the name of Mrs Susanna Ravenhill has been closed, and my modest fortune distributed among my children. I will leave no other will, for I have no possessions. My family will look after me for however long I may have left upon this good earth. To reach the age of eighty would be a fine thing, if God wills it. My greatest pleasure, since the occasion of my reported death, has been to enjoy a little more time to tramp upon the mountain, and to smell its sweet scents and sun-baked rocks, and to watch its changing face, season to season and day by day. If I die with my family around me at the Plas, I think I will be truly content; and when my angels choose to take me, I will try not to slip out of their grasp.

I have left the matter of Brynach, my adopted son, to the very end of this tale, for it will be a very emotional business for me to describe what transpired on his return to Wales.

Unknown to me, it was agreed some time before the famous meeting in the Church Chapel, in the course of much correspondence back and forth across the Atlantic Ocean, that Brynach would buy back the Plas Ingli estate from Wilmot. He had made a fortune in America since his arrival there as a penniless immigrant in 1845, with a certain amount of help from his natural mother, my sister Elen. But in recent months he had become concerned about the widening split between north and south, mostly to do with the treatment of slaves, and he was becoming convinced that Civil War was inevitable. One of the reasons for Brynach's sudden departure to New York, as admitted to me in various letters, had been his failure to find a new wife, following the death of his first wife Anne. That had left him with two small children, David and Rose, to bring up alone. Then there was a brutal refusal by a certain Squire Preece to allow Brynach to marry his daughter Lisbet, with whom he was deeply in love. She had been in love with him too, but had been forced by her parents to marry the eldest son of the Squire of Llys-gwynt near Llandeilo. That was not an unusual state of affairs, but both young people had been heartbroken. Recently, as I learned later from Betsi, circumstances had changed. Lisbet's husband William had inherited the estate in 1852, and had died in a hunting accident a month before my own reported death. There were no children in the marriage, and no other male relatives, and William's will specified that Lisbet should remain as Mistress of the estate. She was now a free agent in possession of a considerable fortune, and was a great deal wealthier than I had ever been as Mistress of Plas Ingli. She and Brynach had re-established contact with Betsi's help, and with Elen's blessing, and it was a convenient thing indeed that Brynach had not, in his decade in America, found anybody to compare with Lisbet, and had remained an unmarried widower. He had proposed to her in a letter in March, and she had accepted in April.

For three months everybody had known about it, except me. Betsi told me the news a few days after the big meeting in the Church Chapel, when we two were out gathering hedgerow flowers, having determined that I was sufficiently recovered from the excesses of the previous weeks to deal with another shock. I had until that moment assumed that Brynach had purchased the Plas Ingli estate from a distance, as a foreign investment, and for the purpose of providing for Rose and Henry. I had not for a moment imagined that he might return in person to the Plas or to the district in which he had grown up. When I was told, I had to sit down on a log on the roadside, for I had never contemplated the possibility of Brynach coming home. I did not weep, but neither could I laugh. "Dear Mother!" said Betsi, knowing that my mind was in turmoil and my emotions in disarray, and putting her arms around me. " It will be a marriage made in heaven, with money on both sides, and with my little brother Brynach and nephew David returning to the land of their birth."

I asked Betsi what my sister Elen thought of this development, and she said that she had lately received a letter from her in which she expressed very great joy, for all she ever wanted was Brynach's happiness. She had had ten years of his love and companionship, she said, and that was more than she ever deserved.

The travellers from America arrived in Milford Haven in the middle of August 1856, and went immediately to Plas Llanychaer where Wilmot arranged a great reunion between Brynach and David and his daughter Rose and her family. There was no reason for me to be there, and indeed

Reconciliation

Brynach had no wish for me to be present, for he still thought me dead. Then there was another reunion at Brithdir, involving Brynach's sisters Betsi and Daisy and their families. I was informed later that those were wonderful, tearful, joyful occasions, and as reports were given to me in my little cottage in Brynglas I too wept tears of joy. Then Brynach jumped into Wilmot's coach with David and Rose, and they travelled to Llandeilo to meet Lisbet. I was heartbroken to learn that he had left the district, but then realized that if I had been in his boots, with a wife-to-be only fifty miles away, after a decade and an ocean of separation, I would have done exactly the same.

A fortnight later, Brynach was back in the area, for more discussions with Wilmot and Wilkins Legal relating to the marriage settlement and to the purchase and transfer of the Plas Ingli estate. He stayed with Betsi and Ioan at Brithdir. Still I did not see him. Then Betsi and Daisy arranged a subterfuge about which I was entirely ignorant. One evening Brynach said that he wanted to visit Cilgwyn Church, on his own, so that he could visit my grave and spend a little time in quiet contemplation in the tranquillity of the churchyard. There, he thought, he could bid me farewell beneath the great pine trees, with the familiar silhouette of Carningli against the setting sun. "When you have done that, brother," said Daisy, "why don't you call in at Brynglas and meet Aunt Susanna, Mother's half-sister, who has recently moved into the district? She wants to meet you, and she deserves your thanks, for she was instrumental in saving the mountain and the estate from the depredations of the Carningli Stone Company." Brynach was at first reluctant, since he knew that he would be in an emotional state following his visit to the graveyard, but when Betsi also pressed him, and said that it was only a five minute walk from the church, he agreed.

At about eight o'clock, as the western sky was starting to take on the colour of the dusk, there was a knock on the door. Myfanwy, Merlin and I had just finished supper, and we were all surprised, since we were not expecting visitors. Merlin sprang to his feet and answered the door. I heard voices, and then he came back inside. "Grandma Susanna, there's a gentleman to see you. He has been weeping."

"Why, my dear child! Who can that be? Well, invite him in!."

He brought Brynach into our little dining room, and I came face to face again with my long-lost son. I recognized him immediately -- the brown eyes and black hair, the upright posture, and the dark complexion. He was less slim than he had been when he left, and he now had the air of a worldly and wealthy gentleman. How I loved him, as my breast was swelled with pride! But there was a redness around his eyes, and I saw at once that Merlin was right -- he had been weeping, for the death of his mother. I had rehearsed this moment a thousand times in my mind, but now I did not know what do do. I wanted to run to him and gather him in my arms, and cover him with kisses, but I dared not do it. He too looked confused and lost, for he saw in me his mother, Martha Morgan, and knew only that I was a stranger called Susanna Ravenhill. His heart, I suspect, told him one thing while his mind told him something else.

"Myfanwy, shall we go and wash the dishes?" said Merlin, who knew that it was the right time to retire and leave me and Brynach alone.

We stood facing each other for a while, and then I found the resources to say: "Brynach, it is very good to meet you at last."

"And you are my Aunt Susanna, I presume?"

I managed to smile. "So they tell me. Shall we go up to my room? It is more private there, with two comfortable chairs, and Merlin and Myfanwy will not disturb us. We have many things to talk about."

Brynach bowed, and allowed me to lead him up the stairs to my room. Once there, I closed the door and we sat down, facing each other. Having promised Brynach that we had many things to talk about, I could not think of anything that might now be appropriate, so I just looked at him, marvelling at his good looks and his fine clothes. My heart was beating wildly, and I had to fight to retain my self-control. At last, I was able to say, in a very feeble voice: "Lisbet is a very lucky woman, Brynach."

"Thank you, Aunt," he replied. "You are very kind. I believe I am a lucky man too, for she is very beautiful, and has had many other suitors."

"And is it good to be home?"

"Very good. I have longed to be back in this place ever since I first landed in America, for this is truly where my heart is."

"And now you have the Plas again........"

"I thank God for it, Aunt. And I have to thank you too, for I have heard of your role in saving both Wilmot's estates and the mountain."

"I have done what I could, and I think it was my destiny, Brynach. But you have been weeping. For your mother, I think?"

"Yes, Aunt, and for myself, for I have not grieved properly until now. She died here, on her beloved mountain, when I was an ocean away, unknowing and uncaring." He looked at me, and there were tears in his eyes. "She truly gave me life, and gave me everything that I know to be good. Now she is gone, and we are still separated, but now by a few feet of sandy soil that might as well be a thousand miles thick........"

"She is closer than you think, Brynach."

He was so wrapped up in his private grief that at first he did not react to my words. Then he looked at me intently, with growing disbelief.

"I do not understand.........."

"Do you think that I look like your mother?"

"The likeness is uncanny. You are older than I remember her, and your hair is not the same as hers, but your eyes, your lips, your complexion, your high cheek-bones, and your voice -- if I was to meet you suddenly in the street I would not just have my head turned by your beauty and your elegance, but also by your familiarity. Excuse me, but I do not know what to think. I am very confused."

He was like a small child grappling with an exercise in algebra. So I decided to put him out of his misery. In one of those impulsive moments which have marked my life, I said: "Brynach, you are a man of the world. Would you be offended if I was to remove my dress?"

"Yes -- I mean no. Whatever do you mean? Now I am even more confused...."

"Don't you worry, Brynach. I am too old for passionate games, and you are perfectly familiar with what I am about to show you. While I take off my dress, will you please light the candles on my dressing table? There are some patent matches in the drawer."

"Well, if you insist........"

So while he lit the candles I stood in the darkening corner of the room and removed my dress, and then my bodice, blouse and stays. I was not interested in showing him my breasts, for they were less beautiful than they had been in my prime, so I stood with my back to him.

"Bring the light, please, and examine my back."

Reconciliation

He still did not understand the game I was playing, so while I stood there smiling to myself he mumbled some apologies and approached as I had asked. At last he saw the marks on my back -- the scars from the cruel scourging I had received behind the whipping cart in Newport, as a young woman in the year 1797. Those wounds had healed long since, but the marks were still there, quite indelible. They were the only distinguishing marks on my body. The only living people who knew about them were my servants Bessie and Myfanwy and my three children.

At last Brynach whispered: "Mother?"

I turned round to face him, oblivious to the fact that if anybody had entered the door at that stage they would have been truly appalled by the scene before them. Half naked old ladies do not normally stand face to face with well-dressed young men. "Yes, Brynach," I said. "I am still alive."

"Can I believe this? But if you are truly my Mother, what of the funeral, the press reports, the inquest, the coffin.........?"

"Full of stones, Brynach."

"But why? Why?"

"It's a long story, Brynach, and I will tell it yo you, all in good time. But first I have to prove to you that I am not a ghost. Come and kiss me, and let me embrace you."

So he did as requested, and I did as I wanted. And we wept, mother and son, locked in an embrace, for a very long time. "There now, *Cariad*," I said at last. "You already have two mothers, Elen and Martha, and now you have a third."

Then I put my clothes back on, and we talked and talked far into the night. When at last Brynach set out for Brithdir Myfanwy and Merlin were in bed, fast asleep. It was three in the morning, and the August full moon was riding high in the sky, with Carningli suffused in a silver glow.

That is really the end of my memoir. Brynach and Lisbet were married a month later in Llandeilo, and I attended as "Aunt Susanna" and as the guest of honour. It was a truly wonderful occasion. The couple then settled on Lisbet's estate near Llandeilo. With the Plas now back in the possession of the Morgan family, it was appropriate for Wilmot's son and his family to move out . That was a great relief to them and to the servants. Wilmot was reconciled with his son Joshua and agreed to let him, Jane and the children move to London, where he was given the opportunity to study to be a lawyer in the same chambers as Daisy's son John. Wilmot , with the proceeds of the Plas Ingli sale, gave the young family an allowance and a house in the city.

And finally, Brynach invited me, old Aunt Susanna, to move back into the Plas. I did that in the spring of 1857. Will retired to an estate cottage, and Gerallt took over as head man. He also got married to his childhood sweetheart Nesta Mather, having previously had inadequate resources and prospects; and his new wife immediately moved into the Plas as my personal maid. Myfanwy also moved back to the Plas, now as housekeeper, and two other servants were also employed.

I moved back into my old room, and was overjoyed to find that all my old furniture had mysteriously returned -- my bed, my chest, my favourite chair, my dressing table and even the writing table in my little dressing-room. In fact, the whole place was furnished just as it was before my reported death. I wondered how this had all been possible, but all people would say was that Rose had organized it.

The ravens are still on the mountain, and so are the skylarks; and the curlews still fly in the dark over the ebbing and flowing waters of the estuary; and the bluebells still bloom in Tycanol Wood. I walk amid the gnarled oaks when I can, but my spirit resides among the rocks rather than among the trees. The mountain is still the place where I walk, and kneel, when my joints allow it, and where I commune with my angels.

Much as I loved Merlin, I was far too old to adopt him and to become a mother again. Indeed, the child had been calling me "Grandma Susanna" since his arrival at Brynglas, as if he knew what was coming. According to the dictates of destiny, when Lisbet met him she immediately fell in love with him, and since she could not bear children of her own, it was inevitable that a ten-year-old freckle-faced boy with extraordinary powers should in due course move to the Llys-gwynt estate near Llandeilo and should take the name of Morgan. Not long ago I decided to tell him the truth about my conspiracy, and the coffin of stones, and my reincarnation as Susanna Ravenhill. I apologized for not telling him earlier. "Why, don't you worry, Grandma *bach*," he said nonchalantly, with a wrinkle on his nose and a sparkle in his eye. "I knew it all the time."

Finale

When I had finished reading this Memoir I knew that I had sufficient grounds for hunting for local information about the last days of Susanna Ravenhill. First of all, I checked the local census records for 1861, and found no trace of her. So I started to hunt through the parish records, and very quickly found an entry in the Register of Deaths dated 30th December 1857 for Mrs Elizabeth (Bessie) Walter. Then I found another entry dated 12th May 1859 confirming the death by natural causes of Mrs Susanna Ravenhill, resident at Plas Ingli in the parish of Newport. Out of interest I also looked for a record of the death of Mistress Martha Morgan of Plas Ingli, and found that too, dated 27th February 1855. That death, more apparent than real, was of course also recorded on a plaque in the Morgan family enclosure in Cilgwyn Churchyard.

So Susanna had enjoyed another two and a half years of life after the completion of her memoir. She had reached the age of eighty, and then eighty-one. I was pleased about that, and I knew that as "Aunt Susanna" or "Grandma Susanna" she would have passed her final years with her family around her. I hoped that she had had good health and ample time to enjoy the greatest of all the pleasures of old age, namely the lovely warmth and quietness of a sleeping great-grand-child on her lap.................

To find out how our heroine had died, I had to hunt through the local press, and I found a report eventually, in the pages of *The Cambrian*. This is what it said:

The Cambrian, Saturday 21st May 1859
A NOTEWORTHY EVENT IN THE NEWPORT DISTRICT
Four years ago, the Cambrian was the first newspaper to report on the earthquake that affected the Carningli and Newport district, and also on a number of singular occurrences which seemed to be connected with the untimely death of a respected local woman, namely Mistress Martha Morgan of Plas Ingli.

Now it has come to our notice that another strange phenomenon has been observed on the mountain on the evening of 12th May. At sunset there was a most vivid display of sunset colours in the far west, but the summit of Carningli was

*surrounded by a halo of bright light so intense that those who saw it could hardly
look at it directly. Those who observed the phenomenon from Newport said that it
seemed that the sun was shining on the south side of the summit, and those who
observed from the south said that the source of the light was to the north. In any
event the summit was silhouetted against the light for some ten minutes. Some
claim to have seen an angel standing on the summit for a little while, but our
science correspondent informs us that that was probably a result of a sort of
hysteria which sometimes affects people who see strange natural phenomena.*

*An hour or two prior to the sighting of the strange halo on the summit of
Carningli, an elderly lady named Mrs Susanna Ravenhill died while sitting in her
favourite chair in the shade of an old white lilac tree, in the garden of Plas Ingli. It
was a warm and beautiful early summer evening, and when her body was discovered by servants the lady was holding a bunch of freshly picked wild flowers on her
lap. Mrs Ravenhill had on that very day celebrated her 81st birthday with family
and friends, and there are no suspicious circumstances.*

*It is noteworthy that both of these reports of strange natural phenomena on
Carningli seem to have been connected with Plas Ingli (the highest house on the
mountain) and with the deaths of elderly ladies. Mrs Ravenhill is believed to have
been the half-sister of the late Mistress Martha Morgan.*

*Carningli seems to have gained something of a reputation as a special and
even sacred mountain. Three years ago there were a number of sightings of ghostly
figures on the mountain, shortly before plans for the establishment of a mighty
quarry and metal industry were abandoned. At the time, Mrs Ravenhill is believed
to have been involved in the campaign to save the mountain. One of our reporters
who lives nearby says that there is still a primitive belief in Cilgwyn that the
mountain is protected by spirits, and that somewhere on its slopes there is an
entrance to the Otherworld..*

*Mrs Ravenhill's funeral was held on 16th May, at Cilgwyn Church, with
interment in the adjacent graveyard.*

*The Cambrian is always first with the local news, and prides itself on its
discretion and respect for the truth.*

After the discovery of this press cutting, there was only one thing to do. I
rushed back to Cilgwyn Church and started to hunt among the headstones,
as I had done with Ben Phillips some years ago when we started our hunt

for Martha Morgan. This time the searching was easier, since the graveyard had been cleared of brambles following the sale of the church for conversion to a private residence. Down near the bottom wall, close to the stumps of a row of recently-felled yew trees, I found two small slate headstones, side by side. They had been tipped over by the expanding roots of the trees, and now leaned at a precarious angle. I had probably seen them before, more than once, but had previously had no reason to take note of them.

The first one said this:

**Here lies the body of
an unknown gentleman
who died on the mountain of Carningli
at least 50 years prior to this date.
Given a Christian burial on this day
15th March 1855
May he rest in peace**

And the second one, just a few feet away, said this:

**In loving memory of
Susanna Ravenhill
late of London
and then resident of this parish
who saved the mountain
and joined the angels
12th May 1859, aged 81 yrs**

Author's Note

The main scenario of this book, namely the apparent death of the heroine and her subsequent full recovery, may seem to be an unlikely one, but it is by no means impossible. There is even a medical name for it -- the Lazarus Syndrome, named after the man whom Christ is reputed to have raised from the dead. In the medical literature there are many instances of successful resuscitations and even spontaneous "awakenings" of those assumed to be dead, and many learned scientific papers on the subject. A key factor in survival seems to be the cooling down of the body and the gradual slowing of all the vital functions to the point where all signs of life appear to be extinguished. The greatest danger in resuscitation is that once "death" has occurred, permanent brain damage will occur if recovery does not take place within a few minutes.

It should be remembered that the three key indicators of clinical death in the mid nineteenth century were lack of breath, lack of pulse, and lack of eye movements. Examinations of "dead" people were often cursory and unreliable. In Victorian times there was a dread of being buried alive, and patent coffins were even sold which would allow "dead" people to alert the outside world if they suddenly woke up and found that they were six feet under! There were many Gothic horror novels in the Victorian period based on the theme of death and resurrection. The Society for the Prevention of People Being Buried Alive (it really did exist!) encouraged a practice whereby the deceased were left lying in their caskets for days or weeks on end before being deemed sufficiently dead to bury. When the Duke of Wellington died in 1852, this macabre postponement ritual reached an extreme. The Duke was not buried until two months after his death.

In some ways this story is a very introverted one with a straightforward narrative form. I had to write it because Mistress Martha suddenly told me, one day in October 2006 when I was up on the mountain, that she did not die! But in writing down the tale as it came into my head, it gave me the opportunity to explore new themes -- the social impact of industrialization, the separation of town and country, the increasing mobility of the population with the arrival of the railways, and the ability of the new industrialists to use technology on a scale large enough to remove mountains.

But most important, I wanted to explore the concepts of identity and personality. What does loss of identity mean? Is it possible for an individual to change personality, to forget the past, and fundamentally to change beliefs and patterns of behaviour? This is a problem faced by informers or spies who are encouraged to "reinvent themselves" for security reasons, or criminals who have served their time and who might be in danger from vigilantes without new names and new locations. What must it have been like for the survivors of Auschwitz to try to leave behind their past, with all its terrors, and to fashion new lives in safety and freedom? And -- a question relevant to this novel -- what would it have been like for Martha, or somebody like her, to change identity and leave behind a life filled with joy and excitement and love, and yet to remain in familiar surroundings with a familiar world of social contacts?

In one of those strange conjunctions, I had already started to write this book when the Carningli Graziers Association and the Pembrokeshire Coast National Park announced a plan to conduct aerial herbicide spraying on the bracken covering the mountain's lower slopes. Their intentions were no doubt laudable, but immediately there was a cry of "Save the mountain!" and a multi-faceted campaign built up a great momentum in just a few weeks. It was a real grass-roots revolt. Local people felt so strongly about the threatened contamination of this special place that many promised to lie down in the spraying zone beneath the helicopter -- in full view of the TV cameras. A petition with over 1,100 signatures was submitted to the PCNPA, and with the officers responsible being placed under relentless pressure, the proposals were at last abandoned.

At the height of the campaign the mountain suddenly produced two guardian angels in the form of a pair of hen harriers which were believed to have nested -- for the first time ever -- in the proposed spraying zone. Hen harriers are the most heavily protected birds in the UK. If the spraying had gone ahead, the graziers and the officers of the PCNPA would have committed a serious criminal offence, and would have been liable for arrest and prosecution. The threat to the mountain described in the novel was of a different kind and was on a different scale, but "economic necessity" was the justification in both cases, and if anybody wants to see the novel as an allegory, that's fine by me.........

Acknowledgements

As ever, I thank my wife Inger and my family for their unstinting support and for their unwavering belief that my novels will one day be up there in the best-seller lists! When that day comes, I hope I am alive to enjoy it. Once again Inger has acted as editor, proof-reader and expert consultant on the female psyche. I thank my readers' panel of Ian Richardson, Irene Payne, Angela John and Robert Anthony for commenting on earlier drafts of the text and for much timely advice. I have to express my gratitude for the wonderful encouragement of a host of readers who have become so immersed in the adventures of Mistress Martha and the fortunes of Plas Ingli that they probably now know my five previous tales better than I do. They have demanded more, and what can one do other than oblige? Finally, I acknowledge my great debt to two scholarly works: Revel Guest and Angela V. John, 2007, *Lady Charlotte. An Extraordinary Life* (Tempus) and Keith Strange, 1980 "In search of the Celestial Empire" *Llafur* 3(1), pp 44-86. They provided me with much of the raw material for Chapters 7 and 8 of this story.

The Angel Mountain Saga

On Angel Mountain, Greencroft Books 2001. ISBN 0905559 80 0. A5 paper back, 328 pp, £6.99. Corgi edition 2006)

House of Angels, Greencroft Books 2002. ISBN 0905559 81 9. A5 paperback, 432 pp, £7.99. (Corgi edition 2006)

Dark Angel, Greencroft Books 2003. ISBN 0905559 82 7. A5 paperback, 432 pp, £8.50. (Corgi edition 2007)

Rebecca and the Angels, Greencroft Books 2004. ISBN 0905559 83 5. A5 paperback, 432 pp, £8.50.

Flying with Angels, Greencroft Books, 2005, ISBN 0 905559 84 3. A5 paperback, 400 pp, £7.99.

Martha Morgan's Little World, Greencroft Books 2007. ISBN 0905559851. A5 hardback, 252 pp, £12.00. The companion to the novels of the saga.